SENTINELS

Book 1 of the One True Child Series

Sentinels is a work of fantasy fiction. Names, characters, places, and incidents are the product of the author's imagination or are used fictitiously. Any resemblance to actual events, locales, or persons, living or dead, is coincidental.

Liminal Books is an imprint of Between the Lines Publishing. The Liminal Books name and logo are trademarks of Between the Lines Publishing.

Copyright © 2018 by L.C. Conn

Cover design by Cherie Fox

Between the Lines Publishing and its imprints supports the right to free expression and the value of copyright. The scanning, uploading, and distribution of this book without permission is a theft of the author's intellectual property. If you would like permission to use material from the book (other than for review purposes), please contact info@btwnthelines.com.

Between the Lines Publishing
9 North River Road, Ste 248
Auburn ME 04210
btwnthelines.com

First Published: 2018
Original ISBN (Paperback) 978-0-9996556-0-3

Second edition:
ISBN: (Paperback) 978-1-950502-75-2
ISBN: (Ebook) 978-1-950502-77-6
ISBN: (Hardcover) 978-1-950502-76-9

Library of Congress Control Number: 2022935431

The publisher is not responsible for websites (or their content) that are not owned by the publisher.

SENTINELS

Book 1 of the One True Child Series

L.C. Conn

Also available from L.C. Conn

Realm of Dragons: Fight for the Crown

For my Father. Thank you for believing in me.

Prologue

The rage knew no bounds as he held the world in his fist. He had created it to be his and his alone, so that the people he had brought to life would worship him, feeding his need to be all powerful and the centre of the universe. For a while it had worked, his needs were satisfied, and he was happy. But they did not appreciate what he had done for them. In time they had wanted more, became more demanding of him. Now his rage would be the last thing they knew. His hand squeezed the world as he brought it all to an end, creating a vast explosion which lit up the darkness that surrounded him. The pinpoint of light grew and spread, blinding his vision, and he roared at his displeasure of it.

The light encompassed all as it sent out waves, pulsating into the far reaches of the universe. Fragments of the old world riding the shockwaves, were flung into the darkness. Fiery-hot chunks burning brightly spun out of control, attracting rock and minerals to circle them. As they spread, the explosion started to slow, and the fragments began to cool. In the centre of the explosion, the bright light continued to shine. Within its core a Being drew her first breath and became conscious as she rose from the wreckage—with the light from the explosion swirling under her skin.

The Being looked around only to find a universe in chaos, and she became sad. Order and stability were lost to the winds. She stood and looked out at the remains of a great world, gathering to herself the memories of those that had been sacrificed unnecessarily for a single creature's whim. The Being stood on one large piece of rock, which circled a star and warmed the ground at her feet. The emotions over ran her, and she began to weep for those who had been destroyed. All the torture and the suffering they had endured under their cruel master, now brought forth great sobs from the Being. The tears she shed dripped down from her eyes and onto the ground. A great flood of tears for the loss of so many, so much so, that a river began to run.

The river flowed away from the grief-stricken Being, and filled all the low spaces on the rock, collecting into great lakes and seas. The sadness the Being had felt turned to rage, and she struck the ground with her fist. The land split, and the great molten core that had not yet cooled, swelled up, bursting out of the cracks she had made. The hot magma grew new land and boiled away some of the water, creating a great steam cloud that hung in the sky.

The distant star continued to warm the small world, threatening to dry up the collected water. The clouds above became sodden with all that they hoarded and released their heavy loads, spreading the life-giving liquid across the barren land. As the rain fell, the sunshine created an illusion: An arc of light, split into seven perfect shades of colour, that stood out from the dark landscape. As the Being stood on an upthrust of rock and wondered at the amazing vision, she did not see the dark one approaching.

"You are not welcome here. This is my world. My universe. Who are you?" the dark one loudly demanded of the Being. She turned to face the form that approached and recognised him as the one responsible for the turmoil that now reigned over the universe.

"I am from the light, and in this place, you shall never have authority. Never again will you oppress a people and use them for your own ends," the Being retorted. She stood tall against his fury, calming her own as the tears still spilled from sad eyes.

"From my destruction came your creation. Therefore, you are my being, and you shall bow down to me and my wishes." The darkness grew before the Being, looming large over her.

"I am the light, the light that will dominate you and put you where you should be. You have no sway over me. The light shall overpower you and keep you at bay. The children I will bring forth onto this land will welcome and grow in the light and will benefit from its kindness. They shall feed from the crops and animals which the light shall encourage to grow, and they will worship you never. They will not know you," she told him slowly.

"You are nothing and weak. I am the great destroyer, the one who rules over life and death. I am the chaos of the universe, and all who reside here shall be my slaves. I destroyed my last creation because they did not worship me the way they were supposed to. If you go against me, I shall destroy you also."

The Being looked past the dark evil to the large rainbow and saw its magnificence. From the single source of light that shone from above, came the dazzling display of colours as it split apart through crystalline drops of falling rain. If this monstrosity that stood before the rainbow declared himself Chaos, then this Being who marvelled at the perfectly arranged spectacle of colour, should be Order.

Slowly Order reached down, drawing from the centre of the world the energy that spiralled there. She pulled it in from the air around her and filled herself up until Order thought she would burst. Order sent out her will and split herself into seven, each figure to be a Sentinel to guard the world that The Great Light wanted to protect. A different nimbus of colour swirled under each of their skins: red, orange, yellow, green, blue, indigo, and violet. The seven Sentinels stood together and faced Chaos.

Chaos stood his ground and stared at the beings before him, his anger rising inside at the defiance of The Great Light and what she had done.

"You shall not overcome me. I will rule you, no matter how many there are, or you shall all die!" he screamed at them.

"We are together, and together we are Order. You will not reign over this world. We have come to protect it, and it shall be beautiful and peaceful. Chaos has no place in this world. We banish you and beg that you do not come back to this place," the seven said together.

"You banish me? You cannot banish me from what is mine! I will crush you and break you. You will bend your knee to me," Chaos declared, his rage increasing at their defiance.

The group lifted, their rainbow dancing high into the sky and each split apart to form their own group of seven, to protect the world from Chaos. They spread across the face of the world, each group taking up an area to defend and protect.

Chaos roared and his anger exploded when they would not bend to his will. He fought against their barriers and defences until the land buckled under the strain of his wrath. He caught up a stone that was floating nearby in his large fist and threw it, seeking to destroy the new world. The lump of rock skimmed the surface, only to be caught up in its pull as the world spun, and there it stayed, to circle the world forever more.

In the land to the north, the first group of Sentinels formed the great stone circle, where Order had first declared herself a conduit for the power of the beings. Each group that had been sent out over the world created their own sacred sites. These sites were to be the focus of their connection to the original group.

The rage of Chaos slowed, and he departed to think on how to deal with the problem of Order and her children. His attack had been useless, and he wandered the spreading universe, destroying stars and planets in his path. Meanwhile, the little world flourished and changed in his absence.

Some of the wounds on the surface of the world had healed and created great open landscapes, while others still wept molten rock. Seeing the bare environment, the Sentinels began to grind the surface to dust, releasing the minerals necessary to start life. The soil bloomed with grasses, their roots holding it together against the wind and rain. Further plants grew. Shrubs and trees they created to bring shelter and sustenance for the creatures to come.

At first the groups worked together, then they became interested only in their own pieces to protect. They moulded the landscapes to their liking. Emptying great seas and moving land, easing the damage the dark one had inflicted. They created animals, who began to roam the world seeking out new, brighter, and fresher pastures to graze on. Not all were plant eaters, some desired flesh to keep a balance.

Chaos was still out there, watching their progress and seething. With the passing of time, he began to feel his own power fade with the lack of worshipers. A large rock swept past him, grazing his shoulder, and leaving a trail of vapour and ice in its wake. He took the speeding rock up in his mighty fist and sent it flying towards the world the Sentinels were creating. It hurtled at great speed, and when it did hit, it was with enormous devastation.

It fell to the earth with a mighty explosion, sending debris and ash high into the air. The flames from the explosion spread out with a concussive force, and almost consumed the tiny planet, destroying nearly all the Sentinels work in a flash. The cloud from the debris blocked out the sun, plunging the planet into near darkness. To help heal the damaged world, the Sentinels called forth ice and snow to cover the land. So thick it lay on the ground that the seas dropped, and the sacred stones were buried deep under its heavy blanket.

Chaos watched with great delight at the destruction it had almost caused. He sent more into the path of the planet, leaving great craters over the surface. Mostly the chunks of rock he hurtled their way hit the moon. The rock Chaos had first used to try and destroy the world, now acted as a shield from his current onslaught. It was barren and grey, but viewed from the planet below, brought welcome light in the dark hours. With each frenzied attack, the Sentinels used their abilities to fix and mend the damage.

The group that guarded the sacred stones met, and together they began to banish the ice and snow that lay over their lands. Great valleys remained from the carving of the ice, and it pleased them to fill some up with the water left by the enormous melting glaciers. The Sentinels walked the earth and were unhappy to find that not all the creatures they had carefully created had survived the great freeze. Some had adapted, and they looked to that as a sign.

One group of Sentinels to the south had created a creature who seemed to be very hardy and adaptable. These they had formed to be very much in their own likeness and called them human. The humans learned quickly and soon grew to dominate their environment. They moved about the earth, exploring further and further afield, meeting with others and merging, always adapting to the changing conditions.

The ice and snow still covered the northern and highest parts of the sacred lands. Very carefully the Sentinels cleared the stones and the valley below, where Order had brought them to life. The great pillars of rock reached up from the earth, seeking the sky, and this is where they met. Each slowly entered the circle and took up their places between the stones. They pushed their robes from their faces, feeling the warmth of the closest star now that the ash and dust was starting to leave the atmosphere. They sat in their places to discuss the plans Order could see the necessity of if the world was to survive and break free from Chaos' wrath. The lights of their colours played just under their skin, swirling, sparkling, and dancing in the rays of the sun.

Their abilities were sharper and more intense than the other groups sent out into the world. As they leant up against the stones, they connected with the other Sentinels and drew in their knowledge, imparting it into the stones along with the enormous energy from the earth itself.

"Order has given her wishes plainly. We must do as she commands. Our purpose is to pass our abilities onto The People to come, as this is important for the survival of our world, and possibly many others," Blue said, sitting forward to address his brothers and sisters.

"It must be so. We must go out and find those humans who wish to live in our lands peacefully," Red added.

"It does not matter if they wish to be peaceful. These humans will fight for survival and to protect their own. I have already seen it," Green told the gathered group.

"Do we all agree that the abilities will be passed to The People, and continue down their lines?" Indigo inquired.

"It is the will of Order that it is to be so, therefore we must obey," Violet commanded.

"My brothers and sisters, our lands are the most sacred and must be protected well, especially this particular spot. There is a need to have one of The People to take up this task. They shall be our connection to those that are to come and impart our knowledge to all who seek it. This line should be constant and unbreakable," Blue spoke.

"I should like to offer one of my line to the task, and they shall forever more be linked to this place. The valley below shall be their home," Red declared.

"It is still barren and bare. There are not enough resources to sustain them," Orange protested.

Yellow stood and quietly stepped to the edge of the hill where the stones pushed their way to the sky. In her hand she created a great staff, and she plunged it into the ground. A mighty crack split the rock, and water that had been stored there since Order's first tears, burst forth. It tumbled down the hill and snaked its way through the centre of the valley below, before joining the river that cut the valley off at the end. When she returned, the staff was gone.

"There, water is necessary for the survival of these humans. As for food, we shall place plants and game generously around the area so they can be sustained," Yellow told them.

"I have studied these humans. They can be like the locust, stripping an area bare and moving on. Leaving nothing of sustainable value behind," Green told the group.

"Then I shall teach them to harvest wisely and only take what they need. If you could all keep your own lines from the area, it will be enough to sustain them," Red said.

"They will need to breed with others. I do not think it wise that they breed within their own line," Violet spoke up.

"Others will come to seek wisdom from The Great Light here at the stones. They will have contact with the outside world," Orange told her gently.

"Are we in accord, then?" Green asked.

"We are," they each intoned.

"We will then part and find those that we need to create The People." Indigo declared, calling the meeting to an end.

The Sentinels wandered the sacred lands. Each giving a part of themselves to the bloodlines they created. Red's line he secured as soon as possible to the valley below the stones. In the river at the end of the valley, fish, large and fat, sustained them, as well as the berries and other fruits found in the forest Red grew to hide the valley from view. The line of protectors he bore was strong in both ability and physical strength, with the common trait of dark hair and bright blue eyes, because of his own vanity. The task to protect the stones, Red entrusted to the female line. The other People he fathered were spread wide, all distributed to guard the ways to the stones. They took to themselves the sigil of a boar, which is tenacious and hardy, but fiercely protective of its young.

Orange went to the west and had the most land to care for. It was mostly rugged and hard to work. Mountainous with great deep lochs, and islands that stood alone far out to sea. The children he created were strong and warrior-like, thriving in the water and mountains alike. An eagle became their sigil, as it flew so high and could see so far. The water People became raiders, and those in the mountains gained a reputation for being giants through their feats of strength.

Yellow had lands just to the south of Red, which were arable and beautiful, with rolling hills and valleys. Her People grew crops, fished, and hunted. They lived in family groups and were creative. They tended to roam the area, never settling down in one place for long. A bear they took for their own sigil. Ferocious in a fight, but tender hearted.

Green headed south and had the smallest of the lands. His People became diplomats and traders. They were wise but also fiercely protective of their piece of the border. They were sometimes slippery to deal with but were never deceitful. A serpent became their sacred symbol.

Blue went north and east. His coastline was rugged and withstood the worst of the heavy weather that blew in from the great sea. Dense forests covered the inland parts, and the game that lived there was plentiful. The People he fathered were hardy, determined, and proud of their lands. A great horned stag they took for their symbol.

Indigo's People were cunning and wily. Their lands were to the south, and they had the largest part of the border, which they protected jealously. Their desire for knowledge was great, and they travelled everywhere to learn as much as possible from others. They were ferociously loyal to those who helped them and their family, so the wolf was a perfect fit as their sacred animal.

Violet's lands were to the east, and the only Sentinel she had no boundary with was Orange. Her People were gentle and peaceful, leaders and planners. Their place in the sacred lands was well protected, with highlands and coastal plains. Their personalities could be big and brash, but their hearts were generous and loving. Bullish sometimes by nature, the great horned bovine became their symbol.

Wandering the lands, the Sentinels grew their bloodlines—each gently protecting the families that would play an important part in the future Order had seen. Red and Orange tampered quite a bit with their descendants, creating many warriors, utilising the strength and mind touch abilities. Indigo and Violet tended more towards intelligence in theirs, creating those who were strong in the mental abilities. Green produced those who became adept at healing and the use of plants, also Whisperers. Yellow and Blue distributed the special abilities to their lines equally. While the other Sentinels sired many sons and daughters, this final pair was very careful on how many descendants they produced.

Chapter One

"And that, my children, is how the world came to be," Tarl'a told the boys, their eyes bright as she pulled the covers tighter over them. The wind howled outside the small hut.

"Ma, we're descended from Red, then?" the oldest of the boys asked.

"Yes, Galen, we are. Our family was created to look after the stones. But that is not for you or your brothers to worry about. It is always the women who watch the stones."

"But we have no sisters," he spoke plainly.

"I am still young enough to have more children Galen. Now sleep, all of you."

Tarl'a kissed each of their heads before moving back to the fire, and to the side of her husband, Mailcon. He put his arm around her as she began to sing a quiet song to send the boys to sleep.

"There have been no more children for some time now, my love," he said to her quietly once the boys were gently slumbering.

"There is still time, Mailcon."

"You should go to the stones and seek the Ancestors' help. I am sure they will help you conceive the daughter you so desperately want."

"I will go in the morning, as it is something I have been thinking about. But Loc is only two summers old now. There is still time," Tarl'a said adamantly.

Mailcon drew her closer and they lay together beside the warm fire. He kissed her gently, and they joined together as they had on so many long winter nights. But in her heart, Tarl'a knew it would do no good. The feeling that there would be no more children was overwhelming her. She had no daughter to pass the task onto, and that worried her the most.

In the morning as Tarl'a made the long trek up the hill to the sacred stones, she stopped at the spring and drank her fill. She stood and looked out at the valley far below. The steep hills, which embraced the long green meadow, were painted with the heather in bloom. The grass was lush and long and cut through with the brook, which was fed from the spring at her feet. She followed the brook with her eyes as it snaked its way the centre to the deep green forest that hid the valley at the end. Movement brought her eyes back to the small round house that sat just below and watched for a moment longer as Mailcon and their boys went about their morning tasks.

Sighing deeply, she turned and went around the large rock, which thrust its way up out of the ground, hiding the sacred stones from view. Standing at the entrance, she waited. Normally her Ancestor would not take long to answer her call, but today she waited for a lengthy time. She was about to give up when a shimmer of light flickered at the entrance and formed into a Being whose white light shone brightly.

Expecting the red hue of her Ancestor, this white one startled Tarl'a, and she took a step back at the overwhelming presence of Order.

"Tarl'a, daughter of my son, you seek guidance?" Order asked her gently.

Tarl'a sank to her knees and bowed to The Great Light.

Order stepped forward and lifted Tarl'a up.

"I do not seek your reverence nor your adulation. I do not set myself up as a god," Order said quietly.

"I only sought guidance from my Ancestor. Never have I thought that you yourself would appear to me." Tarl'a still held Order's hand, feeling herself slowly drawn by her into the circle.

"I came to seek your permission to put a plan into action," Order told her as they reached the centre.

"My permission?"

"Yes, child. I would not force this request onto you. I am not Chaos. This must first be agreed upon and discussed greatly before it can happen."

"What is it you wish from me?" Tarl'a asked, a little confused.

"You came seeking understanding as to why there have been no more children for you in the last two turnings of the seasons. It is as I wish. If you say no to our request, you shall have the child you have wished for—a daughter."

"And what is this request?"

"That, my child, is a great burden that I am afraid may be heartbreaking and hard for you to take on. If you take on this request, there shall be no more children for you and Mailcon. You have your four boys, one of whom the protector line shall pass down to, this Red has allowed. The task I ask of you is to foster a special child—a girl. The hopes and fate of this world shall rest heavily on her tiny shoulders," Order told her with some regret.

"Who is this girl, where does she come from?"

"The child will be born from two of the Sentinels, a true child. It has always been forbidden, this type of union, but the child is a necessity. Chaos will become stronger and more of a threat to this world, and that cannot be allowed to happen. This child shall become even greater in the abilities than my own. She will come to possess the energy of the universe and will hopefully one day help defeat Chaos."

"Why do you wish for us to foster her? She should be trained by her parents—by you." Tarl'a was having a hard time understanding why the Ancestors and The Great Light would entrust such a precious task to mere mortals.

"Tarl'a, through the guidance of you and Mailcon—through your understanding and love for her—she will grow to have the traits that will be necessary. The child would not get that from her parents. She would grow to be too much like them. Though they are not arrogant, their sense of self-worth would be passed to her. I have thought long and hard about this child. You and Mailcon, as the descendants of Red and Violet, are the perfect pair to bring this child up. I do not ask you to take this on lightly. All I ask is for you to go and think about it and talk with Mailcon."

"I will think about it," Tarl'a nodded.

Order placed a hand on her head. "My blessings and love be upon you. Go in peace until we meet again, Tarl'a. I will wait for your answer."

When Tarl'a looked up, Order was gone, and she was left with a singing in her heart. As far as she could remember, no one had ever been visited by The Great Light before.

Mailcon stood at the door as his wife came back down the hill. He could see already that something momentous had been revealed to her.

"Galen, take the boys and go collect deadfall for the fire," he told his eldest son.

"Yes Da." The young boy, only six summers old, gathered his brothers up. Taking the youngest by the hand, he led them down the valley towards the woods that hid the entrance.

Mailcon waited for Tarl'a to get nearer, and she gave him a weary smile.

"There was no need to send the boys off," she said as she entered the small house with Mailcon quickly following.

"The set of your face suggested otherwise to me. What did your Ancestor have to say?"

"It was not Red I met at the stones." She turned to him with a worried frown.

"Which one was it? Was it mine, Violet?"

"No. Mailcon, it was Order," she told him with awe.

"Order? The Great Light?" Mailcon was stunned at her words and stood staring at her with an open mouth.

"Yes." Tarl'a sat by the fire and stirred it to life, placing a pot on the edge.

"Why would Order appear? She has never done this before."

"No, to my knowledge no one has been so blessed. But I was today. The power that emanates from her is immense."

"Are you able to tell me what Order wanted?" he asked as he came to sit beside her.

"Yes. We need to discuss this very carefully. It is a great honour that will be bestowed on us, but one that comes with disappointment, I think, especially for you."

"What is it? You are scaring me."

"Order wishes us to foster a girl, a very special girl."

"Is that all? Of course we'll take her in," Mailcon said with a slight laugh at the easy task.

"Mailcon, it would mean there would be no more children for us. If we refuse, we will have one more child and that will be the girl I have wanted. But if we take this child in, she will become our daughter, and there will be no others after."

"Who is this girl, and why are we being asked?"

"She is to be a true child of the Ancestors. Born of two from Order, not from one of The People. She is needed to battle Chaos. Her abilities will be great and stronger than the Ancestors themselves. We have been asked to take her in and raise her as our own. To give her the necessary human traits that Order thinks she will need to defeat Chaos."

Mailcon leaned back for a moment as he poked the fire. Tarl'a started to place grain and meat into the boiling water in the pot, beginning the meal for the evening.

"Think on it Mailcon. This is something we must agree on together," she told him and then stood to see where the boys were.

In the quiet of the house, with just the crackling of the fire, Mailcon contemplated the great task that lay before him and his wife. The prospect of not having any more children came to him, but either way there would be one child—a girl. He poked the fire one more time, watching the embers flare and glow brightly.

"My son," a sweet voice said beside him. He looked up and saw the softly glowing form of Violet. She sat beside him and smiled.

"My Ancestor, you do me honour by visiting me here at our hearth," he greeted her.

"I sense a great worry in you, my son. I have already talked to the two who have been asked this task and assured them that their child would be in no better hands than those of yourself and Tarl'a. Red is of the same opinion. But I feel your hesitation."

"When you sent me here, I thought I would be given some great piece of knowledge or asked to take on a great task. Instead, I found myself falling in love with Tarl'a. Is this the task you sent me here for? To raise this child?"

"It is, my son. We have been planning this child since Order first made us aware of her necessity."

"I am not worried about having no more children, we have our four boys. I am only worried for Tarl'a's sake," Mailcon told her, a frown creased his brow.

"Your wife will love this child without question or hesitation. She is waiting for you alone to make the decision." Violet looked up at the door and stood. "She comes back."

As Tarl'a ducked under the doorway, her eyes grew wide at the sight of her husband's Ancestor.

"Violet, you do us a great honour," Tarl'a greeted her as she stood.

"No, daughter of my brother, you and my son do us a great honour by even considering what has been asked of you."

"We have not decided," Tarl'a told her, then her eyes strayed to Mailcon.

"No, you have not, and we await your decision eagerly. I will leave you. My blessings on you both and your sons."

"Thank you, Violet. Until we meet again," Mailcon said, coming to his feet and standing with his wife.

The Ancestor disappeared, and they were left alone.

The noise of the boys coming back to the hut floated in through the door, and Tarl'a turned to her husband.

"Was she demanding an answer?"

"No. She would not do that. Only encouraging. I think either way, we will have a daughter. We should be honoured that we have been asked to take on the role of parents to the child. Will you be all right, knowing you did not birth her?" Mailcon asked his wife with some concern.

"A little saddened that the line will not follow my own true daughter's. But Order told me that it shall pass through one of our boys. Are you sure you want to take this on, Mailcon?"

He took her in his arms and held her. "Yes, I am sure. She will be loved and cared for, and she will be well protected until she comes into her abilities."

"Then it is settled. We will go to the stones tomorrow and let them know," Tarl'a declared.

"Da, Ma!" The call came from outside.

Galen put his head in the doorway. "We have visitors." He ducked back out and the couple followed.

Before them stood a dazzling array of colour in a semi-circle around the house. The gathered group walked towards the couple and their children, and as they closed in together, they merged into one light.

Order held out her hands to them both.

"Thank you, my children. It has gladdened my heart to know that you will look after this child."

"It is our honour, Order," Mailcon told him, his hand shaking slightly in his wife's as she held onto it.

"The child will be born, as is the order of these things, in nine months hence. When I depart, I shall leave the two that are to birth her for you to get to know. A protection shall be placed over this valley. Entry shall only be allowed to those who come to seek true knowledge from the stones, shielding you from those of ill intent, including Chaos. The child must grow up here in this valley for the protection to work. She must not leave until she is ready, as we cannot guarantee that Chaos will not find out about her."

"We understand," Tarl'a said nodding.

Order turned and looked at the four boys all lined up at their parent's side. She moved to stand in front of Galen, the eldest.

"Galen, you shall be a great warrior with strength and flight abilities, also a protector." She went to the next. "Ru, I see a guide with stealth and tongues, a peacemaker also. Your life will take you far and wide.

Uven, a healer and mind touch, perfect abilities for an advisor. And finally, Loc. Animals will come from near and far to talk with you, but be careful you don't fall too deeply into their midst. You shall also possess the ability of foresight."

Each child looked up in awe at the magnificent Being. The blessing Order had bestowed on each boy were more than they would have gotten in the normal way.

"Each of these abilities will be necessary for the protection of the child. I must go now and leave you all to your lives. My blessings and love are on you both, Tarl'a and Mailcon." Order's last words floated away as she disappeared, and in her place were two.

Yellow and Blue stood before them, holding each other's hand.

"We find that we are in need of your guidance," Yellow said softly, blushing.

Tarl'a's view of the Ancestors changed that afternoon. While she had always thought of them as being all-knowing and aware, she now found, when it came to relationships between women and men, it was a different story. This confused her and she tried a few times with Yellow to find out how they had mated with The People. But every time she was on the brink of asking, she hesitated, as the question evaded the words necessary to form it.

"Is it always necessary to have affection for the person you wish to mate with?" Yellow asked naively.

"No. Most find that it is a necessary part of the process," Tarl'a said, embarrassed to be talking about it. "Sometimes a man can mate without consideration for his partner's feelings or wishes."

"He can force himself on a woman?"

"It has happened and sometimes the other way around as well. A man can be easily led into that state."

"As you have suggested."

"Yellow, may I ask you a question that may seem to be intrusive?" Tarl'a asked, finally finding the courage.

"You may, Tarl'a."

"How is it you have mated with The People but are so unaware of how to go about it?" she asked clumsily.

"Ah, yes, that word may be a little misleading. We do not mate as The People do, as we are not built the same as you. This form is of my own choosing and I can change it as I see fit." Yellow's body evolved fluidly into that of a tall, muscular, and very good-looking man, and just as quickly changed back. "As you see. When we mated with the nomadic people who came to our lands, we put an essence of ourselves inside each child as it lay in the womb. We passed the abilities that way, some of us more strongly and more frequently than others."

"Is that still the case with each child?" Tarl'a asked curiously.

"No. The abilities are now bound up in The People. They will remain so until such a time as all necessity for the abilities is at an end. That will not happen until Chaos has been defeated and cast out of this world for good."

"Will such a day come, Yellow?"

"We hope with our child, the One True Child, that it will be so."

"You would give up your child to be fostered by us?"

"Yes. It is necessary for us to do so. I am not equipped to bring up a child properly who will be one of The People. I have already seen that I will love and care for her down the ages. Her spirit will remain the same, as will her name."

"You have already chosen it?"

"Very carefully."

"Can you tell me her name?" Tarl'a asked hopefully.

"No, not until I place her into your arms. If I speak her name, she will already be in danger. This name is a great talisman for her. Her true name, when spoken, is a herald of her abilities. There will be a time in the far-off future when she will be called by another name to hide her, but her true name will always be there, written across her spirit."

"You speak of a future—how can she live to be that old?"

"You have foresight, Tarl'a. Cannot you see the future for my daughter?"

"I cannot. I have not met her yet."

"We shall talk again when I bring her to you, and you will then see what I see. She will be a strong woman with a great capacity for love. It is this love she will need to deal with her tasks and trials." Yellow stood from the stump where she had sat with Tarl'a, the meadow all around them.

The sun was beginning to go down on such a strange day. The final rays over the tops of the forest at the end of the valley were orange and golden, laced with purples on the clouds above. Yellow faced the sun and breathed in deeply, the swirling colours under her skin glowed brightly for a moment.

"Thank you, Tarl'a. Now I understand the relationship between a woman and a man. I understand now more greatly the way a child is conceived. How I envy your ability to love a single man."

"You do not feel love for Blue?" Tarl'a asked, standing now before Yellow.

"I feel more affection for my brother than the other Sentinels, but I think not the love you so evidently have for your Mailcon. We are not permitted that kind of love. We are Sentinels. It is our purpose to protect the world, guarding against Chaos, who inadvertently created both Order and us." Yellow looked up and saw Blue and Mailcon walking towards them. "Would you consider Blue to be handsome?"

Tarl'a turned and watched the pair walk towards them. "Some would consider him to be an extremely handsome man, and many a heart would flutter over him. For myself, I find that he is too handsome."

"Thank you for your honesty," Yellow said and went to meet the pair.

Blue held his hand out and she placed her own in his. To Tarl'a it almost appeared as if Yellow was blushing at the physical contact. The Sentinel's lights swirled faster under her skin and seemed to glow brighter on her cheeks. Within moments, both Ancestors had vanished from sight with the last of the sun's rays.

Mailcon came to her side and placed an arm around her waist.

"That had to be the most embarrassing conversation I have ever had." He smiled as they walked back to the house.

"You will have four more to make as they grow," Tarl'a laughed, watching their boys playing around the house.

"At least now I have had some practice," he said, joining her.

Tarl'a sat up in the middle of a stormy night, but it was not the tempest which raged around the hut that had woken her. A voice had called her name in the midst her dream and she was compelled to answer it. She got up and started to gather some things around her.

Mailcon woke with her movements and watched for a moment before speaking.

"What are you doing?" he whispered so as not to wake the children.

"I have to go to the stones," she told him, standing, now prepared.

"It is the middle of the night and there is a storm."

"It is important, Mailcon. It's the child," she said and ducked out the door not waiting for his response.

The wind whipped around, throwing sheets of water into her face and drenching her within moments, pulling and tearing at her clothes. Pushing through the storm, she headed to the track on the hill, knowing where she was going in the inky darkness of the night. At the base of the hill a light shone into the black—a dark and deep colour. Indigo nodded as Tarl'a passed her and followed on up the track. At the next switch was Violet, a soft, warm light emitting from her. At each turn she was met—Green, Orange, Red, and finally Blue. At the last turning she was met with Order, glowing brightly and illuminating the way to the great circle of stones.

In the centre she found Yellow. The swirling colours under her skin raced now with the effort she was feeling of birthing the child. Tarl'a did not notice the drop in the wind or the absence of the rain as she entered the circle, coming to the Ancestor's side.

"How far along are you?" she asked the woman.

"I don't know. Help me, please Tarl'a. I was never meant to give birth," Yellow cried out before letting go an ear piecing scream.

"Let me check." Tarl'a's experience with her own four births came back to her. "It won't be long. I can already feel the head."

Yellow's brothers and sisters all stood around the circle, each one placing themselves in between the great tall standing stones—Order taking the place that would normally have been Yellow's. All the Sentinels raised their hands and started to chant, the language unknown to Tarl'a and unheard as she concentrated on Yellow and the child that was in a hurry to meet the world.

The storm that Yellow's emotions had whipped up continued to rage outside the circle. Inside she screamed out to the world, her hands grasping at the grass underneath her. Until with one great final effort, the child was born into the hands of the woman who would raise her. Tarl'a wiped the child, bundled the little girl up into the blankets she had brought, and then handed her to Yellow to hold.

Carefully, Yellow unwrapped the girl and stood. The parts of her she had changed so she could carry the baby were now gone, no longer needed. The pain she had felt was forgotten and was never to be remembered. But the love Yellow instantly had for the little girl in her arms was immense, and she transferred as much as she could to the child.

Tarl'a stood back as the Ancestors all drew in close to see the girl and to bless her. Yellow passed her into the arms of Order and The Great Light held a hand over her tiny head. With eyes closed, Order saw the potential in the child and all the children down her line. Order nodded and smiled, then handed the child to Blue.

His own blessing he gave to his daughter, as he bent down and kissed her forehead. His own love he passed to her to join that of Yellow's, then gently handed the baby back to her mother.

"Tarl'a, it is time," Yellow said as she gazed into the blue eyes of her daughter.

Tarl'a came forward now and stood before them all. As each passed and stepped out of the circle, they gave her their own blessing. With just Blue, Yellow, and Order standing before her now, she accepted the baby into her arms.

"The child has a name, and we spoke once before of it. It is now passed to you, but still, you must not speak it until you are safely back inside your house. Once her name is tied to your home, she will be protected within the valley, and it must not be spoken beyond those borders. If it is, it would bring her into the notice of those she must face later. Take care of her, Tarl'a. Let her know her parents love her."

"I will, Yellow. I will love and protect her, and I will let her know how special she is," she said, still looking down at the tiny face.

"No. She must grow with no preferential treatment, and no special notice. The girl must grow strong in the love of a family. We place her in your care, along with Mailcon's, to raise her as your own," Order told her.

"We will do so." When Tarl'a looked up, the three had already started to move to the entrance, and she turned to follow them.

As Tarl'a descended with the precious bundle in her arms, the Sentinels once more guided the way in the dark of the night—their lights shining the path for her. The storm had abated, and the clouds gave way to the starry sky above. A meteor shower streaked golden across the inky sky. But Tarl'a had no eyes for the wonder of the sparkly display.

They stayed with her until she reached the little house. Each once more blessed the child as she passed them to the door, last of all Yellow with one final kiss for her daughter.

Tarl'a entered the house and found the fire banked up and glowing brightly. At the side was Mailcon, dozing with his chin on his chest. He woke with a start at her touch, and she sat beside him, unwrapping the girl.

"What is her name?" he asked her with wonder as he took the baby from her arms.

"Carling." The name came to her as clearly as if it had been called out into the room. "Her name is Carling."

"Little Champion. It is truly a fitting name for her. She is so beautiful and perfect," Mailcon said with wonder.

Chapter Two

Carling laughed as she was being chased by her older brother. He picked her up and swung her around in a circle. Galen was her favourite of all the brothers. He would always find time to play and make her laugh, even though he was supposed to help their father. Loc was the closest to her age, but he was more interested in the animals. Ru and Uven would play with her, but they tended to lose patience when she didn't understand what they wanted her to do.

Galen was tall, almost as tall as their father already, and he was strong too. His ability was already showing itself. He could easily pick her up in one hand and lift her onto his shoulders, carrying her up there for a long time while he worked. She loved to help him, especially when he would walk in the forest looking for firewood. Carling loved the trees, but she loved to dart away from him more, so that he would have to find her again.

A large bundle of wood sat on Galen's shoulder, and he held her hand gently while listening intently to his little sister tell him of the otter she had seen at the river. Behind them came the snort of a horse, and the children turned as one to see who had come to visit. Sitting astride a small pony, with his legs sticking out, was a man with a large beard and tattoos over his face and arms. He pulled up short beside them and dismounted the huffing animal.

"You must be Galen, Tarl'a and Mailcon's eldest," the man said in greeting.

"I am. And who are you that knows my name already?" Galen dropped the bundle of wood and pushed Carling behind him.

"I'm your Uncle Gart. Is your father close by? I have important news for him," Gart said jovially.

"He's at the house." Galen picked up the bundle again and put it back on his shoulder.

"How old are you now, boy?" Gart asked, as he walked with them, leading the tired looking pony.

"Twelve summers."

"I would have picked you more to be fifteen or sixteen. And who is this sweet little child?"

"My sister," Galen said as he took up Carling's hand once more.

"I hadn't heard your parents had another child. After you four boys she must have been over the moon with a daughter," Gart said as he walked beside them. "When did your ability come in, Galen?"

"I'm not sure, I never noticed," he replied as they rounded the bend, and the house came into view.

Mailcon sat outside dressing the hide of a deer, when he looked up from his work to see the newcomer to their valley walking with his children.

Carling let go of Galen's hand and ran quickly to her father, her blonde hair flying out behind her.

"Da, Da, we have a visitor," she said, running into his arms.

"I can see that, child. Did he give his name?"

"Gart. He said he is your brother."

"That he is, Carling. Tarl'a," Mailcon called into the house and his wife came out to see what the commotion was.

"I wonder what he wants?" she asked speculatively as she wiped flour from her hands with her apron.

"I suppose we'll find out soon. Carling, go fetch your brothers from the brook," Mailcon told her.

"Yes, Da." Carling ran off without a backwards glance and headed to the part of the brook she knew her brothers favoured.

The three of them were staring into the fast-flowing water, and Loc was down on his knees in the current as he tickled a trout from its hiding spot. It was a fat and lazy fish, one that they had tried to catch since last season. She skidded to a halt and waited to be noticed, knowing better than to interrupt Loc when he was trying to get a fish with his bare hands.

The boy's hands darted quickly and pulled the fish out, struggling to keep hold of it. He tossed it to his brothers, who both missed the fish, and it landed back in the water with a large splash before swimming away indignantly downstream—not wanting Loc to have another chance of catching it.

"You idiots! I got wet for nothing!" he yelled at them.

"Why did you throw it to us? You should have kept hold of it until we could take it from you," Uven said, annoyed at being accused of losing it.

Ru looked up from both brother's when he caught a shadow over them. "Carling, what do you want? We're busy."

"Da wants you all at the house. We have a visitor," she said and turned around, leaving them behind as she ran back to the house.

Visitors were a regular occurrence in the valley. People would come to visit on their way up to the stones. Carling was wary of anyone she didn't know, and she had a suspicion that she was always kept busy when they were there, so she wouldn't be noticed.

She rounded the house and found the man now standing talking to her father and mother. Galen was nearby, already breaking the wood down into smaller pieces for the fire. Carling went to help him, all the while listening to what the man was saying.

"A bit of refreshment wouldn't go amiss first, Tarl'a, then I'll tell you all my news," Gart said.

"I think there might be some ale left." Carling's mother ducked back into the house and the girl came up behind her father, placing a small hand in his and peeking out at the newcomer.

"We hadn't heard you had a daughter, Mailcon. You never sent word," Gart said smiling down at her.

Mailcon looked down at Carling. "I was sure we had sent a message to say our family had gotten larger. Carling, this is your Uncle Gart, he is my older brother."

"Hello," she said shyly.

"Such a pretty child. Her hair is like the colour of the sun, so golden."

Tarl'a came out and the two men sat themselves down. She handed them each a cup and sat beside her husband, pulling Carling onto her knee. Although she was only six summers old, she was small for her age, and many times people thought she was younger. It was something that her parents never corrected them on.

"So, news. To the west have come a new people, and they call themselves Celts. So far there have been no altercations between The People and these newcomers. They seem to be exiled and looking for a new place to settle."

"Whose lands are they settling on?" Mailcon asked.

"The Eagles. They have been wary of them so far and have let them have some land. From what I hear, it is hard land to toil and there is little game, but they appear more fisher folk than farmers."

"The Ancestors will guide you on how to deal with these people, Gart," Tarl'a said.

"Yes, but we also seek your Foresight, Tarl'a. As Guardian of the Stones, you have the greatest ability. What have you seen of The People lately?" Gart asked before taking a deep gulp of his cup.

"I have not sought out that question, so I will have to think on it. But you have come for another reason. I can sense that."

"Yes. I came to seek your permission to foster Galen in my home. Who better to teach him his ability, than his uncle?" Gart asked.

Mailcon turned to look at his eldest son, who had stopped working to listen in to the conversation. "What do you think, Galen? Would you like to go with your uncle and be taught your ability? Maybe have a few adventures as well?"

"It would be interesting to leave the valley, Da." He came walking over to the small group just as his younger brothers came around the house, still arguing about who had lost the fish. They stopped when they saw the stranger and came to stand by their father.

"You have been lucky with your family, Mailcon. They are all fine-looking boys."

"Thank you, brother. Your own must be grown now," Mailcon said.

"Yes, most are. My youngest is still with us. My eldest now has a family of his own. You know, if you wish to betroth your daughter, I know of a prospective match that would be a good one."

"Not for my Carling," Tarl'a said as she hugged the girl closer. "She is too young to betroth just yet. Plus, there are other things in her future."

"I will bow to your wishes, Tarl'a. But if the tradition stands, she will take over from you one day as Guardian to the stones—an honoured and praised one. So, we already know her ability." The large man winked at Carling and she stared at him.

"That's right, and when her time comes to wed, her husband will make himself known. The Ancestors have already seen to that. I remember my own journey here," Mailcon said, smiling at his wife. "Will you be staying with us long?"

"A day or two. I would like to visit the stones while I am here if you would guide me, Tarl'a."

"I would be honoured to, Brother."

"Why does he come now?" Tarl'a asked Mailcon in a whisper later that night. "How did he know Galen had come into his ability?"

"Are these questions to do with a genuine concern about something, or more a mother's protectiveness for her child?" Mailcon whispered back.

"The timing of his visit is unusual."

"No. He knew how old the boy would be. Tarl'a we cannot keep him here in this valley—nor the others."

"One of them is to be Guardian after me. One of them must stay."

"But that is not until a long time off. We must let them go and explore the outside world first. Find themselves wives. Can't you use your foresight to see into their futures?"

"I don't wish to. I will answer travellers' questions and tell them what I see, but for my own sons and Carling I refuse. I will only see heartache and tears. I tried once with Loc, remember."

"Order may have blessed our boys doubly, but I think that may have been more of a curse," Mailcon said sadly.

"No, not a curse. Loc does not get betrothed. His bond with his animal will be too strong."

"He is only one. The other three will marry, though."

"Yes, they will. Though I do not see to who. That is enough, I will see no more. Life is a journey and if we spoil the surprises now, we will not enjoy them later," she said.

"I wouldn't worry about Galen, he's already as strong as three men. He'll be fine out in the world. Gart will look after him," Mailcon tried to reassure her.

Across the house in the darkness, a pair of pale blue eyes watched them through the dying embers of the fire and listened in to their conversation. This time of the night was always when they spoke their worries and fears for the future, and it was then that the little girl would find things out. Now she didn't like what she heard. Carling could not believe her brother would be going away. She struggled with it for a moment before a tear escaped her eye.

Morning dawned, and Tarl'a led Gart up the hill behind the house. Carling followed them on little legs that worked double time to keep up. When she reached the top, she drank from the water as her mother did and went around the rocks, standing to one side. She had never neared the stones. She felt their power and pull, and they frightened her a little.

Gart and Tarl'a entered the stones and stood in the centre. They waited there for such a long time, or so it seemed to the little girl. She sank to the grass and closed her eyes, wishing that the Ancestors would hurry up. When she looked up, they were coming from the other side of the rocks and entering the circle.

She could not hear what they said to her uncle and mother. Their voices were soft, like a faraway bird call on the wind. She had seen them before and was not afraid of the colourful Beings. She would always wait until her mother was finished and they would notice her. It made her feel special.

The Ancestors were now filing out of the circle, and as always, walking towards her. Carling stood and waited for them each to place a hand on her head. The last two stopped in front of her and knelt on one knee.

"She has grown so much," Blue said.

"She has become so beautiful," Yellow replied with a smile.

"Our blessings on you, child, and our love," Blue told her as he kissed her forehead, followed by the same action from Yellow.

"We will meet again when you are thirteen, child," Yellow told her and stood. The pair left with a sigh, a backwards glance, and then disappeared behind the rocks.

Carling stared after them, unsure of how to take this strange greeting they had given. She looked to her mother to ask, but Tarl'a shook her head slightly.

Gart was watching his niece with wonder.

"Why is she is so singled out by the Ancestors?" he asked her mother and they walked through the entrance of the stones.

"Carling was born here in the circle. I had been called to the stones when she decided it was her time to be born. The Ancestors were with me and helped deliver her," Tarl'a answered him. This story was one Carling had not heard before.

"You are going to have to be careful with her suitors as she grows," Gart said with a laugh.

"As Mailcon said, he will know when the time is right to meet her. Her destiny is clouded from my sights." Tarl'a took Carling's hand and led the way back down the hill.

Later that afternoon, Galen was heading out to the wood and Carling ran after. She caught up with him and took his hand. He looked down and smiled at her.

"Aren't you supposed to be helping Ma?" he asked.

"Yes, but I want to go with you. Galen, are you really going away?"

"Yes, little sister, I am. I am going to our uncle's house to start my training."

"Can I come with you?" she asked hopefully.

"No, you cannot. You have to stay with Ma and Da. You are the next Guardian and must learn from Ma."

"I don't want to be tied to the stones. I heard them talking last night. They said that all of you boys will be going out into the world. Why can't I?"

"That is the way of it. You must stay here. Ma has not left the stones since she became Guardian."

"But she did leave before she took over from her mother. Galen, I want to see the world. I want to go to far-off places and meet new people," she told him strongly.

Galen stopped and picked her up, placing her on his shoulders. "You may get to go out of the valley before you take over from Ma. I hope you do, Carling. I am not looking forward to leaving tomorrow, and I shall miss you the most of all."

"Will you be back soon?"

"I don't know. Uncle Gart was saying that it will be over a year for the training of the skills and then there is more. Carling, can you keep a secret?"

"Yes, of course I can."

"I discovered a few days ago I have another ability."

Carling leaned down so she could see his face, so far that he had to react quickly to hold on to her, as she began to slip from his shoulders.

"Another?" she cried out with amazement.

"Yes, I am sure I have Flight."

"Have you tried?"

"No."

"Da said last night that Order had blessed you boys doubly. Do you think he meant that you have two abilities?" she asked seriously.

Galen placed her on the ground and knelt so he was eye to eye with her.

"Who are you and where is my little sister?" he asked with a laugh.

"I'm here, silly."

"You sounded far older than your seasons, then. I was worried that something had taken over you." He kissed her forehead and stood. Taking her hand once more, he led her into the woods.

"I listen when people talk, Galen. I remember things as well. Why do you think you have Flight?"

"Wait until we are in the woods, then I'll show you." They walked on and were soon under the cover of the trees, entering the clearing in the middle

"Will you show me now?" Carling asked, excited.

"Here, watch." He placed the axe down on the ground and looked up into the trees, spotting a branch. He put all of his strength into the leap and landed on the limb, wobbling a moment, grabbing hold of the trunk to keep him upright.

"But you have Strength! Couldn't it be just that?" Carling called up to him.

"That's what I thought, until I did this." He stepped off the branch and controlled the descent to a slow pace. His feet touched the ground softly, and he walked towards her, picking the axe back up.

"You must tell Ma and Da. Maybe Uncle Gart can get you training for that as well," she said sulkily.

"Your turn will come soon enough, Carling. Anyway, we already know what your ability will be. It will be Foresight like Ma. All Guardians of the Stones have Foresight."

"They blessed me again this morning. But Yellow and Blue came and talked to me this time."

"That is because you are so pretty, and because of the way you were born."

"Ma told Uncle Gart that I was born in the circle. Is that true?" she asked.

"I think so. Come on, are you going to help me or not? Or should I send you back to Ma?"

"I'll help." They walked to the other side of the wood and made their way back, picking up deadfall branches along the way.

Gart climbed up onto the back of the pony and hauled Galen up behind him. Carling held her mother's hand tightly, tears already trailing down her cheeks at the thought of her beloved brother leaving them. Their farewells had been long and emotional. She noticed Ru standing a lot taller now that his older brother was going, already taking on the mantle of the eldest son in the house.

With a wave, they were going down the track and Carling watched them go. Her tiny heart was breaking. She let go of her mother and ran after them, her hair loose and flying behind, her little legs going as fast as they could to catch up.

"Galen, Galen," she called out as she chased after them.

Galen turned in his seat behind Gart and saw her running. He slipped from the back of the horse and caught her up in his strong arms.

"Don't go, Galen," she sobbed into his shoulder.

"I have to, Carling. I have to. Stop crying, please! We will see each other again soon. Then we will see how much you have grown." He put her down on the ground and knelt in front of her, pushing the hair off her face and wiping her tears. "I will miss you, Carling, but I will be back. You will have to watch out for me in one full turning of the seasons."

Carling hiccupped and flung her arms around his neck. "Come back safe," she told him before letting go and turning to run back home. She didn't stop at the house, instead carried on up the hill, not once looking backwards at her brother. Without a thought of her fear of the stones, she raced through the entrance and lay down in the centre on her stomach, tears wetting her arms as they cradled her head.

A touch on her back startled her, and she looked up to see Yellow and Blue by her side.

"Why do you cry, child?" Yellow asked, concern in her eyes, the lights under her skin swirling softly.

"My brother is leaving me behind. I don't want him to go," she told the Ancestor through her sobs.

"It is his destiny to leave this valley, but he will be back and you will see him again. This has been seen," Blue told her.

Yellow gathered her up and held her on her knee, wrapping her arms around her. "Do you wish to forget him so you can stop being sad?" she asked Carling.

"No, I just wish he wouldn't go. My other brothers think I'm a pain and don't play with me as much."

"You must get to know them, Carling. They are to be your support. The relationship you form with them now will strengthen you as you grow, and it will help you face your future," Yellow told her.

"You are the Ancestors… can't you make him come back and stay?" Carling looked up into their faces, eager at the thought.

"We cannot change the destiny of your brother. This time apart from each other is necessary, and one day you will understand why," Blue said while he cupped her face in his hand.

"Carling," Tarl'a called, rounding the other side of the rocks and stopping at the sight of the two Sentinels who had given life to her child.

"Tarl'a please join us," Yellow requested.

Tarl'a entered the stones and came to sit in front of the group. Her eyes were wide, and her face was filled with fear at the thought of losing her child back to the two Ancestors.

"We found her crying, Tarl'a," Yellow reassured her. "We were only trying to calm her."

"Thank you, Yellow. I was concerned with the way she reacted to her brother leaving."

"It is a natural thing for her to be upset at Galen leaving her." Blue looked at Carling's foster mother carefully. "You have not looked into your son's future."

"No. I have seen enough to know that he will be happy once his father and I have gone. I do not need to know the rest," Tarl'a told them.

Carling was watching the interaction between the Ancestors and her mother very carefully. She had a feeling something else was not being said, but she couldn't work out what it was, except that it had to do with Galen in some way.

"There will come a time soon that the education of this child will need to be taken further in hand. A fostering such as Galen is doing will not be enough," Blue informed her.

"You cannot take her away from us." Tarl'a instinctively reached for Carling to pull her away from her natural parents.

"We would never do that." Yellow held on tightly to Carling. "Please, just a moment longer." She lay her cheek on Carling's golden head.

Tarl'a sat back and waited for the two Ancestors to be ready to hand her back.

"A mother's love runs deep, no matter where her child is," she told Yellow, who only nodded.

"We must leave, Yellow. We have things to prepare." Blue placed a hand on her arm.

Very carefully, Yellow kissed Carling on the head and handed her back to Tarl'a. Blue leaned in, and as his lips touched her head, Carling could see a great cave with sea all around it. Giant pillars of rock thrust out of the water, like columns holding up a heavy roof. Inside the cave she floated to the very end where she saw a smaller pillar to stand on.

Carling shook her head and the image disappeared, then she buried her face in her mother's shoulder. Tarl'a stood up with her child in her arms, and the Ancestors placed themselves on either side of the entrance as they exited the circle.

"Her thirteenth birthday will be a special one, Tarl'a," Blue said as they passed through the threshold of the ring.

"I understand, Blue. But until then, let her be a child, as Order has asked. No more blessings, no more notice. She was to be brought up as normal as possible."

"We understand, and we will do as you ask. But when she comes to the circle and is so upset, should we leave her to her heartbreak?" Yellow asked kindly.

"I thank you for this moment, and I do understand your feelings. But she is too young and impressionable to deal with it." Tarl'a moved off and headed down the hill with Carling still in her arms.

"Ma, I don't understand," Carling said, pulling away a little.

"I know, my sweet child. One day you will, but not at this moment. You're too young, and you're still upset about Galen."

"Why would they take me away from you and Da?"

"That is a question for another time, Carling, and no not for a very long time, not until after you come into your ability."

"But I know what that will be. Galen said it would be Foresight like you. That every Guardian of the Stones has it."

"Yes, but it is not certain that it will be," Tarl'a replied patiently to her daughter's questions.

"But you can see, can't you? Will you tell me what my ability will be, Ma?"

"No, I will not. Now hush, I do not want to talk about it anymore." Tarl'a put Carling back on her feet and held her hand as they headed down the track.

Chapter Three

Carling followed Loc closely and quietly as he slipped out first thing in the morning. The sun hadn't even risen, and a mist shrouded the ground as she tried to keep her foot-falls quiet, as Ru had taught her when he was home last. It had been over a year since Loc went away to start his training and the visits from her brothers were very rare, leaving the girl feeling lonely.

Loc's form was still visible through the swirling mist as he passed into the trees. The darkness under the great limbs made her pause for a moment. Stepping silently and carefully, she followed her brother into the depths and found him in the same clearing where Galen had shown her his Flight ability. That day came sharply into focus, and she found herself missing him again. Hiding behind the trunk of a large tree, she watched her youngest brother as he stood in the centre. A shadow on the other side of the clearing moved, and a shaggy black wolf stepped into the space and sat down in front of Loc.

"You can come out, Carling. She has already told me you are there, and she promises not to hurt one of my littermates." He turned and looked directly at the spot in which she was hiding.

Slowly, she stepped around the tree and faced both Loc and the wolf. He beckoned her to come forward, and she moved closer.

"This is Wolf," Loc told her. "Hold out your hand so she can sniff you, I promise she won't bite," he encouraged her with a smile.

Carling stepped forward again and held out her hand. The wet nose of the large wolf pressed against her palm, then moved under it to let it rest on her head.

"She says that you are special, and she welcomes you to our pack," Loc told her.

"I'm not special, my ability still has not come in," Carling told her brother.

"No, it hasn't, but I am sure it will soon. Patience, Carling. Now are you going to tell me why you have taken to following me?"

"I wanted to know where you were going. You have only been home for a day, and you are already disappearing." Carling stroked the wolf's ears, feeling the softness of them.

"I was just meeting with Wolf. She has finished hunting and has news for me. There are men camped on the other side of the river. They arrived last night and seemed to be waiting for something."

"Da and Ma should be told," Carling said, looking at him directly.

"Thank you for the advice. How about you go back and tell them, and Wolf and I will go and have a look at the group?"

"Oh, no, you are not getting rid of me that easy, Loc." Carling left him standing in the clearing and headed towards the river that ran across the entrance to the valley, denoting the boundary.

It was only a short distance away, and she pressed herself against a tree to remain hidden. Wolf had been right, there was a group of men camped on the other side. A guard could be seen walking the small perimeter, and the horses nickered on their tethers as he passed. Loc came up behind her and looked over the top of her head.

"Who do you think they are?" Carling asked him.

"I have no idea. There are no markings letting us know which family they belong to," Loc said. "Come away, we've seen them now, and we must go warn Ma and Da. The fact that they didn't come over the ford and shelter in the woods for the night means they may be hostile. Wolf said she would stay and keep an eye on them for us."

Tugging on her arm, he pulled her back into the cover of the trees. He kept his arm on her until they reached the valley, pushing her along as she kept slowing up.

"I'm not as fast as you, Loc! My legs are smaller," Carling complained.

"Says the girl who can run like a rabbit," Loc laughed at her. "When we get to the house, I'll tell Ma and Da—you say nothing. They don't like it when you go that close to the edge of the valley."

"I'm not a baby anymore," she declared.

"We are aware of that, my little sister. You keep reminding us." Loc laughed at her.

They remained quiet for the rest of the walk, but if they were hoping to make it back without detection from their parents, they were sadly mistaken. The greying head of Mailcon came out of the house and stood waiting for them at the door.

"Good morning, Da, did you sleep well?" Loc asked him.

"I did, son. Where have you and Carling been so early in the morning?" He folded his arms across his chest.

"There are men camped on the other side of the river. My friend Wolf called to me this morning to let me know."

"And Carling had to go with you to make sure that this was true?" Mailcon asked, turning his eyes to his daughter.

"No, Da, I followed him. He didn't know I was there."

"I did when Wolf let me know," Loc said. "I tried to get her to go back, but as usual, she wouldn't listen."

"And you, Carling, how close to the end of the valley did you go?"

"Only to the edge of the trees. I have never been further. My whole life seems to be confined to this one valley. I know every blade of grass, every flower intimately, because I have never been allowed to go any further." Carling was getting angry at still being treated like a child who had to be protected. She pushed past her father and entered the house.

Tarl'a was banking the fire and starting breakfast.

"You shouldn't talk to your father like that, Carling," she chided.

"How long am I supposed to be kept here? The boys have all been able to leave; why can't I?"

"Because it is our wish that you stay within the valley, until you are ready to leave us," Tarl'a answered as Carling sat down next to her and started to help with breakfast.

"We have riders approaching," Loc called out, poking his head through the door. The mother and daughter left the fireside and went to meet their visitors.

A group of six horses came down the track towards the family home. No markings were evident on either rider or horse to tell them who these people were and where they had come from, which made Tarl'a and Mailcon very curious. Carling held back and kept behind her mother, watching carefully.

One of the riders broke ranks and rode towards them quickly. As he neared, he raised his arm in greeting with a large smile spreading across his features. The man jumped from the horse and ran to the group.

"Ma, Da!" the man called out, his dark hair flying, and Carling recognised Ru.

He greeted his parents and youngest brother with enthusiasm and then spied Carling. "Little sister!" He enfolded her in his arms and picked her up off the ground. "It is so good to be home."

"Why didn't you come straight to us last night?" Mailcon asked.

"Because we arrived late. I didn't want to overwhelm you with many visitors," Ru told them and went to meet his fellow travellers.

"And these people are?" his father asked.

"Most are our people. But a few are Celts. You remember Uncle Gart telling us about them? Well, there have been more arriving, and they have been moving further inland."

"You have brought them here to this valley?" Tarl'a asked, a little worried.

"They come with a pure heart, Ma, otherwise they would not have been able to cross," Ru said quietly. "They also know about the abilities. There have already been intermarriages."

"But why did you bring them here?" she asked again.

"I wished you to meet my intended bride." The group was now upon them, and Ru went to the only female rider and helped her down. "Ma and Da, this is Nila. She does not speak our tongue yet, but I am teaching her."

Nila was tall and proud looking, with pale skin, and hair as orange as the rising sun. In her hands she held a gift for Tarl'a and she presented it to her graciously. Inside the cloth wrapping was a beautiful and delicate golden torc to be worn on her arm.

"It is beautiful! Thank you, Nila," Tarl'a said, smiling at the girl. Nila smiled back aware she had made her mother-in-law-to-be happy.

"Let me introduce you to the rest of the group," Ru said as the others were all dismounting. "You know Uncle Gart, and this is his youngest son, Elfin." Ru placed a heavy but friendly hand on the young man at his side. They were about the same age and had the same colouring. Anyone looking at the pair could have mistaken them for brothers rather than cousins.

Mailcon greeted his brother warmly and his nephew. Ru turned to some of the other members of his party. "This is Nila's father, Faolan, and this is her brother, Bevan." The young man turned towards them, and Carling stared at him for a moment. His hair was the same colour as his sister's, but his eyes were a soft shade of green and were startling to see. He appeared to be not much older than she was.

"We are honoured to meet the parents of Ru. We have heard many things from Gart about you and this place," Faolan greeted them, his accent sounded lilting and light to Carling, with almost a musical quality to it.

"Welcome to our home." Tarl'a extended the invitation to sit. "Have you eaten yet?"

"No, Ma, we came straight here. I was in too much of a hurry to come home and introduce you all." Ru blushed slightly as he put his arm around Nila.

"Carling, come help me," Tarl'a said and pushed her daughter inside, noticing she was staring at the youngest of the guests.

As the two of them worked at the fire inside, they could hear the others talking outside. Carling helped make the morning cakes of crushed grain and berries, placing them by the fire while her mother made the broth. When everything was ready, they took it outside to serve. As Carling handed the little cakes around, she averted her eyes from them all, especially Bevan.

"This cannot be Carling the Blessed," Gart said as she came to stand in front of him.

"Hello, Uncle," she said shyly.

"You have grown. Has your ability come in yet, girl?" he asked good-naturedly.

"We will discuss that later, Gart," Tarl'a said as she handed him a cup of broth to go with the cake.

Gart raised his eyebrows and looked at his brother, who nodded.

"As you can see, Faolan, my niece is not only blessed with such beauty and the colour of her hair, but also by our Ancestors."

"But you could say the same for me, Gart, apart from the hair," Tarl'a said, sitting and starting her own meal. "As my daughter, she is blessed by the Ancestors, as she will be Guardian of the Stones after I am gone."

"I would be most eager to visit your great stones, Tarl'a, if you would permit me?" Faolan asked her.

"I would need guidance on that and permission from the Ancestors. Carling and I will venture forth to them this morning."

Faolan inclined his head in deference to her, and the conversation slipped into quiet. Ru looked slightly uncomfortable with it, and Carling deduced that he had hoped it would go slightly better than it was. She plucked up her courage and asked him a question.

"On your travels, did you see anything of Galen, Ru?" She felt herself go red.

"No, Carling, I did not. But we did hear that he has travelled past the borders of our lands. He went with a party down into the southern lands to entreat for peace. There had been some dispute with the lowlanders as to where exactly our lands start and theirs finish."

"He went with my eldest son. Galen is large now, and a favourite with the ladies. He will not choose, though, so they are left heartbroken," Gart told them.

"I think my brother is liking the attention too much to settle just yet," Ru put in.

"I remember when he came with me. You chased us, Carling, and didn't want him to go," Gart said with a chuckle.

Nila said something to Ru, and he hastily spoke back. She nodded and looked at Carling, asking a question in her native tongue.

"Nila would like to know how old you are, Carling. I have told her that you are already twelve summers, but she thinks you younger," Ru smiled.

"I will soon be thirteen," Carling said, sitting straighter in her seat.

"Born in a storm and with a temper to match. Do you still have your temper, Carling?" Ru teased her.

"Stop teasing, Ru, or she will knock you on your arse again, like she used to," Mailcon said, grinning. "Our daughter may look small, but she can fight like any man, having been taught by her older brothers."

"Uven sends his greetings, I almost forgot to tell you. His training is going well, and he hopes to visit soon," Ru told them quickly.

"My sons are all grown and have mastered their abilities," Tarl'a said wistfully as she gazed at Carling. "I have only Carling left at home now. Loc here is only visiting as well."

"I would have liked to have fostered you as well, Loc, it is too bad you didn't come to us," Gart said.

"My main ability needs space, Uncle. I could not have learned what I needed from any person around you, and Ma helped with the other," Loc said softly.

"What are these abilities you speak of?" Faolan asked eagerly. "I have heard tell of your people having powers."

"They are gifts from the Ancestors," Gart began. "You have seen me use my own countless times as we came here."

"We each possess a unique gift which only emerges when a child reaches a certain age. Once their training is finished in the ability, then the child is considered an adult, and a ceremony is performed to welcome them," Mailcon added.

"What if one of your people does not have an ability?" Bevan asked, sitting forward.

"That has never happened," Mailcon answered.

"I am afraid it has, brother. Children of mixed heritage are being born without abilities. When you go to the stones, Tarl'a, I must speak with the Ancestors about it," Gart told her.

"I think that might be wise. We will go now, while the morning is still new. Loc, clean up the mess, please." Tarl'a stood and turned without preamble, and Carling followed her, pleased to be away from the strangers that had invaded their home. All through the meal, she had felt their eyes on her and it made her uncomfortable.

"Why did you bring them here, Gart? This of all places?" Tarl'a spoke when they were far enough away and before they started up the hill.

"Nila wished to meet you, the parents of her intended. It is only natural that she should be escorted by her brother and father to keep her safe. They are not wed yet," Gart replied.

"I can see that. Her father seemed eager to learn about the abilities," Tarl'a said. "Does he wish to use them for his own means?"

"I do not think so. He is just curious, I suppose." Gart was breathing heavily now that they were climbing the track.

Carling kept her thoughts to herself. The talk of the abilities hurt her a little, as hers still had not appeared. She was lost in her own mind, no longer listening to what her mother and uncle were talking about, when she bumped into the Gart's broad back.

"She is supposed to be your successor. How can she do that without the ability of Foresight, Tarl'a?" Gart's voice carried up the path.

"I am sure the Ancestors know what they are doing. It won't be long now until it comes through," Tarl'a said confidently.

They talked no more until they reached the summit of the hill and rounded the rocks. Gart drank heavily from the spring and came to stand behind Tarl'a and Carling as they began to enter the circle. Unlike other times Carling had been up to call on the Ancestors, they did not need to wait long until they appeared.

The host came in though the entrance and placed themselves around the stones, waiting to be asked the questions the group had come armed with.

"Ancestors, my greetings to you all. I have come to ask why some of our people are being born without the gift of abilities," Gart started.

Green stepped forward to answer.

"The abilities are always passed through the female, as she is the carrier and giver of life. The ones you speak of are born to mothers who are not of the people."

Red was now standing at his brother's side. "It is perhaps an oversight on our part, but it was thought necessary for the sake of the One True Child."

"One True Child? Who is this person?" Gart was confused with the term.

"You have not told him, Tarl'a? The time has almost arrived for us to take on the training of the child," Red said.

"I was waiting for her ability to appear. It has not done so, so I have not spoken of it to anyone." Tarl'a held her head up high.

"The abilities will not show themselves until the child travels to our home. The location is already implanted in the child's mind." Blue was now with his brothers and spoke gently to her. "It is a journey that is necessary and is now becoming urgent. The time approaches, and the child must be at that place by the next full moon."

"Then I shall make sure that the child is prepared." Tarl'a dropped her head to hide a tear.

"You know who this child is?" Gart asked her.

"We will speak soon," she told him quickly, before turning back to the Sentinels. "There are other questions we have for you, Ancestors." Tarl'a stood straighter now, pushing the problem aside. "There are some who are not of our people wishing to visit the stones. Will you allow them to?"

"We welcome all, Tarl'a. They will be met. These people who come to our lands—the Celts—must be met with friendly and open arms. It is part of the process, and our peoples must merge. They are peaceful on the whole but can be warlike. The time to use your ability is now. You must no longer be reluctant to see the future. It is your duty to warn The People of things to come," Red said to her firmly.

"Yes, my Ancestor. I will do as you ask, though it pains me greatly to see what is to come."

Red came to her and placed a caring hand on her shoulder.

"My daughter, it was left to you to see these things through. Your line was created for a specific purpose and that purpose has grown to cover Order's plan. It will be hard for you to let the child go, but it is time. The child must come into her abilities to face what is to come."

"I understand Red. It will be done," Tarl'a said quietly.

"Good." Red moved from her and stood before Carling. "Go fetch the visitors, Carling, we will meet them now."

"Yes, Ancestor." Carling left them, and as she rounded the rocks she looked back and saw them in heated discussion with her mother. Gart looked stunned at what was being said.

As quickly as she could, she headed down the hill and raced back to the little house. She found the visitors still sitting out front and came to a skidding halt, bringing them all to look up at her as she tried to collect her breath.

"The Ancestors request you come to them now. They will meet with you," Carling gasped, looking at Faolan. His bright blue eyes stared at her until he comprehended and stood.

Bevan joined his father as they followed Carling, but when the young girl looked back, she saw Nila still sitting.

"You are to come too," Carling told Ru's betrothed, who waited for Ru to translate.

"It is not their way, Carling. Women are not involved in these things," Ru informed her, looking a bit sheepish.

"That's silly." Carling went over to Nila and took her hand, leading her towards the hill. They climbed up the track, following Carling to the stones.

Faolan and Bevan stood in awe of the size of the stones, and then they noticed the occupants—a colourful array standing behind Tarl'a and Gart. Carling saw the look her uncle was giving her, and she was puzzled.

"Welcome, please join us," Red said, beckoning them in.

The small group entered the stones and came to meet the host. Faolan looked from one to the other, unable to comprehend the nature of the Beings, while Bevan and Nila stared openly at the swirling lights that played under their skin.

"We had heard of you from others, but we thought you to be like our gods, aloof and hidden," Faolan said, bowing low.

"We are not gods. We are but Sentinels here to protect the world," Red addressed him. "We know of your gods and know what they are like. They do not hold as much power as we, but they are welcome in our lands, and they are respectful of our wishes."

"You speak to our gods?" Bevan was stunned at this news.

"Yes, we have found them to be very helpful and co-operative in our plans. They have promised their protection for certain places and people. We do not seek to rule you or change your beliefs in your gods. We wish a joining, a merging of our people. It is to the benefit of all that this occurs. In some families, our lines will continue, they will be part of The People. In others, they will be lost with the mixing of the cultures. And I think now, in some special instances, we will step in and change things as necessary to help us in our quest," Red told them.

"You have been told of the stories of Order and Chaos and their battle for this world," Yellow said stepping forward. "Chaos already has his plan in place to dominate this world, and it will be coming to our fair shores shortly. Our own is about to blossom. An idea that you have been thinking of this morning, Faolan of the Celts, cannot be. That one is our child and is intended for someone else."

"I understand." Faolan inclined his head in acknowledgement. "We did not seek you out to make such an arrangement, it was just a passing thought. We sought you out to understand this place in which we have found ourselves. We do not wish to dominate your people, but work with them, and with that in mind we seek your permission to do so."

"The permission was granted the moment you set foot on our lands. Your gods had already petitioned us for our help," Green told him.

"Our lands are vast, and there is room for us all. Long have we admired your spirits as warriors and seafarers, and we welcome you," Orange told them.

"Thank you." Faolan bowed once more.

"There is a gift we would bestow upon your daughter, Faolan, to help her assimilate into her new family, if we have your blessing to grant it," Violet said to him, stepping forward.

Faolan looked flustered at having permission asked of him from such Beings, and he faltered for a moment.

"What is this gift?" he asked, still wary.

"The gift of understanding. The process of her being taught our language by Ru will be long and sometimes very frustrating for her. We can give her the help she needs to understand and be understood in turn. Will you allow this gift to be given to your daughter?" Violet inquired.

"It is not our way to educate our women. But as you have said, both peoples must assimilate and learn from each other. I would be honoured for such a gift to be given my Nila," he told her.

Violet placed a starry hand on the hair of Nila and passed the knowledge on to her. She smiled into the face of the girl.

"Welcome to our family, Nila. Ru is a fine son of mine and will make you a great husband. You both will be happy and blessed with many children. I will take the moment now to make the first interference and claim half of them as my descendants."

Nila looked at Violet with large eyes, as she understood every word. She turned to Ru for support.

"Thank you, Ancestor," Ru said, taking Nila's hand.

"It is time for us to leave. Our attention is required elsewhere," Red said as they stepped away before filing from the circle, walking out of sight behind the rocks.

The party was quiet as they descended the hill, Carling bringing up the rear. There were moments during the meeting not only with these strangers, but with her mother and uncle, when something had been talked about, and it worried her. She watched as her mother broke away from the group and went to talk to her father. They were soon joined by her uncle, and they stopped talking when Ru approached them.

"Thank you, Carling, for taking us to such a momentous meeting," Nila said to her as she approached hesitantly.

"I did nothing that I was not told to do by the Ancestors."

"Ru says that you will be Guardian after your mother, such an honoured position. I still do not understand why it is entrusted to a woman," Nila marvelled. "Why a man has not claimed the right to do so."

They began to walk past the house and the brook that ran beside it, out into the meadow beyond.

"It is as the Ancestors wish," Carling explained. "When Red, our Ancestor, made our family, it was with one purpose only, for the protection of the stones. It has always passed through the female line. I feel that our people see roles of women and men differently. But we are all equal. Well, everyone else is equal, I'm not."

"Why do you feel so?" Nila asked.

"I have been forbidden to leave this valley. My parents have always been protective of me, so in that we are not equal. My brothers get to go out to the world and see new things, new people. I have to wait here for people to come to me. I am pleased Ru has found someone to share his life with. But he will not be staying for long, I believe."

"No, we came to make the betrothal before your parents. It has already been performed before mine. Then we will be going back to the settlement to start our life. He has been so instrumental in entreating between our people. But before we go back, I would like to get to know you better."

"There is not much to know. But it will be nice to have a girl nearer my age than my mother to talk to for once. How old are you?"

"I am eighteen summers. Are you really thirteen?"

"Yes, I am," Carling answered.

The girls wandered the meadow alongside the brook and turned when they got to the forest. They talked of many things. Nila explained so much of the outside world that her brothers had never told her. When they got back to the house, Carling could feel the tension in the air.

Chapter Four

That night, the meal that was prepared was more of a feast than their normal simple fare to help celebrate the betrothal of Nila and Ru. The group was enjoying themselves with storytelling and singing. All seemed happy except for Tarl'a and Mailcon. Although they smiled and laughed with the rest, Carling was aware of something else. A sadness was the feeling she got from them, a deep-seated melancholy of something being lost.

The evening wore on, and at one quiet moment Tarl'a stood. "I have a vision for you, my son," she said, addressing Ru. "It is as Violet has told you—happiness with your bride and a great many children. Half your children will be blessed with abilities and are of Violet's line, just as you are."

"Thank you, Ma." Ru put his arm around Nila.

"For my brother-in-law. Your house will be overflowing with grandchildren, and you shall prosper. As we were warned up at the stones, an evil is coming to this land. Your lands will be invaded but know that there are many who will come to your aid, as you aid others. This is the vision I have seen for you."

Gart nodded grimly to her. "Thank you, Tarl'a. Your words will be passed around and your warnings noted."

"For our new friends and family," Tarl'a turned her attention to Faolan and Bevan, "you shall also prosper in these lands, and your descendants shall become some of the great leaders. I have seen some coming from your line who will be important players in historical events. But be aware that they are women, and as such, I advise that all women in your family be educated."

"I thank you for your words, Tarl'a. With those of your Ancestors, we shall be advised by you," Faolan responded with a nod.

Tarl'a then turned to Loc. "My youngest son, your journey has only just begun. You have a special task ahead of you, and I would ask that you take it very seriously and protect that which will be placed in your hands. You and your wolf must make sure this task is complete, and I am sorry to say that I see danger and hardship in your path."

Loc stood and hugged his mother, who he now towered over. "I do not know of this journey you speak of, but I will take it seriously. When does it begin, have you seen?"

"Yes, I have, and it will be soon." Tarl'a broke away from her son and went to sit with Carling. "My daughter, my youngest child and my sweetest. So long have you complained of not being allowed to go further than the confines of this valley. There was a very good reason for your isolation, and now the time has come to tell you that it is at an end."

"I can leave?" Carling asked as Tarl'a caught her hands in her own.

"Loc's journey I spoke of, will involve you. The special task is to see you safely to a place only you know of. Blue has already told me he has given you knowledge of where you need to go. There is so much more to tell you, my child, so much more you need to know to prepare you for your journey. Now, you and I must part from the family, and go up to the stones to talk about it. They are waiting for us."

"Who is waiting, Ma?" Carling asked as her mother pulled her to her feet.

"Mailcon, will you join us?" She held a hand out to her husband. "Ru and Loc, please make sure our visitors are comfortable for the night."

Carling's head was spinning with the news that she could leave. But worry came hard on the heels of feeling stunned with what more her mother would be telling her. Tarl'a and Mailcon walked ahead of her hand in hand. Carling noticed that her Da was almost supporting her Ma as they climbed up the track.

"Why won't you tell me now, Ma?" Carling asked as they came around the rocks.

"Because, my child, they wish to be with us when you are told, as is their right." Tarl'a was becoming more and more upset at the prospect of telling her the news, and Carling could see it.

"Carling, just wait. It is important," Mailcon said as he stood at her side.

Tarl'a walked into the circle and stood in the centre. Her head was thrown back and her arms raised to the sky.

"We have come as you have requested," she cried out and very quickly a nimbus of light shone around them and coalesced into the form of Order.

"I greet you, Tarl'a, daughter of my son," Order spoke. "Thank you for your patience, your understanding, and your love for our child. The greatest of blessings be on both you and Mailcon."

The light soared into the night and split into its many facets, a rainbow of colour each descending down to the stones. Figures emerged from the light and stood before them, their lights dimming in the night.

"Please enter, my daughter and my husband," Tarl'a bade them.

On feet that moved of their own accord, Carling entered the circle and walked up to her mother. Behind her, Mailcon entered and stood behind Carling, his hands coming to rest on her shoulders.

"We bring before you the daughter we have raised, the daughter we have loved. We hope that we have done right by her and have taught her as you have wished," Tarl'a called out as tears started to rain from her eyes.

"She is the daughter of the hearts of you and Mailcon," Yellow said from her position in front of the towering stone. "She will always remain your daughter. The truth must come from you. Her story is to be told this night in your words, and we shall listen to them."

Tarl'a sat down on the grass in the centre, and Mailcon and Carling joined her there. Each took one of Carlings hands in theirs, while clasping to each other. Tarl'a sniffed, and the tears kept coming, unabated. Carling looked between her parents, worried at what was to come.

"Carling, the night you were born, there was a great storm that raged around the land, but not here. Not in this circle. You were born right here in the centre of the circle, but it was not from my body that you came. You were entrusted into our care to love and cherish you, to teach you the ways of The People: humility, love, caring, and courage. We were never to treat you any differently from our own boys. You are the greatest treasure of the lands, born to give hope to the world. You are the One True Child of the Ancestors. Born from the body of Yellow, given from the seed of Blue, your true parents. Created from necessity in answer to Chaos, from the plan of Order." Tarl'a's tears ran unchecked, and so, too, did those of Mailcon.

Carling sat staring at them both. Her mind reeled at the information. The two people she had depended on and loved so much in the world, were telling her that they were not her parents.

"Please tell me that this is not true," she begged quietly, tears filling her own eyes now. "Please, you are my Ma and Da. It cannot be true."

"I cannot lie in the circle, Carling. I cannot lie ever," Tarl'a told her. "Our line has always been truthful.,"

"But if it is true, then you have lied. Every day of my life has been a lie," Carling retorted.

"No, we never told you because we were not allowed to," Mailcon told her. "It was the wishes of the Ancestors that you be brought up as normally as possible."

Four of the Sentinels broke from the stones and came to sit with the little group. Red sat beside Tarl'a, and Violet beside Mailcon. Blue and Yellow each took a seat on either side of Carling.

"It is true, Carling. You are the product of a forbidden act that was deemed necessary by us. You are a true child of the Sentinels, of Order. Your golden light shines brighter than all of ours combined, even brighter than Order. Your golden light is a beacon of hope and love. Your abilities will be stronger and a match for Chaos. You are our champion," Red told her gently.

"You are the greatest gift we could give this world for its protection. You are the sum of all our knowledge, and it is there inside you already. A golden spark of hope that will grow and blossom. We have watched you grow from the moment you were born, and although we—the rest of the Ancestors—love you, Carling, those who bore you love you more. Red and I will leave you, along with Tarl'a and Mailcon, so you can come to know your birth parents," Violet said gently and rose from the ground.

Tarl'a leaned across and hugged Carling close. "I love you, Carling. You are my daughter. You are my child, and I will never stop loving you."

Mailcon gathered them both up and held them, adding his own affirmations, "We are still your family, Carling. We love you."

The couple let her go and stood, moving away from the circle, leaving her to face her birth parents, and a future without them.

Carling now turned to the two she had known her whole life. The pair who had spoken the most to her, whose blessings were given more readily. She saw now why this had been so, and she looked between the two.

"It must be difficult to understand what is going on, Carling, our sweet child," Yellow said as she lay a hand on the side of the girl's face. Carling pulled away from the touch and saw the hurt in her birth mother's eyes.

"It is. Why did you not raise me yourself?" she asked, panic rising in her voice. She took a deep breath and calmed herself.

"It was necessary so that you could grow and understand the ways of The People. We created you, yes, but we could not raise you in our ways. We could not encourage and guide you to have traits such as empathy, humanity, and so many more that you will need when you come face-to-face with Chaos. It is through you and your boundless abilities that we and Order can do our work, so that we can banish Chaos forever," Blue told her.

"I am to fight Chaos? How? I am only me, so little. Chaos is vast and powerful."

"A great deal is going to change, Carling. With our help and guidance through your abilities, we can help you grow not only mentally, but physically. Since you were born, you have been hidden in this valley. Your name was not even mentioned until your mother spoke it for the first time in the presence of your father in the house. You have been guarded, protected, and loved, not only by human parents and brothers, but also by us. At least one of us is always here each moment of the day to watch you grow," Yellow said, reaching out to Carling once more.

"Why do I not look like you if I am your child? Why do I not have the sparkling lights under my skin, and why do I not carry any of your features?" Carling demanded, again fending off the touch.

"You are as you should be, my daughter," Blue said, as he picked up Yellow's hand in comfort. "You carry some of our traits in your eyes and your hair. Golden light is your hue. That magical light at dawn and dusk in the sky is the same pale blue as your eyes, and the sun the colour of your hair. You know us, Carling."

Carling stood and moved away from the couple, almost making it to the entrance before she turned back. "Red said that I am a product of a forbidden act. What did he mean by that?"

Blue rose to meet her. "We are of one being. Our abilities, though greater than those of a normal human, when combined into one vessel or child, such as yourself, grow so vast and far-reaching. That is why it has been forbidden. Until now. Until you. Order did not make the decision lightly, nor did she make the request lightly. Yellow and I both thought very hard and for a very long time before we agreed to the union. Your planning has already taken such a large amount of time, with many discussions with our brothers and sisters, and only occurred after garnering their consent. We are so very proud of you, Carling."

Yellow joined Blue and held his hand once more. The pair had grown closer over the years as they had watched her grow. When Carling looked at Yellow, she could see a fear of being rejected, and she felt sympathy for the Sentinel.

"What of Ma and Da now?" Carling asked. "There is no successor for Ma, who will be Guardian after her?"

"That has already been decided. The line will continue for this momentary time through one of their sons," Yellow said.

"It will be Loc's job, then. He has foresight," she mumbled thinking of her brothers.

"No, it will not be Loc. We cannot tell you that future. Carling, you need to come to us. When you were six, I gave you the knowledge of where to find our home. It is still there. You must be there before the full moon, before the day you were born." Blue came forward with Yellow at his side. Together they embraced her, and this time she did not pull away from their touch. Each bestowed a kiss on her head.

"Come find us, our child, and remember we love you," Yellow told her.

"If you ever need us, call and we will come," Blue said. They let her go and moved out of the circle. Carling followed and watched as they blessed and thanked Mailcon and Tarl'a.

The Ancestors departed, leaving the three facing each other. Carling ran to her mother's arms.

"I want to go home, Ma," she cried out to her.

"Let's go, then." Tarl'a turned her daughter and with Mailcon leading the way, they descended the hill once more.

Morning had broken, and Carling was walking along the brook thinking about the previous night. When she awoke, her first thought was that it had been a dream, but when she looked upon Tarl'a's face she knew it had not. She had left the fireside to seek the solitude of the brook and meadow to think and process the information the Ancestors had given her.

She watched a fish as it swam lazily in the pool, losing sight of it in the reflection of the sun and remembered a fish all those years ago, before Galen had left. She wondered where he was at that moment. He was still her favourite brother. Then she realised he was not her brother. None of the boys were her brothers, and her mother and father were not hers either.

For a moment she felt so alone. It was just her. A creature that should not be. An oddity. A tear stood out in her eye as she felt the enormity of the situation hit her. Her one task was to battle Chaos. Her only objective to banish him from this world. But she was so small, she thought.

"There you are, what are you doing so far out here, Carling?" Loc asked as he trotted up behind her. When she turned, he saw the tear and stopped. After Galen had left, Loc had become her companion and playmate until he too had left to begin his own training. "Whatever is the matter?"

"Ma and Da have not told you or Ru?" she asked as another tear escaped her eye.

"Told us what, Carling?" he asked her as he placed an arm around her.

"I am not sure I am allowed to tell." Carling swallowed hard, trying to push the feeling down.

"Is this to do with what happened up at the stones last night?" Loc asked carefully, trying to pry the information from her.

"Yes. I am so afraid."

"You? Carling afraid? Of what is there to be afraid?" They started to walk back to the house.

"Lots of things, but mostly losing all of you."

"You can't lose us, Carling, we are your family. Even though we are not home anymore, we still have a connection. Even with Galen, who is so far away."

"But I am not family." Carling broke his hold and ran from him. Tears were streaming down her face as she passed her mother, who was sitting outside grinding grain for the morning meal and dashed quickly inside the house.

"Carling?" Tarl'a cried out and followed her inside, finding her wrapping her bedding around herself and covering up. "Come out from there, Carling! You are no longer a child to be doing that. Come out and tell me what is wrong. Did Loc say something nasty to you?"

"No, he didn't. I am confused, I'm lost, and I'm all alone."

"Stop being silly! Of course you are not alone. As for lost, you are in your home." Tarl'a pulled the bedding off and sat her up. "We are still your family, Carling. Who bore you makes no difference. It is those who love you and have been there for you, that make up your family."

Carling saw movement at the door and watched as Mailcon, Ru, and Loc entered the house.

"It is about time we told them. We cannot help Galen and Uven not being here, but they need to know, Tarl'a," Mailcon told her plainly.

"What is this all about? Carling, I am sorry if I made you cry, but I don't know what it was that I said." Loc moved into the house and came to kneel in front of Carling.

"Come sit, boys," Tarl'a instructed them.

The conversation that took place in that little house by the brook, which was fed from the sacred spring on the hill behind them, was long and full of love. The boys took in the information that the girl they thought was their sister, was in fact someone completely different, and not even wholly human. But it did not change their feelings for her. She was their sister, and they declared that she would remain their sister for as long as they all lived.

"Do you know where it is you have to go?" Loc asked her when they had all finished.

"Yes. I can see it clearly, and I can even see the path I need to take to get there. I can also see how long it will take," Carling told him.

"We had better start gathering provisions for the journey, then," Loc declared. "I will gladly help to see you safely there."

"I will help, too," Ru offered eagerly.

"No. You are heading the other way, Ru. You have your betrothed to think about. I am sorry," Tarl'a added, seeing the disappointment on his face. "The Ancestors will not let anything happen to Carling, and with Loc and his wolf at her side, she will be well protected."

"When do we leave, Carling?" Loc asked her.

"Tomorrow," she said definitively. Carling could not have told them how she knew, but it must be so.

The day was spent preparing everything that they would need. Mailcon took over when Tarl'a tried to burden them with cooking pots that would be too heavy to carry. He was practical in his choices for their journey, knowing that Loc was a good hunter, and would provide for them both with game. Carling knew her plants and could identify those that were edible and those that were poisonous.

Faolan expressed doubt and fear that the pair would be too vulnerable in the wilds, until Loc's abilities were explained to him, and Wolf was invited to their fireside. He offered his assistance and guidance to their destination, until Gart reminded him that he and his son were to travel with him and Ru to the east, the opposite direction.

The reason for their travel had been kept within the family. Ru had not even told Nila why there was a sudden urgency in his younger siblings' travel. His explanation to his intended bride, was that his mother had had a vision, and that they must travel for an important and necessary reason. Ru had to do a lot of quick and quiet talking to get her back on his side.

Carling could not sleep that night, the conversations with the visitors still in her head. Turning over in her bed, she looked at the dying embers of the fire in the pit in the centre of the room. A log collapsed, sending up bright orange sparks. Through them, a figure emerged, and she sat up when she saw him. He placed a finger over his lips and touched the sleeping form of Loc, who woke with a start. The figure motioned to the pair and they followed him outside.

"You must go now. Yellow and Blue sent me urgently. There is danger waiting for you the moment you step outside the protection, Carling," Orange told them. He was tall and muscular. "They asked that I stay with you for a little while."

"But Ma and Da! We can't leave without saying good-bye," Carling protested.

"Make it quick, then, we do not have much time. Loc, is Wolf around?"

Loc stopped and concentrated for a moment. "Yes, just within the tree line."

"Good, have her meet us at the ford. Now hurry," he urged them.

Carling re-entered the house and went to her father's side. "Da, Da, wake up! I have to go. I have to say goodbye," she said urgently, shaking him.

"What? It's the middle of the night, Carling. Go back to bed," he told her, trying to roll over.

"Da, please. I have to say goodbye. I have to leave now." She threw her arms around his neck and held on for a long time. "I love you, Da."

"What is all the noise?" Tarl'a asked, sitting up.

"We are going, Ma. Orange is adamant that we leave now," Loc said, coming back inside. He began to pick up their bundles, slinging one over his shoulder.

Tarl'a and Mailcon hurriedly disentangled themselves from their covers and followed their two children from the house. Orange was waiting for them, urging them on.

"What is going on?" Tarl'a demanded of the Ancestor.

"There is some urgency. Some men are coming, and it would be better that Carling be gone before they arrive," he told them.

"What men?" Mailcon demanded, forgetting who he was talking to.

"Da, does it matter right now? If the Ancestor says we have to go, we have to go," Loc said as he passed Carling her bundle and she looped it onto her shoulders. He stepped forward and hugged his father, then turned to his mother.

"Stay safe, my children," Tarl'a said, breaking from Loc and moving to Carling. "Look after each other."

"We will, Ma," Loc told her.

"And you, Orange, look after them. I want to know that they get away safely," Tarl'a said to the Sentinel.

"I will, Tarl'a. As soon as I can, I will get word to you," Orange promised her.

With one final goodbye, the pair followed the Ancestor down the track and disappeared into the darkness.

They did not talk until they reached the ford. The water slipped across their path, and they stopped at the edge. On silent padded feet, the dark shadow of Wolf came and stood between Carling and Loc, her mouth open and tongue hanging out.

"She says they are still a way out but they are gaining quickly," Loc told them.

"Cross over and head west. I will go see where they are and try and find out more about them," Orange instructed the pair and vanished, only to reappear on the other side.

"I wish we could do that. Come on, Carling, let's go," Loc said, tugging on her arm.

They waded across the cold water and up the other side. As Carling pulled her foot from the river, she turned and looked back at the forest that grew beyond. The darkness of the foliage deepened against the sky above, its multitude of stars winking down at them.

"Carling," Loc called to her, realising she hadn't followed him.

"I'm coming," she said, and turned from the only home she had ever known.

The track flew under their feet as they ran, her bundle bouncing against her hip. She followed Loc as they passed the hills that shielded the valley and climbed up the side of another. Carling tripped on a rock and fell onto her hands and knees before pushing herself up and away again to try and catch up with Loc. Her heart was pounding in her ears, and her breath came in sharp bursts. The years of running and playing with her brothers had built her fitness, and she was soon at Loc's side.

"Nice of you to join me," Loc laughed, grinning at her.

"Hurry up! You're slowing me down," Carling laughed back and sped up.

At the top of the hill, Orange was waiting. They came up short in front of him, and stood panting, catching their breath.

"They have arrived at the ford," the Sentinel told them.

"Who are they?"

"They are from a far-off land. They call themselves Romans, and they are Chaos's men. He has helped them conquer many lands and they have gained great power. Now he has turned their attention to our lands. It is only a small group. They are searching for the valley and for you, Carling."

"Will Ma and Da be protected?" she asked.

"Yes. Keep going. I will let Tarl'a and Mailcon know what has happened. You need to get further away before you stop for more rest."

"We only stopped to speak to you, Ancestor," Carling said, smiling up at him.

"You are definitely my brother's child, Carling. Now go, I will find you and let you know what is happening."

"Thank you, Orange." Carling and Loc took off again, not waiting for him to reply.

Chapter Five

The sun was well and truly up by the time they stopped for their next rest. Wolf had found them a cave and was lying in the shade panting when they rounded the rocks that hid it. Carling dragged her bundle from her shoulders and lay down on the ground, her chest pumping as she tried to fill her lungs with oxygen to feed her limbs.

A waterskin appeared above her and she took it from Loc, downing the rest in a few gulps. Pushing herself up, Carling rested her hands on her bent knees and stared out of the entrance.

"Do you think we have travelled far enough?" she asked her brother, still panting.

"For now, I hope. We need rest," Loc said as he slipped down cave the wall and sat.

"Can you see what is to become of Ma and Da?" Carling asked, turned her head to him.

"I need rest first. My visions are still settling down, so Ma tells me. I need quiet and rest before I can call them up."

"Maybe later, then," Carling suggested.

"Yes, maybe later," Loc agreed, then added with a grin, "You still run like a rabbit, Carling,"

"I had good teachers," she replied, laughing a little.

"That is why we placed you with Tarl'a and Mailcon," Blue said, coming from the back of the cave. "Loc and Wolf, can you leave us a moment? I must talk to my daughter alone."

"Yes, Ancestor. We'll go refill the water skins," Loc told Carling as he stood and went to the entrance. He took a moment to look back before Wolf was at his side, and they left.

Blue sat in front of Carling and crossed his legs. "You will not acknowledge me, daughter."

"I acknowledge you, Blue, but do not ask me to call you *father* just yet. It has only been a full day for me to get used to this news. And some of that has been running. Do you have news of my parents?"

"I do. But before I give it to you, you must promise me that you will at least get to know your mother. I spent every moment with Yellow as she carried you under her heart and swelled with love. We were not expecting to have these feelings for you, daughter. We are Sentinels. Our lot was to protect the earth, never to know our own children except to watch them from afar as they grew and prospered. But to have a child of our own was a monumental thing, and it has changed both your mother and me. Our brothers and sisters do not realise how much it has changed us."

"I will make that promise, Blue. I will get to know not only Yellow but you as well."

"Thank you, Carling. That is all we ask of you. Now, Tarl'a and Mailcon are fine. The protection that was put into place to keep you from the eyes of Chaos is still standing strong. It has protected the valley from the Romans."

Carling dropped her head in relief at the news. "What of the visitors, Ru and Nila and her father and brother?"

"We warned them to stay, and Ru is keeping an eye on the situation. This is only a scouting party. It will still be many, many turnings of the seasons before these Romans will be on our lands."

"But if I defeat Chaos, will that not keep them from invading?"

"We can hope, Carling. We will give you all the support and knowledge we can to prepare you to meet Chaos."

"What is Chaos like?" Carling asked.

"Large, angry, and very powerful."

"You are not helping me build my courage," Carling said with a wry smile.

"There is plenty of time for that later. Now I must go and check on your family and relieve Violet. She has her own people she must supervise."

"Thank you for letting me know what was happening with them," Carling told him as he found his feet. He held out his hand to help her up, and she took it.

"Our blessings on you, my child. Our love as well. Your journey to us is only beginning. Remember, if you need us, just call," Blue said, still holding her hand.

"I will, Blue. Thank you."

"Loc, you can come back in now," Blue called out, still staring down at Carling. The intensity was great, and she looked away from it.

Loc re-entered and stood at the opening, waiting for Blue to move or say anything. Carling pulled her hand from his, breaking his concentration, and he turned to her brother.

"Keep her safe and look out for her," Blue charged Loc.

"I will, Ancestor, I promise."

"Our blessings on you both." Blue left them and rounded the rocks.

"Did he tell you what was happening at home?" Loc asked her.

"Yes, they are fine. Those men couldn't get through the protection the Ancestors had placed on the valley. Ma and Da are fine and Ru is keeping watch."

"Good, we will stay here for the remainder of the day and rest. We'll leave when the sun goes down again and travel by night."

"Aren't we far enough away from the valley?" Carling asked.

"No, not for my liking." Loc leaned against the cave wall and slid down it. "I listened in, Carling. I heard all Blue had to say to you. It is really true, isn't it?"

"It seems that way, Loc." Carling sank to the ground where she stood.

"Then how come your ability hasn't come through? Being their child, I would think that you would have had it by now."

"I don't know. I have no idea of anything." Carling gave a great sigh. "You know as much as I do, I have not kept anything from you. The Ancestors have their ways."

"They do indeed. Are you hungry?" Loc pulled his bundle towards him and pulled out a packet wrapped in cloth.

"No, maybe later. I'm too tired to eat." Carling pushed herself to the opposite wall and leaned up against it.

"Get some sleep. When you wake, you can eat, then we will have to be on the move again." Loc bit into one of his mother's grain cakes.

A warm body moved against Carling and she rolled over to find the shaggy black fur of Wolf pressed up against her. The warmth exuding from her body comforted Carling, and she lay her arm around the animal. Her eyes were closing again when the scuff of a foot made her sit up, disturbing Wolf in the process.

"Sorry, I was trying to be quiet," Loc said as she sat up.

"You could never be quiet," Carling told him, pulling her bundle close to her. "I like Wolf, she is lovely and warm to sleep next to."

"She is. Traitor." Loc smiled at Wolf, who made a whiny sound and padded out of the cave.

"That wasn't nice," Carling told him.

"She said you smell nicer," he laughed.

Carling joined him in laughter for a moment before the growling of her stomach made a louder noise. Fishing around in her bundle, she pulled a squashed cake from a cloth packet and took a bite. The taste of berries and crushed grain had never tasted so good, and she finished it off quickly.

"I would go steady with those," Loc warned. "Remember, we didn't get time to pack the rest of our provisions. I am going to have to start hunting a lot sooner than I thought."

"I can help. I helped Da trap while you were gone," Carling told him.

"Good. I was thinking that we should avoid all contact with others."

"Why? They are our people. They will help us if we ask," Carling told him.

"We don't know how far those men have moved through the lands. I have to keep you safe, Carling. I promised an Ancestor and I don't think that is the kind of promise you can break without some sort of punishment," Loc told her with a grin.

"Have you had any sleep?" she said through her laughter.

"A little," Loc replied as Wolf entered the cave. "The men are following. They haven't found us, though. We are going to have to be careful when we leave here. They spent quite a bit of time trying to get into the valley."

"Do you want to catch some more before we leave?" Carling looked out the entrance and noticed the fading light.

"I can sleep later. We'll get going. I've filled the waterskins again. Do you know where we are going?"

"The way is mapped out in my head."

"Can you find it in the dark?" Loc asked.

"I got us this far, didn't I?" Carling stood, placed the cloth packet back into her bundle, and picked it up. "Are you ready?"

"For another night of running, you bet. I'll have Wolf range behind and keep us up to date," he told her shouldering his own bag.

"Let's go, then."

They ran on into the night. She could feel when they were veering off course and would correct it. Her feet were sore, but the need to get further away from the men was overcoming the aches and pains. Wolf kept them informed all the way while keeping herself hidden.

Feeling safe enough, Carling and Loc stopped for a rest. There was no talk between them, but Carling hoped for more news from Wolf. Loc felt exhausted and out of breath.

"They are still following. I don't know how they are tracking us in the dark," Loc told her before drinking heavily from the waterskin.

"I have a feeling I know. I think Chaos has something to do with this. How far back are they?" Carling asked.

"They are at the last river we crossed. They are pressing their horses pretty hard. Wolf can sense that they are under some stress and agitated. If they keep it up, the horses will start dying underneath them. The darkness isn't helping, either. They are stumbling around out there," Loc told her.

"But still they are on our tail." Carling put the waterskin back on her belt. As she was about to rise, Loc's hand flew out and held her down. "What is it?"

"Wolf." Even in the dark, she could see that he was looking off into the distance with other eyes. "Move, move now!" he cried out, and she didn't need to be told again.

They were up and running as fast as they could, despite already having run for half the night. From behind them came the rumbling sound of hoof-beats. With a flash, an image came to her and she turned.

"Loc, this way!" Carling called out, not waiting to see if he followed. She ran on and on. Loc was falling behind, tiring.

Carling pulled up and stopped him. "Hide. It's me they're after. Hide and stay hidden till I call out." She pushed him towards some rocks nearby and carried on.

As she ran, she called out to the Ancestors and hoped they would answer. She was sure they would—they had promised. She only hoped they could hear her over the pounding of her own heart and the gasping breaths she was taking.

"Ancestors…I need…your…help." With fists pumping at her side and her bundle bouncing behind, she carried on.

Now she could hear the horses not only behind her but also to the side, as the men sought to surround her. A crashing and an unhuman scream amongst the rocks to her left let her know that one of the horses had finally fallen, succumbing to the great stress these men were placing on them. She felt sad for the animal, but couldn't help but wish that more would fall the same way.

The image flashed again before her, and she could see that it was not too far away now. A shout cried out in the night as they closed in. As she rounded a large boulder in her path, light flared into the night, and she ran into the centre of the Sentinel host. They closed ranks around her as she dropped to the ground, panting. Hands with bright white sparks glittering under the skin pulled her up and held her.

Through the bodies of the Sentinels, she saw the horses approaching, their sides puffing with the exertion, and the riders still urging them on.

"These are not your lands and not your realm. Go from them now and leave our child in peace," Order called out to the men, who were all around now, circling the group.

"She is wanted by our master," one of them called out.

"Our daughter is not his being," Blue replied fiercely.

A horse stopped in front of him, and the man looked down at Blue. When he spoke, it was not with a natural voice.

"She is an abomination, a creation that should never have occurred. I will destroy her and anyone else who stands in my way. This world will be mine. You cannot stop the spread of my people. They already dominate most of the lands."

The man lifted his eyes from Blue and stared at Carling. They glowed red with anger and with the power of the being who possessed him.

"Are you too afraid of our child to even show yourself?" Yellow called out bravely.

"Your child is untried, untested, and is still young. I will kill her. You cannot protect her every moment of the day. I sense no great power within her, except the fear that now grips her heart. You have created nothing. You have broken your own rubrics for nothing."

"Then why do you chase her? Why do you seek to kill our child?" Blue called out.

"Because of the possible threat she poses. You have taken the trouble to hide her from me to keep her safe. There must be a reason for that. You are very quiet, Order. Have you lost some of your potency by creating these colourful birds?"

"Chaos, I lost nothing in creating the Sentinels. I gained more than you can ever understand. Send your minions away, they cannot harm her while she is under our protection." Order stepped in front of Carling, shielding her from the gaze of the man who was the mouthpiece of Chaos.

"You cannot protect her. I will have her and crush her in my hand. I will snuff out the life you have so carefully created."

Carling did not hear the rest of the diatribe that the voice flung at the Sentinels. Her mind went blank and calm, the fear slipped away, and something else began to speak to her.

"My child, your plan is a good one, and we will help you with it. When we break ranks, run to where you were headed. We will keep them from you until the time is right. You know what to do, it is already there inside you. Keep calm and know that we love you and will protect you," said Yellow.

Coming back out, she heard the man still slinging insults at the host, and she made herself ready. When they struck out with their light, blinding the horsemen, she ran off again on blistered and damaged feet. She summoned all her strength and felt her muscles flexing and straining to carry her away, closer to the place she sought.

Carling sensed the edge before she saw it and came to a skidding halt. The darkness beyond yawned large down the sheer cliff as she stood on the precipice. Out beyond the valley floor, the thin sliver of the new moon and stars illuminated the water filling the great gorge, which had been carved out by the once thick layer of fast-moving ice.

Through her own heavy breathing came the sounds of pursuit from behind her. Carling turned to face them and could see the beasts moving towards her quickly. Standing her ground firmly, she clenched her fists, the heat building inside until it was almost unbearable. Waiting until the moment the riders and horses became too far committed, Carling brought her hands up.

Releasing the energy that she had contained within her fingers, she sent out a great golden sheet of light. It swept before her, pushing out and blinding both animal and man alike. Stunned, they still rushed forward, and Carling dropped to the ground. Hooves barely missed her as they stumbled on in a blind panic until they reached nothingness.

The screams from men and beasts came up to greet her, and she heard the sickening crunch of bone and flesh striking the rocks far below. The night became quiet and still. There was no movement anywhere, not even a whisper of a breeze. The thought of those innocent lives being used in such a way by Chaos, and then wasted by her, filled Carling with great hatred of herself. She had killed.

Guided by Yellow, Loc found her at the edge of the cliff. He struggled to lift her up in his arms, to take her as far away from the drop-off as he could. Staggering under the weight of her, he fell to his knees, her head bouncing against his arm as he held her close.

Yellow knelt beside him and laid a hand on her head.

"She is still there. There are no injuries other than those to her feet. It is a great sadness at what she had to do that has put her in this state," Yellow told him.

"We will stay here for the rest of the night. Are you sure there are no more chasing us?" Loc asked her.

"We are sure. Carling did what she had to do. This is why she was born," Yellow said sadly.

"What did she do?" Loc's eyes darted up to the ancient Being.

"My daughter was born to become a warrior, a champion. This was her first test, but far too early for her, and she passed it none-the-less. Carling had to kill tonight, and it is that with which she now struggles. The idea of killing another human is as abhorrent to you, The People, as it is to us, the Sentinels. I suggest that when she comes around you do not press her to find out what happened. She must come to terms with it in her own time. I am going to leave you now. I feel she will not want my presence when she wakes."

Yellow placed her hand back on the head of her daughter and then bent to kiss her. There was a sadness to her that caught Loc. He could sense the immense love she had for his sister. He placed Carling down on the ground gently and stood with Yellow.

"I will look after her, Ancestor. I will help her understand."

"Thank you, Loc," Yellow said as she left them.

Looking down on his sister, Loc's first thought was to keep her warm. Grabbing the scrubby bushes that littered the hillside, he made a small fire. Large enough for light and a little warmth but not big enough to alert anyone who may still be around. Wolf came padding up and sat down beside him.

"There are no humans around the hill. You and your littermate are safe," she told him.

"Thank you, Wolf." He worked at taking Carling's bundle from her shoulders and making her more comfortable.

"I will keep watch if you wish to sleep," Wolf offered.

"That would be helpful, and I would be very grateful." He took his own bundle off and placed it down beside Carling's, then he lay down close to her.

Wolf headed out into the dark and padded around before coming back and lying down beside Carling. "She needs me more than you tonight," Wolf told him.

"I know and understand, Wolf." Loc watched the fire and added a bit more wood to bank it up. "Wake me before dawn and I will take over."

"I will." The wolf gave a big sigh and placed her large head on her paws.

Once more, Carling woke with the black fur of Wolf pressed against her. The morning air was cold, and she shivered. Wolf stirred beside her as she sat up and looked around at their surroundings. The events of the night before came back to her, and she held her head in her hands. The wolf whined and placed her head on Carling's lap.

"Tell me it was a dream, Wolf. I can't face today knowing it was real." Carling placed a hand on the head of the large animal and scratched her ears. Wolf, in turn, licked her face to comfort her.

The cliff was not too far off to her left. She stood carefully, edging to the drop-off and took a breath. Looking down, she could see nothing, no evidence of the men who had chased them the day before or the horses they rode on. The voice of Chaos came back to her with his threats and demands. Carling took a couple steps back from the precipice and looked out at the view beyond.

"Carling, are you all right?" Loc asked, coming up behind her. Carling turned, buried her head in his shoulder, and burst into tears. "You did what you had to. You saved us."

"I killed those men and horses. I used an ability to murder."

"You used an ability?" Loc pulled her away and made her sit down. "Can you tell me what happened?"

"They were charging… my hands were clenched. I threw a light to blind them, and they went over the cliff." Carling turned her head to the edge, remembering the sounds of the night.

"Let's move away from here." Loc pulled her to her feet and they moved back to where the fire was still burning low.

Carling sat down hard, tears still falling fast. "Yellow was in my head and encouraged me. They helped me. They let me get away and then let those men come after me so I could do that."

"You did what you had to. Yellow was here when I found you. She loves you, Carling."

"Then why set me up to do that?" she demanded through her tears.

"She said you were a warrior. That this is what you were born to do—to rid the world of Chaos. That also means the men that he uses to get to you," Loc said, hoping to ease her guilt.

Carling pulled her bundle towards her. she took out the last cake in her pack and ate it. The hunger wasn't satisfied, as it still burned away at her insides. Loc was watching her carefully, not wanting to upset her. Slowly he pulled his own pack out and handed them to her.

"No, they are yours. You need to eat as well. We will just have to stop for the night early and hunt for our meal." Carling pushed them back to him, turning from him as he ate.

"Do you want to stay here a little longer?" Loc asked when he was done eating.

"I would rather get as far away from this place as we can, as quickly as possible." Carling stood and placed her bundle over her shoulders, setting it into place once more. "At least we don't have to run anymore."

They journeyed on for the next few days at an easy walking pace, with Wolf always at her side. They would stop for the night early in the afternoon to hunt with some success, and the hunger Carling had felt that morning was soon abated. Collecting berries and plants along the way also helped to keep the feeling of hunger at bay.

On the fifth day of travelling, Loc finally got up enough courage to ask Carling a question that had been nagging away at him since he found her on the cliff edge.

"You said you used an ability against those men. What was it?"

"Light. It is not the ability I thought I would have." Carling pulled the head of a long piece of grass and started to play with it in her hands as they continued to walk.

"But it is an ability. Have you tried again to do it?" There was more eagerness in Loc's voice now that she had answered his question.

"I haven't. I'm not sure I want to." She threw the seed head away and carried on. Wolf came up from behind and bumped into her side, forcing Carling's hand onto her back.

"But if that is the ability you are meant to have, then you need to use it. You can't just not use it or it will eventually disappear."

"Maybe that would be a good thing. Light is one of the damaging abilities. It has the potential to kill someone and hurt them in other ways also."

"Only if you use it that way."

"But I have already. The first time I used it—I killed." Carling stopped walking and Wolf raised her head, waiting for her to carry on.

"You did what was necessary. Who knows what those men would have done if they had caught you." Loc came to her and placed a hand on her shoulder. "You have lived a pretty sheltered life in the valley, Carling. Violence happens all through the lands. It may not be what we are taught or how we are supposed to act, but it is a fact of life. We are not the Ancestors. We have our own human faults of jealousy, anger, or hatred. Some of these drive men to harm others and sometimes to kill."

"But that is not The People's way. That is not what is supposed to happen."

"Maybe it is the influence of Chaos. I saw great sadness in Yellow that night when we found you. She did not like what you had to do, but she understood that it had to be done," Loc told her.

Carling pulled away from Loc and started to walk again. Wolf, still at her side, looked back at her companion. He stepped out, caught up to the pair, and they walked on in silence.

The days felt like they all melded into one for Carling. For some, she felt like they had made no progress at all. For others, she could feel the distance between herself and her home, so far behind now, growing.

She missed her mother and father greatly and wished she knew how they were faring.

Night-time was her measuring stick to find out how much longer they had before she needed to be at that cave. The moon and its growing shape each night helped her keep track. She began to worry that they were running out of time, as she felt how far they were away from their goal. She worried as she sat by their fire every night, never once giving voice to those fears to Loc.

It was one of these nights that she found herself still awake tending the fire while her brother slept, Wolf by his side. She stared at the flames, watching the orange tongues as they reached for the sky, dancing over the wood and glowing embers. Through the crackling of the fire, she heard a footstep and felt a presence behind her.

Turning quickly, she saw the softly glowing light of Order walking towards their camp. Carling stood to greet the Great Being, who motioned for her to sit back down. Sinking to the ground, Order joined her at the fire.

"You are having some problems, we understand." Order's voice was soft and low.

"I am, Great One."

"They are problems only if you allow them to be, Carling. It is one thing I did not factor into my plan; I will admit that. Tarl'a and Mailcon did their job very well in raising you—maybe a little too well. Your brother Loc has told you right. Men have their faults. I can only guide them and give them a path to follow. I cannot influence their feelings and how they react to situations."

"I don't wish to kill, Great One. I didn't want to hurt those men," Carling told her.

"And that is to your credit, Carling." Order took her hand, enclosing it in the swirling lights of her own two larger ones. "Take courage that you still feel that way, it will help you. But my dear child, you were created to be the champion, to be my staff and sword. It will never be easy to take a life, and we do not wish it to be. But in some instances, it will be necessary, just as it was then. Would it help you to know that those men were already half dead? Chaos had pushed them so hard that their lives were already ebbing from them. Their souls were in torment as he used them."

"It does not help. They could have survived after he had used them," Carling said adamantly.

"No. When Chaos has his claws into a soul, he does not give it up so easily. Those men were destined to die on our lands one way or another. Their souls are at peace now, I have seen to that."

"Thank you," Carling said simply.

"Tarl'a and Mailcon are well and are missing you. This was the other matter that had you so heavy-hearted."

"Will I see them again?" Carling lifted her eyes to Order and saw the comforting smile on her features.

"You will. They are as much a part of you as we are. You are caught in between the worlds, and I fear you feel it greatly. You are not lost, Carling. You have never been lost." Order let go of her hand, and for a moment. golden points of light darted and swirled under the young girl's own skin. "When Chaos has been defeated, you shall come to us and take up your birthright. We would not let you go adrift. You shall stand beside your brothers and sisters in guarding the world, and you shall know your reward."

"Will it be far off, the battle between Chaos and me?" she asked with a little fear.

"It will take many lifetimes, Carling, for you to battle Chaos. Each time you meet, you will become stronger."

"Lifetimes? I am to do this more than once?" Carling asked incredulously.

"Yes. Chaos will not be defeated by just one meeting. He is too strong for that. Your training will prepare you for all, my child, and the time for it to start is getting closer. You must hurry."

"We are trying."

"We will help. There are ways we can, but the journey there is part of your training. You are already growing into who you are supposed to be, Carling." Order smiled and then got to her feet.

Carling soon followed. "Thank you, Great One, for your visit tonight."

"My blessings on you, my daughter."

As Order's hand touched the top of Carling's head, she could feel the pure energy that was contained within the Great Being. She almost crumpled to the ground under the pressure and force of the touch. Order held her up and gazed into her eyes. An outpouring of energy was passed to her, and she gasped as it settled inside.

"A gift for you. It will be needed to help you grow physically. It is what you should have had from birth. There will be no more moments of people believing you younger than you are. But again, that was necessary." Order released her and smiled. "We will await your arrival eagerly."

Carling sat back down after Order had left her and pondered the words that had been spoken. More questions were raised, and she hoped that they would be answered when she reached the cave.

Chapter Six

With the dawn of the new morning, Carling was still sitting staring at her hand that had glowed and sparkled with the golden lights. There was no trace of them now and she rubbed at the skin. At her side Wolf stirred, lifting her large head and yawning. Slowly she stood and stretched out her kinks, then gave Carling's hand a quick lick with her long tongue before going off to hunt and scour the area for danger.

Loc was still snoring softly, curled up beside the fire, and Carling was not ready to wake him. There was still a lot that Order had told her that she had to think on. The idea that she was to be used as a weapon took hold, and a determination settled over her. Carling heaved herself up to her feet and quietly left the fireside, heading out to the berry bushes she had seen as they made camp the previous night. She wanted to get something for breakfast before Loc woke.

Gathering the juicy, sweet, red berries, she was still thinking about all Order had said. Her mind was so occupied, she was not aware of her surroundings. Suddenly muscular arms clamped tightly around her, and she dropped the succulent berries, spilling them to be trodden underfoot as Carling struggled with her captor. He held tightly to her, lifting her up off the ground and pulling her further away from the camp.

"Loc!" Carling called out.

Legs kicking, she pulled on the arms that held her. The man threw her to the ground, and she tried to roll away from him. As he grabbed her arm and climbed on to her, she got her first look at the attacker. He was shaggy and dirty, an encrusted wound ran down the side of his face, and he had a wild and manic look in his eyes.

Carling lashed out at him with her hand, trying to scratch at his eyes as he held her down. She did everything she could to get him off of her, her mind racing and panic rising.

"Help! Loc! Wolf!" she cried out again.

The man grinned evilly at her as he managed to get control of her flailing arms. "Carling," he grunted, his voice not his own. Carling could feel the fear rising up in her as she realised he was being controlled by Chaos.

He transferred both of her wrists to one of his hands and with his free one, he started to press down on her throat. She felt the fingers tighten around her flesh and doubled her efforts as her eyes went wide with fright.

"I told you that I would find and destroy you," he said, flecks of spittle flying from his mouth.

Carling fought with all her might, using her legs to try to dislodge him and free herself. Her efforts became harder and harder as she could feel her strength waning. With her vision darkening, she struggled less and less. As her vision finally turned almost black, a dark shadow raced from the bushes and flew at her attacker, pushing him from her body.

Carling managed to get to her hands and knees, gasping for breath, hearing Wolf growling at the man. The sounds of crashing and heavy-running feet neared, and Loc burst through the bushes, coming to her side.

"Are you all right?" he asked quickly, skidding on his knees beside her. Carling nodded her reply.

Loc left her side and went over to the man Wolf was now holding down, her muzzle inches from his face and neck. She moved when Loc approached, and he launched himself at the man, his fist already up. Carling rushed to him, trying to stop her brother's knuckles from connecting with the man's shaggy face.

"Loc, stop!" she cried out as she held his arm.

"He was killing you," Loc grunted, still trying to get to her attacker.

"Stop! Just stop!" Carling yelled.

With all her might, Carling pulled him off the man and Loc stumbled back, landing heavily on the ground from the force of her push, looking at her in shock.

Wolf was still snarling at the intruder and had resumed her position guarding him. He lay on the ground panting and had a dazed look in his eyes as he stared up at the sky.

Carling staggered, went to his side and knelt. "Who are you?" she asked the man. Her throat hurt, and it came out as a rasping whisper. She cleared her voice and tried again, this time a little stronger. "Who are you?"

The dishevelled man turned his head to her, his eyes now focused and dark with hate.

"You know who I am, Carling. I am the Being called Chaos," he said weakly.

"This is not necessary; you could just leave. This world does not want you," Carling told him.

"This world is mine, born from my original creation. You do not belong here, Carling. You are the one who should never have been born."

"Can you not see into the future, Chaos?" she asked him.

"I can see that you pose a threat to my plans, that is all. You are just a child." The voice was now just a whisper, the husk of the body fading fast.

"You cannot stop me, Chaos. I will be coming to stop you and banish you from the face of this world." Carling told him, putting as much strength behind her words as she could.

"Is this the future you have been told, child? Is this the lie that Order has told you?"

"Order cannot lie. The Ancestors cannot lie. It will be so, Chaos," Carling whispered to him near his ear. "My family will banish you."

The final breath left the used and damaged body, and Carling leaned away from the rotting flesh.

"You will not defeat me, Chaos," she cried out into the morning air as loudly as she could. "You will not defeat me."

The berries lay forgotten and trampled on the ground far behind them as Loc and Carling moved on from their campsite. They pushed on faster, and the distance to their destination grew shorter. They did not speak about what had happened amongst the berry bushes, but the bruises around her throat were a constant reminder. It had been the first time Loc had truly seen such strength in his sister and the potential she had been given.

There had been a moment when she called out to the heavens, giving her warning to Chaos, when for the briefest of seconds he'd seen golden lights play out on her face. It was the instant that he finally truly believed she was the One True Child. The child he had played with, the sister he'd adored, was no longer there. She was becoming her destiny, and he felt proud to be there at her side.

The quietness from Carling disturbed him. She used to laugh easily, but even his feeble attempts at making her giggle had no success. For four more days they travelled like that, and on the fourth night, he sent out his own silent calls to the Ancestors. He hoped they would listen, and he was not disappointed.

Loc had built a great fire that night, hoping to scare any demons away from Carling's mind. Even the presence of Wolf at her side did nothing to diminish the dour nature she had adopted. He watched her from his side of the fire and sent out another call to the Ancestors.

Two of the host came to their fire that night. Hand in hand, Yellow and Blue approached them and sat beside their daughter. Loc could see that they were talking, but he could not hear their words.

Wolf got up and came around the fire to sit at his side. "Your litter-mate is scared of what the future holds," she told him.

"I saw her strength, her determination. Chaos is the one who is scared. He seeks to kill my sister before she can harm him. He must have seen it to be so afraid of her."

"Fear is a great motivator, pack-mate. Fear of the unknown, fear of pain, fear of seeming less than we are. Nevertheless, your litter-mate is scared. When I first met her, I sensed that she was special, and each day it grows stronger in her. Already she is changing and growing. The Ancient Ones knew what they were doing when they created her."

"I cannot go with her, can I? I cannot stand with her when she faces him." Loc said, putting his arm around Wolf, seeking comfort from her.

"I do not have the ability to see into the future as you do. But I believe we can only be with her for some of her journey and while we are with her, we must support and guide her as best we can. The dealings of men and ancients are complicated." Wolf sighed and lay down beside Loc.

"So it seems, my friend. If only the world worked in the way of wolves, we would all know our roles and know where we stood in the order of things," Loc said, scratching her ears.

"It is an easier concept to live in," Wolf agreed as she leaned into his touch.

"You are halfway to your destination, Carling. The moon is waxing, and the days are passing quickly," Blue told her.

"Why do I have to be there by the full moon? What is so important about that time?" Carling asked them both.

"It is the night that remembers your birth. It is the night when your abilities will come to you, and you need to be with us so we can support you. There is no way of knowing how you will cope with so many at once descending upon you. We fear that if you are not with us, it could drive you mad—as mad as Chaos is," Yellow finished quietly.

"Do you fear that I may become like Chaos?" Carling's eyes went wide, and the blood drained from her face at the thought of the madness she'd seen in the eyes of her attacker. Chaos's eyes haunted her dreams, and his voice wove through them, causing her to wake shivering.

"That is only one possibility, Carling. A very small one. Which is why we need you to be with us when it happens." Blue took her hand and held it gently. "You are growing so much on this journey. Your actions spoke so much louder than any word that could have been uttered. Your protection of your brother was a great deed."

"You are growing in strength and in purpose. Your declaration to the Great Darkness was your first step in acceptance of all that has been thrust on you," Yellow said as she took up the girl's other hand.

"I was angry that he would not listen to reason," Carling told them quietly.

"There is no reasoning with Chaos. Order has been trying since the moment of inception. There is only one course with Chaos. Your use of the word *family* has angered him greatly. He does not understand the concept of support and strength from a family," Blue told her with a smile.

"I am understanding and accepting more. I am afraid of what is to come, afraid of facing him when he has his full strength at his disposal. I am afraid my brother does not understand what is happening. But most of all, I am afraid of losing all those I love," Carling told them in a small voice.

"Fear is natural. Embrace the fear, my child, and use it to your advantage. It is a small component that will help gather your courage to you. And I think you will be surprised at how much your brother Loc understands. He is the one who called us, Carling. That is why we are here. He was worried about how quiet you have been, and he is more astute than you realise. It's almost as if he is part wolf already," Yellow said.

"Ma once said that he would not marry, that his bond with Wolf would be too strong," Carling mused, remembering that fireside chat she had listened in to all those years ago.

"That is correct. But she did not see the type of bond they have. It is something that is necessary—not only for your journey—but for his as well," Blue told her.

"Carling, there is enough time to ponder these matters and all that has happened to you since you left the valley. Take the time to really get to know your brother and enjoy his company. He still has many things to teach you," Yellow said with a smile.

"He has taught me so much already; all my brothers have." Carling raised her eyes to look at Loc across the flaring flames of the fire. His eyes were full of hope and love.

"We will leave you now, Carling," Blue said, rising to his feet. Yellow stayed, holding her hand for a moment longer.

"I thank you both for your words and care," Carling said as she stood, gripping Yellow's hand tightly and looking her in the eye. "Mother."

Yellow rose and enfolded her into a loving embrace, holding her near. "My child," she said softly.

Carling then turned to Blue. "Father."

In his eyes of startling blue, a glistening tear formed. "My daughter." He kissed her forehead, and the pair departed.

Carling watched the couple leave, their glowing colours fading into the night. With a sigh, she made her way around the fire and sat beside Loc. "Thank you, brother, for your assistance. Thank you for calling them to me."

"You are welcome, little sister," he said as he smiled back at her.

With lighter hearts, they carried on with their journey. Carling was no longer afraid to talk of the matters that lay ahead of her, and she found that Yellow was right. Loc did understand far more than she had given him credit for.

Although their father, Mailcon, had taught her how to trap, Loc gave her some of his own secrets for finding game. Rabbits and birds made up their diet, along with berries and other plants as they came across them. Carling insisted they spend one afternoon harvesting a patch of wild grain. That evening, after grinding the soft seeds, she made up the cakes they both loved so much to fill their bundles with once more.

They laughed together and competed against one another in most things. It helped to while away the hours and make the journey less tedious. Wolf would join in some of their antics, jumping and running between them, her tongue lolling from her mouth and a grin on her long face. She was a great help when they stopped in the afternoon to hunt, driving game towards them and gratefully taking her share of the catch.

Loc came back from one such hunt to where they had decided to stop in for the night. He held in his hand a brace of rabbits, already cleaned and ready to be skinned. He lay them down in front of the fire Carling was starting. He stopped when he realised she was not starting it with the flint and steel as she had been taught. From her hand came a light, bright to look at and already crackling as it leapt from her palm to the kindling she had placed down. Blue tendrils of smoke curled up from the dried tinder, and a small flame appeared.

"I sometimes listen to advice, Loc. Close your mouth, the flies will get in." She smiled up at him.

Wolf came loping into the camp then and stopped at Loc's side. She looked up at him and he concentrated for a moment. Carling watched the pair and wished she could understand what was being said between them.

"Wolf says we're being watched. There is a man to our north," Loc told her.

"What should we do?" Carling automatically turned her head and scanned the hill to their north, but she could see no one there.

"We do nothing but wait. He will come to us, and then we'll see what he wants." Loc crouched down and pulled out his knife, starting to skin the rabbits. "There is no point worrying about it right now, Carling. We are not doing anything against anyone. We pose no threat."

Carling fed the fire and built it up, all the while looking around her at the slightest of noises. Wolf had left them and was keeping Loc informed of what the man was doing, and he in turn, passed the information onto his sister.

"He comes," he warned her later as the meat was cooking over the fire, the smell of it wafted onto the breeze as it sizzled.

"He may just be a traveller like us, and hungry," Carling suggested.

"In that case, he will be welcome to share what we have." Loc turned the rabbits over and he heard a low growl come from Wolf in the darkness that now surrounded them.

"I mean you no harm," a deep voice called out.

"Come closer. Wolf will not hurt you, unless you mean us harm." Loc stood and waited for the man to enter the firelight.

He was tall and older than Loc, but not by much. Carling judged him to be nearly the same age as Uven—about eighteen. As he reached the light, he stopped for the pair to look him over. He carried no weapons that they could see, except for the knife at his belt.

"Welcome to our fire. What is your name, stranger?" Loc asked him.

"I am Arilith, of the Deer," the man said, eyeing the rabbit that hung over the fire.

"Come sit with us. The meat will be cooked soon, and you are welcome to share with my sister and me," Loc told him.

The man's eyes left the sight of food and landed on Carling for a moment before he came forward and sat apart from the brother and sister.

"I am Loc of the Bull, and this is my sister, Carling of the Boar," Loc introduced them.

"Two Ancestors. A mixed family, then," Arilith said.

"Yes. Violet and Red make up our family," Loc responded

"Where are you headed?" he asked.

"West. And yourself?" inquired Loc as he turned the meat once more.

"To be honest, I'm not sure. I had a dream and was told to go to the west, but not my destination. I had just finished my training and have been wandering this way ever since, begging what food I could, and surviving on what I can find out here in the wilds. I am most fortunate to find myself in the presence of a whisperer whose animal is a wolf. Your hunting is a wonder to behold," Arilith prattled on.

"We work well together, yes." Loc pulled one of the rabbits off the fire and cut it up, handing a portion to their guest.

"Thank you," he said, accepting it. "And yourselves, is there a purpose for your travel?"

"Family. My sister is about to start her training, and we travel to where we need to go," Loc informed him, handing another portion to Carling.

"The Eagles are a hard people. Will they take you in?" Arilith asked as he bit into the juicy flesh.

"They will, as any of our people will when a child needs to be trained. The ones we seek are very adept at her particular ability," Loc told him.

"I have seen many with light before. I did not know they had to be so specifically trained," Arilith said between mouthfuls, flicking his eyes back over to Carling.

"How long have you been watching us?" Carling asked, her suspicion of the man still growing.

"All of today. I saw you pass me down in the valley. I have been keeping to higher ground," he told them as he tore more of the cooked meat from the bone.

"It is harder going up there. Are you hiding from someone?" Loc asked.

"No, just following the dream," Arilith said with a shake of his head. "It still comes to me each night, telling me where to go. I believe it's one of the Ancestors, but I cannot work out which." He tossed the bones into the fire before licking his fingers.

Loc passed him another portion and he took it readily.

"When was the last time you ate well?" Carling asked him.

"I cannot remember. There was a settlement quite some time ago where I traded my ability for food. I am a healer," he added.

"We have no need of your skills, Arilith, but we are willing to share what we have," Loc told him.

"Thank you. It is good to eat well again," he said.

"There are plenty of plants and berries you could have eaten. They should have been enough to sustain you," Carling spoke.

"Yes, and I have been, but nothing beats the taste of meat, young one. Your hair is so beautiful. I have not seen that colour before, so golden. If you are going for your training, you must be twelve summers?"

"Yes, she is," Loc said protectively.

"You can stand down, Loc, she is too young for my taste." Arilith grinned and finished the rabbit, sending the bones to follow his last. "I prefer my women to be taller and more well-built, if you know what I mean."

"I do know." Loc became as wary as his sister at that point and sent a message out to Wolf, who came and sat beside Carling.

"And with such a guardian, I would not like to try my luck even if I were interested," Arilith laughed. "You have nothing to fear from me. I only seek a warm fire, food in my belly, and company on this night. I find that solitude does not sit so well with me. To be able to talk to anyone is infinitely better than talking to myself. I envy you both, being able to journey together. You must be close to each other."

"As close as brother and sister can be," Carling spoke up. "Of all my brothers, Loc and I are the closest in both age and likeness."

"You are lucky, I never got on with my siblings. My sisters were much older than I, and my brother did not like my following him around," Arilith told them with a small smile.

"Has it not changed now that you have grown and finished your training?" Carling asked him.

"No, I have not seen them for many turnings of the seasons. My brother travels to the south with a group from the Wolf and Snake, dealing with a border dispute," he told them as he stared into the fire.

"Our brother also is in the south, with our cousin of the Bull," Carling said eagerly, her thoughts turning to Galen.

"It is a large group, I understand. Many of the people are represented," Arilith told them, yawning deeply.

"I'll take first watch," Loc offered.

"That is very kind of you, Loc. Wake me for my turn," Arilith proposed through another deep yawn. He turned his back to the fire and made himself comfortable.

Loc banked up the fire with more wood and asked Wolf to watch over Carling. "I don't fully trust him. Get some sleep; Wolf will look after you," Loc whispered to his sister, not taking his eyes off the newcomer.

"Wake me in a few hours and I will take over," Carling said.

"No wandering away from the fire, then." Loc grinned and settled himself in for the long night.

Carling pushed at the logs that were half burnt, moving them further into the fire. She sat cross-legged and stared up at the sky, watching the light that played on the heavens. It glowed green as it danced and moved above them. The stars twinkled in and out as it covered them up and revealed them again. She remembered the stories of how the world was made, that her mother told her when she was young, and now she imagined those tiny points of light having a world like this one circling it. It was something she had not considered before, and she tucked the idea away to ask Order or the Ancestors about it when she next saw them.

The thought of seeing them turned her gaze to the moon, which was swelling greatly in the sky. It was only a matter of days now till she had to be there. She could feel the cave beckoning her onwards, awaiting her arrival with anticipation. She drew her thoughts away from it and worried.

"So my dream is at an end," Arilith said from his side of the fire, startling Carling with his words.

Carling looked up and saw him still lying on the ground where he had slept, his eyes open and staring at her. She looked to her side, where Loc still slept soundly.

"My dreams have been pushing me on, and now they are silent. I finally saw the Ancestor that has been sending them to me. I believe you know him, Carling." He sat up and stretched without taking his eyes off her. "Blue."

"I have had dealings with Blue," she told him honestly.

"More than dealings," Arilith said. "Normal people do not hear from the Ancestors. They can go their whole lives without knowing or talking to them. Yet I find myself driven by the image of my Ancestor to meet you. And it is you and not Loc I was to seek out."

"Our mother is Guardian to the Stones, so on many occasions have I seen the Ancestors," Carling replied.

"But you are not to take over from her. You have light as your ability, the Guardian must have foresight," he said.

"That is correct. There is another who will take over from her."

"Why would Blue wish me to seek you out?" Arilith pondered. "That is the part that I do not understand. I tried asking in my dream, but he only smiled cryptically."

"Who knows what the Ancestors' wishes are," Carling said, poking the fire once more.

"I believe you do. Would you mind if I travelled with you and your brother for a while?"

"What you do is of no consequence to me," Carling answered. "The world is not mine to order about. If you wish to travel in the same direction as Loc and me, there is nothing we can do to stop you."

"But would I be welcome, child?" He flashed her a half smile that gave her a moment's pause.

"You must do what you think best," she said carefully.

"A child of your age should have already started her training," Arilith said. "You are older than you look."

"No, I am twelve summers old, soon to turn thirteen."

"Then you think like a person who is a lot older. The way you speak…" Arilith tried to explain, "it's like I'm talking to one who is already trained and has come into adulthood."

Carling stirred the fire once more and placed another log on it. She did not respond to him but kept her thoughts to herself.

"Blue, guide me, let me know why it was that you wanted me to seek out this child. You make my life a puzzle and then leave me to guess what it is you want me to do," Arilith called out.

"Shh, you will wake Loc," Carling cautioned him. Wolf looked up from her paws and stared at the newcomer to the pack.

"I called you to seek Carling out, so that you may get to know her," Blue said, coming into the circle of firelight. "There is a task you need to perform for her. I am sorry, Carling, that I did not warn you of Arilith's presence. I should have when we last spoke."

"That is all right, Blue."

"I had hoped the other name would stick, Carling."

"I thought we were just being cautious, Father." She smiled at him.

"The time for all the truth to come out is now, Daughter." Blue smiled back and sat beside her.

On the other side of the fire, Arilith's eyes widened at the revelation, and he stared between them. "I thought you said you were of the Boar?" he stammered.

"It is an understanding we have with our brother," Blue told him. "She was fostered into the Boar. Her mother and I could not raise her. She is the greatest of our gifts to the world."

"Why have you sent him to me, Father?" Carling looked at Arilith, who was still coming to terms with the news.

"Daughter, he will become one of your advisors when the time comes, and you need guidance."

"I thought my brothers were to guide me?" she asked curiously.

"And they will, but there will be others who come from our brothers and sisters whom you need to listen to as well. Your brothers have all trained you well as you have grown, but sometimes they will want to protect you a little too much, you being their younger sister," Blue advised her.

"What if I don't trust him, Father?"

"You will not meet with a more trustworthy man, Carling, that I can promise you. He, like you and your family, cannot lie. It is something we all agreed upon. That those who come into your life and give you guidance will only ever tell the truth, no matter how painful," Blue informed her.

"That is true, I have never lied. Every time I go to, I choke up and the truth spills out before I am aware I have spoken it. Sometimes it is very distressing, especially when I bring pain to people with my words," Arilith exclaimed. "This was your doing, Ancestor?"

"It is, but not only mine. Order's plan was laid out to us, and we have followed it. You are part of a greater plan, Arilith, a plan that begins with my child. The idea of her is far older than you can ever foresee. She may seem young now, but she will grow and come into her abilities. Journey with her and her brother Loc and get to know them. Then you must wait for her to come back from her training. Our wishes will become known to you then."

"I will, Ancestor. It will be as you ask." Arilith bowed his head to Blue.

"Listen to him closely, Carling. There will come times when I shall have need to speak through him," Blue advised his daughter.

"It shall be as you ask, Father. Before you go, how are Ma and Da?" she asked.

"Missing you a great deal. Your Da is tracking you and knows you are well. We are keeping them informed, Carling."

"Thank you, Father. Please give my love to Mother."

Blue looked at her in surprise and smiled. "I will, Daughter. It will gladden her heart to hear your words, as it does mine. Go with my love and blessings, my child." He kissed her forehead and turned to Arilith. "Blessings on you also, son of my line." Blue walked out into the fading darkness.

"A child of the Ancestors." Arilith shook his head.

"It is a long story, Arilith, and one that can wait until we are walking once more. I am warning you now, my time is short. I need to be at my destination in three days' time, and there is still a long way to go. I hope you can run, because we may need to," Carling told him plainly.

"Can I know your destination?"

"At the moment, no. I am still not sure how to get out to the last part. But I am sure that we will find a way."

"Who is your mother? You told Blue to pass on your love."

"All in good time, Arilith."

The sky above was lightening, and the stars were slowly winking out one by one. Carling stirred the fire up again, and Wolf stood and stretched. She bade Carling good morning with a lick on her face and then trotted out into the fast-growing morning light.

Carling had done what Blue asked of her; she had gotten to know Arilith better as they travelled. Between herself and Loc they told him the story of her life, the story of Chaos, and the reason she had been born. For the first couple of days, Arilith went between thinking it all a fantasy to believing ardently. Now he had accepted it as truth, remembering Blue's words about her family.

The first view of the coastline came into sight, and they travelled beside it for another day before coming to a small settlement. There was a mix of The People and Celts living on the edge of the water. Boats and fishing nets lay on the shore, and the smell of dried fish wafted on the breeze. The huts were all close together, and a large jetty had been built out over the water. Children playing on the sand spotted the travellers and ran between the huts to tell the elders of the village.

A group of men came from behind the first hut and stood in their path, arms crossed and waiting for them to approach. Carling stepped back behind her brother and Arilith, waiting for them to speak first.

"We come with no ill intent," Arilith spoke for them. "We are on our way to take this child to her tutor."

"Who are you?" the first man asked. He was tall with lengthy ginger braids hanging down each side of his face, and his beard was long and bushy. Carling could see the muscles moving under his shirt as he tried to work out whether they were friend or foe.

"I am Arilith of the Deer. My companions are Loc of the Bull and Carling of the Boar."

"So many families. You are welcome for the night. We will feed you and give you our protection. But in the morning, you must be gone."

"Thank you for your hospitality. May we know your name?" Arilith stepped forward and held his arm out in greeting.

The great man grasped Arilith's forearm tightly in return. "I am Lucan."

Lucan brought them into the main hut with a great firepit set in the middle. A large pot was already cooking something that was decidedly fishy smelling but made the mouths of all three travellers' water. They sat as they were bade and talked of their travel. Arilith did most of the talking, and Carling marvelled at how he never once gave too much away about who they were.

As the day waned, she became sleepy and dozed beside the fire. The cave she had to get to was nearby, she could feel the pull of it. She woke with a start and yawned. Getting up, she went outside to get fresh air and looked out at the surf. Somewhere out there in the distance was where she needed to be.

"The sea is a dangerous place," Lucan said as he walked towards her. His braids were blowing in the wind, which was picking up and driving the waves to shore.

"How long have you been in these lands?" Carling asked him.

"Long enough. Many turnings of the seasons. We find that your Ancestors are welcoming, and our gods seem to like the place," he told her,

"I once met a Celt like yourself. His name was Faolan, his daughter is my brother's wife."

"The young man inside?" Lucan asked.

"No, one of my other brothers."

"I remember Faolan," Lucan said with a nod. "He left the shores and went inland. We came over on the same boat."

"I need to get to a specific place," Carling started, feeling like she could trust this man. "But it is over the water."

Lucan crossed his arms and looked at her hard. "A curious dream came to me a few nights ago. Our goddess of the sea told me I needed to make a boat available to one with hair of gold," he told her, looking at her windblown, glowing locks that were now picking up the hues of the setting sun.

"The Ancestors and your gods work together sometimes." Carling smiled. Despite his gruffness and his imposing figure, she liked this man.

"Where is it you need to go?" he asked curiously.

"There is a cave out there somewhere. I can feel it. It has mighty columns holding up large rocks. It thrusts itself out of the water and is a hard place to live. Do you know of such a place?" Carling asked as she stared at the horizon, her eyes seeing what was so far off.

"I do. It is a deadly place, and very difficult to get to. Why would a child need to get there?" Lucan asked curiously. "No one lives on that rock."

"I am called by the Ancestors."

Arilith stepped out of the hut at that point, quickly followed by Loc. "Our charge is a very special person, Lucan. The Ancestors do not call those who are not. She is already blessed by them," Arilith told him.

"This child?" Lucan asked in disbelief.

"She is no mere child, Lucan," Loc said, coming out as well. "In your dream, did your goddess tell you a name for this one of golden hair?"

"Yes. It made no sense."

"Was the name the One True Child?" Loc asked him.

"That's it. How did you know that?" Lucan asked.

"My sister is the One True Child of the Ancestors, born of Blue and Yellow. She was raised by our parents to be the staff and sword of Order," Loc told him proudly, looking at his sister.

"Then no mere child at all," Lucan agreed. "A boat will be made ready for you for when you wish it, Child."

"Thank you, Lucan. If we could leave in the morning, I need to be there by nightfall. Will that be enough time?" Carling asked hopefully.

"I will have my strongest rowers on board, and they will get you there before the sun dips over the horizon," Lucan promised.

Chapter Seven

The wind whipped around the island, bringing with it the hint of the coming spring. Birds with bright red legs squawked loudly as they clung to the rocks and rode the gusts and thermals. The sun shone brightly down on the bare rock, bringing some warmth as the winter began to ease its grasp. Waves crashed up and over the strange rocks that encircled the island. Like great pillars they rose from the water, dark and hard. At the gaping entrance, the water rushed into the upper reaches of the cave, making a booming sound as it crashed at the back.

Carling stood at the top above the cliff and looked out to the mainland, which was a dark smudge on the horizon through the hazy air. Her hair got caught up in the wind and whipped across her face. For three full turnings of the seasons she had been here, and she remembered arriving like it was yesterday.

The boat, pulled by eight strong men, had made the trip out to the island easily in the calm conditions. The water that day had been quiet and still. There had been no wind to beat against them. The island was—as she had seen—dark and foreboding. There were no trees, only scrubby grass, and there were only few places they could pull into to put her to shore. Carling had held tightly to her bundle, which only contained the bare necessities. Lucan and his family had tried to press food provisions on her to take, but she had insisted that they were not necessary.

Carling had watched as they pushed away again from the rocky shore they'd left her on, taking up their oars and heading back to their homes, wondering at the craziness of a child wanting to stay on such an island. Carling almost called them back, the feelings of isolation and desertion taking over her, until a gentle voice called to her.

Following the sound of the voice, she made her way around the island, carefully making for the cave she knew was there. She leapt and climbed the large columns, feeling the rough stone under hands. They had the same feel as the stones from the circle. The cave came upon her as she rounded the outcrop, and she stood panting and staring at the dim yawning mouth.

Stones very much like the ones she was standing on were pushing their way down towards the sea. The water below was crystal clear, and she could see the rocks' counterparts underneath the waves. She entered the shadows and along a ledge, stepping up and down on the tops of the torn-off rock. As the ledge suddenly narrowed, she came to the end. The slight swell inside sounded like the breath of a giant as it rose and fell.

A single finger of rock with swirling water all around it, stood before her. Carling took a breath before stepping over to it to stand on the top. She stood facing the back of the cave and closed her eyes.

"Mother, Father, uncles, aunts, I come seeking your wisdom, your knowledge," she said aloud, her voice echoing off the many facets of the rock.

"Welcome, our child. Join us," the voice of Yellow called out.

When Carling opened her eyes, a path had appeared in front of her. She stepped from the rock and entered the space, the door closing behind her. Yellow and Blue were there to greet her, gathering her up in their arms.

"Welcome home, Carling," Blue said.

"We have waited so long for this day," Yellow told her.

The home of the Ancestors was deep under the rock. It was a simple place, with no extravagance or palatial feel. It felt like a home. There was no real entrance, only a carved arch in the wall where Carling had first entered through from the cave beyond the thick walls. There were rooms for each, and a large common room with a table set in the middle. She found out that it was not used much, as the Ancestors had better things to do out in the word. But the day she had arrived was the day that they all joined together to make her welcome.

The training took time. They did not force the abilities on her, and she found that there were far more than she was aware of. They each took a turn with her to train her in their own particular ones. Violet was gentle and taught her to Track, Seek, and use Stealth to her advantage. Indigo's ability was in the mind, her touch so light that sometimes Carling was not aware she was there. Green shared his knowledge of Healing and the many uses of plants, as well as how to talk to animals. Orange and Red together helped hone the other abilities for use in attack. Yellow and Blue held back their training until later. To her they passed on their knowledge of Strength, Flight, and Light, along with their love. They were the constants in her presence—always there in the morning when she woke, at night for the evening meal, and as she slept. They were a comfort for her, as she missed her own little family.

Now the time was coming for her to re-enter the world, and she began to fear. The island, while isolated, had become her home. She had not thought about how she had been confined. There was always someone around to help her or something to practice. But the training was ending.

As she stood now at the top of the island, she wondered about her family out there. Using the skills that had been taught her, she sought them out. It was something she had not wanted to do, knowing it would give her pain and make her miss them even more. But the hunger to know how they fared was urgent now, and she sent out the thoughts.

Ma and Da were easy to find. Still in the little valley, they lived in the small hut—just the two of them now. Da's hair was greyer than she remembered, and he looked aged. Ma was still hale and hearty. Carling watched her trooping up the hill to visit the stones, and she saw her smile when Blue appeared to her.

Carling turned her vision to Loc and found him walking with Wolf. They were still wandering the lands, and she could sense that they were far from home. Their parting had been hard on Carling. He was the closest of her brothers, and he had become even closer on their journey. He was happy, she could see that now, and she felt that he was searching for someone.

The image before her changed again, and she found Uven. He was closer to her than she realised, sitting in a hut talking to Arilith in the fishing village where she had left him. They were debating something over the prone figure of Lucan, who lay in agony on the giant table in the main hut. Uven had filled out a bit since the last time she saw him, no longer the skinny youth of her childhood.

Ru was next, and she found him with a baby in one arm and a child on his knee. He was laughing at something, and Nila was nearby. Her stomach was already swelling with the next child. Violet had spoken true. Many children would come to the pair, and they would be happy.

Carling then went looking for Galen. She searched for him but found the vision clouded and unable to read. No matter how hard she tried, she could not see her eldest brother, the once favourite of the little girl Carling. She could sense that he was a long way from home and that Loc was near him. She tried again to see him, but again it was blocked to her. Finally, she gave up in frustration.

"You will see him again when the time is right, our child," the voice of Order spoke to her from behind.

Carling turned and greeted the Great Light. "Why can't I see him now? I see the others in my visions. I can even sometimes hear what they are saying."

"As I have just said, when the time is right. And right now, is not that time. What it is time for, Carling, is your final training. For that, it falls to me. I will be teaching you all the wonders of the universe, for daughter, you are special. You can do things we cannot," Order told her with a smile.

"But you are the Great Light," Carling exclaimed, stunned at her words. "You're the highest of the high!"

"No, that is you. But even you have limitations. Come, I wish to show you something." Order lifted off the ground and soared into the air. Carling followed her up and up, leaving the earth far behind.

As Carling rose, she felt the air get progressively thinner in her lungs, and when she reached Order, there was no air to breathe. Working through all she had been taught, she found the solution and put it into practice. Almost like breathing underwater, she changed her body to suit the conditions. As she made these changes, tiny points of light began to swirl around under her skin, small at first but growing brighter and stronger with each breath.

Looking down at the world, she could see how beautiful it was. The work her parents, aunts, and uncles had created took her breath away.

"It is so large," she said to Order.

"It is. There is so much more than just the sacred lands. This world started as a piece of rock, floating in the vastness of space. The sun warmed it and caught it up in its orbit. It is this that I wish to show you. Carling, you have the power to stop the world in its path, to stop time itself."

"Why would I want to?" Carling asked, a bit aghast at the thought of doing so.

"It may become useful at some point. It is something we cannot tell you how to use, or even how to go about it. This world is eventually to be left into the care of you and those of your line."

"No. I cannot take that on. I am only one."

"There is only one and will only ever be One True Child. This was the plan. The creation of a child who would take over from the Sentinels and Order, once Chaos has been dealt with. It will take time, Carling, and many lifetimes before you can truly become The One. Even then, you will need help—and that help is already in the planning. There is to become one Ultimate One after you. A child of love, a child of whose lineage is starting with you. The Sentinels of the south will join those of the north to bless her. You shall be her guide, along with two others. A brother and a sister shall come to you in one of your lifetimes."

Order gave her a vision of her lives, so many down into the future. She saw herself, always the same.

"These are your lifetimes. This shall become the age of the One True Child," Order told her with a smile.

"But what of the Sentinels? What of you—what will become of you all?"

"We shall be here to see you through, to guide you and love you. Our child, the dawning of this new age is for you to shape. This new age is for you to defeat Chaos, to leave this world to the one to come. It is the order of it all. Our time is almost done, and my light will eventually dim. So, too, will those of the Sentinels."

"I don't want you to go," Carling said desperately at the thought of losing them and being set adrift by herself.

"We won't be going anywhere while you are in this lifetime, Carling. But in the subsequent ones, we will be pulling back, until eventually you and The People will not know us. The world the Ultimate One will come to know will be completely different from this, and her power will be so great that she will not need us."

"So we are working towards this Ultimate One? To give her the guidance she needs?" Carling asked, trying to piece it together.

"Yes, child. Your guardianship of this world is to deal with Chaos, so that he is no longer a factor in her life. So she can put this world back onto the course that was originally planned. This is why you were created, Carling."

Order descended back down to Earth, and Carling took one final look at the beautiful planet. It sparkled blue, green, and white in the sunlight. She followed and landed beside the Great Being, changing the structure of her lungs to breathe the air once more.

"Order, how much more is there to learn?" she asked the Great Being.

"We will only be a little while longer with you, Carling. One more turning of the moon and then you will begin your journey home. I feel we have kept you long enough from your foster parents. They still feel your absence greatly."

"Thank you. Shall we begin?" Carling asked hopefully.

"Are you in so much of a hurry to leave us, Carling?" Order laughed.

For a full cycle of the moon, she stayed with Order. The knowledge of the universe and how it was created and worked, stretched her mind further. The possibilities that were presented to her were so great, occasionally she had to take a break just to come to grips with them. At those times, she would again bring forth visions of her family, and as in the past, those of Galen were still hidden from her. She would take her frustrations out in her work.

The time finally came when she was finished. Carling did not feel ready. She did not know if she could still take on the role for which

Order and the Sentinels had trained her. Her self-doubt ate away at her the night before the ceremony. She stood looking out at the ocean once more. It was almost a full moon, and the light that it gave made the sea look silver. Up on the cliff it was calm and peaceful, and she sat cross-legged, looking out.

"Are you worried about something, Carling?" Orange came and sat beside her, and on her other side, Red appeared.

"The seasons seem to have slipped by me. I'm not sure I'm ready to leave," she told them.

"We know you are ready. You have been ready for some time now to go back to the world. It's fear that is holding you back," Red told her.

"You could always look into your future and see what it holds," Orange suggested.

"I cannot. I will not. If I do, it may taint how I go about things," Carling told them.

"See, you are ready. A lesser person would have taken the easy option and sought out the answers," Orange said.

"We have all worked very hard to get you to this point, Carling. We know you are more than ready and capable of doing what needs to be done. And never forget we are with you. You are one of us. You are a Sentinel," Red told her.

"But you each have your colour. Your names are all colours. Mine means *little champion*," she told them, not understanding.

"It does, and it was chosen very carefully for you. If it helps, we can call you Gold or Golden One. So shines your beacon of light," Orange suggested with a smile.

"No, I have my name. I don't need any other than that," Carling said with a laugh.

"There is something else that concerns you, and it is not this fear of yours. You are worried what your foster family will think of your changes," Red said.

"Is it that obvious?"

"A little, child. They will love you no matter what," Red assured her. "The daughter of my line and her husband could never reject you. You are their daughter still, Carling. And as for your brothers, they are the same."

"But I can never see Galen. Why is he being kept from me?" she asked the pair.

"There are some things that even we do not know. You are the greater being here. Maybe it is something you must figure out yourself," Orange told her quickly. "Now come, your parents have prepared a special meal for you, and they are waiting." He stood and helped her to stand.

At sunrise the next morning, the host and Carling were gathered on top of the island. They stood around her, and Order was at her side. The first golden rays hit them, and Order placed a hand on her head.

"Our child, your training is at an end. It is now time for you to leave us and the protection of this island to face the world and your future. Your destiny awaits you, and we send you off now no longer the child who came to us. Our blessings and love go with you as you journey far. Our support we pledge to you as you face the darkness that wishes to rule this land and the whole of the world. Into your care we place this world and the lives of The People. We are in your charge."

The lights under Order's skin burst forth with a dazzling display. As each Sentinel came to give their personal blessing, their own lights flared. When they had each passed, Carling turned to face them all. A rainbow of colour was before her, brighter and clearer than she had ever seen it before.

One by one, they winked out as the host left, leaving only Yellow and Blue standing with Carling. They approached their daughter and enfolded her in their arms.

"Our daughter is now grown. Your potential has been achieved. We are so proud of you, Carling," Blue said.

"Thank you, Mother. Father. I promise to do my best and try to protect the world from the darkness."

"That is all we ask of you, Carling," Yellow said, kissing her forehead. "We love you and we will be there when you need us, just as Order has pledged."

"Now is the moment for you to leave our home. We have enjoyed having you with us, and we have loved every moment we have been able to spend with you. To live as a family, to grow as a family. Our lives are more complete than ever. Remember, this is your home also, should you ever need it," Blue told her.

"Go with our love and our blessings." Yellow kissed her once more, followed by Blue. They moved apart from Carling and left her standing on the island by herself.

The moment they left, she felt the loss. She turned with tears in her eyes and steeled herself. There were no more farewells to be made, and the future lay before her. She had brought with her the bundle from three summers prior, and now she pulled the clothes from the bag and spread them out. They were stained and ragged, and as she held them up against her, she realised how much she had grown.

Order had promised that she would grow physically, and she had. Though the time spent with the Sentinels had hidden from her exactly how much—not only in stature but also in ability. Within a few moments, she had bundled the bag back up and sent it back to her room under her feet. With another thought and wave of her hand, Carling slowly transformed the soft flowing material of the gown worn by the

Sentinels, to that of the hard-wearing and practical clothing made of animal hides and woven cloth The People wore. They were comfortable and familiar, and she sighed as she felt them.

With one last look around at the island she had come to call home, she lifted up and flew across the water. Once more the sea was calm, as flat as the day she had arrived at the island. She dipped down, trailing a hand in the water. A seal broke the surface and she matched its speed as it swam, smiling when it dived down out of sight.

Carling lifted herself up again and got her bearings, finding the little settlement where she had left Arilith and seen Uven. The settlement was no longer small. A broch had been built, and there were more huts and even more boats out on the water and up on the shore. Carling circled around it and landed a little way out of the village.

Walking in, she found in her mind where Arilith was, and was pleased to see Uven still with him. As she strolled into the village, she was stared at by both children and women. Near the centre and the stone broch she found Arilith and Uven sitting outside his hut. Before she reached them, she was hailed by the tall and imposing figure of Lucan.

"There once was a young child who came to our village. Her hair was golden, and she had the hope of the world hidden behind her eyes. Have you come back to us, then, Carling?" Lucan greeted as he limped towards her. She noticed that his leg was turned slightly inwards and was stiff.

"I have, Lucan," Carling replied with a warm smile.

"You have grown. Welcome. I believe there are two here waiting for you." Lucan steered her over to the two men and sat down on the bench, stretching out his bad leg.

"This cannot be Carling, my little sister? You have grown so much," Uven said, getting to his feet. He embraced her and held her out. "When did you get so tall?"

"It must have been while she was on that island, because she didn't reach my shoulder when she left," Arilith said, getting to his feet and greeting her. "Welcome back."

"Thank you. It feels like a lifetime ago. What happened to your leg, Lucan?" Carling asked.

"It was broken, and these two have mended it so I can at least walk on it once more," he said, rubbing the leg.

"Hold onto something," Carling told him. "This might be painful." As quickly as she could, she ran her hand down the leg. Lucan cried out in agony and went to push her away until he realised the pain was there no more. He looked down at his leg, and it was straight.

"It may be a little stiff for a few days as the muscles remember where they're supposed to be, but it should be good as new," Carling told him.

"A Healer. My sister is a Healer," Uven said proudly.

"It is one of the abilities," she said shyly.

"He does not believe what your parents and I have told him, Carling," Arilith told her. "He will only believe it if he sees it for himself."

"Do you wish me to bring Order to the village and confirm the story, Brother?" Carling asked him.

"No one can call Order. The Great Light goes where she likes," Uven scoffed.

"You can call your gods, Carling?" Lucan asked.

"They are not gods, Lucan. They are as much my family as Uven is here. And Order has replied already." Carling pointed towards the edge of the village. Uven turned to where she indicated, and his jaw dropped.

"Was there a reason you called me, Carling?" Order asked her.

"I am sorry, Great One. I needed to make a believer of my brother," she said with some guilt.

"Uven, it is all true. You have been told three times of the reality. I believe even Red has spoken with you. Being the son of Tarl'a, I would think that you would believe who your sister is and would have accepted it by now. I blessed you myself when you were but four summers old, and now I bless you again," Order told him.

"Please forgive me, Order. I should not have doubted the word of my mother and father." Uven bowed.

"Lucan, for your help of our child, I bless you and your village. You welcomed her and her companions into your home and made available transport to the island. For this, you and the village shall prosper and become great," Order told the Celt. "Now, Carling, you have no time to waste. You know where you need to go, and you should be on your way."

"I will, Order," she told him. "It will not take me long to fly there."

"No, you need to take your brother and Arilith with you. You will be going in the same way you got here. My authority has not waned that much, Carling." The Great Being smiled at her.

"I will Order." She bowed her head to her authority.

The group left the village with the well wishes of Lucan and the elders fresh in their minds. Arilith had become sedate and unfit in the time he had spent in the village and was soon complaining about sore feet only part way through the first day. Uven was still in awe of the person Carling had become and said very little to her or their companion.

Carling looked at him that night as he stared into the flames of their small fire. He had changed so much since they were children. He was now a man. The brothers all looked alike, all various shades of their father, and she loved them dearly still. But his quietness had given her pause.

"Do you not like me anymore, Uven?" she asked and passed him a packet of fish that the village had given them.

"I love you, Sister," he said with surprise as he accepted it.

"You have been so quiet. It has been such a long time since we saw each other."

"I have been quiet because I cannot get a word in with this one talking." Uven smiled and indicated Arilith.

"You can talk." Arilith accepted his own pack.

"It has dawned on me how much the world is not what I thought it was," Uven began. "When Ma and Da told me, I remembered the little girl and found it impossible to believe. Now I see this tall, beautiful woman, who is a child of the Ancestors, in a much closer way than we are. I am still making myself believe. I am in awe of you, Carling. When Order came yesterday, I saw how you were with the Great Light. There was no shyness, no hesitancy on your part. Order greeted you like an equal."

"That's because I am. Does it make such a difference to you that I do not act the way I used to?" she asked him, forgetting the meal in front of her for a moment.

"It will only take a little getting used to. We all grow and change. I'm sure I'm different from the way you remember me," Uven said.

"I have the advantage over you. I have been keeping watch over you while I was doing my training. I can see vast distances and pick out people I wish to know about," she told him.

"Could you find someone for me?" Uven asked suddenly and eagerly.

"Who is it you wish to find, Uven?" Carling smiled at him. "And I cannot promise that I can. I have not tried to find someone I've not met before."

"Please. I have not seen her since Red sent me to find you," he said quietly, his eyes looking into the fire.

"I will try. Who is she?" Carling was eager to please him.

"Her name is Cait, she's of the Snake. She is the daughter of the man I trained with at Uncle Gart's broch." Even in the dim firelight, Carling could see Uven blush.

"Uncle Gart I can probably find. Let me try first." Carling closed her eyes for a moment and searched for her uncle.

Finding him easily, she was surprised to see how much he had aged since she last saw him. He was sitting inside at a table surrounded by stone walls, and a storm was building. Across from him, Loc was urgently trying to tell him something, with Wolf at his side. There were many men around them, and they all seemed to be arguing.

Carling opened her eyes. "I found Uncle Gart. Loc is with him. Uven, I want to try something, and I don't want you to panic. I promise I won't hurt you." She reached out and took his hand in hers, then searched again.

Once more, she found Gart and Loc, and this time and she felt that she was standing amongst them. She slowly drew Uven into the vision and settled him as she felt his fear rising. The group was still arguing, but they could not hear what about.

"Show the way to this girl of yours," Carling said in Uven's mind, and he nodded. Still holding her hand, he led her out of the building and into the night. Although the storm raged around them, with lightning ripping through the air, the brother and sister felt none of the effects of it. Their hair and clothing remained firmly in place as they saw the effects of the wind howling around them.

A lone hut was set out by itself near the cliff. Smoke rose from the top of the roof and was swept away by the wind. They passed through the wall and found themselves in the midst of a family scene. A woman was sat near the fire sewing by the flickering light. Beside her was a younger woman with black hair and dark eyes. Uven stopped in front of her and knelt down. His face was full of wonder and love for this girl.

"She is beautiful, Uven. This is Cait?" Carling asked.

"Yes, she is, and so kind and sweet," he replied with a smile as he stared at her.

"Have you asked for her hand?" Carling asked him.

"I made mention that I would when I returned. I have been away so long. I'm afraid she will not wait for me. There were others who were hoping to catch her attention," Uven said worriedly.

"She is of the Snake, you said?"

"Yes."

"I will speak to my Uncle Green. I will see what I can do for you, brother," Carling told him gently.

"Can you? Will he help?" he begged as he looked up at his sister.

"I can try. I want to see you happy, like Ru."

"Loc did not look happy just now, and neither did Galen." Uven was still gazing on the face of his love and did not see Carling's expression change.

"Galen was not there. I would have seen him. There was only Loc, Uncle Gart, and some other men."

"He was there, sitting beside Loc." Uven looked up and then disappeared as Carling let go of his hand. She ran back to the stone building and stood in the middle of the room. She looked directly at Loc and at Wolf, and on the other side she could not see anyone. The space that was there kept slipping past her eyes.

She tried again and again, but still she could not see him. With each attempt she became increasingly frustrated. Carling screamed out with exasperation, and the energy she released shook the building. The sudden shuddering stopped the men surrounding her in their tracks as they stared in fright at the stone walls that surrounded them. Leaving as fast as she could, she felt herself slide back into her own body.

Scrambling to her feet, Carling headed off into the darkness, trying to get herself under control and ignoring the calls from both Arilith and Uven to come back. She fumed and stumbled around in her anger at being unable to see Galen. The air surrounding her crackled, and she sent out fireballs from her hands.

"That is enough, Carling!" a voice called out behind her. She spun on the spot, her arms up, ready to defend herself. Before her stood Yellow. "Are you quite finished?"

"No! I am angry and hurt. Why can't I see him? Why has he been blocked to me?" Carling demanded.

"Who?" Yellow came closer.

"Galen. Every time I go to see where he is, what he's doing, and how he is faring, I am blocked. I cannot see him."

"There is a reason for this, my child. You will see him when you need to. At the moment, there is no reason for you to check up on him," Yellow said calmly.

"But I can see my other three brothers, I can see Ma and Da, and I can even see the woman Uven loves—yet I have not met her," Carling cried out.

"You saw her because you wished to help Uven. Please calm down, daughter. It is very hard to talk to you when you are like this."

Carling took a deep breath and tried to do as Yellow asked of her. The anger was ebbing away, and she started to feel hollow inside. There was nothing else there to take its place. Tears stung at her eyes as they formed and spilled.

"I miss him, Mother. I've missed him the most," she cried out, running to Yellow.

"It is not surprising, my child," Yellow said, taking her into her arms. "You loved him more than the others. But in your mind, he has remained the boy you used to know. He is no longer that boy, but a grown man who has seen and done much in the world. He has changed, just as you have, Carling."

"That does not explain why I cannot focus on him," she said through her sobs.

"It will become clear soon. These things take time to adjust to. It could be that your mind is not willing to see the changes in him. Seek out Loc with your mind," Yellow suggested. "He can tell you how your brother fares. He will be able to pass on a message for you." She smoothed her daughter's hair from her face and wiped her tears.

"Thank you, Mother." Carling pulled away and wiped her eyes, sniffing loudly. "Is Uncle Green nearby? I have a request for him first."

"Is it something I can help with?" Yellow asked hopefully.

"No, the girl is of Uncle Green's line. Uven wishes to know if she still waits for him. He loves her."

"I think you will find that Green is already at your camp waiting for you. So are Uven and Arilith, who are both anxious over you," Yellow told her.

Carling looked to the scene, seeing the glow from the fire, and sighed. "I'm sorry, Mother."

"There is nothing to be sorry about. Love—so I have found out—is a wonderful but sometimes frustrating emotion. Be well, my daughter."

"You also, my Mother." Carling left Yellow standing in the night and headed back to the flames.

It was as she had said, Green was sitting beside Uven with a hand on his shoulder.

"There is no other in her heart, son of my brother. She still waits. I will let her know you are on your way back to her tonight. I think that the news shall give her great pleasure," Green told her brother.

"Thank you, Ancestor. It gladdens my heart to know that she still thinks so highly of me." Uven blushed.

Green looked up as Carling approached, and he smiled at her. "Not gone from us for two days and you are already causing problems, my niece." He gave a chuckle.

"It was unintentional. I am sorry, Uven, for leaving you so suddenly. Were you hurt?" she asked, concerned, as she sat back down.

"No, Carling, I was only shaken a little," he reassured her.

"Thank you for coming, Uncle Green. It was one thing to be on the island and using these abilities. But out here, I feel like I am floundering a little without the guidance of you all."

"You will find your feet soon, I am sure of it, Carling. It is the human side of you that is having such a hard time keeping your emotions in check. Now I must go. There is a certain young lady I must visit this night to give some news to. Be well, Niece, and my blessings on you all," Green said with a smile before he vanished in front of their eyes.

"So many blessings in such a small span of days. I must remember to keep my head screwed on, otherwise it is likely to puff up and blow away in the wind," Arilith laughed, placing another log on the fire.

"Do you wish my blessing as well, Arilith, to add to the others?" Carling smiled.

"Not until we part, Carling. I could not use any more until that time," he said, smiling up at her.

Later that night, after all had settled beside the fire, Carling slipped into the dream state and sought out the mind of her brother Loc. She followed him back to the broch of her uncle and called to him in his dreams. At first his red beacon of light was dim as he clung to the dream he was having, but slowly he became aware of her.

"Loc, can you hear me?" Carling called to him as he finally noticed her.

"I can. Why am I dreaming of you?" he asked, bemused.

"Because I am calling out to you. Brother, it is good to see you again. Are you well? Is Wolf well?" she asked.

"We are both healthy and hearty. But you, Carling, you have changed—or is this the dream you?" Loc asked her, smiling.

"No, this is me. I am changed. A lot has happened to me since I last saw you on the shore."

"Carling, Galen is here with me," Loc told her.

"I know, that is one of the reasons I have sought you out. I cannot see him. I can find you well enough, but Galen is hidden from me," she said with a frown.

"I don't think you would recognise him anymore, Carling, even if you could see him. He has changed so much. He is tall now—so very tall. Taller than any man I've seen before. He is also intense and does not smile much anymore. I have not heard him laugh once since finding him again." Loc told her and Carling could hear the worry in his voice.

"That does not sound like our brother. I remember him laughing often," she said, concerned.

"There is little to laugh at, Carling. Do you remember those men who chased us, the Romans?" Loc asked.

"I do. I remember them and who controlled them well."

"They have landed on the shores to the south in great numbers. Galen came riding in two nights ago with the news. He has travelled far, all over the land to the south. He has visited with kings and great warriors. No one has ever bested him," Loc told her with some pride for his brother.

Carling stopped for a moment and looked into the future. The coming of Chaos' people worried her. "Tell Uncle Gart that they will not arrive at our borders until well after our lifetime, Loc."

"Your training is finished, then?" he asked as he felt her use Foresight.

"Yes, though I am still a little new to it all. Loc, can you pass a message on to Galen for me?" she asked, now getting to why she had called to him.

"Of course, what do you want me to tell him?" he asked her with a smile.

"Please tell him that I still remember him. I still remember how he played with me when my other brothers ignored me. I miss how he used to make me laugh. Please tell him he is loved by his sister," she asked a little shyly.

"I will, Carling. I will pass it on word for word. But why not tell him yourself?" Loc asked confused.

"It's complicated," she told him with a sad smile. "Thank you, Loc. I'll let you sleep now. I can hear Wolf grumbling. We are talking too loud for her. Let her know I miss her warmth and comfort."

"I have. Good night, Carling. I hope we see you soon," Loc replied with a smile.

Carling stepped away from Loc and helped to ease him back into his dream. She looked about her at the place he slept, and for a moment, a bright blue beacon flashed before her, and then it was gone.

Chapter Eight

The trip back to the hidden valley did not take as long as the journey to find the Ancestors. This confused Carling, and when she examined it, she found that she had helped them along without knowing. Great chunks of distance had been covered with one step in her haste to get to her childhood home and see the parents who had raised and loved her unconditionally.

Now, standing on the edge of the river ready to cross the ford into the valley, she felt her heart start to race, and she became nervous. Uven placed a hand on her shoulder. "If you want to see them, Carling, you are going to need to cross over," he said, grinning. He waded into the swift-moving water, giving an involuntary grunt at the cold.

"I am very much looking forward to meeting them," Arilith said as he passed her, shooting his own grin in her direction.

Stepping into the water, Carling did not feel the cold at all as she pushed her way through the knee-high river. Her feet did not stumble once on their way across, and she climbed up the other side with her eyes still firmly fixed on the trail through the trees.

Nothing had changed on this side of the river. The trees still stood tall and strong, and the wind still whispered through their upper branches. When she was younger, she used to imagine that they were talking to each other, and a small smile played on her lips at the memory. One foot moved and then the other, carrying her closer and closer to her home.

One moment she was walking beside the two men, and then she was running. Her blonde hair flew and bounced behind her, arms pumping at her side as she raced to the little hut just over the rise and around the corner. She burst from the cover of the trees and felt her feet carrying her closer and closer, and then there it was. Carling stopped and stared at it.

The little house had not changed one bit. The wood was still neatly piled to one side of the door. Smoke still rose from the centre of the roof. Hides were still stretched out on racks in the work area, and the door stood open to the warm breeze that spring was bringing with it.

Out of the door, a grey head came along with the still-upright figure of her Da. He looked up the track, a hand raised to shield his eyes from the sun that was behind her. He gave a cry and came running towards her. Tears flooded her face as she raced to meet him, flying into his arms and holding on tightly.

"Carling," he said into her hair. "My little Carling."

She could hear his sobs of happiness at her homecoming. He pulled away and held her at arm's length looking at her, drinking in how much she had changed.

"Da. I'm home," she said, laughing. "I was afraid you wouldn't recognise me."

"Of course I recognise you. Come, Ma will be surprised. We had no knowledge of your homecoming. The Ancestors had not said anything to us," he told her through his happy tears.

"Ma is still not looking into the future, then?" Carling laughed.

"Not where you are concerned. She cannot see your future." He placed an arm around her shoulder and kissed the top of her head. "Welcome home, my girl. Welcome home."

They walked together towards the house, and now Carling could see her Ma emerge to see why Mailcon had called out. Tarl'a waited patiently for Carling to get close and opened her arms as her daughter ran to her.

"I've missed you, Ma," she said.

"We have missed you too, our sweet girl. Let me look at you." Tarl'a stepped back and looked Carling up and down. "So tall, almost as tall as your brothers now."

"I think I am taller than Uven," Carling said, smiling broadly. "You will see when he gets here. I left them near the ford. I was in too much of a hurry to see you."

"The Ancestors have been keeping us informed of how you were doing. We are so proud of you, Carling," Mailcon said as he guided her to a seat.

"We were scared those first few nights after you left, with those men chasing after you. Then Blue came and let us know you had fought them off," Tarl'a said sadly.

"Yes, I did." She looked out over the valley, remembering back to the time when all was innocence and laughter.

"You have come into your abilities?" Mailcon said, searching for some other topic.

"I have. Though I feel I have not used them very wisely since I left. Only once can I honestly say I thought of someone else when using them. A village chief who had helped me had a broken leg and it was not set properly, so I mended it as a way of thanking him," Carling told them. "No, there was one more time—when I helped Uven search for the girl he loves."

"Uven has a girl? This is news," Tarl'a said. "He never told us when we saw him last. It was when he was heading off to find you."

"You can ask him yourself. Here he comes now with Arilith." Carling smiled when she saw the two men talking as they came around the corner.

"Is this stranger a friend of yours, Carling?" Tarl'a asked as she looked carefully at her daughter and the stranger with her son.

"Yes, a good friend, I hope. Blue sent him to me. He is supposed to be some sort of an advisor, but so far, he has done no advising. He waited for me in the village while I trained."

"Are you two close, then?" Tarl'a hid a small smile.

"I am not in love with him, Ma, if that is what you are thinking. He is a travelling companion and friend, that is all. I have also been helping them both with their abilities while we travelled. The limitations of their teachers were great," Carling told her.

"Are you sure of your feelings? You seem to be smiling a lot while you talk of him," she teased Carling.

"Yes, Ma. Now stop it. There is no man for me," she said sadly and believed it. It was something she had come to accept while she trained. The Ancestors lived a solitary life; only Blue and Yellow had formed an attachment, and that was only because of her.

It was early morning when Carling and Tarl'a walked up to the stones, three days after she had arrived home. They were arm in arm, and Carling had not left her mother's side for long since coming back. The air was misty on the valley floor, and they climbed above it, watching it move slowly in the morning sun.

"Are you sure there will be no man for you, Carling?" Tarl'a asked. Since her daughter had first told her this piece of news, it had worried her.

"I'm sure, Ma. I am a tool, a weapon to be used for safeguarding the way for the Ultimate One. I am to join the Sentinels, and their life is a solitary one. My life was not meant to be shared, and I could not give myself to a man wholly with what I need to do," Carling told her mother.

"You are young yet to be making these sorts of decisions. Unless you have already sought guidance from the Ancestors about it?" Tarl'a asked.

"No, I have not. It is not something I have discussed with them. I just know within my heart. But I have the love of you and Da, and that of my brothers. That is enough for me." Carling looked out at the blanket of white and silently wished it were otherwise.

They reached the summit without saying another word, and Carling drank from the spring. As always, the water tasted sweet and crisp. She stood and was surprised how fast the Ancestors had arrived to greet them.

"Good morning, Tarl'a," Yellow greeted her. "Our daughter has changed much, hasn't she?"

"She has indeed, Yellow. You and the Ancestors have done a wonderful job with her."

"We only built on what you and Mailcon had already started." Yellow gave her a beaming smile.

"I wish to talk to you, Ancestors. I need clarification on a vision I have had," Tarl'a started.

"The vision is true, daughter of my line," Red spoke with a smile. "I am pleased to see that you are using your ability."

"Then it will come to pass?" Tarl'a asked him hesitantly.

"Yes, it will. Without it there will be no line to follow. And there must be a line—two lines actually. The necessity of it is great," he told her.

"This surprises and concerns me," Tarl'a straightened a little. "I thank you, Ancestors, for answering my call."

"You are not going to say more?" A smile played on Yellow's lips.

"No. I think the surprise will be greater when it happens," Tarl'a said, returning Yellow's smile.

"The surprise will also be a nice one for you, Tarl'a. The one you seek nears, along with one of your line," Yellow said.

"Thank you, Yellow. We shall watch for them." Tarl'a gave the Sentinel a nod.

"Who is coming?" Carling asked and tried to see the event Yellow had alluded to.

"You will not see them, Carling. In this I have decided it is best you don't," Yellow told her firmly.

Carling looked around the group gathered at the stones and found them all to be either smiling or trying to hide grins. There was something afoot, and she did not like to be kept out of it. She tried again to see, but there was nothing—only haziness and shadows.

"Carling, stop trying. You will only get frustrated again. I don't think a light display up here would be a good thing," Blue said as he came to Yellow's side.

"As you wish, Father. But I will find out. Ma cannot tell a lie." Carling found herself grinning now. "She will have to tell me if I ask her directly."

"What if I were to forbid you, Carling? Would you still ask the question of your foster mother?" Order appeared in the midst, and the smile faded from Carling.

"I would abide by your word, Order. I will not ask Ma. But I find the limitations you all place on me to be greatly frustrating, considering you have placed this world in my hands," she told the Great Light.

"Even a baby bird must first learn to fly, Carling. You are testing your wings only for the moment. Very soon, the limitations—as you call them—will be off and you will be free. We still hold the balance of power, and you are still our child for a little while yet," Order told her gently.

"It shall be as you wish, Great Light," Carling said giving in to the inevitable.

Three more days she stayed with her parents in their house. The waiting was becoming tedious and boring. Twice she had made her way to the brook and looked for the large fish that had eluded them all. Twice she had pulled it out of the water, only to put it back. Not once did she let Uven know she had done so. He was still trying every afternoon—and failing.

It was peaceful and quiet, and she remembered when she couldn't wait to leave. That feeling was coming back slowly. It crept up on her in moments when her thoughts drifted to all she had seen and done outside the confines of the hills and wood.

On the third night, Carling woke with a start. A voice had called to her. A harsh and guttural voice. She recognised it and shivered as she remembered the sound of her name on his lips. Then it came again.

"Carling!" Chaos called out into the night. The others around her slept on, their snores and breathing were of those deep into their dreams already.

Slowly she got to her feet and dressed, pulled her boots on and laced them up around her legs. Outside was cold and the mist was already forming around her, rising from the warm earth as the cool air hit it from above. The faint tendrils curled around her legs, illuminated by the moon far overhead. They swirled as she walked through them towards the hill at the back of the house and then left them below as she rose into the air.

Landing softly at the top where the two hills met, she waited. It was all quiet. The only sound that came to her was the water as it escaped the spring and cascaded down the side of the hill, splashing as it tumbled down. The upthrust of rock stood before her, a guardian in its own right as it protected the sacred stones from view. Carling lifted off the ground once more and flew to the top of the rock.

There was no one around. He was not there, but she had heard him. Carling looked over at the land beyond, the hills that rose and fell like a sea frozen in time.

"Carling." Again he called, and she turned to face the place it had come from.

"I am here, Chaos. What is it you want?" Carling called out.

"As always, you. Come face me Carling, and let us test how well Order and her children have taught you," he challenged her.

"It is not the time for us to meet, Chaos. That is still many summers away," she told him.

"Are you afraid? Are you still a child? Is the fear that I sensed in you when we first met still gripping your heart?" he taunted her.

"Fear is a natural thing, Chaos. I embrace my fear and use it to drive me on. Do not think that it makes me weaker." Carling called to him, still searching the landscape for any sign of the Dark One.

"Then come and face me. Let me test you and see how strong this fear makes you," he ordered her.

"No. I will not come to you. If you wish to see me, you come to me. You know where I stand," she said bravely, hoping that he wouldn't.

"So be it," he said with a laugh.

The vision of the true Chaos grew in front of her on the ground at the base of the rocks. He was a large muscular man with dark hair and eyes that had a glow of red about them. Carling could see his muscles rippling under his shirt as the Being kept on swelling in size until he was looking down into her face.

"Am I all you had hoped I would be, Carling?" he sneered at her, holding his arms out and turning so she could see him fully.

"A trick—one I know well." Carling jumped from the rocks and made herself grow to match his size. "As you can see, Chaos, we are equally matched."

"This is my world, Carling. You will not be defeating me anytime soon," he told her with his arrogant self-confidence.

"Do you always have to waste time with words, Chaos? Or do you not want to test my skills?" she asked calmly but felt her fear rise.

Chaos roared and immediately fired the first shot at her, a large ball of intense darkness, hoping to envelop her. Carling countered with an equally large ball of her own, one of light—an intense and brightly burning golden light. It blinded Chaos for a moment and he growled again at her.

Reaching out, he enclosed her in his arms, squeezing with all his might. Carling smashed her head into his and swelled again even larger, breaking his hold. Chaos matched her, and they now stood like giants in the landscape.

"Come get me, Chaos," Carling taunted him, running towards an open area in the hills, where she turned to face him.

"This is not a game, Carling," he called to her.

"All tests are games in one way or another." She watched as he walked towards her, his eyes burning red as they bored into her. She found her mind starting to haze up and become foggy. Carling shook her head and slammed her defences up. "Is that all you have?" She smirked at him.

"Who are you who thinks you can defeat me where seven already could not?" He circled her carefully.

"I am the One True Child of the Ancestors. Born of necessity, and Guardian to the Ultimate One to come," she called out to him.

Chaos stopped for a moment and stared at her.

"The Ultimate One? Who is that?" he demanded.

"Your limitations are hindering you, Chaos. The Ultimate One shall guide this world—One born from my line and that of the Sentinels," Carling told him pleasantly, as if telling a child she had a treat for him.

"There shall be none from your line, Carling. I shall take your life this night." He grinned at her. "But first I think I shall have some fun."

Pushing off from the ground, he left two great dents behind and launched himself at her once more. She ducked out of his way, striking him with a fist to the side of his head. Chaos fell onto his knees and looked up at her.

"You fight well for a girl." He stood to face her once more. "Are you not going to attack?"

"Why should I do all the work when you are doing it so well for the pair of us?" She grinned at him, her body tense and ready to strike again.

Chaos lunged and caught her. Swinging her around, he threw Carling as far as he could. Tumbling through the air, she came to a skidding halt on one knee—the dirt underneath scraping away from the rock it hit—and looked up to face him. From her hand a great staff appeared as he bore down on her. She raised it up and caught him in the stomach with the end, stopping him abruptly and knocking the wind from him, making him stumble back.

This time Carling was circling him, waiting for him to catch his breath and stand to face her once more. He watched her as she moved gracefully around him, her long golden hair loose and flowing around her shoulders.

"You are beautiful, Carling. You should join me," he said, getting to his feet.

"No," she told him as she spun the staff in her hand and lashed out at him with it, hitting him in the back, thigh, and shoulder all in quick succession. He cried out.

"But we could rule this world together," he tried again, watching her warily.

"No." She spun the staff again, feinting to strike a couple of times before landing more blows to his face and stomach.

Shaking off the hits, he turned on the spot as she circled him.

"We could be the most powerful Beings in this world," he suggested as he tried to cajole her.

"No, no, no." With each word she landed a blow—one to the back of the head, one to the back of the knee, and finally, one to the heel. Chaos collapsed to one knee. "You only wish to own me, control me. You do not wish to rule with me, Chaos."

Chaos roared once more and slammed her to the ground, the earth splitting underneath her. The heavy impact shook the surrounding area, sending nesting birds crying out into the night as they escaped their trembling nests. Carling roared from where she lay and started to lash out at him with light and fire. Each blast caught him and made him wince. The flashes were so bright they lit up the night sky and exploded against him with the sound of thunder. He staggered away from her, his feet catching the exposed rocks, sending them crashing down the hill as he brought up his arms to protect his head and eyes.

Carling got to her feet and changed out her staff for a sword. She flew at him, slashing out and slicing through his flesh, cutting him over and over. The dark blood that flowed through his veins splashed onto the ground, scorching it, leaving a rotten and acrid smell to curl up with the smoke. She stepped back and found she was breathing heavily.

"I will never bow down to you, Chaos," she declared to him, her sword out before her.

"I will have you or I will kill you!" he screamed. Rushing at her, he pushed the sword aside and grabbed her around the waist, lifting her up off the ground. She pounded at him with the hilt of the sword, trying to get him to let her go.

Leaning in, he brought his face close to hers.

"You will be mine, Carling." He kissed her, his lips cold and harsh.

She pulled away from him, and her hand slashed down with the sword. She sliced at his shoulder, and he released her, grabbing her arm in the process. Taking the sword from her grip, he turned it to her, thrusting it through her shoulder, and Carling screamed out into the night.

"I will defeat you, Carling. But not tonight. Your test is over." He pulled the sword from her body, bloody and dripping, and threw it to the ground. Standing over her, he blasted her once more with a large ball of darkness.

The last thing she saw that night was Chaos's grinning features.

It was that noise Galen awoke to, the loud, thunderous concussions booming over the land. The night was clear, and the stars shone brightly in the sky above. There was no reason for the sound. Wolf padded out of the inky darkness and nudged the sleeping form of Loc. Coming awake, he moved his head and watched the display over the hills.

"Wolf says it is a battle," Loc said urgently.

"Where?" Galen asked. "Who?"

"She does not know, only that it is a battle," Loc replied.

Galen was up and moving before Loc had finished telling him. Weapons in his hands, he raced off towards the lights and noise.

"Go with him Wolf," Loc urged the large animal.

His even breathing and the speed of his feet carried him far in a short amount of time. Galen heard their voices before he saw them. He crested the hill that hid the two great figures fighting in time to see the sword thrust into the woman's shoulder and hear her scream. He saw her fall and the other pull the mighty sword free, throwing it to the ground. The large man snarled and then he walked away, disappearing.

Off and running again, Galen was at her side within seconds. He found her shrunken to normal size and unconscious. Her hair was splayed out around her head and blood was oozing from her shoulder. Wolf came up to his side and sniffed at the woman, whining momentarily as she nudged her undamaged shoulder. Lifting her muzzle when she got no response, the wolf howled into the night.

Without thinking, Galen picked her up and headed for the one place he knew he could get the help she desperately needed. The bloodied sword he ignored and left lying where it fell. He did not see it disintegrate into a thousand golden points of light and wink out of existence until it was needed again.

The woman weighed nothing in his arms, her head bouncing against his shoulder and her golden, flowing hair covering her face. Galen made it to the hill with the sacred stones and passed them without a backwards glance. Down the hill he ran, not bothering with the easy track and switchbacks. He stumbled and almost fell near the bottom. He juggled her into a better position and made his way to his childhood home. It was a place he had not seen since he was twelve, a place that held wistful memories of sad blue eyes saying goodbye.

"Ma, Da," Galen called out into the night as he neared the house. "Hello! I need your help."

He kicked at the wooden door, and it splintered into pieces. Shouts of alarm came from within, and bodies moved inside as he entered. He lay the inert form of the woman down beside the dying fire.

"Who?" Mailcon managed to get out before Uven yelled.

"Galen, what is going on?" Uven called out, then noticed the woman at his brother's side and rushed over. "Ma!"

"Carling!" Tarl'a cried as Uven placed his hands over the still-bleeding wound.

"Arilith, help me," Uven called, and a tall figure moved with great speed to her other side, joining his hands with Uven's. They both closed their eyes and concentrated.

"So much blood," Arilith muttered as sweat started to bead on his brow.

"Try to find the source," Uven told him.

Galen watched his brother and the stranger work, his mother coming to his side. The woman was pale, and the name she had cried out had not quite caught up with him.

"Where did you find her, Galen?" Mailcon asked. "Galen!" he called out sharply to get his attention.

"In the hills, there was a battle. They were large," he said stupidly.

"Who were, Galen? You are not making sense." Tarl'a took the face of her eldest, long-lost son in her hands. "Tell us what you saw."

"She was battling a man. They both stood so large, like giants. He wrestled the sword from her hands and ran her through. Who is she?" Galen asked them, still looking down on the woman.

"It is Carling, my sweet boy," Tarl'a told him and held him close.

When his mother let him go, he dropped heavily to the floor and stared at the pale form, finding little that he recognised of his sister.

"Yellow, Blue—we need you. Please come. Your daughter is in peril," Tarl'a called out into the darkness outside.

Within moments, the small house became tight with the large presence of two of the Ancestors. The inclusion of the two baffled Galen, as had the words his mother had used to summon them.

Yellow removed the two pairs of hands from Carling and placed her own over the wound. Within moments she had stemmed the flow and knitted the flesh back together, leaving only a faint, silvery scar behind.

Blue placed his hands on either side of her head, then he nodded and pulled them away. "She is stable. It will take a while for her to replace the blood she has lost, but our daughter will recover." He sat back with some relief.

"Galen said she was in a battle. She can't have been fighting him, can she?" Tarl'a asked Blue desperately.

"We have no knowledge of this. It was not foreseen. We would have advised her not to face him, not to risk everything in a futile meeting. She is still too young yet. Her abilities are still growing, still developing into her full potential," Blue told her.

"He was large, vast, and threatening. But so was she," Galen told them, still staring at her, confused. "Carling?"

The fire flared as Mailcon fed the embers. The light played across her features and hair, then Galen recognised her. It was his beloved sister lying there so pale and so changed by the years.

"We will find out the story from Carling when she wakes," Uven said, looking at his hands, coated in his sister's blood. He got up and started to head outside. He stopped beside his brother. "Welcome home Galen."

Chapter Nine

The dreams flitted from one thing to another, and through them all, the harsh, threatening words and voice of Chaos threaded them together. Faces and people flashed in front of her, talking, calling out, and frightened. She looked around at them and wondered what they wanted, why they couldn't let her just rest and be at peace.

The pain in her shoulder still stung and she rubbed it, her hand coming away red with the blood she felt there. It did not scare her to see it, not even really registering that there was something to be concerned about. She felt more ashamed at having Chaos beat her. She had felt so confident of her abilities. So sure of her strength. But he had taken the sword and used it against her.

Carling turned away from the faces of her family, both celestial and earth-bound. She wandered away from them and their concern. She felt them seek her out, searching for her. She did not want to go back to them just yet. The moment was not right. It was not time. The longer she slept, the longer they fretted and worried, but in her dreams, she did not have to face them.

Carling wandered the world in her mind, seeking out those special sacred spots that had been put in place by the Sentinels, feeling their power and energy. Until she came to one. In a tiny land in the southern seas, hidden away in the depths of a dense forest, in a valley very much like her own, she found a circle.

The stones were small and green as the grass, polished and standing proud out of the ground in a clearing near a spring. Carling circled the stones and felt their energy and the knowledge they contained within. Touching each stone, she saw glimpses of the future. Her lifetimes stretched out before her, her many forms.

Seven men and women came to stand before each stone and greeted her.

"The One True Child is welcome to the lands of the south," one intoned and came close to her. She was Yellow, but it was not Carling's mother.

"Daughter of our sister and brother, your life is not ready to start in our lands. It will be a far-off time before you are born here," the southern Blue told her, coming to stand beside Yellow.

"There are still many tasks for you to perform, many trials and battles against Chaos, our ancient foe. You still have growing to do and strength to build. Our energy and knowledge are yours to use. We will be with you when you face the test in these stones," Indigo told her.

"Child of the Great Light, we shall protect this place as the sacred valley is protected. These lands will be ready to be used by The People when they come to our shores in preparation for your birth," Violet told her.

"All will be ready in preparation for the Ultimate One when she comes. From one of our people will she come, from the joining of one of your line. We watch over the line carefully and faithfully," Orange spoke as he came forward.

"Our faith and love go with you. Our blessings also. There is still much for you to do, Child of our hearts," Red said.

Finally Green stood before her. He raised a hand and placed it on her head. "It is time to wake now, Carling. Wake and live your life. Your wound is healed, rest your mind and let those who love you most help heal the wounds that are not physical."

A flash of light, and she felt herself spinning through space and back to her body.

Carling gasped as her eyes flew open. Sitting up, she coughed, a great, wrenching cough. Hands held her, rubbed her back, and embraced her. She pushed them off and stood, staggering outside into the warmth of the day and the fresh air. She felt hot and stifled, her hands coming up to strip the outer layers of her clothing off, pulling and tearing at them. She made her way to the brook and dived into the deepest pool. The icy water it contained washed over her and dispelled the dreams and images. The words of the Sentinels still with her, she held onto them dearly.

Large hands pulled her up out of the water and pushed her to the bank, where she lay staring into the blue sky above. Her arms were outstretched and panting, water dripping from her face and hair as she breathed in the sweet air of her home.

"What are you doing, Carling?" a loud voice called beside her, and she turned her head in the direction it had come from. Standing waist-deep in the pool she had just been dragged from was a large man. His long dark hair was dripping, plastered to his face. His eyes, so blue, so familiar to Carling, were concerned and mystified.

She sat up and stared at him. "Galen?" she asked quietly.

"Yes, it is me. What were you thinking plunging into the pool like that?" he asked as he waded towards her.

Carling threw her arms around him, sending him off balance and back down into the cold water. Her brother, her favourite, was home. They came back up for air, and Carling became very aware of him—how he felt against her and how close he was. She pulled away slowly.

"Maybe she thought you were the fish we've all tried to catch at one time or another," Loc called from the bank, laughing.

Carling crawled up the bank and sat on the grass, watching quietly as Galen came up to sit beside her. She pulled her hair from her face and squeezed the water from it.

"Do you mind telling me why you did that?" Galen demanded.

"I was hot. I needed to cool down," she said and blushed. "And Loc, I have caught that fish many times. He and I are old friends. He even comes when I call now." Carling laughed and stood to hug her youngest brother.

Loc stepped back, not wanting to get wet, but she was too quick. He hugged her back.

"Where's Wolf?" she asked him.

"Nearby. She says she will come soon," he told her, pushing her away.

"You should be resting, Carling." Galen stood, still towering over her, even though she had grown tall.

"How long have I been asleep?" she asked.

"Four days. We were beginning to worry. Uven couldn't reach you, and the Ancestors all said that it would take time for you to recover. They have all been here, including Order," Loc told her.

"I go away for a few turnings of the seasons, and I find when I come home that all has changed. Most of all my little sister." Galen smiled and pulled her back into a hug. "I have missed you," he said quietly.

Carling felt herself go red again and pulled away. "I have missed you too, Brother." She headed back to the house and found Tarl'a waiting with a fresh change of clothes for her.

"Are you in pain?" her mother asked.

"No, there is no pain, Ma. I am fine."

The little house was feeling very small to Carling as she changed. Her mother bundled up the wet things and laid them outside to dry. As she came out, Tarl'a insisted she sit and brought her a bowl of broth and a berry cake. Carling ate both quickly and sighed as the food hit her stomach. She had not realised how hungry she was.

"Some things don't change, then. You still eat like it is going to disappear," Galen said. He had stripped to the waist and sat barechested in front of her.

"With four hungry brothers, what else was I supposed to do? If I didn't eat, it would have been snatched from my hands," she said, trying not to look at him too closely and giving a small laugh.

"Everyone has tried to tell me the story. It was only after Red came to me to explain it that I understood. My little sister." He shook his head and smiled at her.

"*Our* sister, Galen," Uven said as he and Arilith came from behind the house. "I am pleased to see you awake, Carling." He dropped a kiss on her head.

"How is your shoulder feeling?" Arilith asked as he sat near her.

"It is fine. To which of you two do I owe my thanks?" she asked.

"For what? We did nothing. Galen found you and brought you home, and Yellow healed you. We were floundering trying to find the source of the bleeding," Uven told her.

"We have just been to the stones for some more tutelage. It appears our knowledge is lacking a great deal more than we thought. Green has been very helpful with providing that which we don't know," Arilith said. His eyes had not left Carling once since they arrived, and it was noticed by more than one person.

Carling stood and looked up the hill. "I should go and give my thanks to them," she said distractedly.

"Are you going to tell us what happened first?" Galen asked her.

"Not yet. Later." She started to head towards the hill and they watched her go. They all noticed that she had lost her focus while she spoke, and it left them with an eerie feeling.

The climb up was slow, and when she reached the top, she was breathing heavily. Her strength was still not back, and she felt it now as she struggled on shaky legs. She stood at the entrance and held the stones on either side, feeling their energy swirl into her hands and through to her inner core. The stored energy sustained and renewed her as she garnered its benefits.

Looking up, she saw Yellow and Blue already there waiting for her. She ran into their arms and sought their comfort.

"I was so stupid," she told them as she sank to the ground. "I thought I could match him."

"Why do you think we never suggested you seek him out when we finished your training, dear daughter?" Blue asked.

"He called to me in the night, and I foolishly accepted his challenge." She shook her head at her own recklessness.

"It is his way. He thought to best you and he thinks he has. He thinks he has weakened you in some way, and hopes that when you meet again, he will have the upper hand," said Yellow.

"It is going to take time to build my strength up again, isn't it?" she asked them.

"Yes, Daughter, it will. We take a longer time to recover from injuries than humans do. And although you are human in many ways, in many more, you are a Sentinel," Blue told her proudly.

"And you are not alone in this quest. Your foster brothers are your guides, companions, and sometimes teachers along the way. And one shall become dearer to you over the others," Yellow said to her with a secretive smile.

Carling was still too busy thinking about the battle with Chaos to notice this smile or hear her words. The battle came back to her fresher and brighter in her memory. She heard his words again—his offer to rule together—and Carling shuddered at the horrible thought.

"He called me beautiful and kissed me," she said screwing her face up at the memory.

"You are beautiful, my daughter, but he seeks to flatter you. To win you to his side. If that were to ever happen, he would use you, dear one. He would own and control you. You must never give into him," Blue said emphatically.

"I told him that night that I would never bow down to him," Carling told them.

"You risked a great deal that night. We were so frightened when Tarl'a called to us. We could not see what had happened," Yellow said.

"I'm sorry to have frightened you." Carling felt the admonishment keenly.

Blue kissed her forehead and held her close. "We are still learning how to be parents as well. This is all new to us Sentinels," he told her gently.

"We have heard from our brothers and sisters in the south that you visited them," Yellow prompted her.

"It felt like a dream. They were you, but not you. Their sacred land is so far away, so isolated. They said that some of The People would settle there. Is this true?"

"In one of the visions, yes, but a lot has to happen for that version of you to be born. A lot is at stake, Carling. If you were injured more with this meeting, then that Carling would not be born," Yellow told her.

"I understand. I will not accept any more of his challenges until I am ready. I just hope that I know when that will be," she said with a smile.

"You will know when the time is right, our child. Now it is time to go back to the family you have below. Ru will be visiting shortly, and you must help your Ma prepare. This time with all your foster family around you is important. Learn from them, grow in your knowledge of what it is like to be a part of a large family. Get to know them again. You have all been apart too long." Yellow stood and helped her rise, then kissed her.

"Thank you, Mother and Father, for coming to my aid, thank you for healing me." She held onto their hands tightly.

"It is what parents do," Blue grinned.

"Can you thank Green as well for taking Uven and Arilith's education in hand, and giving them the knowledge they need?"

"It may be an oversight of ours to let the abilities run their course, and not add to the information that is passed down. It is something that we will look into and change. Perhaps that is one good thing to come from your injury," Yellow surmised.

"Perhaps. Thank you."

"Always, Daughter. Go with our love and blessings on you," Blue told her. They each kissed her again and left her standing in the circle.

On the way back out she touched the stones and felt them fill her once more. She felt the vibrations as they communed with the world outside the sacred lands, and she was happier. For once she felt like she was a part of something larger, something more than just the little valley down below and the family who had raised her. Carling smiled.

Contented, Carling walked back to the house at a slow pace. The energy had been replaced, but she could feel that she was still not quite right. She was stopping and picking the wildflowers along the way for her Ma when the sound of wood being chopped came to her. She closed her eyes for a moment, and memories of childhood and Galen chopping wood flooded back to her. But the image of the child Galen was now replaced by the man.

Carling blushed. He was her brother; she should not be thinking of him in that way.

Lost in thought, she headed away from the house to walk along the bank of the brook. The water tumbled over the rocks and into the deep pools where the larger fish liked to hide. It sparkled in the sunlight and the sound soothed her soul. Home.

For a long time she walked, not really seeing the brook anymore. The flowers were still in her hand but were forgotten. Carling looked down the valley to the dark wood and felt the comfort of the embracing arms of the hills. She felt safe and secure. The closer she got to the forest, the more the world seem to encroach on their solitary valley.

A dark shadow moved under the first trees and came out to stand under their large limbs. With her tongue hanging from her jaw, Wolf began bounding towards Carling. She stopped and sat before her.

"Well met, pack-mate," Carling greeted her.

"Well met, pack-mate. You are healed. We were so worried about you," Wolf said to her.

"I am sorry to have made the pack worry. Are you well, Wolf?"

"I am, Carling. You have changed much, but I still recognised you by your scent that night. I have tried to guard you as much as I could since then, but you made it difficult for me to do so. Why did you try to hide from us?" the wolf asked.

"I was ashamed of myself and not ready to face all that has to be said," Carling told her.

"Are you still feeling that way? Is that why you are here, so far from the den? They look for you again—Galen especially." Wolf's manner was teasing, and Carling could not understand why.

"Why do you tease me?" she asked as they walked on together along the bank.

"Your littermate is having confusing thoughts, as are you. As you are not really of the same litter, it is allowed." Wolf looked up at Carling with her tongue hanging out and a wide grin.

"But he is my brother," Carling said, alarmed.

"Then if he does not please you, there is the other. The one who joined us on our journey."

"Arilith? No, he is not for me. I am not meant for anyone," Carling told her.

"Then how can the Ultimate One come from you and your line, Carling? You humans are not the only creatures to talk to the Ancient Ones. The one you call Indigo spoke with me. She explained it all. And it seems to me that it is impossible for you to have a pup without a male."

Carling sensed that she was amused, and she was sure that Wolf would be laughing if she could.

"And what about you, pack-mate? What about pups for you?" Carling asked.

"I cannot answer that, pack-mate. The one I would mate with is not able to. I will be content to be in his company." The wolf sat for a moment and seemed to sigh.

Carling stopped and looked at Wolf. "Would that be my brother, Loc?" she asked, stunned.

"It would be your littermate, Carling. The Ancient One said he is my mate, and I am his," the wolf said sadly.

Carling dropped and threw her arms around the neck of the large, shaggy wolf. "I will ask Order about it."

"There is nothing to be done, Carling, but thank you for your care." The wolf pulled away. "Speaking of my mate, here he comes. He knows nothing of this, Carling, and I would prefer he did not."

"You wish me to lie to my brother? I cannot do that, we are unable to, Wolf."

"The concept of lying is foreign to wolves as well. I just wish you to not tell him," Wolf said sadly.

"You have my word." Carling stood and turned to meet Loc.

"There you are. I was wondering if you could show me this amazing fish that comes when it is called." He was laughing, but Carling could see that there was worry behind his eyes.

"He is a big jack and is in one of the pools over here." She smiled back at him. "And I am fine. I just needed time to think and talk to our-pack mate here."

"Arilith was wondering where you had gone," Loc said with a sly smile.

"Is there something you are trying to say?" Carling asked, appearing to be unable to understand him.

It was not until later that night that she finally built up her courage and told them all about facing Chaos. And as she had expected, there were many voices telling her how idiotic it was of her to do it.

"Next time you have this kind of death wish, call one of us to go help you," Loc told her, lying on the ground with Wolf at his side.

"It was not something I thought about," Carling said, staring into the flames.

"That was obvious," Uven said. "I thought you were dead when Galen broke down the door and brought you in."

"You broke the door down?" Carling asked Galen.

"I was in a hurry. I didn't have time to put you down and open it gently," he said with a grin.

"Thank you for the new door, Son. I am pleased to see that your skills are more than just war craft," Mailcon said.

"We are almost complete." Tarl'a looked around at them all.

"Ru will be here in a day or two," Carling spoke without thinking. When she saw her mother's look, she clarified for her. "Yellow and Blue told me this morning. I forgot to let you know."

"I don't know where we will put you all. The house is already overflowing." Tarl'a looked at the small house illuminated by the fire outside.

"We can sleep out here, Ma," Galen offered.

"Or we can make a new lean-to for you to sleep under. I have been thinking about it for a while now, as somewhere for visitors to sleep. With you all home, the work will go quickly and easily. What do you think?" Mailcon said, stretching out and leaning against the wall of the house.

"I'll be happy to help, Da," Galen offered.

"Of course we will." Uven and Loc spoke at the same time.

"I would be happy to help as well," Arilith also offered.

"Your help will be more than welcome, thank you, Arilith." Mailcon smiled at him and then threw a look at Carling. "And you, Carling, what about you? Will you help?"

"Try and stop me," she said enthusiastically.

"I'm not sure that is such a good idea, Carling. Yellow told me you need to rest and take things easy for a while," Tarl'a said, placing a concerned hand on her arm.

"I'm fine, Ma. I have skills that can help."

"Like bossing us around," Uven laughed.

"I have never bossed you around," she protested.

"Not much," Loc said, laughing. "You've always ordered us around."

The next couple of days were a hive of activity at the house. At first, they didn't let Carling do anything, and she found that annoying and patronising. She headed to the forest after hearing her father tell Galen what he wanted in terms of wood, and she found the perfect tree to fell. It was tall, and she asked its permission first; she heard the acceptance, and she brought it down easily. With a wave of her hand, she dressed the log and split it, turning it into planks and posts.

Carling sat on the pile waiting for Galen to arrive, and she heard him whistling as he came down the track. He did not miss a beat as he approached her and looked at the wood, checking it for straightness.

"It is still too green," he said critically.

"What do you mean?" Carling asked, jumping down from the pile.

"The wood is still too fresh," he said.

"But it would be exactly the same if you had cut it," she protested, looking at the pale, golden stack.

"Since you have taken my job away, how about we waste some time?" Galen bent and picked up a stick from the ground, tossing it to her after examining it.

Carling caught it with one hand and looked at it, puzzled. "What am I to do with this?" she asked.

"The reason you got run through, little sister, is because you don't know how to handle a sword properly." He searched the ground for a stick of his own.

"I had training in sword fighting." Carling swished the stick in front of her.

"Who taught you?"

"Red and Orange." She stopped and leaned on the stick, watching him.

"There is your problem. Two Beings who cannot kill, teaching an untried girl the art of sword play," Galen shot at her.

"I think they did a good enough job," she said defensively.

"An unarmed man took your sword from you, and ran you through with it," Galen said, standing up and facing her.

"I wasn't prepared for it," Carling told him in a small, ashamed voice.

"I know you weren't. That is why we are going to practice," he said as he waved the stick in front of him, then threw it to the side.

"Ma is not going to like it."

"Is Ma going to be the one to face Chaos next time? I don't think so." Galen continued his search for the perfect stick.

"If she finds out about this, she will have your hide," Carling warned him.

"Found it." He picked up the stick and hefted it in his hand. It had a few kinks in it.

"You know, I could quite easily make something out of this wood that would probably be better than this deadfall," Carling suggested as she flexed the stick in her hand, and it cracked under the pressure.

"You can do that?" Galen asked, walking towards her.

"How long do you want them, how thin, and how heavy?" she asked, pulling one of the planks out.

Galen looked between the wood and Carling, then held out his hands. "About this long and about this thin." He measured it out with his fingers.

Carling placed a hand over the wood and ran it along the grain. A storm of wood chips flew, and when she had finished, a perfectly formed wooden sword sat on the planks. Galen picked it up and studied it, turning it in his hands and feeling the balance and weight.

"It's a bit light, but it will do for a starting point," he said.

Carling took it from his hands and concentrated a little. When she handed it back, he tested it again.

"Perfect." He grinned at her.

With the same motions, Carling made another for herself of the same dimensions and weight. She picked it up nervously in her hands and turned to face him, the tip of the sword pointing to the ground.

"For a start, raise it up to me," Galen said, showing her how with his own. "Right. We will start with the movements first. Step forward like this and then back like this," he said as he crabbed forward and backwards, never lowering the sword in his hands. "Now you do it."

Galen watched critically as she moved, and then he corrected her, showing her again.

Carling leaned on her sword and smiled. "There is another way we could do this. I could just take the knowledge I need from your mind," she told him.

"No, I do not want you up here," he said as he pointed to his temple.

"Why not? It would be easier. I would then know what it is that you want me to do," she argued.

"There is no substitute for good, honest hard work, Carling. It will train your muscles and your mind to work together until it becomes second nature."

"Is killing second nature to you, Brother?" she asked him sadly.

"It is not something I take pleasure in, Sister. But at times I have had to kill to defend myself. Never have I taken a life for any other reason," Galen assured her, staring into her eyes.

Carling pulled her eyes away from his gaze, having those uncomfortable feelings again. She moved away from him for a moment and held the wooden sword up. Slowly she crabbed forward and then back again.

"Good. Again," he instructed her.

For the next few hours he drilled her on how to move. Never again did they speak of him using the weapon against a human. She felt that the times he had killed weighed heavily on his mind, and she did not want to bring up painful memories. She worked hard that morning, and when she had finished, she was hot and sweating.

"We had better hide these. Ma already doesn't like my real ones in the house." Galen collected up the swords and walked to the other side of the clearing, placing them inside a fallen tree.

"Da will be wondering what's taking you so long," Carling said as she picked up a bundle of the planks.

"How strong are you?" he asked, amused at the sight.

"Probably a little stronger than you." She grinned as she headed back to the house.

Chapter Ten

The new room was coming along nicely, with Carling and Galen feeding the supply of wood to Mailcon, Uven and Arilith. Each time they headed back to the clearing and the stockpile; they would train some more. For two days, they kept this up without raising suspicions until they were interrupted.

Galen had finally relented, and they now were in the process of trading blows. He showed her how to block first, and they started out slowly. As they sped up, the sounds became loud cracks as they moved faster and faster. She blocked each blow while retreating and trying to withstand the force he threw at her. Her arm raised up for one more blow, and he reached around her and pulled her close.

Their eyes met. Carling was breathing heavily, and the blue of his eyes held her spellbound for a moment. The thoughts she had running wildly through her mind caught her off guard and she almost let herself go. The sound of horses approaching brought her up, and she pushed him away. The sword still hung loosely in her hand, and she moved her hair from her face, looking to see who was coming up the track.

The horses approached, and Carling recognised Ru at the lead. Sitting in front of him was a small child with dark hair and brown eyes, the image of his father. Ru pulled his horse up and dismounted.

"Who are you to be harvesting wood in this forest?" he demanded, coming closer to them.

"I knew your sight was going, Ru, but you can't be so blind that you don't recognise your own brother," Galen laughed.

Ru came closer and peered at Galen. His hand came up to his brother's face, and he felt the lines on it. "Galen. You made it back," he cried out, embracing his brother. "I was not expecting you to be here!"

"Ru, Carling is with me. Here." Galen led Ru to Carling and lifted his hand to her face.

"You have gotten so tall, Sister. I am pleased you are home safely," he said as he embraced her.

"Ru, welcome back." Carling pulled away. "You cannot see?"

"I fell from a horse. I see shapes, but nothing real. I have gotten used to it, it's nothing now," he told her.

Carling raised her own hand to Ru's head and searched for the problem that lay there. She found it easily enough and called for Green's guidance. The area was small, and she pressed on the nerves that helped him see. As slowly and as carefully as she could, she released the pressure. She looked into his face as she worked, and she could see his eyes open wide as the vision gradually returned to him.

"This is a sight to behold! You have grown so beautiful, Sister," Ru said and kissed her on the cheek. He turned and spotted his son and the rest of his family coming up the track. Nila saw him and smiled as he walked towards her unaided, pulling her down with the baby still strapped to her. "I can see, Nila, I can see!"

"Did you hit your head again?" she asked, concerned.

"No. Carling healed me," Ru said, picking her and the baby up.

Nila turned to the couple standing by the pile of wood. She walked to Carling and stared at her. "You cannot be little Carling. You were so small last time I saw you. You've grown." She hugged Carling to her.

"I have, Nila. It is good to see you again, Sister," Carling said shyly.

"Thank you for helping my Ru. How can we thank you enough?" Nila pulled her into another hug.

"There are no thanks needed. It was an easy thing, even Uven or Arilith would have been able to do the same thing," Carling said, embarrassed.

"Our Healer at home could not help. He said it was too risky to do it, that he may lose his sight altogether," Nila told her.

"We have been getting special training and knowledge from the Ancestors. That knowledge will be passed on." Carling looked down into the sweet face of the baby in the sling, who gazed up at her with pale blue eyes.

"Ma and Da will be happy to see you," Galen said as he moved to take the sword from Carling's hands.

"What is going on? Why do you have these things?" Ru asked, finally noticing the practice swords.

"Just a little bit of fun, Ru," Carling told him. "Galen was showing me a few things."

"You are teaching our sister to fight?" Ru rounded on Galen.

"I wish you hadn't fixed his sight, Carling, now he can find me. Yes, and she needs it. You will understand more when you hear the full story." Galen bent down and picked up a bundle of wood. "Mount that horse again, and I'll tell you all about our sister's adventures while we haven't been watching."

The new room was finished and the single men moved into it. Ru, Nila, and their children stayed in the main house, and Carling found that the addition to the group was making the valley suddenly seem very small. Ru had promised not to tell their parents of the drills and practice Galen was teaching Carling, and she was grateful for his silence.

What she was not grateful for was the fact that they now had an audience when they went to the forest to practice. When Uven and Arilith had finished their training for the morning, they made their way to the clearing via the hills so that Tarl'a and Mailcon would think they were still up at the stones. Loc made the excuse that Wolf needed to hunt and would follow shortly after. Ru took his eldest son for long walks, which just so happened to include going through the clearing at the same time Galen and Carling were practicing.

With each session came an improvement in her movements and the way she handled the sword. Each time Galen would attack, she held her own. But she got the feeling he was holding back on her. Finally having enough of him treating her as less than an equal, Carling took matters into her own hands.

The simplicity of it was beautiful. She grew. Just as she had changed her size to match that of Chaos, she stood in front of Galen and stretched herself out so that she was looking directly in his eyes.

"Now, will you please treat me as an equal and not hold back? You know how strong I am," she demanded.

"You want to be treated as an equal? Then, little sister, I will treat you as such. Are you ready?" he asked her, grinning.

Carling moved away and turned to find him already charging. Instinctively, she brought the sword up and met his first blow. He was as good as his word, and he had put all of his ability into that strike. Deflecting him and moving to the side quickly, she rounded on him and slashed at his unprotected back. The spin was quick, and his own wooden sword pushed the point of hers away from hitting him.

On light feet she circled him, looking for the first opportunity to attack, but Galen came on first. Carling defended herself well, keeping him at bay, and then pressed on her own flurry of blows. She pushed him back, grinning as much as he was. With a flick of her wrist, she caught his sword with hers and kicked it out of his reach, disarming. She did not expect him to keep up the attack without the sword in his hand.

Just as Chaos had done, Galen charged and lifted her off the ground. Only this time, Carling knew what to do. She brought the hilt down hard onto the space between his shoulder and neck, causing Galen to cry out in pain and drop her, his arm hanging loosely at his side.

"Do you yield?" she called to him, panting.

Galen stretched and moved his shoulder, flexing his tingling fingers. His eyes darted to the sword on the ground not far from him, and he rolled to it quickly, bringing it up to face her. Carling knocked it out of his hands again and shouldered him to the ground, a look of surprise evident on his face. She placed the tip of the sword at the base of his throat.

"Do you yield?" she asked him again, grinning.

"I yield," he told her, and she helped him stand.

"So, this is where you have all have been hiding for the last few days," Mailcon said, coming up the track. "I see you took the Ancestors at their word and have been teaching Carling." He crossed his arms across his chest and stared at them all.

"Da, she needed—"

"I know she needs to know this, but Ma will not be pleased. Do you want me to tell her, Carling, or are you going to have the courage to tell her yourself?" he demanded.

"I will tell her, Da," Carling said, shrinking herself to her normal size.

"I do not like it, and I do not condone it. Fighting is never the way of The People. You five should know that already, coming from the family you do. But if it stops her from getting hurt—or even worse—killed, then you have my blessing to carry on. Ru, Nila is looking for you, you may want to get back to the house. Carling, make that conversation soon with your Ma, otherwise I will have it with her," Mailcon warned then turned and walked away.

Ru gave them an almost apologetic look as he hurried after their father, taking his son with him. The clearing was quiet again as Carling picked up Galen's sword and bundled the two into the fallen log.

"There's no point, Carling, she won't let us practice anymore," Galen told her.

"Yes, she will. And even if she doesn't give her blessing, I still need the practice." Carling did not head down the track back to the house but the opposite way to the ford. Turning left, she headed upriver to a secluded pool she knew about and began to strip off her clothing.

Diving down deep into the pool, she swam and felt free in the cold water. It was clear, and she could see the fish that resided in it. Bursting back up to take a breath, she cleared the drops from her face and saw movement amongst the trees. Thinking of it as nothing more than Wolf keeping an eye on her, she dived again and swam to the opposite bank. A large rock sat just under the surface, hidden enough for her to sit on it and still be immersed modestly.

The current pushed on her back, and she hugged her knees against the cold. In her mind she went over how to go about talking to her Ma about the practice. Her thoughts wandered again to the image of Galen—his arm muscles rippling as he held the sword—when her daydreams were interrupted.

"Carling?" a voice called from the other bank.

Her eyes came up quickly and she slid off the rock, so that only her head stuck out of the water. On the other shore, Arilith sank to the ground, crossing his legs under him.

"What do you want, Arilith?" she called out across the river.

"Can I join you?" he asked suggestively.

"No, you cannot. I don't want you to," she told him, trying to keep herself covered and becoming very uncomfortable with him being there.

"Well, then I'll just wait here for you to get out." He smiled, and there was something in it that startled her.

"I don't like you that way, Arilith," she said to him.

"What way is that?"

"I have seen you watching me. I can see your thoughts now," she told him.

"Can you? How embarrassing! Can you also see how you affect me? How much you torment my every waking moment?" he asked her.

"So you decide to follow me and talk to me when I am at my most vulnerable?" she asked him.

"I did not know you planned to go swimming. I thought you were taking the long way back."

"Do you often follow me?" Carling asked.

"I would follow you to the ends of the world if you would let me," Arilith declared grandly. "And then throw myself off the edge if you told me to."

"The world is round, Arilith," she told him plainly. "There are no ends."

"Figures. I can't even do that now. I waited for you at the village for three turnings of the seasons. Then you came back and greeted me the same as your brother. I knew then that you did not love me, but I hoped, Carling. I hoped that you would look at me just once," Arilith told her.

"I have looked at you. I am looking at you now," she responded, a little confused.

"No. I mean as you look on Galen. I came to find you to say that I'm leaving in the morning. There is nothing for me here now," he told her sadly.

"What of your lessons with Green?" Carling felt pity for him.

"They are finished. I am to go out into the world to teach others the knowledge that has been passed on to me." He stood, ready to walk off. "I only thought to tell you this news myself."

"Arilith, wait. Don't go just yet." Carling began to swim to the other bank. "Wait for me by the track, I'll walk back with you." She watched him carefully as he walked away, nodding that he had heard her.

Pulling herself out, she dressed quickly and ran to catch up with him. She found him not too far away and walked at his side.

"I have grown fond of you, Arilith, but I do not feel the same as you. And I greeted you the same as my brother because that is what you have become. Please don't go away and become a stranger again," she begged him.

"I have a feeling we will see each other again, Carling. You and Galen will make a wonderful pair," he told her.

"Galen is my brother," Carling insisted.

"Only in name."

"No. He is my brother. And he will always be my brother," Carling said impatiently.

"You can keep telling yourself that, Carling, but you will never truly believe it." Arilith laughed a little.

They walked on in silence for a bit, entering the clearing and finding it deserted and quiet. The wind rustled the trees above them, and birds hopped from one to another.

"Carling, how broad are your abilities?" Arilith asked, breaking the silence.

"I have been told that they are vast, why?"

They had just about reached the other side when he held her back and stopped her. "Can you change how people feel?" he asked, a little desperately.

"No, I cannot do that. I will not do that." Carling placed a caring hand on his arm and looked to the future, hoping to see him happy. "Arilith, you will find someone who will take your breath away. Go to my Uncle Gart's house. She is there, a Healer who needs your training. She is sister to the one Uven is so besotted with."

"My heart is too full of you to see anyone else," he told her, stepping close.

"Let me show you, then." Carling reached up and placed her hand at the side of his head. The image of the girl she had seen she transferred to him, and he stepped back, shocked.

"I thought you couldn't do that, change how a person feels?" he gasped, pulling out of her reach.

"I only show you the one you are supposed to be with. If that has changed your feelings towards me, it is because they were not true feelings to start with," Carling told him.

"Thank you, Carling."

"For what, helping you see what is real? There is no need for thanks, I just wish you happiness, Arilith." Carling started to head towards home, and he ran to catch up.

"What is her name?" he asked eagerly.

"I don't know. Uven may help you there. I think it is time he went to claim her hand. You two could travel together," she suggested.

"And what of you, what do you do now?"

"I have no idea. I don't know where I'm supposed to be, or even what I'm supposed to be at the moment. I cannot see my future, even the Ancestors cannot. I only see possibilities," Carling told him.

"Promise me that you will listen to the advice of your brothers and the Ancestors, and not go after Chaos," Arilith asked carefully.

"Believe me, I do not want a repeat of that. I must say, I will miss your loving gazes from across the fire," she gave him a half smile to tease.

"No, you won't. You'll be too busy making your own at Galen." He laughed as she blushed. "I won't tell him. I promise. But you might want to look up a bit more and see the ones he gives you," he teased her back.

Her brothers were waiting for them when they got back, and she had to defend Arilith to them. Around the fire that night after the meal, she suggested that Uven may like to go visit Gart. His eyes lit up at the thought of seeing Cait again.

"Does she have many brothers and sisters?" Carling asked casually.

"Who?" he asked.

"Who do you think she means, idiot? The girl who is still waiting for you," Ru teased his younger brother.

"Cait has many," Uven blushed.

"Any she is close to?"

"She has a twin she is close to, Ila. She is a Healer. Cait often helps her with her work," Uven said.

"Such a pretty name. Ila," Carling said and shot another look at Arilith. "She would need help with training, will she not, to learn what Green has taught you and Arilith?"

"I suppose so," Uven replied.

"Then that should be our first stop, Uven. You could finally take Cait as your betrothed," Arilith said eagerly. "I was thinking of leaving in the morning. Will you travel with me?"

"So soon, Arilith?" Tarl'a asked him. "You do not wish to stay longer here?"

"No, but I thank you and Mailcon for your generous hospitality. I feel like I am one of the family. I also feel that the road is calling me again. It is time I went out and taught all that has been imparted to me," he said honestly.

"You will always be welcome back, Arilith," Mailcon said, and Carling caught an almost relieved sentiment to the words.

"Then we shall leave tomorrow," Uven declared.

The fire crackled merrily, and Carling caught the smile that played on her brother's face at the thought of seeing Cait again. She looked around her whole family, felt the love that was there, and then she stopped on the face of Galen. His eyes were bright in the firelight, and they were on her.

As they waived Uven and Arilith off the next morning, they were all smiles at going, but Ma was feeling their loss already. She held onto Carling's arm and steered her away from the group. The mother and daughter made their way up to the circle, and as they climbed, Tarl'a had a few questions for her daughter.

"I am sorry that nothing came of Arilith's affections for you, Carling. Are you heartbroken?" she asked gently.

"No, why would I be? Arilith and I were never meant to be. He goes to meet the girl he will be betrothed to. I have seen it and already shared it with him," Carling told her.

"But I was so sure he was in love with you," Tarl'a said.

"It was not love, Ma," Carling laughed. "No, you couldn't seriously see me and him together? He is too much like my brothers."

They remained quiet for a moment as they climbed.

"Your Da tells me that you have something you need to share with me. He said last night that he was disappointed that you had not come to tell me already," Tarl'a told her.

"I'm sorry." Carling stopped and looked ashamed. "I should have come to you, and in dealing with Arilith I completely forgot. Ma, Galen has been teaching me how to wield a sword so that I may better defend myself."

Tarl'a looked at her for a moment, then reached out and took Carling's hand in hers. "If it will help you defend yourself against that monster, then I can see no harm in it. I know you would never harm a person on purpose or without reason. Thank you for telling me, Carling," Tarl'a said and then continued walking.

Her mother was so calm that Carling blinked for a moment. "You aren't mad or annoyed that we did it behind your back?" she asked, as she followed.

"I am mad you did that, but children will do these things. Carling, you are almost fully grown, and you have so much to deal with. This is something you must know. The Ancestors cannot teach these things to you, so Galen is the perfect person." She held onto Carling's hand for a moment. "Go back down. I find that I need to talk to the Ancestors by myself this time."

"Is something wrong, Ma? Have you seen something?" Carling asked her.

"No, my girl. I have questions that I would rather ask without you being near. And before you ask, yes, they are about you. I need guidance before I can guide you, Carling. I need the answers that the Ancestors can give me before I can truly give you advice." She gave Carling a weak smile.

"If you are sure Ma. I will go." Carling quickly hugged her mother close. "I love you, Ma."

"I love you, too, my daughter." Her eyes sparkled upon hearing the words. "Now go and tell that lot that the new room needs to be aired out. With so many males inside, it stinks." She turned and continued up the path. Carling watched her go for a moment and then headed back down.

She was still mulling over what her mother could possibly have to ask the Sentinels when she made it back to the house. Loc was coming out of the new room with Wolf at his side, and Ru's eldest boy came running up to the animal. With a great lick of her tongue, she had him in giggles and running away to play.

"I keep telling her she needs to go and find a mate," Loc said. "She needs to have pups of her own."

"But she does not listen?" Carling asked, coming to his side to watch the play between wolf and child.

"No, she does not. Typical female, it doesn't matter the species, they are all the same."

"Speaking of which, Ma wants that room aired. She says it stinks," Carling told him with a grin.

"You're not with her at the stones?" Loc asked as he glanced up the hill.

"No, as you can see, I am here with you, passing her instructions on to you and Galen."

"What I meant is, why aren't you at the stones?" her brother asked.

"Ma didn't want me there. She needs to talk to them alone this time," she told him. "And I am not tied to them. I am not the next guardian."

"No, I am," he said almost regretfully.

"No, you're not. The line does not continue with you. You may have foresight, but the guardian is one of the others. The Ancestors have told me," Carling informed him.

"That's a relief. I think I would have made a bad guardian. I cannot seem to stay in one place for long." He laughed.

"Just like your wolf." Carling grinned at him.

Loc looked out at the large black animal as it bounded through the long grass, keeping the little boy from the edge of the brook. His face lit up as he watched her, and it pained Carling that he would never know proper love.

"Are we practicing today, or are you just going to let those muscles of yours go to flab as you jabber away?" Galen asked as he came out of the room. In his hands were his own precious swords.

"I find I have some free time, Brother, so yes. Have you grown slow since coming home?" Carling asked.

"No, I am still as fast as I was. Why?" he asked, confused.

"Because I'm going to beat you there." She took off as she finished the sentence and raced across the long grass, her legs and arms pumping as fast as they could go. Behind her she could hear him as he raced after her and was catching up. She sped up and made it to the trees, cutting through to the track and the clearing.

Carling turned as he entered, panting, and she laughed at him. "See, I told you that you had slowed up some since coming home."

"Get the wooden swords," he told her as he caught his breath.

"I thought we were using the metal ones." She headed over to the hollow tree and pulled them out.

"Warm up first, then we will see." Galen grinned at her disappointment.

The pair went through the drills, and he didn't let up on her. He made her perform the movements over and over, barking orders and criticizing when she got it wrong.

Carling's frustration at it was building, and finally she broke. She lashed out with the wooden sword over and over, beating him back and pushing him down. Even when he held his hands up, she carried on, letting her anger fly with the extension of her arm.

"Carling, stop," he cried out, managing to grab the sword away from her. He threw it to one side and jumped to his feet to face her. Even without the practice weapon, she continued to attack him.

Galen held up his arms to protect his head and tried to get her to calm down. He recognised the blood rage that had overtaken her. He reached through and grasped her, pinning her arms to her sides.

"Carling, calm. Carling." He kept his hold on her and tightened his grip until she relented and became limp in his arms. "Carling," he whispered to her.

Carling became aware of her surroundings once more and felt his body pressed against hers. Her arms encircled him, and the feelings she had tried so hard to push down swelled up. She relaxed into his arms, her breathing slowed, and her heart rate dropped.

"Are you back?" he asked her, looking down into her eyes.

"I'm back," she responded quietly.

"Good. You need to watch that. I have seen it before in men in the middle of battle. They lose all sense of where and who they are. They battle until they drop," he told her in a whisper.

Carling pushed him away from her, the embrace becoming too much for her to deal with. She turned away from him and picked up the discarded wooden practice sword.

"With your abilities, it could become dangerous for those around you. If you truly lose control, Carling, it could be dangerous for yourself." He placed his hand on her shoulder and turned her around.

"I can't do this, Galen," she said, shaking off his hand and starting to walk away.

"Carling, what do you mean? You can't do what?" He went after her and took her hand.

"I can't explain, please let me go," she begged him.

"No, I won't. Tell me what the matter is," he asked gently.

"The matter? Only the biggest problem I have at the moment," she said, her voice rising.

"That is why we are doing this, so that you will be prepared when you meet Chaos," he told her, obviously confused.

"I am not talking about Chaos. Please, Galen, just let me go. I need to leave."

"No, don't leave. Carling, don't leave." He pulled her towards him, and she did not resist. Still holding onto her arm, he looked down at her. "Don't leave," he repeated quietly.

"We can't do this, Galen." She refused to meet his eyes.

Galen reached up and placed his hand behind her neck, drawing her even closer. Still she would not look at him.

"Look at me. Tell me what we can't do." He spoke so softly, so tenderly.

Carling turned to look up into his bright blue eyes. "Us," Carling uttered. It was only one word, but it held so much more. "Please let me go."

He searched her face for a moment more before releasing her. Carling moved away and placed the sword back into the hollow tree. Without a look back at Galen, she left the clearing. Her heart was racing again and breaking at the same time.

Chapter Eleven

At the edge of the trees, Carling lifted off the ground, flying high into the air. Using the hill as her guide, she made her way to the stones, and in her haste, landed heavily beside the large rock that guarded them. She rounded it and found the ring empty. Tarl'a had already finished and gone back down. In some ways she was happy about that. She would not have to tell her mother what was bothering her, and in another way, she felt the need of her mother's arms for comfort.

Carling entered the familiar and special place, taking solace from the stones around her. She circled them on the inside, trailing her hand along their rough surfaces. The turmoil that raged inside her was beginning to ebb away as the stones spoke reassuring whispers across time and space, letting her know she was not alone.

There was no way of knowing how long she communed with them, how long she was held by their murmurs, but it was late in the afternoon when she woke from where she sat leaning up against the largest of the stones. Carling moved away from the stone, feeling them drawing her back to them. She stepped into the centre and turned to face the sun as it slid down towards the horizon.

Before Carling could see him, she felt Galen near as he rose up the side of the hill, following the spring and landing beside it. He made his way carefully to the entrance and waited for her to say something.

"Go away, Galen," she told him weakly.

"No. Ma and Da are worried about you. You disappeared on me. What has you so frightened? I still don't understand." He stepped into the circle. "We are in the most sacred of spots, Carling. You have to answer me truthfully."

"I wish it wasn't you who had come to find me." She turned to face him and shook her head.

"Why? Because you have something going on in that head of yours, and it involves me? Why are you pushing me away, Carling?" There was pain behind his eyes and question.

"Because I don't want to get hurt. I don't want to feel the pain of losing you again." It was true, but he could tell she was still holding back. Carling began walking around the stones again, hoping to get to the entrance and leave.

"Will you just tell me what it is?" Galen asked, keeping his eyes on her.

"I would rather not. I don't want to ruin the family. It would rip us apart, and I can't lose you all again," she told him quietly.

"Just a simple answer is all I ask, Carling. Please," Galen begged her.

"You are going to make me answer, aren't you?" She stepped closer to the entrance, nearer to her escape.

"Just stand still, Carling. I know you are trying to get out of this. We may not have been together for the last ten summers, but I still know you," he told her.

Carling stopped walking and faced him once more. She took a deep breath and let it out slowly. There was no getting away from it now, and she had to tell him.

"You must understand first that I never meant for these feelings to surface. I never meant to give in to them," Carling told him, her voice starting to crack with the effort. Galen stepped towards her, reaching out to touch her. Carling pulled away. "Please don't, it will only make it harder."

"Just tell me, please," he begged again with a whisper.

"Galen, the feelings I have for you, a sister shouldn't have. When I'm with you, I don't see you as my brother," she said, looking towards the entrance.

"Carling, I have—" Galen didn't get the chance to finish what he was about to say, as Carling suddenly launched herself into the air. He followed her, keeping her in sight and trying to catch up. "Carling!" he called out to her.

Galen saw her stop and hover as a cloud passed between them, and when he broke through, she was gone. He searched for her, turning and twisting, going higher than he had ever attempted before. But she had disappeared from view.

Galen dove back down to the ground as fast as he could, the speed dizzying, pulling himself up short just before he hit the ground. Upon landing, he was already running towards the house. He rounded the corner and found them all still standing outside, his father concentrating.

"I lost her. She took off and I lost her," Galen told them desperately.

"She's heading southwest," Mailcon said, coming back to them.

"What did she say, Galen? Why is she so upset?" Tarl'a rounded on her eldest son.

"She would not tell me straight out. She kept speaking in circles," he told her, the words still spinning in his mind and the information was too personal. Carling had been right; it would be too hurtful to the family.

"There must have been something," Tarl'a said desperately.

Seeing his mother so distraught, Loc called out with his arms raised high into the air behind them. "Ancestors, come to us in our time of need. Your Guardian has need of you, your daughter has need of you." He hoped they could hear him, hoped they would answer.

"You cannot ask them here for this," Galen cried out as he rushed at his brother, trying to force Loc's arms down.

"Who better to help us find her? She could be anywhere by now!" Loc yelled, taking a step back from his eldest brother.

"She doesn't want to be found," he roared back.

"What aren't you telling us, Galen?" Mailcon asked, trying to get between his two sons.

"He is trying to say that Carling is upset, and her mind is unsettled by something that she has finally discovered about herself," a female voice said behind them.

The small group turned as one in time to see Violet walking around the house and stand before them.

"Where is she, Violet?" Tarl'a asked her.

"She is safe and is at our home, where we trained her. She will be safe there. Tarl'a we need to talk privately," Violet said gently.

"No. You can say it in front of everyone here," Tarl'a responded defiantly.

"It is about what we discussed earlier, Tarl'a. Are you sure you wish them to know now, while they are still so upset?" Violet asked.

"Sister of my Ancestor," Tarl'a began as she pulled herself up straight and clasped her hands together in front of her. "I, the Guardian of the Stones, request you reveal to them, that which was revealed to me."

Tarl'a's request was formally made, and in return was formally acknowledged.

"Daughter of my brother's line, I will do as you have requested. Although I do not agree." Violet turned her attention to the three men before her. "This afternoon, Tarl'a asked us some specific questions, and we in turn answered them. The line of the Guardian shall be passed through Galen. Although he does not have foresight, the one he marries shall."

"I cannot do it. It cannot come to me," Galen said, stunned for a third time that day.

"This has been seen, Galen, son of my brother's line. The second question your mother asked of us today is to see who you shall marry," Violet told him.

"No, I don't want to know. I don't want you to say any more," Galen begged her.

"My son, you know. She told you," Tarl'a said gently, reaching up to hug him. Galen sank to his knees, and she held him like he was small again.

"It is the only certainty in her life. It is the only thing we can see," Violet told him with some compassion.

"Who? Who is it? Tarl'a? Galen?" Mailcon asked, confused, looking between them before he finally turned to his ancestor. "Violet, who is it?"

"Galen shall marry the daughter of my sister and my brother. The daughter you have fostered so lovingly. Galen and Carling are destined to be together. It has been written in the Book of Destiny, and it will be so," Violet said as softly as she could.

"Our Carling and Galen? Why are we only now learning this?" Mailcon asked.

"We did not see it before she was born. It was only recently that it has been revealed to us," Violet answered.

"But they are brother and sister!" Mailcon exclaimed.

"No, they are not. She is not of your flesh and blood, but ours," Violet responded.

"Tell her to get home now, we need to sort this out." Mailcon was floundering, and he had no idea what he would say if Carling were standing in front of him right now.

"I cannot do that, son of my line. Every day she becomes more of a Sentinel than a human. I cannot order her around," Violet told him gently.

"What about Order? Couldn't the Great Light tell her?" Tarl'a asked, her arms still around the crumpled form of Galen.

"It is a request I can make to Order, and I will try for you." Violet moved towards the mother and son and crouched down. She placed a hand on Galen's head. "My blessings on you, Galen. Your mind will know peace, but the answers you seek are already in your heart. The love you feel for Carling has grown."

"Violet, please make her see reason and come home. There is no need for her to take off," Mailcon pleaded, trying to sound calm.

"I will try, my son. Take care of your little family." As Violet stood and turned, she disappeared from sight as she took her first step towards the hill.

Inside the island, deep within the earth, protected and shielded from the outside by the giant pillars of basalt rock, Carling lay huddled on her bed. At her side was Yellow and Blue, trying to comfort her and calm her as best she could.

Violet walked into the girl's room and laid a hand on her sister's shoulder. "It did not go well, I fear. Tarl'a insisted I tell them. They are asking that she return to them soon," she said quietly.

"I can't go back. I can't love him; he is my brother." Carling's crying renewed.

"But it has been seen, Carling. We have been over this," Yellow said, rubbing her back.

"Mother, I can't." Carling shook her head as another wave of sobs wracked her body.

"Let things calm down and reasoned heads accept what is to come. You can stay here for as long as it takes you," Yellow told her.

"I will get Red to go reason with Galen. He is a stubborn one, just like our brother." Violet left them to comfort Carling.

The tears flowed, and eventually Carling slept. Her dreams were invaded by images of her family. She walked the dream path and looked in on them, surprised to find that she could now see Galen. She saw him sneak out in the middle of the night; his bag slung over his back. She watched as he was confronted by Loc and Wolf at the edge of the forest that guarded the valley. She could not hear what was being said between them, but Carling witnessed the look of sadness on Loc's face as he nodded. They embraced as they parted, and she followed Galen out of the valley until it was too painful to watch anymore.

Carling could imagine the reaction of her parents in the morning when they discovered he had gone. She had split the family like she knew would happen. Her sadness deepened. For days she stayed this way, unable to eat, and escaping into the world of dreams. Despite her resolve not to, her mind was always searching for Galen. Finding him alone on the road, wandering. Invading his dreams while he slept and witnessing his pain.

"It is about time she faced up to her responsibilities." Carling heard one morning when she woke. The voices that were drifting to her from the larger communal room were loud and becoming heated.

"Give her more time. She needs to sort through these feelings she is having. We cannot send her out while she is so unsettled."

"Her spirit is still so young and is still learning. It is necessary for her to go through this to understand how to cope with situations like this later. That is the reason she was fostered with Tarl'a and Mailcon, so she could be more like one of The People."

"Is she to be so tormented each time she lives?"

"But what about her responsibilities to the world? Chaos is out there creating havoc. His armies are already spread wide in our brothers' and sisters' lands. They are there fighting, why can she not also?"

"She is not ready, that is why. We have already discussed this when she was training. The human side of her is simply not ready to cope with the pressure and the horror of it all."

"Many of the people dying out there were also not ready to handle the horror spreading across the lands. Very soon his army will be landing on the shores to the south. I have been out to see for myself. Already a great force is amassing across the channel. Chaos will have them here soon."

"One invasion has already been stifled. I helped my brother to create a rebellion that saw the troops' need to leave their staging point. But Orange is correct. Another force is building, and they will come."

"This is not getting us anywhere. We are all aware of what Chaos is doing by manipulating these Romans. But Carling is still too young to defeat him. Still too young to face an army by herself."

"Then we need to help her."

"We are not equipped to battle, to kill. That is why she was created in the first place."

Carling lay there listening as they argued around in circles. It was always the same, some wanting to push her out to do something and the others wanting to protect. So much anger was building that she could feel the storm raging outside as the air began to react to their energy.

"Am I able to go and see these Romans?" Carling asked from her doorway, unable to keep quiet any longer as they discussed her.

"Carling, it will not be safe," Violet told her.

"I have ways of hiding myself. I have all these abilities, and as some of you have said, it is about time I started to use them for the reason I was born," she said stubbornly.

"I can guide you, Carling." Red stood eagerly and faced her.

"You are just reacting to your emotions, Carling. You need to sort those out before you rush off recklessly," Yellow said from her seat.

"I thank you for the comfort you have given me, Mother, but Orange and Red are right. I have duties and responsibilities to The People to protect them. I have an enemy who is taking the lands one piece at a time at the end of a sword. How can I lie there day after day feeling sorry for myself when the threat is now becoming too real?" she asked her mother.

"You are sure you wish to take this on right now, Daughter?" Blue asked from Yellows side.

"I am, Father. I am sure," she said nodding.

"And what of Galen?" Green asked her carefully.

"Given time, he will hopefully marry another, and then I will be free of my feelings," she said, lifting her chin, determinedly trying to believe the words she spoke.

"As I understand it, love does not work that way," Blue told her.

"It must this time. For both of our sakes," Carling told her father.

"If you are sure, then Red and Orange shall escort you to what you want to see. You can only observe at the moment, though. You cannot attack them," Blue relented to her wishes.

"That is all I want. I know I will not purge them from our lands in this lifetime. I know it will be my next. I have already felt that life and seen through her eyes," Carling told the gathered group.

"How, when we have been blinded to your future?" Indigo asked.

"The stones have shown me. They reached back from the future to calm and give me reassurance. They showed me my next life," Carling replied quietly.

"And what about this life, Carling? Did they show you anything of this?" Violet asked curiously.

"No, they did not," Carling told the Sentinel.

"Galen is still in your future, my daughter. It has already been written," Yellow told her, indicating the book on the table.

"When can we leave?" Carling asked, ignoring her mother.

"As soon as you are ready," Red said enthusiastically.

"Then we shall leave now." Carling started to prepare to transport herself from the room while Red and Orange immediately went to her side.

"Carling, wait," Blue called out. With Yellow holding his hand, they went to her. "You can't leave without saying goodbye. We will not let you."

"I don't want to argue with you, Father, or you, Mother," she pleaded.

"Not another word shall be spoken about Galen until you are ready, Carling. But running away and being reckless is not the answer," Yellow said gently.

"For me right now it is. I love you both. Please, I don't want to lose another set of parents over this issue," she begged them, taking a hand of each parent and hold them tight.

"Go with our love and our blessing," Blue said, kissing her on the forehead.

"We are but a call away, Carling, if you need us. You will never lose us," Yellow told her. "I will keep Tarl'a and Mailcon informed of how you are. And yes, they do want to know." She kissed her daughter and held her tight.

Flying high over the land with Orange and Red on either side of her, Carling marvelled at the colours that passed underneath them. Further to the south, the land was being cultivated and the patchwork made it interesting. Carling soared higher and higher above the world and felt the freedom clearing her head. The land ended abruptly with cliffs, giving way to a turbulent channel of water. The waves were breaking white, cutting across in long lines that stretched far over the deep, dark blue beneath them.

The smudge of the vast land to the east was fast approaching through the mist of ocean spray, and the trio dropped down. Orange led the way and they landed on a hill above a large valley near the coast. A wide and deep river meandered its way down the middle, with ships moored out in the water and up against piers that jutted out from the bank. A vast camp appeared, with tents and shelters neatly lined up and men all in similar dress.

"This is only one of their staging areas. We have found another three," Orange told her.

"Are they all this big with so many men?" she asked as she sat on a rock.

"No, the other two are larger. They have already conquered this land," Red responded to her question.

"You said that you helped to create a rebellion. Couldn't we do something similar?" Her eyes roamed over the display down below, taking in every detail she could.

"I don't think so. Chaos will not fall for it again." Red said, already standing and ready to leave. "They are coming, Carling. In fact, they are already in the lands to the south of ours. Come, we will show you."

Lifting back up, they raced across the channel once more to the top of yet another hill. Sitting along another river, a town was growing.

Carling could see many buildings under construction and a busy port on the banks.

"They have been building communities like this one and trading with the tribes, bringing their gold and silver with them and spreading it around to the kings who rule here. These Romans have also brought their gods with them, and they are not compatible with the Celts," Orange informed her.

"Are the gods of the Celts being pushed out?" Carling asked him as she carefully watched the scene down below.

"In some places they are. Many of the kings are turning their backs on their traditions and old ways. They are being enticed by the lure of gold and power," Red told her. "That is how the Romans start. These lands are rich in resources, which is what drives them to conquer. But of course, their true goal—and the only one that Chaos has—is you."

"I think Chaos is spreading himself thin with these people. How can he tend to their needs and care for them properly?" she asked as she watched the group of buildings down below.

"He doesn't care for their welfare, Carling. He gives them his wishes and demands that they carry them out. If they do not, then he is swift in his justice and anger. Many of their leaders have been struck down because they were too slow to do as he wanted. Chaos is not kind and benevolent, Carling. You know this already," Orange said as he placed a hand on her shoulder.

"I had hoped that it was not the case, that with the people he created, he would be gentler." Carling gave a sigh and shook her head.

"Those men that chased you and Loc down were his men. Look how he treated them," Orange reminded her.

"This world and the universe that surrounds us were created from the fragments of his last domain, which he crushed because his first creations did not worship him the way he wanted," Red reminded her.

"What else can you tell me of him? What else must I be aware of? I want to know all about these people—these Romans—about their ways. I need to know how they feel about him," she told them as an idea began to form.

"They do not know him. They only know their gods, his minions who do his work. Carling, are you sure you want to know them? It could be dangerous for you," Red warned her.

"It is the only way," she said nodding her head slightly.

"But as your mother and father keep reminding you—you are only young yet. If we were to leave you here, they will be very upset," Red responded, already guessing what she had in mind.

"How else am I to find out what I need to know? I can't go back to the home of the Sentinels—"

"It is your home also, Carling," Red told her gently.

"I am not truly a Sentinel yet, Uncle Red. And it is not my home. I can't go back to Ma and Da either. Instead, I can spend my time constructively in learning about them," Carling said, arguing her point, pushing down the sadness that was wanting to overwhelm her again.

"They do not see women the same as we do, Carling. You will be perceived to be a lesser person, a nobody without a voice. Someone who will be used, and—as a woman—someone to be abused," Orange warned her.

"Then I had better learn quickly how to use my abilities to my advantage." She smiled sweetly at them.

"Carling, you are going to have to work harder if you want to learn to flatter and charm your way through these people," Red said to her.

The invasion came, and they spread out swiftly. The Romans were soon in total control, and they changed the landscapes of the towns with the building of roads and camps. Order they liked, which amused Carling, considering who was guiding them. Not wanting her to be considered a slave, her uncles had set her up as an independent woman, and there was no end of suitors after her, attracted first to her wealth, and then her. She learned a lot over the next few years.

Carling found that she had a power over the men who came calling on her and that she enjoyed the game immensely. She had servants who had been sent to her by various members of the host, but she was always monitored by The Sentinels. They were frequent visitors to the villa she owned, bringing news of her brothers and parents. As the seasons turned, she only used her abilities to check on them herself in the moments when she was feeling lonely.

Loc was the same as always, wandering with Wolf in between visiting their brothers and parents. Uven was now married, and his wife was expecting their second child. Ru was surrounded by children, as Nila seemed to be pregnant constantly and happy with it. Her parents, Tarl'a and Mailcon, were aging. Carling saw how hard the winters were treating them, but every day her Ma would troop up to the Stones to talk to the Ancestors.

Carling refused to even think of Galen. She had tried to push him out of her mind, and when she talked of her family, she only ever mentioned having three brothers. By doing this, she hoped that the feelings she felt would fade and leave her forever. But only if she did not acknowledge his existence.

This became her life. Carling watched as the town grew around her. The influx of Romans brought with it more trade, new and different foods from across the channel, cloth to make clothes, and entertainments. The more barbaric types of spectacles she did not attend, the fighting and blood still going against her upbringing.

But she discovered music and a talent for playing instruments. Theatre also amused her. It reminded Carling of the stories of her childhood, except now told in front of her eyes instead of in her imagination.

If Carling had wanted to immerse herself in the world of the Romans, then she had gotten her wish. The ways of The People were fast becoming a memory, as she adopted the Roman ways.

"Carling, what exactly is it you are doing here?" Yellow asked one morning after a night of hosting a feast.

She was tired and not feeling well. The intrusion of her mother was not welcome, and she felt short-tempered. "I am getting my education, remember?" Carling snapped.

"It looks like you are trying to lose yourself. Galen is still out there, Carling. He has not wed, and he waits for you to find him," Yellow told her bluntly.

"I don't know who you mean, Mother." Carling walked out of the room and into the courtyard garden to the rosebush that grew there. Blood-red blossoms covered it, and she breathed in their rich fragrance.

"Do not walk away from me, Carling. You know very well who Galen is. It is time to come home. Time to put all this nonsense behind you," Yellow insisted as she followed her daughter.

"But I'm not done yet. There is still so much to learn. Their way of governing is particularly fascinating. There is a supreme ruler, but the governance of the laws is all done by a group."

"I am not interested in the politics of these people, Carling. Your Ma and Da miss you a great deal. They worry over you."

"I check on them. I know how they fare," Carling spoke sullenly. "I know what my brothers do also."

"Including Galen?" Yellow demanded.

"No. I will not have this discussion again with you, Mother. He does not exist to me, and I should not for him. We were brought up as brother and sister, and he can be nothing more than that to me. I will not allow myself think of him in any other way," Carling said forcefully, then regretted it as her headache sharpened.

"You are so frustrating, Carling. I do not anger easily, but you are starting to push my boundaries."

"Then maybe you should go, Mother, and leave me to my work."

"Was it work last night while you debauched yourself?" Yellow asked.

"I did nothing that I am ashamed of. I drank a little, yes, but I did nothing else," Carling responded.

"It did not look that way to me."

"Were you spying on me?"

"We have been keeping an eye on you, Carling. We have been keeping you safe," Yellow told her.

"From what and from whom?"

"From Chaos, or did you forget about him?" her mother asked with frustration at her daughter's attitude. "You did know that Chaos is aware of your presence down here in the lowlands? That he is searching for you?"

"No, I was not aware. Why didn't you tell me sooner?" Carling sobered very quickly at that news. The memory of fighting Chaos was still fresh in her mind, as were his words. Her hand went immediately to the silvery scar on her shoulder.

"Orange and Red have been running around creating sightings of you, along with help from Blue. But it will only be a matter of time before the charade is discovered. Carling, you need to be more careful whom you let near you," Yellow said, now standing before her.

"I am always careful, Mother. I promise I am. I always look inside a person's mind before I engage in any sort of talk."

"How can you if your own mind is so addled with the wine you have been drinking?" Yellow placed her hands on her daughter's shoulders.

"You are nearly twenty, Carling. The responsibilities for your life are now in your own hands. If Chaos comes knocking on your door, we cannot help you."

"I know, Mother. I will try to be more responsible. Thank you for your warnings."

"It is all I can do. And I will tell you again, daughter of mine, you cannot hide from destiny. Once something is written in the book, it cannot be erased."

"Mother, he will not have me. I know this to be true. I am—and will only ever be—his little sister. I saw it in his own eyes." A tear bloomed from her eye and spilled down her cheek.

"We shall see," Yellow said cryptically and kissed her forehead as she gathered her up in an embrace. "Stay safe, Carling. I leave you now, but another shall be watching over you. I leave you with my blessings and my love."

"My love to you as well, Mother, and pass it on to Father." As Yellow let her go, she stopped her one more time. "Mother, if you should be speaking to Ma and Da anytime soon, can you tell them that I miss them, and that I love them still?"

"I will, Child."

Chapter Twelve

Carling sat in her garden, enjoying the summer sunshine and the beautiful smell of the many rose bushes that surrounded her. The roses served two main purposes. The first was that she loved the blooms and the splashes of colour against the deep green of the leaves. And the second was that their scent helped to blocked out the other smells of the town—the sweaty bodies, the animals, and their droppings, and all the other unpleasant industrial smells that filtered through the streets. Her eyes were closed as she dozed on the seat, but her peace was soon to be disturbed.

"Claire, where are you?" a feminine voice called out from the confines of the house. "Claire?"

"I am out here, Livia." Carling sat up and waited for her newly made friend to find her.

"Do I have some news for you, my friend," Livia said excitedly as she sat beside her. While the young girl was the same age as Carling, she seemed younger. Livia was plump with dark hair, tender-hearted eyes, and she loved to gossip. She was also the new governor's youngest child.

"Well, I'm waiting. What is it that has you so flustered all of a sudden?" Carling asked with an indulgent smile at her friend's enthusiasm.

"A party has come from the north seeking an audience with my father. It seems that they wish to do some trading," Livia told her excitedly.

"There are parties like that arriving every day, Livia, what makes these so different?" Carling asked, laughing a little.

"It is that the chief or king, or whatever they call themselves up there, has come himself—not just a delegation. Father is very excited about the prospect of trade with the north. They say they are mighty warriors and that they stand seven feet tall." There was awe in Livia's voice at the prospect of meeting such giants.

"Not all are seven feet tall," Carling told her. "Some are quite short."

"How would you know?"

"I have not always lived here, Livia. I came from the north originally, before I was sent away. I have already told you this." Carling marvelled how this fact had slipped her friend's mind.

"You never did tell me why you were sent away," Livia pressed.

"There was a prospect of what I thought was a very unsuitable marriage, and now I am in disgrace for objecting to it," Carling told her with a smile.

"Was he awful?" Livia asked in a hushed tone.

"No, I felt we were just not meant for each other, and I did not wish to marry at the time."

"Anyway," Livia carried on. "There is to be a feast tonight. I asked my father if you could come and keep me company. If you come from up north, maybe you speak their tongue?"

"I do. But it has been many years since I have spoken it," Carling said.

"Please say you'll come. You have been very quiet lately, not attending any parties or feasts. You used to give the best of both."

"I grew bored of all of that, but for you, I will come tonight," Carling promised her friend.

"I'm so pleased. Will you come now, so we can prepare together?" Livia asked hopefully.

"If you insist. But I really have nothing to wear."

"Whatever you wear will look good on you. Your golden hair is the envy of many women."

"Including yourself?" Carling smiled at her friend.

"No, I couldn't deal with all the attention you get because of it." Livia blushed at even the thought of being noticed by a man.

In a short amount of time, Carling had chosen a dress and set out with her friend. As they neared the governor's house, a great commotion erupted behind them, and they hastily stepped out of the path of several horsemen. In the flurry of activity, Livia knocked the basket from Carling's hands, and she bent to pick it up. When she stood they had already passed.

"Did you see them, Claire? It must have been them," Livia said, still staring after the group of men. "They're headed straight to my father's office."

"No, I didn't. I was too busy picking up the basket you knocked from my hands," Carling laughed.

"Never mind, you'll see them tonight. They're so handsome and rugged looking." She linked her arm with Carling's, and they carried on to the residence.

Livia and Carling walked into the room that night with their hair piled on top of their heads in the latest style. All the pins that held it together made Carling's head itch and ache. They found themselves a seat in the corner, and a slave brought them each a cup. Carling took hers and smiled her thanks at the young boy. The idea of slavery was one that did not sit well with her.

"They haven't arrived yet," Livia said, a little disappointed.

"Who?" Carling asked, knowing full well who Livia was talking about.

"The Northerners. The whole reason for tonight," Livia said quickly, then laughed when she realised Carling was teasing her. "Here comes Father, please be nice to him tonight."

"I am always nice to your father," Carling protested.

"Well, then, don't tease him so much. Mother does not like it," Livia said quietly.

"I will be the perfect guest, just for you, my friend."

The pair stood as Livia's father approached with her mother at his side.

"Mother, Father, you remember Claire," Livia said.

"Yes, we do. Welcome to our home, Claire. I hope you will favour us with some music tonight?" Livia's father asked jovially.

"I have promised to be on my best behaviour, Governor. So, I must beg you to spare me from the embarrassment," Carling told him.

"I have heard so much about your musical ability, Claire. I had hoped to hear it for myself," Livia's mother said, looking down her nose at the young woman.

"I would then like to invite you to my villa, Serena. Perhaps tomorrow afternoon with Livia, and I shall play for you then," Carling said humbly.

"I am sure I can get you to play, or maybe Livia's brother can persuade you. I know he was a favourite of yours at one stage," the governor said.

"If she says no, then we must not press her, my husband. I look forward to tomorrow afternoon and a private concert from you, Claire," Serena said and guided her husband away from the pair.

"That went well," Carling said with raised eyebrows as she sat back down, watching as Serena and her husband took the couch at the opposite end.

"And here comes Benedictus. He asked if you were coming tonight before I came to fetch you," Livia told her quickly with a knowing smile.

"I wish he wouldn't. I know he is your brother, but I am not attracted to him," Carling said with some annoyance.

"Thank goodness. Although it would be nice to have you as a sister," Livia said and greeted her brother.

"You look lovely tonight, Claire, as always," he said, reaching for her hand.

"Thank you, Benedictus. But I would not like for your mother to hear you say such things, as she does not approve of me." Carling pulled her hand away.

"It's only jealousy, since you are so much younger and more beautiful than she is, as well as independent." He smirked suggestively at her.

"You flatter me, as always," Carling said, cringing at his attention.

"Where have you been for the last few months? The parties have been far less enjoyable without you," Benedictus carried on.

"Resting. It's been too hot recently. I find I am preferring the cool shadows of my own house far more than the stuffy rooms of other people's homes."

"Claire! They're here," Livia said beside her, grabbing Carling's arm and becoming very excited.

Carling looked beyond the large form of Benedictus towards the door. Through the opening came a group of four large men, looking very out of place. All were tall and all of them Carling recognised. She ducked back behind Benedictus and searched for a way out, but the only door was being blocked by very men she did not want to see.

"So very good of you to join us, Chief Gart, welcome," the governor said, hurrying forward with his wife at his side. "Come, please, let me introduce you to my son, Benedictus. He is an officer in the army and a fine one at that. He has just been promoted again—haven't you, my boy?" the governor said proudly.

"Yes, Father, I have. It is a pleasure to meet men of the north. We have heard you are fearsome fighters," Benedictus said eyeing the newcomers up.

"We have been known to fight from time to time," the large and deep voice of Gart spoke.

"This is my youngest child, Livia, and this is a friend of hers, Claire," the governor introduced the girls.

"Ladies, it is a pleasure to meet you," Gart said, looking at the pair. His eyes opened slightly wider when he took in 'Claire,' but he did not say a word.

"Sit, please, relax and enjoy yourselves," Serena said to the men.

Livia and Carling reclined on the very end couch in the U-shaped formation around the feasting table. Livia had taken the very end, as her shyness began to overtake her in the presence of the men. Carling found herself sitting next to the one man of the party she wished she did not.

"I'd better introduce you to my men," Gart said to Livia and Carling. "This is Arilith, my Healer." Gart placed a large hand on Arilith's shoulder, and the man inclined his head to the two. "This is Ru, my Translator. Sometimes I don't know quite how to say things in your tongue. And the dark one beside you, Claire, is Galen. My bodyguard."

As the last two were introduced, they nodded to the ladies. Carling picked up her goblet again and drank deeply from it. The talk began and stayed on the other side of the table, mainly between Gart and the governor. Carling tried to look at anything in the room besides the four men.

"Aren't they handsome?" Livia said quietly to Carling.

"They are probably all married, Livia. Most marry young up north," Carling told her.

As the first course was brought out, they were also joined by dancers and musicians to entertain them. Carling, used to the lifestyle by now, could see her brothers and Arilith all blushing at the suggestive nature of the dance.

She tasted the first dishes as they were laid out, still aware of Galen next to her. She was not paying attention to the conversation, as she was so distracted. But she came back to it when Livia elbowed her.

"Sorry, I was far away in my own thoughts," Carling said.

"I was saying that we were hoping you would play something for us later," the governor said smiling at her.

"I have not yet agreed, Governor. I am sure your visitors will have heard far better than I can offer," she told him, looking down into the depths of her cup.

"You are too modest, Claire. I have not heard anything as sweet as her playing the harp and singing." Benedictus grinned at her.

"I am untrained and self-taught, much unlike the master musicians you have hired for the night, Governor. Please do not pit my skills against theirs," she said, blushing now.

"Let the girl be, husband, she does not wish to perform," Serena said, unhappy that Carling was the focus of everyone.

They carried on, and Carling snuck a glance at Galen. He was looking down the table at Benedictus, his face was an unreadable mask. She turned her attention to Ru, who sneakily winked at her, and she looked away quickly.

The next course was brought in, and this time the entertainment was tumblers and acrobats. They were highly entertaining and had everyone enthralled. Carling did not eat much, only picked at the food before her.

The slave boy came and refilled her goblet. Carling smiled and thanked him again. When she looked at Benedictus, he was laughing at her and her ways. As the slave made his way around the others, Galen followed her lead and thanked him. All down the line of guests was the same response. Benedictus was not smiling when the boy got to him.

The last course was served, and still Carling had not said a word to the guests. Neither had her friend. Livia's shyness was legendary in their group of friends, and she was often teased for it. Carling had taken to her for that reason.

Under the cover of the singer that accompanied the final part of the meal, Livia leaned over to her friend. "Why did the one called Ru wink at you?" she whispered.

"I don't know, shall I ask him for you?" Carling whispered back.

"No, I would be too embarrassed. The one next to you is very good-looking. Did you notice his muscles?" Livia blushed even talking about him.

"I have not really looked," Carling told her.

"I wish I had your confidence, Claire."

"It is all bluster, Livia. You just have to think you are confident and make others believe you are. I am only here for you, my friend." Carling smiled at the girl.

The singing ended, and the musicians began packing up as the dishes were cleared away. Carling happened to be looking over at her uncle when he called out. "I believe you said the one called Claire can play and sing. Could I request a performance from you, young lady?" he asked, looking at her.

"I would rather not, Chief Gart. I am a poor substitute for the ones who have just finished," she told him, once more hoping that the matter would drop.

"It is a custom with our people that the family of the host entertain the guests," her uncle responded.

"I am a guest myself. I am only a friend of the daughter of this house."

"You are near enough part of our family, Claire, if Benedictus has his way, that is." The governor laughed and toasted his son, who beamed at her.

"Please, Claire. I would like to hear how a Roman woman sings." Arilith looked at her mischievously.

"I am not Roman. I come from the north, like yourselves," she reminded him.

"Then in that case, it is a must that you sing for us," Ru added with a grin.

"Please, Claire," Livia pleaded with her.

Carling rose from the couch and stood in front of them. She accepted the harp that the musician handed to her with a smile and sat down to play. Although she knew the song very well and had performed it many times, she felt nervous. There was a temptation to play badly and sing out of tune, but her voice and fingers betrayed her. The music that poured from her was sweet and had them enthralled. When she came to the end, loud applause burst forth.

"I think I will decline your offer of hearing you tomorrow, Claire. Your performance tonight will be sufficient for me," Serena told her, with an undertone that spoke volumes of her jealousy.

"As is your privilege, Serena. I completely understand." Carling felt relieved that both the current performance and the following day's were now at an end.

More wine was brought round, and Carling declined. The governor and Gart were talking trade again, with Ru helping with some of the translations. Carling was uncomfortable with the way Benedictus was looking at her, and she could tell he had already had quite a bit to drink.

"Livia, I would like to head home before your brother embarrasses himself and me. Could you ask your father for leave, please?" Carling asked quietly.

"I couldn't possibly interrupt him, Claire. He's talking business. He would become angry with me," Livia said shaking her head, to Carling's disappointment.

"I understand," she replied and looked at her hands.

Slowly Carling crept into Benedictus's mind and shuddered at the grubbiness of it. After releasing the suggestion, she gently retreated and looked up. His eyes were shutting very slowly, and the goblet in his hand began to tip as his fingers relaxed. It was almost in slow motion that he tumbled from the end of the couch and onto the floor, in all appearances very drunk.

Serena did not look happy that their son had shown himself up in front of strangers. Her embarrassment deepened even more when her husband yelled for the slaves to carry him out.

"Boys will be boys won't they? He'll have plenty of time to settle down when he marries." He looked at Carling as he said it, and she blushed.

"Are they betrothed?" Gart asked, surprised.

"No, we are not, Chief Gart," Carling said quickly. "Governor, I would ask to be excused. I feel a headache coming on and would like to get home before it hits."

"Of course you may, Claire. Let me call for someone to see you home." He prepared to call out.

"I will see her home if it is allowed," Galen volunteered, speaking for the first time that evening.

"I can personally vouch for Galen, Governor, he is one of my nephews. You would not meet a more honourable man," Gart told him.

"Thank you. The offer is gratefully accepted," the governor said on Carling's behalf.

"Thank you for a lovely evening, Governor and Serena. I have enjoyed myself immensely," Carling said, getting to her feet and ignoring the hand Galen held out to help her.

"Come see us more often," the governor told her. "I know Livia is always happier when you visit."

"I will, thank you." She stood and was aware of Galen following. She turned to her friend and hugged her. "Come see me tomorrow as planned."

"I will. I am jealous," Livia whispered, smiling

Carling did not wait for Galen to catch up as she walked from the room and out of the house. When she stepped out onto the street, he caught up with her and walked at her side. They were quite a way down the street before he spoke.

"Are you not going to say anything to me, Carling?" he asked her.

"Please do not use that name here. I am only known as Claire," she said softly so others could not hear her.

"Claire, then. Please, I so desperately wanted to talk to you all through that meal. From the moment I saw you," Galen told her, and she could hear the urgency in his voice.

"I have spent the last three years trying to forget you, Galen. What are you doing here?" She turned to face him.

"I am Uncle Gart's bodyguard. You heard him."

"What I heard was a cover-up. Not one of you, except for Uncle Gart, even reacted to my being there," she hissed at him. "If I find out any of the Ancestors have had anything to do with this, I will obliterate the lot of them."

"Carling—"

"Claire," she corrected him.

"Claire. They had nothing to do with us being here. Uncle Gart saw an opportunity and decided to take it," Galen told her.

"Tell him, then, to be very careful about what he agrees to. This new Governor is well known for extracting promises and agreements from people, which they come to regret later. The Romans have their eyes firmly on the north," Carling warned him.

"That is good to know. Uncle Gart will want to talk to you. Can we come and see you?" he asked hopefully, more for himself than their uncle.

"I would be happy to see Uncle Gart, Ru, and Arilith. Not so happy about you," she told him quietly, continuing to walk

"Claire, please. You need to listen to me." Galen stopped her again by holding onto her arm, which she looked down at. "Please listen."

"No. There is nothing you could tell me to change my mind, *Brother*," she said emphasising the word.

"You are so set and determined?" he asked her.

"I am. I have to be." Carling started to walk again.

"And you will not listen to me?"

"No, I will not. Especially not on this subject. Please don't bring it up again," she asked, determinedly looking ahead.

"You have changed, Carling," Galen told her.

Carling stopped and quickly looked around them at the people that were in the street. "You cannot say that name here. We are surrounded by his people," she hissed at him.

"He is searching for you again?" Galen immediately became worried and on guard.

"He is. Mother told me a few months ago." She nodded, keeping her eyes on the men and women around them.

"I understand why you don't want to talk about the issue, but please talk to me as your brother, then."

"I am sorry if I have been short with you, Brother. It was not my intention, but I do not like surprises."

"I remember a little girl who used to squeal at surprises," Galen said, taking a small step towards her.

"Not now. A surprise could end my life, so surprises are not welcome anymore," she told him and started to walk again.

"Do you hear anything of him from these people?" It was Galen's turn to look at the crowd, as he kept pace with her.

"No. They do not know him, only their own gods, which puzzles me greatly. We were brought up to understand that he destroyed the last world because they would not worship him. This hiding is not what I would have expected from him," Carling said.

"Do the Ancestors know where he is?"

"Yes. They're trying to keep him away from me. They set sightings of me around the lands, and he follows. But one day he will stop. And when he does, then I need to be wary." Her steps had slowed as they talked.

"I take it his name is another thing that cannot be mentioned?" Galen asked.

"No, it cannot."

"So why Claire?" he asked her, enjoying the change in tone.

"I don't know. It sounds similar to my own name, and I like the meaning. Bright and clear," she said with a little smile.

"Ma and Da miss you," Galen told her.

"I know. I miss them as well. I send messages to them through Mother and Father when they visit. Orange and Red cannot be relied upon," Carling said. "They sometimes do and sometimes don't remember. Of all the Ancestors, they are still the most childlike."

"That is some way to talk about the Ancestors," Galen laughed.

"But it's true. When they come to visit, they insist on an occasion," she smiled.

"Do the other Ancestors know about this?"

"Of course. I have told Mother and Father, and they have talked to them. But I feel my uncles are shameless." Carling looked up at the house that they had come to. "This is my home."

"It's large. You live here alone?" he asked.

"Yes, along with seven servants," she replied turning back to him.

"No slaves?"

"I do not believe in slavery, Galen. People are born free and should remain so, with the ability to rule themselves and make their own choices. There is so much here that I do not like. I do not like their blood sports, their laws that protect the rich and powerful while oppressing those who need help with food and health. I do what I can for those who need it most, but there is a lot that I cannot do, abilities I cannot use to help them."

"Why do you stay here, then?" he asked quietly taking a step forward.

"Because I hope to make a difference. I befriended Livia firstly because she was being teased, but then I found she was the new governor's daughter, and I hoped I could bend his ear. I wanted to convince him that there is much that can be done for the poor."

"But he won't listen," he finished for her.

"No, he won't. Galen, bring our uncle, brother, and Arilith to see me in the morning—early. No one accepts visitors before noon here, they're usually too ill from the night before," Carling told him

"Why early?" Galen asked.

"Because I am a single woman, and to be entertaining strange men from the north will be unseemly for someone in my position." She looked up into his face for the first time.

"It is good to see you, Claire." He reached out to touch her face.

"No, Galen. Please." She stepped back. "I will see you in the morning."

Carling turned and left him on the road. As the door to her villa closed, she saw him still standing, watching, and the old pain filled her heart once more.

"Mistress, you have visitors," Carling's man servant said, slightly disapprovingly.

"Show them to the rose garden, Fet. They are expected. They are my family." Carling rose from her seat at her mirror and followed him out.

Fet had come to her, following a dream sent to him by Yellow. It was her mother's way of ensuring that her daughter had some protection. After much arguing between them, Carling had agreed to keep him on. Her other servants had come to her in a similar way.

Carling reached the garden only minutes before Fet showed them in. They walked in, looking around at the unusual surroundings they found themselves in, and Ru was the first to see her. He ran to his sister and picked her up in a large hug, placing a big kiss on her forehead before putting her back down.

"Claire," he grinned. "Galen warned us. You are a welcome sight, Sister."

"It is good to see you too, Ru. I have missed you all," she told him, beaming.

"Is your uncle included in that, Niece?" Gart asked, coming towards her with his arms extended.

"He is, Uncle." She was enfolded in a large hug that she thought would last forever.

"And an old friend?" said the next in line.

"Arilith, I am really pleased to see you too." She accepted his embrace warmly. "How is your wife?"

"Pregnant again. I hope we will be back before the birth," he said eagerly.

"You will be, my friend." She smiled up at him.

"Good. Now that is all out of the way, do you mind, Niece, telling us exactly what you are doing here? You nearly gave me a heart attack last night," Gart told her as he sat down heavily on a bench.

"I did not expect you either, Uncle. I have been living here for four turnings of the seasons, studying these people," she said and indicated to the others to sit also.

"Isn't it dangerous for you?" Ru looked up as Fet came in, carrying refreshments. "Are we able to talk freely?"

"We are. Fet here, was sent by Mother. There are no spies in this house," Carling told them.

"Isn't it about time that you came home, Claire? Each time I visit Tarl'a and Mailcon, they grow more and more weary and worried about you," Gart said, accepting a cup from Fet.

"My Ancestor and I are of the same opinion," Fet said as he handed Galen a cup.

"I like this man," Gart said.

"And as I keep telling Mother, Fet—and anyone else who asks that question—it is not time yet. I cannot go back until after I have met with him once more," she told them, waving her own cup away when Fet stood in front of her.

There was silence in the garden, and Carling plucked a rose from the bush and smelt it. She wandered over to the pool in the centre of the courtyard and looked down into it.

"Is it soon, Claire?" Galen asked her quietly.

"I don't know." She turned to face them all, but her eyes only sought those of Galen, who stood at the back of the group. "I wish with every fibre of my being that I could say it will be in this many turnings of the moon or seasons, but I would not be telling the truth. And you know I can only speak the truth. I do what I can while I wait. I live in plain sight in amongst the enemy and pray every day that no one questions who I am. At first, I lived recklessly, I drank too much and lived life on the edge each night, almost in defiance of him. The world is changing with the coming of the Romans, and it will be a permanent change. We cannot put it back to the way it was, but we must ensure that they never reach our lands. Our people must be kept safe from their ways. They take what they want, they make treaties and break them just as easily as the wind changes. They are a violent race. The tide is flowing to these shores with more and more of them, and they will not stop until the world is under their rule. Our only hope to stem the flow is to defeat him. And that is down to me. I am scared. I am afraid. I am not ready. I am not worthy of the hope that has been placed on me." The rose fell from her hand and hit the ground.

Galen pushed his way past Ru and stood in front of her. His hand came up to her face to cradle it, and she didn't pull away. "You are our hope, Car—Claire. It may weigh heavily upon your shoulders, but we are with you. Our love and our lives are with you. You are not alone in this world. You never have to be alone as long as I draw breath. Let me be at your side. Let me love you." His eyes searched hers for some hope for a return of the feelings he knew she felt.

Carling looked into his blue eyes. Her breath caught in her chest, and she could hear her heart beating loudly in her ears. The world did not exist in that moment he declared his love. The others in the garden who had witnessed it were not there. She let out that breath, and as she reached the end, she was torn from the moment by the voice of Fet.

"Mistress. Mistress Livia is here to see you," he said loudly and formally.

Blinking and moving away from Galen, Carling tried to settle her heart rate and collect her thoughts before answering. "Show her in, Fet," she called back.

"We will leave you, Claire," Gart said getting to his feet.

It was then she realised how her words had not only affected Galen, but the rest of her family as well. "Please come back and see me before you go," she said formally as Livia entered the garden.

"We will. Thank you for seeing us." The men all bade her farewell and trooped past Livia.

As Galen passed Carling, he handed her the rose that she had dropped. His eyes pleaded with her, but he did not say another word.

"I'm sorry, if I had known you had visitors, I would not have come. But I was worried how you were feeling after last night," Livia told her as she watched the men go.

"I'm fine this morning." Carling sniffed the rose in her hands.

"Why were the Northerners here?" her friend asked, turning back to Carling

"They didn't realise last night that it was me they had messages for. So they came this morning to deliver them from my family," Carling told her quickly.

"Oh. I hope they were good tidings. You seemed shaken when I came in." Livia sat down and looked up at Carling.

"Some were good, but some were sad. It is the way of the world. I hope my leaving did not put a damper on the rest of the evening?" Carling asked.

"No, Father and Chief Gart talked long into the night. When the man who escorted you home came back, I found out he is the only one unmarried," Livia said blushing.

"Did you actually talk to the strangers?" Carling smiled teasingly at her friend, the rose still in her hands as she sat down.

"Yes, I did. The one called Arilith. He is very nice, but married. I must warn you, Claire, that Benedictus will be coming to see you this afternoon. He wishes to give you an offer of marriage. He was going to do it last night, but then had too much to drink," Livia told her.

"Thank you, Livia. I will make sure I am not at home."

"Mother is not happy about the match, but Father is delighted," Livia continued on, not really hearing what Carling had just said.

"I do not wish to marry him, Livia. I have no wishes to marry anyone at the moment." She pressed the rose to her nose again and drank deeply of the fragrance.

"Not even the one who escorted you?" Livia asked impishly.

"Galen? No. He and I were brought up together. I did not recognise him until he walked me home last night. He was my foster brother."

"The way he looked at you just now as he handed you that rose, I don't think he sees it that way," Livia told her.

"I did not notice." Carling placed the rose on the bench beside her.

"But he was standing so close to you."

"He was giving me news of Ma. My foster mother wishes me to go home and see her."

"You do not get on with her?" Livia asked.

"I love her dearly, but I did not leave in the best of circumstances. It is my own pride that keeps me from going to see her. Let's not talk of that anymore. What shall we do today?" Carling asked her brightly, desperate to change the subject from her family and Galen.

"Now that my mother is not coming to visit you, we could go to the market. And this afternoon we could go see the new gladiators fight," Livia suggested hopefully.

"You know I don't like the fighting. I had heard that there was a new play on at the theatre," Carling countered the suggestion.

"I always fall asleep. There must be something we can do together."

"I'm sure we will find something." Carling stood and picked the rose up. "Shall we go to the market? Then we can look for something to occupy us while we are out."

"I'm always happy to visit the market, you know that," Livia said with a laugh.

As Carling moved into the house, she handed the rose to Fet, who had been waiting by the entrance. "Can you please put this in a vase and in my room, Fet?" she asked him quietly.

"Yes, Mistress," he responded with an understanding nod.

"Oh, and when Benedictus comes calling this afternoon, please throw him out vigorously. I do not want to see him still here when I return," Carling instructed him.

"Of course, Mistress. It will be my absolute pleasure." Fet grinned back.

Chapter Thirteen

The two women spent a lovely morning walking through the market and making small purchases. The afternoon they spent calling on friends and gossiping, though Carling did not join in. Her mind was still on the early morning visit. Still on those blue eyes that had stared at her with such intensity—with such love.

"Claire, it's your turn," Livia prompted her.

Before her lay a board with counters. She picked up one of the pieces and moved it, only to be greeted by laughter and cries of victory.

"That was the easiest game I have ever played against you, Claire," a young woman across the table from her declared.

"I'm sorry, my mind was miles away," she said, giving up her seat for someone else to play.

"I can imagine where it was," Livia said with a cheeky smile. "With blue eyes and muscles upon muscles."

"He *is* very good looking," Claire conceded and blushed slightly.

"Even better than Benedictus?" the girl who had bested her at the game asked.

"The Northerner is very handsome, and it seems our friend here has caught his eye," Livia told the group.

"And soon he will be gone again. I told you this morning, Livia. He is my foster brother." Carling stood. "I think I will be going home. It's been a long day."

"But we were just starting, Claire," the young woman said.

"And you can continue without me," she responded, collecting her things.

"Do you mind if I stay?" Livia asked her.

"You are your own person, Livia. You can do as you wish. I will call on you soon." Carling left the villa of her friend and headed down the road. It was only a short distance to her own home, and there were not many people on the street at that time in the late afternoon.

The day was still warm, and she was enjoying the walk as her thoughts returned to Galen. A dreamy looked played on her lips as she gave in to the feelings, allowing herself to enjoy them. Carling did not see the man approach her, and she was surprised when he bumped her shoulder.

"Carling, welcome to my world," he said harshly as he rounded on her.

The man was tall and very Roman, muscular, and obviously a soldier. She stepped back from him and his almost manic grin.

"Those fools sought to keep me from finding you, but here you are, amongst my people and living as one of them. Is this your way of preparing yourself for me?" he asked.

Carling sent out a searching thought into the mind of the man and found it blank. She shuddered at the emptiness. The man laughed at her efforts.

"How did you find me?" she asked, stepping further back from him.

"How else? Your name, when it is spoken, is like a beacon for me, Carling. It has not only been spoken but thought of so much in the past day. You should have hidden yourself a little better, so those who know you could not find you."

"You should not have come here. You know it is not time," Carling told him, shaking her head defiantly.

"It is time when I say it is, Carling. But I do not wish to fight you. My offer when we last met, still stands. Join me. You will be my equal, and I will love and care for you. Our child shall be all-powerful," Chaos told her, his voice dropping low.

"You are incapable of love, and you do not wish me to be your equal. Why do you control these people? They do not even know you!"

"They do. I am each and every one of their gods, so they worship me. I am enjoying listening to their wishes, and sometimes I even grant their dreams. I can be benevolent when I wish," Chaos told her.

"I can't say it has been nice chatting with you, but I really must go." Carling moved to leave, but a large hand shot out and clamped tightly onto her arm, his fingers biting deeply into her soft flesh.

"Home to an empty house and only your servants to protect you?" he asked.

"Let me go," Carling demanded, trying to pull free.

"I don't think so, Carling. Don't make me obliterate your mind to make you compliant," he hissed at her.

"Do not make me strike out at you," she said back.

"Get your filthy hands off her!" Benedictus roared as he raced down the street towards them. "Let her go!"

Carling was still staring at the man who held her when she saw him coming back to himself. She could feel his mind racing, trying to figure out what was happening. He released Carling quickly as he took one look at the angry Benedictus running towards him, then took off in the opposite direction.

"Are you all right, Claire?" Benedictus asked as he stopped beside her.

"I'm fine." Carling shrugged his hands off and began walking towards her house.

"That man, what did he want?" he demanded.

"He was drunk, and what do men want when they are in that state?" She walked rather quickly, trying to be away from him as soon as possible.

"Do you want me to go after him?" Benedictus offered.

"No. I was handling it. I can look after myself," she told him as fear began to grip her soul.

"Why are you unescorted?" he demanded.

"I do not need a man to protect me," she said, rounding on him.

"I would like to protect you," Benedictus said, coming to stand close to her.

"I think you should go. Livia will need your help getting home." She turned away and rounded the corner to her street.

"Claire. With you at my side, we could run this town," he said, chasing her.

Carling did not reply until she was turning into her house. She stopped him with a hand on his chest. "I will never be at your side, Benedictus. I am too strong a woman for you. You need a little mouse who can be the perfect hostess and flatterer of your friends. I cannot be that person for you. I would make your life difficult, and you would not be happy." As she told him the words, she reinforced them through her touch in his mind. "What I can be is a friend."

When she removed her hand, he stumbled back from her. "If that is the way you feel, Claire, then a friend is always welcome. If you will excuse me, I must fetch my sister home," Benedictus replied, a little dazed and confused.

"Livia is very lucky to have such an attentive brother in you, Benedictus. Look after her well."

"I will. I'll see you later, Claire." He turned and left her standing in the walkway to the house.

"Mistress, you are wanted inside," Fet said from behind her.

"Thank you, Fet. I will be there right away," she told him, still watching the retreating back of Benedictus. When he was out of sight, Carling turned and entered, handing her basket to him.

"You have a visitor. I placed him in the garden," Fet told her with a hint of a smile.

"I will go right out. Can you ask Loxa to prepare something quick to eat, please, and if we could have some wine also?"

"Yes, Mistress."

"One other thing, Fet. It's time. You know what to do," Carling told him with a nod.

"Are you sure, Mistress?" he asked as his smirk faltered and turned to a frown.

"Yes, it is. It will have to be tonight," Carling replied, pleased she didn't need to explain anything to him.

"I will organise everything, Mistress. It will be as you have planned," he told her and turned quickly to carry out her wishes.

Carling made her way to the rose garden and found Galen there waiting for her. He turned when she came through the door and surprised him by flying into his arms.

"He knows, Galen. He found me," she said quietly into his shoulder.

"When?" His arms came up protectively around her.

"Just now. He stopped me in the street. He was using my name as a beacon," she told him.

"And us finding and talking about you has not helped. We can get you away to safety," he said quickly.

"No, it would only put you all in danger. I can get myself away. It's all been planned for some time now, since The Sentinels sent their people to protect me." Carling pulled away from his embrace.

"Carling, I want to help." He drew her close again, his hand tracing the side of her face.

"I know, but I can't let this happen. Until I know what the outcome is, I can't allow myself to. Please understand," she begged him.

"I have waited four years and longer for you, my sweet Carling. I can wait a little longer. But this won't wait." He leaned down and met her mouth with his. Years of pent-up feelings were released in that kiss, and when they broke, Carling didn't want it to stop.

"What is this plan you have then?" he asked breathlessly into her hair.

"I leave town and this house burns," she told him.

"The oil is ready, Mistress," Fet said coming into the garden with a tray of food and wine. He placed it on the bench. "All we need is your word and the house will go up."

"Thank you, Fet. Please activate the other provisions I have made for you all. Tell the girls they can take what they like of my jewellery, then they can go." Carling left Galen's arms and walked up to her manservant. "You have all been so faithful and helpful to me. Give them my thanks and appreciation, Fet, and I wish you well in your lives. I will try to keep an eye on you all and make sure you are safe."

"Thank you, Carling. May the Ancestors protect you now," he said and then looked past her. "Protect her well, Galen."

"I will do my best, Fet," Galen said, nodding to the man before he left them alone.

"You had best go, Galen. This next part will be upsetting for you to watch," she told him, taking his hand.

"What are you going to do?" he asked her, his hand moving around to her back.

"I am going to make it look like I have been attacked and my house set on fire. I have worked hard on the illusion. Then I will be leaving town by the fastest way possible. Flying. But you must be with Uncle Gart and Ru when it happens. You are a foreigner here and you have been seen in my house. There will be suspicions raised," she told him quickly.

"Gart, Ru, and Arilith are all with the governor. I'll go be with them now. But I don't want to leave you again," Galen told her, his lips brushing hers gently.

"You must. I will find you again, Galen. But it won't be until after I have confronted Chaos," she said determinedly.

"Please make it before. Meet me at home, at the stones. I think it's time to accept this, Carling, and we make it official," he pleaded with her.

"I will be there at the next full moon," she agreed with a nod, and against her better judgment.

"Thank you," he said before he kissed her again. Carling walked with him to the door and kissed him one final time before she opened it for him. As he left the house and walked down the street, she sent out a suggestion to her neighbours, so that they would not see him leave. Now all she could do was wait.

Loud and prolonged screams rent the air, and the calls for help pierced the dead of night. Carling stood in her rose garden, a bag already strapped to her back, playing out the charade for the city watch and neighbours. Her loyal servants had all departed after taking what they wanted of her possessions and getting her grateful thanks.

Now standing alone for the first time in the building, it felt hollow and empty. It had never felt like home, like the small house in the valley, but she had spent a long time there. Carling looked at the blood that had been sprayed over the ground at her feet, and once more she let fly the sound of screams and the noise of someone trying to defend her. Shouts from further up the street let her know that the watch had been called, and now it was time for the final act.

Releasing the lights from her hands, they went in search of the oil that had been placed around the house at various points. They burned brightly and merrily as they flew, dancing almost like little bugs on the wind. They found their marks and dove into the viscus liquid, catching it alight and bursting apart to spread the oil far and wide in their respective rooms.

Flames caught at the fabric that had been draped so artistically, but very strategically in decoration and the fire spread. All around her the flames began to grow and the heat became too much. Plucking one last rose from her favourite bush, Carling leapt into the air and rose above the heat and smoke of her burning home, into the cooler air of the sky. The flames burst through the roof and reached up into the night, spreading their glow out into the darkness.

The members of the watch were running down the street to stop the spread of the fire to neighbouring properties. An idea formed further, and Carling encouraged the flames to release sparks, hot and bright, to float to the houses around hers. The fire caught and soon the inferno grew. Satisfied, she left her vigil of the blaze for one last mission before returning to make sure her neighbours were all safe.

A cry went out through the house of the governor, and a soldier came running in. "A message, sir, from the commander. There is a fire, and it is spreading fast. It cannot be controlled. It is advised that the governor and his family retreat over the river to a safe place, until it is brought under control. A guard has been made ready for your protection, sir," the man said from his kneeling position.

"By the gods. Is it that bad?" the governor asked rising, from his seat.

"Yes sir. If you would but look north, you will see for yourself," the soldier said, leading the way outside.

"My god, that is close," Serena said, shocked, looking out at the glow the fire was creating in the dark sky.

"That's close to where Claire lives," Livia said, suddenly frightened.

"I'll go find out where it is. I am sure she is fine, Sister," Benedictus said at her side. He raced off and the others kept watching the flames climb higher and the smoke boiling upwards, covering the stars in the sky.

"Do we know how it started?" the governor asked the soldier, his eyes not leaving the glow and flames that could now be seen over the tops of the roofs of nearby houses.

"No, sir, we do not. The watch was called for something else, and then they found the fire," the man replied.

"It was probably caused by a simple accident," Serena said.

They remained quiet for quite a while until Benedictus came back. He was out of breath.

"It is the same street as Claire, her house is fully engulfed. The neighbours say they called the guard because they heard screams and shouting inside. Father, I caught a man trying to attack Claire this afternoon when I went to fetch Livia. It may have been him."

"Who was it?" Livia asked.

"A soldier. I am sure I can recognise him again. The fire is moving this way, Father. I believe we should go, for the safety of Mother and Livia," he told his father.

"Yes, it might be wise," the governor said, turning towards his family and guests.

"We will go, too. We thank you for your hospitality, Governor, and we hope we can resume our talks once this crisis is dealt with," Gart said with a little worry at the sight of the fire.

"Of course, Gart. Go with the blessings of the gods," the governor said distractedly.

Gart, Arilith, Ru and Galen all trooped from the house and headed to the inn where they were staying.

"Gather your things together, we leave tonight," Galen told them.

"What is this about, Galen?" Gart asked him as Arilith and Ru raced off.

"Later, when we are out of this place." His face was set and grim.

Bursting into the room he shared with Gart, Galen gathered his gear together and stopped when he noticed something unusual. On the bed lay a single blood-red rose. He picked it up, smelled it, and smiled. Tucking it inside his tunic, he ran out the door after Gart and down to the stables.

"Towns are not a safe place, especially where fire is concerned. Everyone is too close together," Gart told the innkeeper who trailed after him. He stopped and handed the man a bag of coins.

"I am sure the fire will not spread here. You do not have to leave," the innkeeper spluttered.

"We thank you, but yes, we do. I suggest you get to safety also." The saddles were soon on the horses, and they were away as quickly as they could. Racing through the streets with the fire to their backs, they headed north and home.

Carling watched the town as the fire spread and concentrated on protecting those that needed to be saved from the flames. No one was to die, only herself and staff needed to seem to. She floated upwind away from the dirty great plumes of smoke that choked their way into the air. She saw that Galen and the others had gotten away safely and was also relieved that Livia and her family were unharmed.

So hard was Carling concentrating she did not see the darkness as it swelled up behind her and a figure emerge from its swirling midst. Slowly the figure began to clap in appreciation of her subterfuge, and she spun in the air.

"Well done, Carling, well done. Masterfully performed. I even like the spread of the fire, but do you really have to save everyone?" Chaos asked her.

"They are your people, Chaos. You should be protecting them," she spat at him.

"Why? They are but insects, grubbing around on the ground, doing my bidding. They do not live for long and they breed so fast. Speaking of breeding…" He looked her up and down.

"You are not my type, Chaos. I prefer a real man. One with actual love in his heart."

"You mean someone like this?" He waived a hand and his body shimmered as it changed. Floating in front of her was the image of Galen, smiling. But he had got one detail wrong. The eyes. They glowed red.

"Not quite good enough, Chaos. I shall have to be wary now to make sure I am speaking to the real man and not the cheap copy," she flung the words at him.

Chaos reacted just as she had anticipated and was ready for him. As he rushed forward, Carling gathered the energy necessary to her and expelled it at him with a great force. The energy burst into life and flared brightly in the sky. The blinding light encased Chaos long enough for Carling to make her getaway. When he broke the hold and the fragments of light splintered and winked out, she was gone. He roared his frustration into the dark sky and took it out on the town below. Where Carling had tried to save people from the large inferno, he now threw them into it, taking great delight in their pain and deaths.

For days now Carling had followed her family north, keeping watch over them. Even after reaching the border of their sacred lands, she continued to stay nearby. Up in the hills that surrounded her uncle's broch, she found a suitable cave to hide out in. Working hard, she placed every protection she could think of to keep everyone away from the hill. Inside she built a fire and a pallet bed. It was bare but enough to meet her needs for now.

Carling still had time to think about her next move before the full moon. There was still the rest of the waning of this one and the new one to swell. Each night she sat by the fire and looked in on those that had come to mean so much to her. Her servants had all been presumed to have perished in the fire and were now scattered as they made their way north again to their previous homes.

Her brothers Ru and Uven were with their wives and enjoying fatherhood again. Arilith doted on his wife as she grew larger with their child. Loc was still wondering the world and heading towards her. Ma and Da were still secluded in the valley, happy in their love for each other and still missing their children. And finally, Galen.

Galen, she had always left until last to check up on. The rose she had left for him he had cherished and smelled often. When the rose had started to wilt and fade, he had made a pouch to hold the petals inside and Carling had placed a charm on it so that they would continue to smell just as strong as they did when the rose first budded. Galen, she also noticed, smiled more and laughed heartily, and it made her feel happy to know it was because of her.

As she searched the hills for food during the day, Carling was always wary of the possibility of being approached again by Chaos. She hoped she had lost him, leaving him behind at least for a little while. It was hard to know where he might be, but she didn't want to tempt fate by searching for him either.

It was one of these times that she was searching for the last of the summer's berries that Carling was found, but by one she was happy to see.

"Niece, you have been hiding from us," Indigo said, coming through the thorny bushes.

"Aunt, it is good to see you. Have you been well?" Carling asked as she kept up her task.

"We are well. Your protections are strong and have kept you from us. We have had to learn of your meeting with Chaos from others," Indigo told her with a raised eyebrow.

"Yes, I am sorry about that. I should have come to you. But I wanted to make sure that those that had visited me were protected," she said as she pulled more berries from the bush.

"Would that be one in particular, Niece?" Indigo asked with a secretive smile as she began to help Carling harvest the fruit.

"That could be true, Aunt," Carling replied, trying to keep a straight face.

"Your mother and father are very happy about this development."

"So I can imagine." Carling's own grin could no longer be contained.

"But it is not that one I come to talk to you about, Carling. There is a matter, which I believe you are aware of, that has to do with one of my children," Indigo told her.

Carling stopped what she was doing and looked at the Sentinel. "Would this child be a wolf, Aunt?" she asked.

"The child is a wolf. A very special wolf."

"What can I help with? She is your child, and although their love is a strange one, they are dedicated to each other," Carling told her.

"It is exactly that dedication that stands at the centre of the problem. Just as we watch over our human children and protect the lines that will be of importance in the future, so we do the same with our animal children. You say you can see your next possible life, Carling. Have you seen those that are around you?" Indigo asked as she placed berries into the basket.

Carling picked up the small basket and started to walk back to the cave. "I only saw small pieces, there was nothing really definite," Carling answered.

"Can you look more closely, then? I would not ask, only that it is important for you to understand what I am about to request of you."

"I will then for you, Aunt. Shall we wait until I get to the stones at the full moon, or do you want me to do it now?" Carling asked, curious at her aunt's behaviour.

"Now, please. I need all the decisions before the full moon."

Carling entered the cave mouth with Indigo closely following. Putting the basket down, she set herself by the fire and crossed her legs. Carling closed her eyes and concentrated, casting her mind to the future. At first there was only fog and indistinct shadows. She took a deep breath and pushed at it, trying to clear the mist away from the visions.

Slowly it cleared and focused for her, and she looked out of eyes that were hers, but not quite right. Before her was a campfire in a wood and across was a young man, full of life and love for her. At her side was a large grey wolf, who raised her head to her.

"Pack-mate?" the wolf asked curiously. The question was only meant for her and not her next life.

"Eventually," Carling told the wolf, who lay her head back down.

Coming back to her cave she let out the breath she had been holding for so long and opened her eyes. She looked at Indigo and smiled.

"You wanted me to see the wolf?" Carling asked her.

"I did, Carling. You can see my problem."

"I can, Aunt. That wolf is descended from Loc's wolf. Do you wish me to talk to her and get her to find a mate?" Carling asked.

"She will not leave Loc. I have even spoken to him to get him to try, but she will not listen."

"There is another way, Aunt," Carling said quietly, looking deeply into the flames.

"I know, but I am unable to do that. My abilities cannot change that which is already formed," Indigo told her.

"I am not sure I can change it either. There are certain laws. Have you asked Order?"

"No, I did not want to ask the Great Light for fear that the answer would be no. Wolf must have pups for this special wolf to be born at the right time. Please, Carling. Please search inside yourself and see if it is possible for you," Indigo begged her.

"It is not just a matter of being possible. Loc must also wish it. I cannot just change him," Carling told her carefully. "My brother would need to want to."

"That was the other thing I was going to ask you."

"Loc is Violet's child," Carling said. "Have you asked her? The change would also change his line to yours as mother of wolves."

"I know all this."

"Indigo." Carling shook her head and got up from where she sat, taking a long drink from her water skin.

"I can stay and keep watch over your brothers while you travel to our home to speak to Violet and Order first," Indigo offered hopefully.

"We will go together, Aunt. I can place a protection on Uven, Ru, and Galen. You need to be there; you can't run from this question."

"Like you did?" Indigo asked her with a smile.

"I was young and inexperienced." Carling came and sat back down.

"We still consider you young. Orange and Red would come back and describe what they saw to us."

"My uncles enjoyed visiting me in the south, sometimes I think too much. The ladies enjoyed their company immensely."

"Really? They never told us that piece of news," Indigo said with almost a jealous note to it.

"Aunt, which of the two is your most favoured?" Carling asked, her suspicions growing.

"Neither, they are equal in my eyes and my favour. That is forbidden remember," Indigo replied, a little too quickly.

"And we have a prime example of that with my parents, Yellow and Blue. They hold hands and sit near each other when they can. They show affection for each other."

"That is because of the bond they created bringing you into this world."

"But they show each other love," Carling continued.

"It is still forbidden," Indigo said sadly.

"I will talk with Violet and Order for you, Indigo, on the problem of Loc and Wolf," Carling told her.

"And the matter we were just talking of?"

"What matter, Aunt?" Carling grinned.

Chapter Fourteen

Carling sat patiently at the table while she was waiting for the other Sentinels to arrive. Out beyond the thick walls of the cave she could hear the waves as they crashed against the sides of the island and feel the slight shuddering under her feet with each impact. The stormy seas were a result of Indigo's impatience and pacing up and down the room at Order and her sister's delay after her call. The room was well lit by large candles, which never seemed to burn down, and now they flickered each time Indigo passed them, sending dancing shadows over the smooth floor and walls.

"Why are they taking so long?" Indigo asked nervously.

"Relax, it is only a question at the moment. We will need to call the others as well. This is a decision that needs to be made together. The change has never been done before," Carling told her as she picked up an apple that sat in the bowl on the table, then bit into the juicy sweet tasting flesh.

"Is it really necessary to involve all of them just now? We have not even talked to Loc."

"I think it may pay to discuss this as a group. It does raise some serious questions," Carling said around her next bite. "And I have already called them, and they are on their way."

"I think their coming will have more to do with your actions of late Niece, than this question." Indigo came to sit with her.

The pair did not have to wait long to find out what the other Sentinels thought as they joined them one by one. Their greetings were warm, and Indigo had been correct, they each asked what she had been up to. Yellow and Blue were last, bar Order, and they hugged their daughter close.

"You have grown stronger daughter," Blue told her proudly.

"Thank you, Father. Since Mother's last visit I have done a lot of growing. I am sorry I spoke to you that way, Mother," Carling told her.

"You are forgiven," Yellow said. "Is this why you have called us together?"

"No. Indigo has a special request that needs to be discussed." Carling led them back to the table and sat down as the Sentinels took their places.

The discussion, though seemingly simple to Carling, did take a long time. Well into the night they talked over the problem. All the possible outcomes and pitfalls were brought up. Just as all the positives and benefits were used to counter the arguments. There was no heat to their discussion, no anger. It was all very civilised and calm. Carling found herself thinking that if this had been talked about between her brothers, it would have finished in blows.

"I think we have reached an agreement," Green spoke to the table. "It is a necessary thing that must be done. Violet, this is one of your sons we speak of. Are you in agreement?"

"I am, Green. For the sake of the future, it should be done. But as we all know, our children have their own minds and free choice. I will gladly give parentage over to my sister if my son wishes it." Violet turned to Indigo.

"Thank you, Sister," said Indigo.

"Carling, you mentioned that you did not know if you could do this. I think you had better talk to Order and get the Great Light's advice," Orange told her.

"I will, Uncle. Order was asked to join us, and I am surprised that she hasn't come," Carling said.

"There is still time," Blue said. "It has been a while since we have all been together. It seems over the last few turnings of the seasons we have had other things on our minds. This is a great opportunity to talk and share the information we have gathered." As he spoke, he looked directly at Carling.

"You want to know what I have learned of the Romans?" she asked her father.

"If you wish to start, I think you will find we are willing to listen," he grinned at her.

Carling told them of her time in the south, of living amongst those they considered their enemy. Their beliefs, their customs, and their way of life were all discussed with help from Orange and Red, who had spent the most time with her. When she spoke of what she had learned in regards to how Chaos saw the Romans, there were more detailed questions. And they dissected her more recent meeting with Chaos, down to the last inflection in his voice.

While they were talking, Carling sat back and watched the dynamics of the table. Orange and Red were all action and their voices rose above the others, as alike as twins. Green was calm and serene, always the mediator. Violet could be as passionate as her brothers, but just as quiet as Indigo in other ways. Indigo rarely spoke, her quietness sometimes puzzled Carling, until she realised that her actions and posture spoke volumes and were more wolf than she realised. Carling found that the others turned to Yellow and Blue for confirmation of a fact or agreement to a decision. They sat together, as normal, hands held discreetly under the table, and she caught them looking at each other adoringly.

This brought to mind the non-discussion she had with Indigo earlier, and she watched her aunt closely. There was one of her uncles Indigo preferred over the others, and now that Carling was aware of it, it was very plain to see. It amused her to see that he returned her looks when she was not watching.

Carling yawned, stretched broadly, and excused herself to go lie down and sleep. There was also another reason she wanted to be by herself. The issue of her aunt had put her own mind to the man she now accepted she loved. As she lay on her bed, she found him easily and slipped into his mind. She stood back and watched as he acted out a strange nightmare. He was fighting off something that was indistinct and dark, and Galen was working with all his strength to push it back and away.

Recognising what it was, Carling was stunned and inactive. It took her a moment before she leant her strength and might to force Chaos from his mind, and keep him from attacking Galen, trying to take over him. With the darkness expelled, Carling turned to find a surprised Galen staring at her.

"I was winning," he said, not realising this was not exactly a dream.

"I'm sorry for helping you, but Chaos would have taken over your mind and used you against me," she told him gently. "Galen, I am here in your dream. I came to see you, to make sure you are protected."

"You are here?" Galen asked brightly.

"Not physically. With Mind Touch I can find you wherever you are, and we can talk here inside your mind."

"Where are you?" he asked, a little disappointed.

"With the Sentinels. I wish I was with you," she told him, walking towards his dream form.

"I still had it," he told her grinning.

"You don't understand. Chaos was really trying to take over your mind." She stopped, concerned he did not comprehend the seriousness of what had just happened. "I thought I had protected you properly, but he has found a way to get to you."

"That was him? He wasn't trying very hard, then. And thank you for protecting me," he conceded, giving her a little bow.

"You are welcome." They were now only a short space away from each other. Galen brought his hand up to caress her cheek but stopped only a millimetre from her.

"I cannot let you do that Galen," Order said from beside them. "I will not allow that kind of bond just yet, as Chaos could gain access to Carling through you. You will both have to be a patient just a little longer."

"Order, I've been waiting for you," Carling said stepping away from Galen.

"I am aware of your impatience, Carling," Order smiled a little. "I'll let you say goodbye and will be waiting for you when you return to us."

Order turned and disappeared from the dream. When Carling turned back to Galen, he was stunned that Order had appeared and was shaking his head.

"I'm leaving tomorrow for the valley and home, Carling. Will you be there?" he asked hopefully as he turned his eyes back to her.

"I have said that I would be there, and I shall. I'm nervous about going back, about seeing Ma and Da again."

"Nervous also to tell them about us?" he asked her gently.

"Yes, that also. Between now and when we see each other, you cannot think of my name or that of Chaos. They will draw him in, and I worry he may try again to attack you."

"I will try, although it will be difficult," he told her with a look that suggested so much.

"Thank you. I must go. I can't keep Order waiting," Carling told him, almost unconsciously leaning into him, wanting to be in his arms.

"I will see you on the full moon," Galen said.

"Safe journey." Carling pulled away from his dream and re-entered her own world. She lay for a moment looking up at the ceiling made of hexagonal columns, thinking of him.

"The Sentinels have told me of your questions, Carling, and it surprises me that you have asked it. You are already aware that you can do this task. So now I am wondering why it is you still ask it," Order said as she emerged from her room.

"I ask, Order, because it is proper to speak to you first about it. You are still the Supreme Being of this world. It is in your care, as are all the creatures, be they human, animal or celestial," Carling replied formally.

"That is soon to pass. Carling, there is a place that I need to show you. Will you come with me to see it?" Order took her hand and waited for her nod.

The room shifted and fell away, to be replaced by a dazzling bright, white light interspersed with flashes of rainbow colour. The columns in this room Order had brought her to were clear and shone with a brilliance. The light from the small opening above reflected off each surface and the room seemed to shimmer with it.

"This is a very special place, Carling. Even in the moonlight, this room is illuminated and only on the darkest of nights will there be no light," Order explained.

"It is so beautiful. Do the others know of its existence?" Carling asked as she turned to take it all in.

"No, they do not. I have protected this little cave well from both human and Sentinels," Order replied.

"Then why have you shown it to me?" Carling asked as she came to stand before her.

"Because you need to know where to find it. I have been pondering on the problem of Chaos for a long time, Carling. Light is his greatest weakness. He feeds on darkness and despair, while he hungers for the hurt and pain of others. In here he will be diminished." Order looked around at the room and placed a hand on the one of the columns.

"You wish me to imprison him here, instead of killing him?" Carling asked, a little confused.

"It has been revealed to me that you are not destined to kill Chaos. That is the task of the Ultimate One. Your destiny, Child of the Light, is to confine and reduce Chaos," Order informed her.

Carling pondered this a moment, and she was ashamed to feel the easing of the burden that she had felt in killing Chaos.

"Even if I imprisoned him here, would he not still be able to have influence over the world in the times of darkness?" Carling asked.

"Yes, but to a lesser extent. Confined in here, he will not be able to confront you personally in your next lives. From in here he will only be able to control those less powerful. And this room will not be in complete darkness. You have the ability, Carling. Search your mind and find it. It is connected with the Light. It is the reason I allowed this ability to be passed through to The People. Light dispels the darkness and keeps you safe." Order stood back a moment and waited while Carling searched.

Carling turned her thoughts inwards and walked through the confines of her mind until she found the Light ability. It hung there as a bright orb of light, sending pulses out to the far reaches of her mind. Carling stared at it as she walked around the orb before stepping inside. Swirls and sparks exploded and sped past her as she made it to the centre of the ability. Golden and white they glowed, making her squint to see what lay hidden inside.

It was at the very centre she found it—a small speck of light. Burning bright and glowing golden on the outside, sparkling in her hand like a beautiful crystal. It almost appeared to be made of the same material as the giant crystal columns in the room. Studying it, she found how it worked and gently placed it back. As Carling left the ability and came back to the room, her brow was still furrowed while she contemplated the matter.

"I see what it is that must be done, and it will be so. The confinement will be a long one before She who comes can deal with him," Carling told Order.

"Yes, it will be a long one, but only a moment for Chaos. The world is older than the humans know. They cannot feel its history in even a grain of sand."

"Most humans, Order. Some do feel it weighing heavily upon them," Carling said.

"And from them come the lines that will be the most important in the future. Including yours, Carling, with Galen. It has taken you some time to get used to the idea." Order gave her a small smile.

"It has, as I had to change my thinking from brother and sister to the opposite. You may have sought to bring me up as normally as possible, Order, but you blundered there. You should not have put me with his family," Carling told her with a sigh.

"The idea was that you felt love from the moment you were born. Love comes in many forms, Carling, but love should always be a constant in your lives. Love is what will save mankind and is the greatest protection you have. Go home and see Tarl'a and Mailcon. Surround yourself once more with the love of your brothers and accept finally the love you were meant to have from the beginning. That of Galen," Order told her.

"I am blessed to have so much love given to me. But there are others who do not get to feel so blessed," Carling hinted.

"You speak of Indigo and Orange," Order said, tilting her head a little. "You wish them to be able to love as Yellow and Blue are allowed to."

"You wish love in this world, Order. Yet you deny it to those who come from you, those that could spread love to the world. Their kind of love will not result in another True Child. I have seen that when I looked at the possibility. And what I have seen is an innocent love, a mutual kindness and affection. They already feel it, why give them pain in denying it?" Carling asked.

"That kind of love I have never denied them," Order said with a shake of her head.

"But you do not tell them that they can. I had not thought you capable of hidden truths," Carling said with some wonder.

"I have not told them, because it will give you pleasure to do so." Order told her, with a twinkle in her eye.

"Is this my reward for acknowledging my own?"

"I do not work on a reward system, Carling. They love, and even if they do not realise it, feel love in return. They had only to acknowledge their own to accept it, just as you had to," Order told her gently.

"I will pass your words on then, Great Light." Carling walked around the room, feeling the coolness of the crystals, and an image came to her as she made her way.

"Yes, they are there under the ground ready for you to raise them up and be used. You can do it now, or will you wait and keep them hidden from his view?" Order asked as she watched Carling's movements.

"I think when I return with him will be best," she said, thinking. "Is it wrong for me to say that I am pleased it isn't me who is going to be killing him?"

"It is not wrong, Carling. Long have I known that it has weighed heavy on you. The idea of you as staff and sword—as champion—has clouded your judgements for some time. Now you can see what must be done and do it with a clear and open conscience, unhindered by dread. This will also help you in your next battle with Chaos. He will not be able to feed off your anxieties and your fear of killing." Order placed both hands on Carling's head. "Our child, you are blessed, you are honoured, and you are loved. May the light of the universe grow inside you and light your path. May your golden light shine out to the world and warm it with love. May your children be blessed down through the ages. May they come to know peace and prosperity. This is my last blessing on you, my dearest of children." Order released her and Carling noticed for the first time a diminishing in Order's light.

"You're leaving this world so soon?" Carling asked with some dread as she saw what was to come.

"I am. The light in this room I will feed for as long as necessary, as Chaos and Order belong together. It is time for the One True Child to come into her own and lead the Sentinels. You have your knowledge and the guidance of your family, and I place them in your care."

"Do they know?" Carling asked, concerned.

"No, they do not, and that is the way I wish it. Now, let us return to them and spend this day in their company."

Order held out a hand, the lights flashing brightly for a moment before dimming down again. Carling took it and kissed it quickly before the Great One transported them back to the family gathering. A single tear drop fell from Carling's eye before they left, and it dropped to the ground. The droplet splashed onto the hard basalt floor, shattering into a thousand shards which embedded themselves into the rock, sparkling in the sunlight that filtered from the world above.

Carling quickly dispelled anymore tears that might have shed when they returned and sought out the comfort of her parents. They gave it to her readily, not understanding what had made her feel sad, but there to give their love. Carling sought out Indigo next and pulled her away from the others to talk privately.

"Do you remember when you came to me, we spoke of a matter?" Carling asked her.

"I thought we had not spoken of it, Carling," Indigo said with a little laugh.

"That matter has been resolved, and I believe he feels the same way." Carling looked over to where Orange and Red stood talking to Order.

"It is forbidden, Carling. Even if he did, we cannot," Indigo protested.

"No. What is forbidden is the act that results in a One True Child. The other—that which you feel for him, and he feels for you—is allowed." Carling gave her an encouraging look. "I spoke to Order about it."

"You spoke to The Great One about us? Order knows?" Indigo asked, a little shocked at Carling's actions.

"Order has always known. You only had to speak it and acknowledge it between you to have it. Order has been waiting for you and Orange to find each other."

Carling held Indigo's hand gently and brought her back to the group. She led her on past Green and Violet, past Yellow and Blue, to stand between Red and Orange. Gently she picked up Orange's hand and placed Indigo's inside it. Not a word was spoken in the room as she did this simple act. Only love grew in their hearts for the two who had loved for so long and had kept themselves apart.

Order left them quietly and gently later that night. Only Carling seemed to have noticed that the Great One had slipped away, feeling the passing. But she knew that the light would still be there, shining brightly in the room of crystals. Looking around the room, she found that the pairs were talking quietly to themselves. Of Green and Violet, she had not been aware of their regard for each other, that they had already accepted and acknowledged it. Now she sat alone, and Red came to sit beside her.

"My niece, you have taken my brother from me," he said with a great sigh teasing her.

"He is your brother still, Uncle Red. I have taken nothing from you." Carling placed a hand on his arm affectionately.

"I will have to be content to be alone, then." Red sighed once more dramatically.

"There are always the ladies you left behind when you visited me. You left a trail of broken hearts in that town," Carling said, laughing at him.

"I could start to corrupt Chaos's people. I like your thinking, Niece." Red brightened a bit and placed his hand over hers. "My son Galen is a very lucky man. You will be very happy together."

"Thank you, Uncle," Carling said, then quiet descended between them as they watched the others in the room.

"Our world has lost Order, hasn't it?" Red asked quietly.

"Order has not left, only goes to do that which must be done. When I confine our enemy, its opposite will help give light to his imprisonment. Order will be in the world for as long as Chaos is."

"So, the age of The One True Child is truly upon us now." He sighed a little before taking on a mock air of seriousness. "I welcome you Sister to the Sentinels. Long may you lead us and guide us."

"Why am I not surprised you knew? Order thought none of you knew that she was leaving."

"Order created us, and sometimes the plans were as plain to us as they were to her. The Great Being gave us life and intelligence," Red said with a wink.

"Uncle Red, I have a fear—that when I meet Chaos again, it will be in the dark."

"Sister, you have to only call us, and we will lend assistance. If it is the dark you fear, then we shall light up the sky and dispel that fear for you. As my son keeps telling you, Carling, you are not alone, and you are loved. Your golden light is our beacon and our banner."

"Do you fear being alone?" Carling asked.

"No. I am never truly alone. I have my brothers and sisters and the children of my line. I have the creatures I have created. I have my niece, who has given me no end of worry and grief." Red grinned at her. "I am looking forward to helping you in the future, and eventually we will go too. The passing of time, Carling, even we cannot avoid. There are ways we can go and not be gone, but that is for later—much later. In the future we will have different names and be hidden, but you shall always know us. Remember, when it seems the darkest, there is always light if you look for it. You must be brave, Carling. There will be times when you feel the world is against you, when you feel lost and alone." He waived his hand over the top of his other palm and held up a beautiful yellow rose for her to take. "But remember you will always be a part of our special family."

Carling took the rose from his hand and sniffed deeply the rich perfume that came from it. It calmed her, and she felt at peace. "Thank you."

"What else is a doting uncle for?" He asked, giving her a wink.

The few days she spent with them flew past. The realisation that Order had pulled back from the world filtered through the group, each accepting it in their own way and looking to Carling as their guide. A role she was finding very unsettling, especially now that she was also finding the days running out until she had to be at the stones to fulfil her promise to Galen.

Carling decided a few of days out from the appointed time to go off into the lands by herself for a while. She left the Sentinels with a nervous heart and headed out over the water. The weather was still warm and the sea, as she travelled over the top, was calm and clear. The seals dove and played under the water as she passed over them, popping up for breath and then racing under the surface again.

Landing on the beach, she found the village of Lucan had grown larger. She entered the maze of streets that lead out from the harbour that had become busy with boats and sought him out with her mind. She found him easily, his loud voice a clarion call that heralded his presence.

"I don't care whose children they are, if they are hungry then they are to come to this house and be fed. That is what I have decreed and that is what is to be done," he yelled at a man who walked away stiffly. Lucan turned, muttering under his breath, and then noticed Carling in the doorway.

"The most beautiful woman in the world has come to pay me a visit again. You are not a child any longer, I see." He grinned at her.

"No, Lucan, I am not." She greeted him warmly and was retuned the same.

"What brings you to our town? We have none of your brothers here. At least I don't think we do, anyway."

"No, I am not in search of my brothers. I came looking for you, my friend. I wanted to see how you are doing?" Carling told him.

"I am healthy and attempting to keep the rest of them well. Sometimes I think your god cursed us the day she blessed us. We have prospered as you have seen, but that prosperity breeds problems. No end of them." He gave a little laugh. He may have lamented the perceived problems, but Carling saw he revelled in them.

"Order is not my god. Order is the Supreme Being, The Great Light. And Order has gone from us. I bring you news of a new age, Lucan. It is the age of The One True Child of the Ancestors. Many changes will come to these lands, many more men of different beliefs and religions. It will be a time of wars and disputes."

"Why are you telling me these things, Carling?" Lucan looked confused.

"I tell you so you can prepare your people. So far they are away from all the dramas, and safe. But the world will become a smaller place, Lucan, and I am afraid that it will catch up with you and this town. I also tell you because there is a task I need to set for you and your descendants. There are many of The People here. You yourself are married to one and have five grown sons, all of whom have abilities," Carling told him.

"What is this task?"

"There is an island—you know the one I mean. It must be protected, and in due course, it must be hidden for a while. I can set protections on it, but I cannot always keep my eyes on it. You and your family welcomed us in and fed us when we first came here. You took a young girl you knew nothing about to an island and left her there at her request. You never questioned us. Now I make another request. All I ask is that strangers and your own townsfolk alike do not step foot on that island. They do not use it and do not go near it. You and your family are the only ones permitted to."

"Carling, we welcomed you and your brothers because that is the way of the Celts and The People. Though we thought it strange a young girl would want to be left on an island, I felt there was something very special about you. I had also been visited by one of our goddesses, telling me to do what I was told." He gave a little chuckle. "It is a funny thing, One True Child. You need never worry that you request too much from us. I know who you are and where you come from. It has already been explained to me by the one you call Order. She came again five days ago."

"Again, I am unsurprised by the actions of my family. I thank you, Lucan, and your boys. This is a hard task I ask. It binds you to this place and to the island."

"We will defend it, my friend, till there is no more breath in our bodies. The island shall remain a secret for as long as we can keep it. Order told me of the secret it shall hold and has passed onto me and my line the protection we shall need from it. Now that all the serious business is out of the way, Carling, will you stay for the night and eat with us?"

"I would be honoured, Lucan," Carling replied with a smile.

Chapter Fifteen

Carling spent a very enjoyable evening with Lucan and his family. He called upon her after they had eaten to tell the old stories for his boys. The men and their children sat and listened carefully to the history of The People. After the story was told, Lucan asked her to tell of the Romans and what she had seen in the south. The education they gained that evening was passed down the lines of his sons and kept the family well down the years as they looked after the island.

The call for home was now urgent as the moon was nearly full. Carling farewelled Lucan and his family and made her way out of the town. When she had walked far enough away, Carling closed her eyes and concentrated on the stones. The pull from their energy she latched onto and followed it carefully back to them. When she opened her eyes again, she was standing in the middle of the circle.

Carling breathed in deeply the fresh air and looked about her. The stones were the same, and the hills had not changed at all. She walked out of the circle and to the spring, drinking her fill from the cool, clear, sweet water. With hesitant steps she made her way down the hill, keeping an eye on the house at the base.

Reaching the bottom, she made her way across the little meadow towards the house. A man came walking from the other side and stopped when he saw her, dropping the axe which had just been resting on his shoulder, and running to her. Mailcon picked her up and held her tight, tears streaming from his eyes as he went from hugging to looking at her to hugging again. He kissed Carling's forehead.

Mailcon had aged, Carling realised as she looked at her Da. His hair was now more white than dark. The lines around his eyes had deepened and his beard was tinged with the same white as his head.

"Ma will be so happy," he said to her finally, when he had calmed down and got a hold on himself.

"Where is she?" Carling asked, eager to see Tarl'a.

"Inside. Carling, she's not well," he said gravely. "I was going to call the Ancestors and ask them to force you home, but you came on your own."

Carling took a moment to understand what he was telling her. She looked towards the house and took off at a run. She opened the door to the stuffy room with the fire banked high and found her Ma bundled up in her blankets.

"Ma, I'm home," she said softly, taking her hand, alarmed at how cold it felt. "Ma," she whispered.

Tarl'a opened her eyes and looked on the face of her daughter. A weak smile crept across her face. "Carling," she said quietly.

"Shh Ma."

Carling placed a hand on her head and went inside her foster mother's body, searching for the cause of the fever. She found the toxins in the blood and discovered where they were coming from. Very carefully she scourged them from her body and repaired the tear in the bowel where the infection had started. Carling searched further, and as tenderly as she could, worked on healing her mother.

When Carling finished, she sat back and pulled her hand away from the head of her mother and breathed deeply. The energy she had expended to bring her mother back from the brink of death was great.

Sweat poured from her brow, and she lay down on the ground looking up at the ceiling.

Mailcon knelt between the two and called out to Carling. His voice sounded so far away, and she could not focus on him well at all. Her eyes began to close, and her mind reached out for the help she desperately needed, using the last of her energy to do so.

Red burst through the door and picked her up immediately, disappearing with her in his arms. Up at the circle, he reappeared and placed her gently against the largest of the stones. One by one the others began to wink into existence, and all stood around her, their hands stretched out, adding their own energy to feed her used up stores.

Carling's breathing eased, and her body relaxed against the stone as she pulled the energy from it still. The Ancestors sat and waited for her to wake.

"Why did she call for you and not us?" Yellow asked as she held Carling's hand and smoothed the hair from her face.

"I don't know. I heard her call and came quickly. It was so faint I feared for her," Red told her.

"What was she doing to lose so much energy? What was so important to nearly waste herself away?" Violet asked suddenly.

"Again, I don't know. She was on the floor of the house. Keep watch over her. I'll go talk to Tarl'a." Red stood and left them. When he returned, it was obvious that he was feeling shocked. "Tarl'a was ill, and Carling healed her. It should have taken two to do what she has just done," he told them.

"Is she cured?" Blue asked

"Yes, fully." Red sat at Carling's feet. "Thoughtless, silly, woman. You almost killed yourself," he quietly told her.

"I couldn't let her die," Carling said, opening her eyes and shifting where she lay. The energy was feeding into her, but she still felt weak.

"Lay still, Carling," Blue said, holding her down by her shoulder.

"Let me sit, please," she said and tried to push herself up. With help from her father and uncle she was soon sitting with her back to the stone.

"To expend so much energy by yourself was dangerous," Blue said by way of admonishment.

"I know that now. It was not like when I fought Chaos. I was weak afterwards, but not like this," Carling told them.

"That was more to do with the blood loss than the energy you expended. Healing someone takes a lot. You did not see how Uven and Arilith were almost spent when they tried to close your wound, and they were still having trouble finding where you were bleeding from," Yellow told her.

"I promise I will take more care next time, Mother. I wasn't thinking, except that I couldn't let her die before…"

"Before you and Galen become betrothed?" Yellow asked.

"Yes." Carling moved into a more comfortable position.

"You almost ruined all the plans. You were thoughtless. I thought you were reckless down south, but this was worse Carling, so much more," Red said, raking his hand though his hair, the disappointment evident in his tone.

"I'm sorry, Uncle Red, but Ma would have died. She would have gone without a replacement. There would have been no guardian," Carling defended herself.

"You are the next guardian, Carling. Have you not worked that out by now?" Red stood and moved away from her. "My son Galen may pass the line down, but you are the next guardian, not him. It is you who inherits the title from Tarl'a."

"I thought it would be one of our children, not me."

"That is enough, Red," Green said, standing to face his brother. "She understands now."

"Does she? Because I don't think that she does. How many times does she have to risk her life before it sinks in that she is important? Important to so many." His voice was loud, and Carling stared at him.

"This is not helping, Brother," Green said calmly, placing a caring hand on Red's shoulder. "It would be best if you left for a while. Go tell Tarl'a and Mailcon that she is recovering and will be down soon."

Red threw her one last look—a look that was mixed between concern and anger at her actions—before he vanished. The others took their leave also, until it was only Carling, with Blue and Yellow at her side.

"To some extent, Red is right. You do throw yourself into these situations without thinking them through first," Yellow told her firmly.

"I don't intend to," Carling said, still stunned at how Red had spoken.

"We know you don't, but you are not a child anymore and you need to recognise the consequences of your actions. You should have called for our help before you even started to heal Tarl'a. You may have abilities that are far greater than ours, but the energy stores in your body are still the same. They become depleted easily," Blue informed her.

"Can't we increase the capacity to hold more?" she asked, looking between them.

"No. As you can see, your own are now reaching their peak once more," Blue said, picking up her hand. Under the skin golden lights began to flicker and swirl.

"We will take you down. I want to check on Tarl'a," Yellow said, getting to her feet.

Blue helped Carling stand, and they both took her hands. Again, the world around her faded and slipped, and she found herself looking at the door to the house. Letting go of her parents, she pushed the door open and found Tarl'a, Mailcon, and Red sitting inside. Red looked up when she entered and got to his feet.

"I'm sorry for the way I spoke, Carling. I am pleased to see you revived. I will leave you now," he said with a sad note in his voice.

"You did not say anything that I did not deserve to hear, Red. It was reckless and thoughtless. I am sorry," she said, going to stand in front of him, reaching up and kissing his cheek.

"You need to look after yourself. My blessings on you, Carling, and my love as well." He disappeared without another word, and Carling felt his sadness.

"Carling," Tarl'a called, gaining her attention.

"Ma. How are you feeling now?" she asked, taking the small frame of her mother into her arms.

"Better, thanks to you. Red told us what happened."

"Please, I have already been told off for what I did. I am just pleased that you are well," she said, finally letting go.

"Tarl'a, I know Red has probably checked already, but I want to make sure, my friend, that you are healed," Yellow said, coming to sit beside Tarl'a.

"Yes, he has, like a boar ripping through the undergrowth he was as he tore through me. But yes, you may. You will whether I say yes or not," Tarl'a assented.

Within a minute, Yellow had performed the scan of her old friend's body and nodded when she had finished. "It is as it should be. You did a very good job, Carling."

"Thank you, Mother," Carling said from where she stood.

"Come Yellow. It is time we left them to their reunion," Blue said, taking her hand. "We will see you soon, Carling, when the moon is full." He winked at her and they shortly departed.

"What is happening at the full moon?" Mailcon asked, confused.

"There have been a lot of changes in my life and many adventures. Do you still have some of your excellent ale, Ma? I think I am going to need some with everything I need to tell you," she said, sitting down.

The lights in her hands had diminished and were now only very faint. If a person did not know they were there, they would have missed them.

Two days before the full moon, Carling could feel someone searching for her and she reached out for them. She joined the person in their mind and found Uven waiting for her.

"Thank you for answering, Carling," he said with a smile.

"It is good to see you Uven, where are you?" she asked.

"We're not far away," Uven told her.

"Who is 'we'?"

"The whole family is coming. We are travelling together, children and all. Arilith and Ila are with us as well."

"What about her baby?" Carling asked, concerned for her welfare.

"She wasn't going to be left behind. Besides, she's a Healer, as is he, and yours truly as well."

"I guess she is well looked after then," Carling laughed. "When will you be home?"

"If it were up to Galen he would be there now. Where are you?" Uven asked.

"I'm here already. I got here yesterday."

"Then I won't tell him that, he's already getting rather snippy," Uven laughed.

"Be nice, Uven, and travel safe. If you don't get here by the full moon, you have my permission to tell him that I can wait."

"I don't think Galen will stick around with us if we are delayed. We'll see you soon. Let Ma and Da know so it isn't so much of a shock for them."

"I will. Before you go, Uven, are Loc and Wolf with you?" she asked him.

"No, we haven't seen them, and Ru hasn't been able to find them." Carling could tell that this was worrying Uven.

"I'll see if I can find them," Carling said with concern. "I'll get Violet to help as well and maybe even Indigo."

"It sounds so strange hearing you talk like that," Uven said.

"There is more to tell. See you soon." Carling pulled away from the connection and pondered the problem with Loc.

Quickly she moved herself from the house up to the stones. The more she used this method of transportation, the better and faster she got with it. Calling out, she brought Violet and Indigo to her. They arrived and greeted her quickly.

"Do either of you know where Loc and Wolf are?" she asked urgently.

"He is close." Violet's eyes went distant as she located him.

"So is Wolf, and as usual, they are together. Carling, we need to do something very soon about them," Indigo told her. "Time is running out for Wolf."

"Where are they?" Carling asked.

"They are in the forest, in the clearing near the ford," Violet said and followed Carling when she made the switch of locations.

Indigo joined them, and Carling found Loc sitting under one of the large trees along with Wolf, who had her head in his lap.

"Loc, what are you doing here? Why haven't you come to the house?" Carling asked as she sank down beside him.

"Because I didn't want to leave her," Loc said sadly.

"Ma and Da have always welcomed wolf."

"Hello, Violet, Indigo. Is there a reason you three have come looking for us?" Loc asked them.

"Yes, there is, Brother. This includes you, pack-mate," Carling said to Wolf.

"I am aware of what it is you speak of pack-mate. But I cannot go and leave him," Wolf whined softly.

"We are aware of that, my child," Indigo said very carefully as she sat beside the wolf.

"Loc, an agreement has been made between myself and Indigo with regards to your line. We are here to discuss it with you, and we wish you to think carefully on our words," Violet told him.

"I will, Ancestor. What is it you wish to discuss?" he asked curiously.

"My dear litter-mate," Carling started and picked up his hand, holding it gently in hers. "We are aware of the love you and Wolf share. We wish to allow you to be together as you should. I can change you into your long-wished-for form, but only if it is what you truly desire. Once I change you, I cannot change you back."

"You can change me to a wolf?" Loc asked slowly.

"Yes. Violet has agreed to give your line over to Indigo's care, and she will no longer be your Ancestor," Carling continued.

"I would welcome you, Loc, as a child of mine," Indigo confirmed for him. "He would be the mate you need, Wolf."

"Why are the Ancient Ones so concerned with a wolf's need to have pups?" Wolf asked her curiously.

"There is a need, Wolf, in the far distant future. One of your pups' pups will be companion to someone who is needed," Carling told her.

"I will not be around, and neither will my pack-mate. What does it matter to us if this pup is there?" Wolf's head came up as she looked between Carling and Indigo.

"It will matter to me, Wolf. She is to be of importance to my next life, and I will need her."

"This matter is best decided by my pack leader," Wolf said, looking up at Loc and licking his face.

"It is an amazing thing you offer me, Carling. I will need to think on it a great deal, and I will need to talk to Wolf, because it is not something to be decided on alone." He lay a hand on her head and scratched her ears.

"Will you come to the house? Ma and Da will love to see you. The others are coming as well—Loc, Uven, Ru, Arilith, and Galen." She smiled as she said his name. "I would like you both to be there."

"Be where?" her brother asked.

"At the stones, in two nights' time with the full moon. Galen and I will be betrothed." She blushed and tried to hide her grin.

"About time. You should never have run off, Sister." He threw his arms around her and hugged her tight. "We will be there. But for now, I think we will stay in the forest and discuss your proposal. I will let you know tomorrow night."

"We will leave you then." Carling stood and followed the Ancestors as they left the clearing.

Carling walked out of the shade of the forest and into the bright sunlight. The warmth of the golden rays did nothing to brighten her mood as she pondered the problem of Loc and Wolf. Violet and Indigo walked at her sides, their quiet companionship welcome to her. As they reached the rise and turning in the road that would take them on to the house, Violet stopped her.

"We will leave you here, Carling. Tarl'a and Mailcon do not need to have more fuss and the disruption that we Ancestors bring them," Violet said with a smile.

"You are never a fuss or a bother, either of you," Carling told them.

"Nevertheless. You have news to impart to them, and we have other duties," said Indigo also smiling.

"Or is it you wish to be in another's company, Aunt?" Carling grinned.

"Orange and I still have things to talk about, yes," she conceded.

"Red is feeling left out and alone. I'm worried about him," Carling told the pair.

"Red will find his way, Carling. You and your family will be closely guarded by him. That will keep him occupied for a while," said Indigo.

"But he deserves—"

"Our brother knows he is loved by us all. He knows he has the love of your family and yourself. But if it will help you to be more at ease, then we will take care of him more closely." Indigo embraced her and kissed her cheek.

"We will all be with you in a few nights time," Violet told her gently. "Get some rest tonight, the next few days are going to be a bit hectic."

With the final word, they both left her, and she wished they had not. Carling happily sighed when she realised they had become like sisters to her, and she carried on home.

Tarl'a was just coming out of the house, dragging the bedding with her. Carling went and helped her to lay it out in the sun to air. She then swept the house and helped to tidy things away. They worked together like they had when she was young. Never needing to be told what to do, always just knowing. The house was opened up and the sweet summer breeze wafted through.

Carling went out into the meadows and picked wildflowers to bring inside to sweeten the house, including the new room. This, too, got the once over, and Tarl'a watched her.

"You have done a fine job, Carling. I hope the family appreciates it." She stood in the doorway inspecting the work.

"I figured I didn't need to tell you they were coming. There is something else Ma, something about Loc," Carling started hesitantly.

"This I know, too, my dear girl. I have seen and am pleased he will be happy at last. Da knows as well. I have not kept anything from him."

"It's a big decision—one I hope he is ready to make. I can't bring him back once I do this, Ma. It will be permanent."

"We know." Tarl'a came and laid a hand on Carling's cheek. "You worry so much about everything and everyone. Come. I have something to show you." She took her daughter's hand and led her into the main part of the house. From a chest pushed up against the wall, she pulled out a cloth bundle and laid it on the floor. Carefully she unwrapped it and pulled out a dress in a soft shade of green.

Embroidered around the neck and sleeves were the most delicate chain of flowers in reds and yellows. Tucked inside another cloth was a belt of worked leather, etched with boars. Tarl'a laid them out for her to see.

"What do you think? Da made the belt for you just after you left us, when we understood what had caused you to leave. The dress I have been working on for some time now."

"Ma, it is beautiful. I don't deserve parents like you," she said, a tear coming to her eye.

"You will wear them for your betrothal?" Tarl'a asked, wiping her tears away.

"Yes, I will wear them with pride." Carling leaned into her mother's arms and enjoyed the comfort she found there.

"All we need now is our groom. I have seen you both so happy, Carling. I tried for a very long time to not see what was coming. I will tell you honestly, at first I did not like the idea of you and Galen together. But I understand now. You needed to be with us to get to know him and he, you. Carling, I love you both as my children, and I am so happy my daughter will be guardian after me."

"Order paid you a visit?" Carling asked and Tarl'a nodded. "It seems that the Great Light has been doing a lot of talking recently."

Later that night as they sat around the fire, Loc and Wolf came walking into the light. He greeted his parents warmly, as well as his sister, and he sat down beside them with Wolf at his side. They did not talk of the problem; they did not ask him questions. They had already accepted that he would make the decision and were just waiting for him to come to terms with it.

Instead, they talked of other things—of childhood memories and stories from the road. Carling told them of the Romans, and Loc told them of far-flung communities. They talked long into the night, laughing and sometimes quiet. And then Tarl'a began the story they had all loved when they were children. The story of how the world was created and how Order was born and confronted Chaos. How the Ancestors came to be and protected the world. But the ending this time was different.

"Order decreed that Yellow and Blue should conceive a child. This child came to be and was placed in the care of the Guardian of the Stones and her family. The child was raised and was loved—so beautiful and caring. When time came for her abilities to be trained, she learned her fate. In the company of her foster brother Loc and Wolf they travelled to the home of the Ancestors.

"Her training was vast and took many turnings of the seasons. She learned to love her birth mother and father and found love with the Ancestors. She returned to her foster home and reconnected with her parents and brothers and fell in love. Running away from her true love, she did not understand she could not run from her destiny. It took her many seasons to realise that he was the one for her, and she came home. Home to the valley where she was protected and hidden as a child.

Home to where her destiny lay. The One True Child of the Ancestors wed her true love."

"I think it needs a bit more polishing, Ma," Carling said, blushing.

"Maybe just a little. I will wait to hear the stories from the boys. They can fill me in on a few more details," Tarl'a said, smiling at her. "Now to bed with you."

"Goodnight, Ma, Da. Goodnight, Loc and Wolf." She stood and headed towards the house.

"Carling, can I have a word before you go in?" asked Loc as he got to his feet from where he sat on the ground.

"Of course." Carling changed direction and they walked out into the darkness behind the house. "What did you wish to speak of?"

"You know what. I would like to take up your offer. I want to become a Wolf," he told her.

"Are you really sure about this, Loc? You have thought long and hard about what it means? You understand that I cannot bring you back?" she asked, her hand taking his.

"Yes, yes, and yes. Carling I have never been so sure. I love Wolf. I know to some people it seems strange, but I love her and want to be with her. And Wolf loves me."

"Ok, I am just making sure you understand it all, and that it is not some whim."

"A whim? To change my life completely, totally, and utterly. To sever the ties of family and be lost to you all forever? It is not a whim, Carling," Loc said, shaking his head.

"You will not be lost to us, Loc. Remember, I will still be able to talk to you. Ma and Da will not want to lose you either. We understand, Loc."

"But our brothers won't," he said sadly.

"Yes, they will. Why would they deny you the right to be loved and give love? They will be here tomorrow. Talk to them—we can help them understand."

"Thank you, I would like you there. You are the best sister a man could ever have. I love you, Carling, and I wish you and Galen so much joy and happiness."

"I wish you and Wolf the same. Now it is time for me to go to bed. I will see you tomorrow." She kissed him on the cheek and left him to the darkness.

Wolf passed her on the way. "Thank you, pack-mate."

"No, thank you, pack-mate for making him see sense," Carling told the wolf.

"It did not take much to convince him."

Chapter Sixteen

All the next morning Carling kept an eye on where the travellers were. Feeling them nearing the ford, she flew to the clearing to wait for them. She was nervous and excited all bundled up into one, and she could not settle. Loc came to join her and found it funny to watch as she paced up and down, going from talking quickly about any topic—seemingly to fill in the silence—to pale and quiet in quick succession.

"Will you calm down? You have known him your whole life. It's not as if you are only just meeting for the first time." Loc laughed at her.

"But you don't understand," she said, getting annoyed with him. "This is different. Totally different,"

"Relax. Put your mind on something else. I know—tell me what's involved in changing me to a wolf." Loc tried to get her attention.

"It's not that hard. I just pour my energy into changing your structure and all the other bits," Carling replied quickly, still distracted.

"Please don't forget the bits." He laughed even more.

Carling looked at him blankly for a moment before she realised what he had said and then blushed before joining him in laughter. "No, I won't, I promise."

"What else? Will it be painful?" With this question Loc's laughter was gone.

"I don't know. I've never done it before—no one has. You will be the first and hopefully the last," she said quietly, coming to sit beside him on the fallen log.

"Just make sure you get it right. Indigo came back to us after you left yesterday and talked it through with us again. So, one of my child's descendants will be helping you in the future?" he asked her brightly.

"Yes. I quite like that idea. That I will keep bumping into those that I love or those that are connected with our family. In some ways it's quite comforting to think about," Carling told him.

"Indigo said that when we pass, our spirits will join them, and we can choose to come back or stay. I'm not sure if I want to come back, if I can't be with Wolf." Loc looked over to where the large black wolf was lying in the shade.

"That is up to you and Wolf. As she said, you can choose. I've not really considered that just yet. At the moment, I don't really want to know what happens after we die."

"With all the time spent with the Ancestors, you don't know it all yet? You do surprise me, Carling," Loc teased her.

"I have never claimed to know it all. I'm stumbling through life like everyone else. Except my mistakes seem to have more effect than others." Carling frowned as she thought of them.

"You'll be fine, Carling. I have faith in you," he told her, placing a caring hand on her shoulder.

"Thank you," Carling said and then turned at the sound of horses. Eagerly, she leapt from the log as she looked up the track towards the ford.

"Oh no, daughter. You cannot see your groom on your wedding day. You are coming with us," Yellow said, stepping in front of her view and taking her arm.

The world slipped again, and she was transported elsewhere. When she opened her eyes, she saw she was in the Ancestors home on the island.

"What are you doing? I was about to—" she started.

"We know," Indigo said grinning.

"But—" Carling spluttered.

"No buts. Look who has joined us," Violet said, stepping aside and revealing Tarl'a. In her arms was the dress and belt, and she was looking very wide-eyed at the room around her.

"Welcome to our home, Tarl'a," Yellow said, putting an arm around her. "As her mothers, I thought that it was our right to get her ready."

"I think that is a very good idea, Yellow," she said, smiling at Carling. "Is there something we can do with her hair?"

"Like comb it, maybe?" Violet said, producing a comb out of thin air and advancing on Carling.

"How about some curls?" Indigo said as she tilted her head slightly

"I was thinking flowers," Tarl'a suggested.

"How about all of them." Yellow grinned.

The primping and preening seemed to take all day. Orange, Green, and Blue visited the home of the Sentinels at one point or another to see how the preparations were going and were all shooed away quickly. Carling noticed that Red had stayed away.

Carling endured their pulling at her hair and combing it out when it did not look right, or they could not agree. She smiled at the fussing they were doing and enjoyed her time with them. When she could, she spied on Galen and discovered where Red had got to. They were sitting outside the house with cups in hand, drinking along with Mailcon and the other three brothers and their wives while the children played around them with Wolf. The scene was such a lovely one, Carling could not help but smile with contentment.

"And just what do you think you are doing?" Violet asked her.

"Nothing much, just a bit of—"

"You can stop that now. Yellow, can you put the block back in place? Our young lady here has been spying," Violet told the others.

"Has she? Yes, I will put it back in place now. It is bad luck to see him before the ceremony, Carling." Yellow's eyes went distant and then came back smirking. "There, that should stop you. It worked before."

"It was you? You stopped me seeing him all those years?" Carling demanded of her mother.

"You were not ready to fall in love with him. If you had been able to keep an eye on him, you would have only seen him as a brother. So it was for your own good," Yellow told her simply.

The ladies carried on, but Carling had another way of getting to Galen that they did not remember. She sent out the thought and found Red.

"I know this is an imposition Uncle, but I just want a word with Galen. Mother has put a barrier up so I can't contact him," she said quickly.

"And you think I will allow you to talk to him through me?" Red responded with raised eyebrows.

"Yes, I had hoped so."

"Daughter of my sister and brother, I know what is good for me and I do as I am told. So, I cannot let you do this." He was grinning now, and she could feel him stifling a chuckle. "Enjoy your time with your mothers and sisters. I look forward to seeing their handiwork in making you even more beautiful."

Red was laughing as he pulled his thoughts away, and Carling sat fuming in the chair. She heard Yellow whisper something to Tarl'a and the two giggling.

"Serves you right, Carling. Just for once, sit, be happy, and do as you are told," Tarl'a told her.

Eventually the time came, and the messing around with her hair came to nothing in the end, except as a way to pass the time. Her hair hung down her back in golden waves, and around her head a garland of deep red and yellow roses sat. The perfume of both complementing each other and filling the room with their scent.

The dress was draped and fastened by ties and the belt placed around her waist. The four stepped back to take in the effect and smiled.

"You are the most beautiful bride in the world," Violet said, beaming.

"Galen is waiting," Indigo said brightly.

"My daughter," Tarl'a whispered through her tears as she clasped Carling's left hand.

"Are you ready?" Yellow asked taking the other.

Carling did not trust her own voice and nodded to them. The world slipped once more, and she found herself on the other side of the rocks that guarded the great shards of stone which made up the circle. The rocks also hid the valley below and the house she grew up in. She could hear voices getting closer on the other side.

Following Violet and Indigo, with Tarl'a and Yellow still at her side, Carling walked around the rock towards the sacred stone circle. The Ancestors left her side to take their own places around the stones, and Tarl'a joined the rest of the family in the ring they had formed around the centre. Standing just outside the entrance was Galen, waiting for her. Carling stepped forward and took the hand he held out for her and together they entered the circle, making their way to the very centre. The Sentinels sent up their lights to meet in the middle, creating a dazzling rainbow canopy over everyone.

Carling and Galen faced each other, their hands clasped, and their eyes locked together as a white light formed beside the couple. Order herself had come to bless the couple and their marriage. Placing one hand on top and one hand under their joined hands, Order threaded a golden cord of light around them, holding them fast.

"These two come to the sacred circle to be blessed and become one. May their love shine like a beacon on a dark night. May no one sunder their joining. As it is written in the book of destiny, these two shall be linked forevermore. Down through the ages their lives will come together when they need it most—to support and guide each other, to love. From this day you shall be as equals in everything. The blessings of the Sentinels be upon you. Our love we gift you. You are now one, tied for eternity," Order sang out the blessing. When she had finished, the sound of a bell ringing out a single note came from somewhere distant.

Order removed her shining hands, and the golden cord tightened for a moment before winking out—the feel of its touch still playing on their skin.

As Order stepped away, Violet stepped forward. "My blessings and my love, I share with you both," she said as she lay her hand over theirs.

Indigo came next, and she intoned the same blessing. Each Sentinel stepped forward, giving their blessing and love until Red. As he stepped to their side he lay his hands on each of their shoulders.

"Carling, daughter of my brother and sister, niece, and sister. Do you freely take my son Galen as your betrothed and husband?" he asked her.

"I do so freely take Galen," Carling replied, still looking into Galen's eyes.

"Galen, son of my line, do you freely take our One True Child as your betrothed and wife?" Red asked of Galen.

"I do so freely take Carling," Galen said, his voice low and deep.

"Then my blessings on both of you and my love for always. I shall guard your line and protect it to the very end," the Sentinel told the couple.

Red stepped back to his stone and resumed his place. The hands of the Ancestors all raised, and the light brightened around them.

"Go now and for all time live your lives together in love," they all intoned, and one by one they blinked out.

It was the time for the family that remained to congratulate the couple who still stood in the centre. Their eyes were still on each other, and their hands still clasped. Galen leaned in and kissed her gently at first, letting go of her hands and placing his around her waist. Hers snaked up his chest and around his neck, holding on tightly as he picked her up and swung her around. He placed her down again and kissed her one more time before taking her hand and leading her out of the circle and towards the path.

Carling stopped and placed an arm around him while looking up into his face. "I want to fly," she said with a grin, and they lifted off the ground. The couple soared up into the air and revelled in the freedom they felt up there. Holding each other tightly, they celebrated together as they broke through the clouds and the stars took over the sky, stretching from horizon to horizon. They hovered with the clouds at their feet and Carling sighed as she rested her head against his chest.

"Are you ready to go back now?" Galen asked, his voice almost lost to the wind that danced around them.

"Galen, I love you," she told him, looking up into his face.

"I love you too, Carling," he said, kissing her again. Slowly they descended in a careful and gradual spiral, landing a short distance from their childhood home.

They broke apart and waited for the group to join them, watching as they threaded their way down the hill—their arms around each other. As the group approached the couple, they led the way around the house and found the host of Ancestors waiting for them. They joined together for a feast and enjoyed the happiness and the love they all shared.

"Are you happy?" Galen asked, leaning in and whispering into her ear.

"Extremely," she whispered back.

"Shall we go?"

"Go where?" Carling asked, a little confused.

"Come, I'll show you." He took her hand and they stepped out of the firelight and the family group. They walked out into the meadow and towards the brook.

"Where are you taking me?" she asked.

"You'll see," Galen grinned at her.

Their way was lit by the bright full moon, and she let him lead, just happy to be at his side.

"Careful." Galen lifted both himself and Carling up off the ground to cross the brook. They touched down on the other bank, and he steadied her. Still further on into the meadow they walked, and Carling looked back. The glow from the fire flared into the night, and she saw the figures around it and heard their laughter.

"Not much further," Galen said, seeing where she was looking. "Red thought we might like a little privacy tonight."

Carling turned back to face where they were going and tiny lights began to blossom on the ground that led to a tent. It was a dull red under the moonlight, and as they neared, the light flared to life inside, making the fabric look dazzling. Galen held back the tent flap, and Carling stepped in.

On the floor lay carpets of amazing designs and softness, situated around a large bed which was made up of furs she did not recognise, silky and deep. On a table sat two goblets and a jug of wine, fruit, and other food she had never seen before. Two chairs sat at the small table, and the ceiling was draped in richly coloured fabrics. She turned as Galen stepped in and dropped the flap behind him.

"Red did this?" she asked.

"Yes, he called it his wedding gift to us. Do you like it?" Galen stepped up to her and placed his hands on her hips.

"I do." Carling suddenly became very nervous, and her heart raced as she realised what was about to happen.

Galen lowered his head and kissed her, his hand moving to her throat and up to her hair. Gently he took off the garland of roses and placed it on the table. Again, he kissed her as his hands found the clasp on her belt. Sliding it off, he placed it over one of the chairs.

Carling tugged at his shirt and helped Galen pull it over his head. As it fell away, she noticed the fine stitch work on it and smiled at Ma's work as she lay it on the other chair. Turning back, she blushed at his half-nakedness and lowered her eyes to start unclasping his belt, pulling it off and adding to the chair. Her hands went up to the neck of her dress and started to undo the lacing that held it closed. Slowly and carefully, she loosened it enough to push it off her shoulders. His hands gently helped as he exposed her soft skin, kissing each shoulder as he went. Carling stepped out of the dress and placed it with her belt, keeping her back to Galen.

She heard a thump and turned to find him on the floor, having tripped trying to get his boots off in a hurry, forgetting to unlace them first. Carling burst out laughing and tried to hide it.

"Just for that—" he said, grabbing her hand and pulling her down with him. He held her gently and kissed her again.

All shyness now gone, Carling relaxed and was lost in their love.

The red glow of the sun's first rays striking the side of the tent woke Carling the next morning. She stretched out on the bed and remembered who was with her, looking to her side to find Galen still asleep. His long, dark hair covered his face a little, and she pushed it back so she could see him better. The movement of his hair tickled his face, and he swatted her hand away. An impish grin played upon her lips as she picked up a long lock and held it at the tip, then tickled his nose with it. Again, he swatted at the irritation. Grinning broadly at how he reacted, Carling once more brought the little tuft of hair up to his nose and tickled it.

"Do it again, Wife, and I am going to have to do something about it," he grumbled, opening his twinkling blue eyes to her.

"And what will you do, Husband?" she asked, laughing.

Under the covers he reached out and pulled her close to him, kissing her soundly. "I can think of only one thing," Galen said and claimed her mouth again.

Much later, Carling rose from the bed and poured them each a goblet of wine. She passed one to Galen and sat back down on the bed.

"I could get used to this," he said, smiling up at her, his hand resting on her thigh.

"I will have to ask Red if we can borrow this when we want some privacy from Ma and Da," Carling said.

"We'll be in the new room. Isn't that private enough?"

"No, I could hear you snoring from the house," she teased him.

"That was not me," he smiled. "That was Loc."

"Oh no it wasn't. After last night, I know it was you." She drank from her cup and smirked at him before getting up and pulling the dress back on.

"No, do you have to? We have food, we have drink, and they are not expecting us out there just yet," he told her as he watched her body disappear underneath the soft fabric.

"We cannot stay here in this tent all day. They have come such a long way, Galen," she said as she straightened the folds and started to lace the front.

"We have come a long way," he replied as he rose from the bed and cupped her chin with his hand. She reached up and kissed him again.

"We have indeed. But we have our whole life to be together and spend alone. Our family is spread wide and for once we are all together. Plus, there is something that I need to do today. We are not the only ones to be betrothed," Carling told him seriously, enjoy his embrace.

"Loc and Wolf," Galen said, nodding. "You want to do it today?"

"Would you want to wait?"

"No, waiting until last night was torture." He grinned, reached for his leggings, and pulled them on.

"Good decision, Husband." She laughed as she fastened the belt around her waist.

"But we will be back in here as soon as we can get away again," he said, doing up his belt.

"You will have to race me back then." Carling threw his shirt at him, and cried out in delight as he caught her, lifting her off the ground.

They walked out of the tent hand in hand, Carling breathing deeply the morning air and raking her hand through her hair. The golden tresses caught the sunlight and gleamed brightly as they floated on the wind. When they came upon the brook, Carling could feel Galen readying himself to fly over the running water, and she held onto his arm and brought him to a halt.

"Are you afraid to get your feet wet?" she challenged him.

"All right, I bet you I can jump further than you can over the brook," he accepted the challenge. "No cheating by using our abilities."

"I don't cheat." Carling dropped his arm and moved away from the brook in order to make a runup. Hitching the skirt up on the dress, she smirked when she saw him looking. With a flash she was off and leapt through the air, landing on the other bank with plenty of space to spare.

"Your turn," she called to him, dropping the skirt, but still holding the fabric. Carling waited for the perfect moment, then lifted the skirt in a deliberate action aimed at distracting Galen. It worked well and he landed in the water.

"You cheated," he called out over her laughter as he climbed the bank and picked her up, putting her over his shoulder.

"Put me down." She was still laughing hard.

"You want down, then down you shall go." Galen placed her down in the long grass and lay on top of her, his wet clothing seeping through to hers.

"Get off me!" Carling was still giggling and struggling, but not trying very hard to dislodge him.

"I wish you would make up your mind. First you want down, and now you want me off?" He was laughing and rolled off her, lying beside her in the sweet-smelling grass of the meadow.

"Are you two quite finished? Because Ma wants to know if you would like something to eat." The head of Ru loomed over them and blocked out the sun.

"I could eat. Actually, I'm starving," Galen said as he stood and helped Carling to her feet.

"You know, Carling, he was a mess yesterday when we arrived and found that you had been whisked away before he could see you," Ru told her.

"Really, how much of a mess?" she said, eyeing Galen.

"There was a lot of shouting, and I think there may have been a few tears," Ru continued to tease his older brother.

"Don't forget it is not only flight I have as an ability, Ru," Galen said, pushing his brother gently.

"It was only when Red arrived that he calmed down," Ru said laughing, but keeping his distance.

"You see what I have had to deal with all this time," Galen said with fake exasperation.

"You do know who you are talking to, don't you Galen? I haven't forgotten what it was like when we were younger," Carling told him.

"Yes, but Ru has gotten worse in more recent times when you've not been around." He placed his arm around her shoulder and pulled her in close.

"Every chance I get, brother. Why should you have all the fun?" asked Ru.

"Fun? What fun was he having, Ru?" asked Carling.

"Never you mind. I wasn't having any fun as I was missing you too much." He kissed the top of her head.

"I believe that is what is known as bullshit." Ru laughed and skipped further out of Galen's reach.

"You can tell me later, Ru," Carling called after the pair of them as Galen left her to chase after his younger brother and she carried on to the house.

"Some things never change," Tarl'a said, coming out of the house to see what all the noise was about, shaking her head at her two eldest boys.

"Would you want them to, Ma?" Carling asked as she watched them with her.

"No, I would not. How are you this morning? I did not think we would see either one of you today." Tarl'a grinned.

"We have a task to do, an important one that cannot wait any longer," Carling said, turning to her.

"I wondered when you would do that. Do they know it will be today?" Tarl'a asked, concerned.

"I don't think so," Carling said quietly.

"Give us this last day, Carling, please. Let me have my boy for one last day," Tarl'a begged with a catch in her voice.

"I will, if that is what you wish, Ma." She put her arm around her mother.

It was obvious to everyone that something was happening as Tarl'a and Mailcon singled their youngest son out for the day. The whispers between the brothers soon spread the word of the change to come. Carling was helping her mother, along with Nila, while Ila and her sister Cait sat nearby.

Soon Loc came searching for his sister. "A word, Carling?" he asked after fending off an offer of food from his mother.

Carling followed him out to the brook and she could see he was not happy.

"Loc I just want to—" Carling started.

"Wait," he said impatiently.

Carling was startled. Loc did not talk like this normally, and she became concerned.

"I realise what you are doing, Carling, and I thank you, but there is something that is concerning me. Wolves only live for a certain amount of time." The furrow between Loc's brows was deep as he spoke.

"You are worried that you and Wolf will not have much time left together?" Carling asked.

"Yes. She is already old for a wolf," he told her quietly.

"It's all in hand, Loc. You and wolf will spend many, many years together. I had already considered that problem when Indigo first came to me, and I've worked it out," Carling reassured him.

"You have no idea how relieved I am to hear that." He pulled her into a hug and kissed her cheek. "I'll thank you now, for your help and support."

"I haven't done anything yet. Talk to me when it is all over, you may find it a different matter," she replied, returning his embrace.

"I was born in the wrong body, Carling, I should have been a wolf to start with."

"That was not my doing. Talk to Violet. For the moment you are still her son," Carling laughed and linked arms with him as they walked back to the house.

For the second night in a row, the group climbed the hill behind the house. At the end of the line came Wolf and Loc, followed closely by Violet and Indigo. Carling had spent the afternoon up at the stones going through exactly what she needed to do, practicing it in her head to make sure she left nothing to chance. It was a daunting task she was about to take on, and as she neared the stones once more, she began to feel nervous. Her steps began to slow a little the closer they got to the top. Feeling her slight reluctance, Galen gave her hand a little squeeze and a smile of encouragement. Carling breathed deeply and continued on.

The stones now loomed large before her, and she sent little balls of light around them to brighten the night. She entered with the family following, and they arranged themselves very much the same as they had the previous night. This time it was Loc and Wolf who were in the centre.

The Ancestors, led by Violet and Indigo, walked into the circle. Instead of positioning themselves by the stones, they arranged themselves around Loc, Wolf, and Carling, taking each other's hands and bowing their heads. Carling could feel them drawing in energy from around the stones in order to sustain her in the task. Her lesson had been learned. She would need all the aid they could give her.

"Are you and Wolf ready, Loc?" Carling asked them.

"We're ready, Carling," Loc told her simply, with a deep breath. He slipped the unadorned robe he wore from his body, standing naked before her.

"Then we shall begin," she told him with an encouraging smile.

Carefully, Carling placed her hands on Loc's shoulders and closed her eyes. The energy she would need to perform this feat would be great, and she was pleased they were there at the stones. She felt them thrum with the energy she pulled from the ground and the air around them, channelling it slowly and deliberately into the body of her foster brother.

With her next thought, Carling began to change him slowly from his feet up. She could feel the muscles and tendons realign themselves as the bones stretched and changed. Under her hands, Loc began to tremble. The pain of the change began to hit him, and he stifled a groan. Beside him Wolf whined, concerned for her mate.

"Violet, help him with the pain," Carling pleaded as she breathed heavily. Like a gentle touch, she felt the Ancestor add her own efforts in easing the agony Loc was going through.

Further on she pushed, sweat now dripping down her face with the effort, and drawing on more energy from the centre of the earth. The change of the internal organs was harder than she thought it would be, and she took a deep breath and held it as she made the adjustments. Another thought joined that of Violet's, and Indigo was there calming and supressing his pain.

The process was long and she hated giving him so much agony, hated the changes that were necessary to make him happy. The final moments were on them, and Carling opened her eyes to look on the face of her brother one last time before pushing on.

"Thank you," he said to her softly, through a grimace of pain.

Carling closed her eyes and began the final change. From his mouth a snarl escaped, as it stretched and pulled. The combined efforts of Violet and Indigo were not enough for this part, and he lashed out unthinkingly, biting down on Carling's arm, sinking the sharpened teeth into her flesh. Galen rushed forward but was held back by the ring of Ancestors.

So much concentration did she have in making sure the brain was perfected, she did not notice the jaws clamp down and did not call out. Carling's grip on what used to be Loc's shoulders was firm and strong, and she kept them there until she was satisfied that everything was where it should be. Finally letting go, she stumbled back and was caught up by Blue who held her up.

"Breathe, Daughter," Blue whispered to her as he lowered her to the ground gently.

Yellow was at her side and inspected the bleeding and torn flesh from bite Loc had inflicted on her. Carling's eyes were still closed as she gulped in the cool night air. Her mother lay her hand over the puncture wounds and healed them, leaving slightly silvery scars. A tongue licked her face, and she opened her eyes to see a large grey wolf whining slightly and nudging her.

Carling reached up and felt the fur around his neck and hugged him close. "Litter-mate, I am sorry it was so painful for you," Carling said into the fur.

"Littermate, I am sorry I bit you. It was unintentional," Loc spoke to her.

Sentinels

"Carling, we are not finished yet. I still need to transfer his line," Violet said to her gently. "Can you stand?"

"I can, Aunt," Carling replied as Blue helped her up and she accepted a lick from Wolf.

"He is as magnificent as I knew he would be," Wolf told her.

Carling joined the Ancestors in the circle, holding a hand of each parent in hers as the wolves stood in the centre. A soft glow came from each of them as the lights swirled under their skin, including Carling's. It was the first time her human family had seen them, and they gazed in wonder at the golden light that swirled there.

"Son of my line, son of Mailcon and my brother's daughter Tarl'a, you are now under the care and protection of the mother of wolves, my sister Indigo. You are human no more, but fully wolf. My blessing on you and your mate," Violet intoned, and from a distance the soft sound of a bell peeled out once.

"I welcome my son, formally known as Loc, into the family of wolves. I will watch over you, your mate, and the pups that are to come. My blessings on you both," Indigo spoke softly to the pair and the bell peeled again.

"A gift from the Ancestors to the two that stand before us," Carling called out, "A gift of a long life together. The years shall be kind to you, and you shall know true companionship and love."

Carling let go of her parents' hands and cupped her own together. From within, a bright golden light began to shine and blossomed out. Releasing the light, it floated and expanded, encompassing the two wolves in the centre. The light brightened and then faded slowly. When it had diminished, a golden fleck could be seen in the eyes of each wolf. Carling took her parents' hands once more, and they all bowed their heads to the wolves.

"Our blessings to the two here," they intoned together.

Each Ancestor greeted the wolves, laying a hand gently on their heads to give their own blessing, and then left the circle. Carling was alone in the centre with them, and she hugged each one.

"My blessings always and my love. Remember you are welcome here, you are our brother still," she said to Loc.

"I cannot begin to thank you, Sister," he said to her.

"Live well and enjoy the love you deserve," she told him.

Standing up, she stepped back for the family to greet them. Carling stumbled to the largest of the stones and placed her palms to the cold surface, leaning against it, feeling it feed her energy. A hand on her shoulder made her turn her head. Bright blue eyes met hers and were smiling at her.

"You are amazing," Galen told her, pushing her hair back behind her ear.

"Not me, the universe," Carling said, giving me a weak smile, still feeling the energy flowing into her. "I just asked it, and it did the rest through me."

"I don't believe that for a moment, Carling. I saw the lights." He traced a finger over her hand and a trail of lights flared and danced where his finger had lingered.

"I am still me," she said quietly.

"You are." Galen leaned in and kissed her.

The family started to move out of the circle and down the hill. Galen remained with Carling until she was ready and fully back to strength. The lights had brightened the longer she drew in the energy from the stones, and they played under her skin. As she pulled her hands off the stone, Carling hid them in her sleeves.

"This is you," Galen said, pulling them out and kissing each one. "You need never hide them."

"They will fade."

"I don't care if they fade or not. I am still in awe of your abilities. Please, never stop surprising me," he begged her.

"I'll try." Carling looked around, and she found that they were alone. "How about now? Would you like a surprise now?"

"Here?" Galen asked, and his eyes widened a little as Carling nodded and took his hands, placing them around her.

"I am sure we'll not be disturbed." Her eyes went distant for a moment as she checked where everyone was. "They are all otherwise engaged in something else," she grinned again.

Chapter Seventeen

If Galen had hoped that they would have a child within the first year of their marriage, he hid his disappointment well. He and Carling travelled greatly in the years after their betrothal, first going to see Gart and his broch. They stayed with him for two years, comfortably together, enjoying each other's company. Gart had never broadcast his niece's true nature to anyone, not even to his own children

It was while they were with him that they heard news of the Romans to the south. They were on the move, both heading to the east and to the north.

"I'm just thankful I never made a deal with them," Gart said heavily when he heard the news from his son. "Elfin, are you sure of these reports?"

"I am, Da. It has been told to me twice by two different men. They mean to be here soon, and there are more reinforcements landing every day." Elfin was the image of his father, both in looks and height, as well as temperament.

"I don't like this one bit," Gart said, with a worried frown.

"Uncle, do you wish me to go and check on this? There are many who still owe me favours in the south," Galen offered.

"Yes. Take Elfin with you. The more eyes we have on them the better," Gart told him. "If it will be faster, take a boat."

"We can run faster Uncle," Galen said, grinning.

"That you can," Gart said with a laugh. "Leave in the morning at first light. We already know that their goal is here in the north." Before Gart's eyes returned to the charts in front of him, they darted to Carling who was listening in from where she was seated with the other women of the house. "But I don't understand. Why do they go east? There is nothing there, apart from mountains."

Carling excused herself for a moment and headed to the chamber the couple shared. As soon as the door was closed, she leaned against it and sent out her thoughts. Red joined her more quickly than she had expected.

"How can I help my beautiful Niece?" he asked with a bow.

"You can cut that out for a start. I do not need anyone bowing to me," Carling said irritably. "Why are the Romans intent on the east. What's out there?"

"There are only the Celts and their druids. There is a concentration of them there. The people out that way are simple, hearty folk. There are also a few deposits of resources in the lands there that the Romans could covet, but other than that, it is hilly and mountainous," Red replied.

"So why the push to the east? I need to see it for myself. I fear he is up to something, and I don't want to be surprised by his actions," Carling said, still mulling over the problem as she paced the room.

"Are you finding the lifestyle in your uncle's house to be a bit confining?" Red asked with some mirth in his voice.

"A little. Galen would understand, but the others would question my absence if I were to leave. I know Uncle Gart means to keep me safe, but their lack of knowledge is a hindrance," she said heatedly with some frustration.

"So tell them. Elfin already suspects something strange. You use your abilities sometimes without knowing it," Red told her.

"Can you go for me, Uncle?" Carling asked, stopping in her tracks. "I can then see through your eyes."

"Why not go with Galen and Elfin? He can be trusted, Carling. You are going to need to trust these people." He placed a hand on her shoulder.

"I do trust them. Thank you."

"You're welcome. I will go now and have a look at what is happening. See if I can stir up a wasps' nest." Red grinned.

"Do not irritate him unnecessarily. But you might give him a few headaches if you wish, though nothing that will send him north. I'm not ready to face him yet. The time isn't right. Order is still working on his prison," Carling told him, chewing on her lip.

"I know. I have visited it. I think it will be a fitting place to end his days," Red said grimly

"It's not a permanent solution. My job is to be gaoler, not executioner."

"But such a pretty executioner you would make," Red teased her.

"Goodbye, Uncle."

"My blessings, Niece." He grinned as he left her.

Carling returned to the room and found the men still talking and making plans. She walked up to Galen and pulled him aside for a moment, talking urgently and quietly with him. "I have just talked to Red. He's taking a look for us as to what is happening to the east," she whispered.

"When did you do that?" Galen asked, looking around to see who might be in earshot.

"Just now. Galen, I want to come with you," she told him.

"I don't want you anywhere near the southern borders, Carling. It's too dangerous. You are too far away from the stones as it is," Galen told her, shaking his head.

"I can get there in a blink of an eye, and you know it," she shot back.

"What if you are with child?" he asked with a little hope.

"Are you looking for excuses to make me stay?" Carling asked him, pulling away, then adding sadly, "I am not pregnant."

"Carling, no. I know you can handle yourself. I trained you, remember? I just don't want to risk you unnecessarily, and it will be hard out on the road."

"I have travelled before. I dealt with the Romans who chased us. Galen, I am coming with you whether you like it or not," she told him emphatically.

"I cannot change your mind?" Galen asked when he realised she would not give up.

"No, it is made up. And Elfin needs to know. He needs to be aware of who I am."

"Then we will tell him on the road. There are too many ears in this place. Even now, our conversation has been noted and guessed at," he said as he looked around the people gathered in the room.

"I know we have caused gossip, and I know it stems from jealousy. Until I came here, I had no idea my husband was such a favourite with the ladies in this part of the lands. Some have even taken great delight in telling me all about it." She grinned up at him, feeling relieved he had agreed.

"And none of them could ever catch me properly. My mind was always on you. You know Red used to show me images of you as you grew?" he said as he returned an equally large smirk down at her.

"Why am I only now hearing this?" Carling asked.

"Because I was not supposed to tell." Galen kissed her, and she blushed.

The trio ran at a constant pace, and as all three had strength, they made good time that morning. When they stopped at a river to refresh themselves, Carling told Elfin of her status. At first he was surprised and a little disbelieving, until Galen came up to her and ran his finger up Carling's arm. The light display that played under her skin gave their cousin every indication that she was telling the truth.

The small group carried on running long into the afternoon, only stopping as the sun dipped down behind the hills and started out again just as dawn was breaking. Late that afternoon they finally reached the border of the sacred lands. Before she stepped over that invisible line, Carling gathered as much energy as she could to herself and then slammed up her defences, locking herself away from all who could find her—including the Ancestors. She did not want to take any chances.

As she stepped over the line, it was like she stepped through an invisible barrier, like a gauzy drape parting around her. Carling could feel the difference on the other side. When she had come back from the south last time, she had not noticed it, as she had been more concerned in keeping her family safe from evil eyes. The change was only subtle, and she stood while she tried to get a hold of it.

"Are you alright, Carling?" Galen asked, coming to her side, concerned at her hesitation.

"I'm fine. Let's go," she said, pushing his hand from her arm.

"No, wait. Something happened just then. We can rest if you want to."

"Galen, I am fine. I just noticed a change between our lands and the south. I didn't feel it last time," Carling told him.

"You were a little upset the last time you left. We can stop here and rest for a bit," Galen suggested.

"No, we need to leave. I can sense something here," Carling said with a frown as the feeling intensified, and she looked at the problem further. "We have to go now," she exclaimed as she felt the full force of the trap Chaos had set take effect. She did not wait for either of them but took off at great speed to put as much distance as she could between them and the barrier.

The difference she felt was the alien protection Chaos had placed there. She felt stupid for having stayed the small amount of time she had already and hoped fervently that it would not trigger any activity around them. She pressed on, and soon Galen and Elfin were at her sides, both wary and alert at her warning.

Carling's hopes faded as she saw not only horsemen but foot soldiers, all bearing the armour of the Romans, racing towards them from a thicket of trees ahead. Galen pulled both his swords from the scabbards at his sides as Elfin did the same. In Carling's hand, the sword she had used against Chaos coalesced in bright golden sparks, shining in the sunlight as she raced to meet the foe.

"Stay back, Carling," Galen warned and pulled in front of her.

The horsemen met them first, using long spears as they charged towards the three travellers. Galen knocked the first aside and cut out at the legs of the horse, making it fall taking its rider with it. The man screamed as it rolled over the top of him. Another horse reared up in front of Carling, and she reached out with her mind to calm it, while bringing her sword up to meet the blows from the rider. Mollified by her, the horse raced away carrying the man with it as she had asked it to. Turning back to the fray, Elfin and Galen were taking on unseated Romans.

Carling saw a sword slash down onto Elfin's shoulder from behind. Although the action seemed to be carried out in slow motion, the warning screamed from her lips came too late. The world around her stopped, and all were frozen in place. She raced over to her fallen cousin and placed a hand on his wound. The blood was not flowing, but she knew he was mortally wounded and needed help urgently. Holding him close, she transported him to the stones and used the energy stored there to hastily stem the blood as it oozed out through her fingers. Crying out, she begged for help from the Sentinels, and they came.

Yellow took over from her and she left them to return to Galen. The scene around her was still, like the frescoes on the walls of the Roman houses. Carling's blood began to boil up and the anger began to overflow. Her mind was taken over, and with a wave of her hand she unfroze the scene, slashing out at the nearest Roman to confront her. She felt the sword as it slashed through his armour, hitting the bone under the soft flesh while his blood spurted out and over her.

In Carling's other hand, another sword grew from the pure energy she had gathered from the stones, and she used both with lightning speed and deadly accuracy. The grim determination in her face set fear into the eyes of her enemy. The sun glinted off her blades as they blocked and slashed out, bringing down each foe that came at her, pushing them back and cutting them down.

Her body and weapons moved together, an extension of herself as she stepped and danced around her attackers. On they came until there was only one. The last to succumb to her sword fell to his knees first, and she stood over him while he pressed his hands over the wound in his stomach, trying to stem the flow of blood and hold his guts in. The rage still on her, she raised her sword to finish him off, and her hand was stayed by his words.

"You have been taught to fight well, Carling. You have bested me this day, but there shall be others on your trail. I know where you are now," the guttural voice called out from the dying man.

"I shall meet them with the same anger I feel now, Chaos. This is a waste." With one final blow she disconnected the head from the body and watched as it bounced along the ground, spraying out bright-red blood on the green grass.

"Are you hurt?" Galen asked, wiping his sword on the cloak of a dead horseman.

"I am unharmed." The swords in her hands dissipated into the air in a glittering array of sparks that winked out and died. Carling fell to her knees and sobbed, crying out into the air at the destruction she had inflicted on these men.

"Carling." Galen was there with her, holding her, cradling her into his arms as she dealt with the grief of their deaths. "I told you to stay back."

"Elfin," Carling said suddenly, sitting up and holding onto his arms. Without thought, she transported both herself and Galen to the stones. When the world righted itself, she found her cousin alive, still being worked on by the Ancestors. Green was now at his side, his hand pressed onto the wound and eyes closed with concentration.

"How is he?" Carling asked of her mother.

"The healing is slow. There is so much damage done to his shoulder. The bones have splintered, and there are major veins and blood vessels that have been severed. If you had not got him to us so fast he would surely have died. You did well, my daughter," Yellow said wearily.

"No, I have not, Mother. I have killed." Carling gasped back a sob and Yellow caught her up in a comforting embrace.

"We have had this conversation, Carling," Red said, coming to stand before her, his hand reaching out to her head. "You are our sword and staff, our champion, remember," he said gently.

"I still do not like it. It is wrong to take a life, no matter what the cause. He placed a trap and I triggered it. They would not have died if I had not insisted on going south."

"Carling, you were not to know," Galen said as Yellow released her to him. "You did not know. Your actions were brave today. You saved our cousin. If you had not been there, we would have been overrun, and

Elfin and I would have perished under their swords," he said to comfort her.

"You would have got through them. They would not have been alerted to your presence," she protested into his shoulder.

"Shh. We will talk about it later," he said, trying to calm her.

"Will you stay here, or will you go back?" Red asked him.

"I will leave that to Carling. But we need to know what is going on. What did you find, Ancestor?" Galen asked him.

"Those in the East are as I have told her, druids and Celts. Most have been pushed from their homes already. It is why there is a concentration of them. I could not see why he would want to harm them," Red told him.

"Because he knew it would lure me out of our lands. That I would want to know what he is doing and see it for myself," Carling said.

"Red, I need you," Green called from the side of Elfin.

Red left them and replaced his brother in healing their cousin. Green sat back against the nearest stone and closed his eyes. Already the strain of the work was showing on Red's face.

"I need to go on," Carling said from Galen's arms. "I can transport us elsewhere. But Elfin must go home. I cannot protect him."

"And what about me? Do you protect me?" Galen asked her.

"I did protect you, but I was too late for Elfin," she said, looking down at their cousin's pale and unconscious face.

The Sentinels worked on Elfin well into the afternoon. Red was replaced by Indigo and then finally Blue. Carling, even though she trusted them, checked Elfin's injuries, and was satisfied. She stood and went to Violet.

"Can you prepare Gart for the return of his son?" she asked her.

"I will go now, Niece." Violet nodded and she vanished before Carling's eyes.

"Galen, I will take Elfin and come back for you. Then we will go on," she said to him.

"You are tired," Galen said, concerned. "You need to rest."

"I can rest later. I need to do this."

"Alright. I'll wait for you here." Galen kissed her gently. "Come back soon."

"I will."

Carling went to Elfin and raised him into her arms. The image of the broch and Violet came to her, and she concentrated on getting them to her side. As she appeared, she found the room had been cleared, and Gart was standing anxiously, waiting. The weight of Elfin in her arms became suddenly very heavy, and she dropped to her knees.

"My son," he said, taking him from her arms and laying him down.

"He has been healed, Gart, but the blood loss was great. He will need to rest to recover," Violet told him tenderly.

"What happened?" Gart asked, looking at Carling.

"There was a trap. We were set upon by Romans just after we crossed the border. Chaos sent his people East to lure me out. I am sure of it, Uncle. I tried to protect him, tried to keep him safe, but I was too late. I'm so sorry," Carling explained from where she knelt.

"It was her quick thinking that brought him to us to heal him, Gart. She did save him," Violet informed her uncle.

"Are you yourself hurt?" he asked, alarmed. For the first time, Gart truly looked at Carling and took in the blood that was splattered over her.

"None of this is mine. Neither is it Elfin's," Carling replied, looking down at her clothing.

"You battled?" Gart asked with astonishment.

"I did. Uncle I—"

"Carling, there is no need to go over it again. It is time you got back to Galen," Violet said, placing a hand on her shoulder.

"Galen! Is he injured also?" Gart demanded.

"He is not," Violet told him.

"But my son…" Gart turned back to Elfin and held him.

"I will be back, son of my line. I will sit with you and Alauna until he wakes," Violet offered.

"Your presence will be welcome, Ancestor." Gart looked at Carling and growled, "Go back to your husband, Carling."

"I am sorry, Uncle Gart." The harshness of his voice did not surprise Carling, and she nodded.

With great effort, Carling stood and took Violet's hand. Within moments they were back at the stones, and she collapsed into Galen's arms.

Carling stirred under the blankets, rolling over onto her side and hitching up the covers to her shoulders. Nearby, the comforting sound of Tarl'a's gentle voice intruded into the quiet, and she frowned. Her eyes opened slowly and looked deep into the small fire in the hearth. The dancing flames licked at the wood, and the embers glowed warmly while sparks crackled up to the ceiling, winking out before hitting the wooden roof above her. The smoke drawing up to the opening in the ceiling coiled and curled blue, and she saw another time through younger eyes, blue smoke from the ruins of a house.

Carling closed her eyes again and dispelled the vision of that version of herself from the future and came back to the present. She shifted onto her back and opened her eyes again, lying there staring up at the ceiling. The light from the sun outside filtered through the gaps and she wondered what day it was. Then the memory came back to her.

"Elfin," she whispered and searched for him in her mind. She found him safe at home, being tended to by his wife and mother. He was awake and healing, his colour back in his smiling cheeks, enjoying the attention he was being given.

"Carling?" a whisper came to her, and she travelled back to her own body. Opening her eyes, she saw Galen beside her. "Good morning. How are you feeling?"

"Sad. Uncle Gart blames me for Elfin almost dying," she said quietly. Her throat was dry, and she began to cough.

"You have been asleep for two days, Carling. We've been worried." Galen helped her to sit and passed her a water skin. She drank deeply and long from it.

"What happened?" Carling asked, once her thirst had been sated.

"You came back with Violet and collapsed. The Ancestors could not tell me why."

"I can't tell you either. Does Ma know what happened?" Carling asked with some dread.

"I have told them both," Galen informed her.

Carling placed her face in her hands. Tears escaped her fingers as she cried. Galen wrapped his arms around her and held her tight.

"They understand, Carling. They understand. And as for Uncle Gart, he should be grateful you were there to help Elfin. He sent us out there."

"But I tripped—" Carling began.

"Enough. No more blame. These things happen, and you handled yourself in the battle with honour and great skill. I was so proud of you—I am so proud of you. Elfin is alive because of your actions. You kept us all alive. That was not me, not the Ancestors, but you." Galen pulled her hands from her face and tilted her head towards him. "You are the One True Child of the Ancestors. The greatest Being in the world, and you stopped time to save Elfin. I love you, Carling. Don't think of the other things, just my love for you," he told her gently as he pushed stray strands of hair from her face.

"Galen." Carling reached up and placed her hands on either side of his face, kissing him. "I love you."

"You are special, Carling. Your skin glows like the Ancestors. You wield a sword like a great warrior. The world will never know your like again. And your love knows no bounds for the world and all the people in it, including the Romans. My sweet Carling, you are special," Galen carried on.

"All right—stop. Enough. No more please." Carling pushed the blankets from her and tried to get out of his grasp.

"No, you will hear me until you believe in yourself." He held onto her shoulders. Carling stopped moving and leaned forward. "That is why I am with you. This is the plan of Order. I am your support and your love. I am here for when you are at your lowest, to build you up and make you whole again. To love you completely, totally, fully. Use my love as your shield. Let it protect you and keep you safe. Let it be there in the times that you must do the things you hate. Let it shine for you, just for you."

"It does shine, Galen. It shines the brightest blue, the same colour as your eyes. When I look for you in the dream space, you shine so brightly. Now, here in this room, I look into your eyes, and I see it. The blue flame behind your eyes burns so fiercely, and I feel so honoured that it burns for me. I love you, Galen, so very deeply, so completely."

"Then get up and fight, Carling. Fight for our people. Fight for our way of life, for our beliefs. You are the only one who can do this. The staff and sword of Order."

"No, not the only one. I need you at my side," Carling told him.

"Always," Galen said solemnly.

Carling spent the next couple of days being tended to by Tarl'a, Mailcon, and Galen. Every day she spent slowly gaining back energy and shifting her thinking. They did not tiptoe around the issue but talked to her about it and forced her to confront it. Galen was at her side each and every moment, showing how much he loved her.

They lay together in the new room early one morning. Carling was held in his arms, and she rested her head on his shoulder. "It's time we went back out into the world," she said quietly, not even sure if he was awake or not.

"We could stay here. You are supposed to be the next guardian." He kissed her head.

"No, we have the problem of Him. I know he is searching for me, and this is just a way of luring me out, but I need to find out what he is up to and try and stop more people from being harmed," she said quietly.

"We will leave today, then," Galen agreed.

"That is one good thing about the abilities. The way I can transport us," Carling said and then added slowly, "And I have been thinking that I should do this alone."

"No, you will not. I am not letting you out of my sight, Carling. Remember, I am your support." Galen shifted and leaned up on an elbow, looking down on her.

"I thought you would say that." Carling reached up and stroked his face.

"Don't you dare disappear on me. I will call the Ancestors to track you down." He moved her hand from his face and held it.

"I meant that I am pleased I will not be alone, that you still want to go with me. I need you by my side Galen—always."

"I am so pleased you have finally come to your senses." His face brightened, and he kissed her once more.

With their goodbyes to Tarl'a and Mailcon, they left their valley home. Carling transported them to a safe distance just inside the border of the sacred lands and stood looking at the space they crossed over only days before.

Galen placed a hand on her shoulder. "We know what to expect. I trust you to get us out of whatever we come across," he told her.

"We could always fly," she suggested.

"We could. Do you want to?" Galen asked her.

"I would prefer. Then we wouldn't have to confront what we left behind," Carling told him, remembering the carnage.

"Then let's go flying." His hand slipped down to her waist, and he pulled her in and grinned.

They lifted off together and soared into the air. Higher and higher they climbed, and she propelled them forward over the border, once more feeling like she had passed through a gauzy veil. Far below the land stretched out before them, and she looked to the south. Clouds, dark and threatening, were building and pushing north, and she knew they were not natural.

"He's trying again," she called to Galen over the wind that was beginning to buffet them.

"We'll head west a bit, see if we can go around." Galen pulled her along with him and angled away from the onrushing storm.

Lightning crackled at the edges, and the thunder caught up with them as it boomed out. Flashes of light illuminated the clouds from within, making them glow briefly. It was coming on them fast.

"Hold tight to me," Galen cried out as he strengthened his grip on her.

The wind now tore at their hair and clothes, pushing and battering away at them. The air caught the couple, throwing them up on the thermals only to drop them from a great height. Carling grasped Galen's free hand tightly, starting to feel fear at the pressure that was building around them.

"We have to go down. We're going to be swallowed up soon," Carling yelled over the noise of the wind and guided them down to the ground.

They landed halfway up a hill, just shy of a stand of violently swaying trees. Galen kept hold of her hand and dragged her under their broad protection. They hunkered down under the large branches, waiting for the storm to pass. Great bolts of lightning slammed into the earth, leaving round scorch marks on the lush green of the open fields below them, and the oppressive crack and booming of the thunder shook and vibrated the ground at their feet. The rain started to fall in great curtains of water, drenching everything in its path within seconds.

The gales blew across the landscape, bending the trees to breaking and stripping the leaves, exposing the branches then sending them flying into the tempest. Small rivulets of water cascaded down the side of the hill and poured into the river down below, swelling it rapidly. The flood spread out over the fields and destroyed the crops, sweeping away the cattle and sheep that grazed there. The racing water sank into the ground and loosened the soil on the rocks underneath, carrying it down the hill and leaving great brown scars against the green of the rich grass. Rocks now stood out and protruded from where arable soil once stood.

The storm raged on and on, seemingly to stay over the top of them. The trees above their heads were bending over and cracking, deadfall branches landing heavily in the undergrowth of the forest that surrounded them. The tree they had pushed themselves up against gave way halfway up with an almighty crack, tumbling down towards their heads.

Without thinking, Carling pushed back with her mind, forcing the wood to move aside. The old trunk narrowly missed the couple and landed with a great thump on the ground, bouncing a little. The branches and foliage created a protected area and Galen quickly pulled Carling up and then pushed her under the newly fallen wood.

Under the protection of the branches, they huddled together. Galen pulled out a blanket from his pack and wrapped it around them both as the temperature began to drop suddenly. The air went from midsummer warmth to a freezing winter cold in a moment. Their breath began to condense, and they watched as the frost crept along the branches, coating them with a lacy whiteness while the water that still ran from the tree froze before their eyes, leaving delicate icicles dangling from the twigs.

Carling began to shiver and pressed closer to Galen. Squeezing her eyes closed, she pulled what energy she could from the surrounding area and cloaked them further, hiding their abilities and their light. Dimming his blue beacon saddened her, but it was necessary to shield them from Chaos and the war he was raging with the weather. She pulled the energy closed and tightened any gaps she could find, slamming up her defences.

As she finished her work, a mixture of the wind and the rolling thunder sounded like a roar of frustration at their sudden disappearance from Chaos' sight. The storm increased in intensity and continued through the rest of the day. Carling held on tightly as he threw everything he could to lower her defences and show him where they were.

"Hold on, Carling," Galen begged, holding her tightly and trying to support her. He could feel the effort she was putting in to keep them safe and began to worry she was expending herself too much again. "Do you want me to call the Ancestors?" he asked in her ear.

"No." She shook her head determinedly.

"You are not alone, my love," he told her.

Outside their makeshift shelter, the night was descending quickly, helped by the black clouds that boiled away above and around the pair. Galen did not want to leave her side or let her go for one moment, not even to light a fire to warm them. In his mind he began to call Red, hoping his Ancestor could hear him. The dark clouds above them were racing now, moving away to the horizon, taking the rain and the wind with it. As the last shower had been rung from the inky blackness above, Red came striding to where they were hidden.

In short order, the Sentinel had a shelter built and a blaze going inside. Galen picked a still-shivering Carling up and placed her beside it. Red entered after and set about making sure everything was dry, creating a bed out of thin air for Carling to lay on.

"The storm has passed," Red told her. "You can let go now."

Carling opened her eyes and found Galen at her side, Red hovering over his shoulder. "So cold," she said, shivering violently. She had been so engrossed in protecting them that she was only now realising how she felt.

"You are wet through. You need to get warm and out of those things," Galen said, trying to help her.

"So do you." She winked at him.

"And that is my cue to leave you." Red was heading out the door when Galen stopped him.

"Wait, I need a word with you, Ancestor, in private." He then turned back to Carling. "Start stripping. I'll be back in a minute."

Galen followed Red out into the night, and Carling did as she was told. As she knelt by the fire and started to pull off the drenched tunic with fumbling fingers, she could hear their low voices, Galen's sounding troubled. Carefully she focused, tuning out the outside noises and the crackle of the fire.

"But it has been two turnings of the seasons, Red. I would have thought by now—"

"I am the wrong Sentinel to talk to about this, Galen. You should have called Yellow. Or better yet, talked to your own mother," Red replied.

"Ma just said the same thing that Yellow did. That sometimes it takes time. Is it because of who she is?" Galen asked.

"I really couldn't tell you, my son. There are children, Galen. They have been seen. Two important ones especially. Stop worrying about it, and just enjoy being together. Carling will fall pregnant when the time is right for your children to be born, and now is not that time," Red told him gently.

Carling pulled back from the conversation, feeling embarrassed that Galen had gone to not only Red, but also Yellow and Ma for advice on her lack of producing children. Never once had he raised the issue with her, and now she felt disappointed. Dragging off her undershirt, she pulled on a dry one from her bag and pushed the leggings off while she thought about what she had heard.

She was still struggling with them when Galen came back in. He knelt beside her and started to undo the laces of her boots, pulling them off one by one. Carling watched him the whole time he worked, staying his hands as the leggings finally slipped from her legs.

"Why couldn't you ask me?" she whispered.

"Ask you what?" Galen put the leggings by the fire to dry and acted as if nothing were wrong.

"Galen, I heard," Carling told him, touching his arm, trying to get him to turn towards her.

"I couldn't. I didn't want to worry you," Galen replied, refusing to meet his wife's eye.

"So, you kept it inside and talked about me to others?"

He turned his head to face her, his hair hanging down and dripping at his shoulders. Galen's eyes were full of pain and worry. "I was worried you were doing something to keep you from carrying a child," Galen told her honestly.

"I would have told you if I was. It will happen when it is supposed to happen, Galen. Our children will be born, and I will do everything in my power to make sure they do. I would never do anything like that, not to you." She held onto his arm tightly, trying to reassure him.

Galen pulled her close and started to kiss her. Carling tugged at the shirt he wore and pulled it over his head.

"Next time you have a concern about us, don't discuss it with others. Talk to me first," Carling told him between kisses.

"I will." He pulled the shirt she had just donned off and lay down by the fire with her.

Chapter Eighteen

After a long night spent in the shelter, Carling emerged to find the world had changed around them. Trees that had once stood tall and trailed their tops in the sky were now snapped and broken, stripped down to bare branches and jagged stumps. Further down the slope, gouges had appeared in the side of the hill as if some giant had scraped away at it with their fingers. Stretches of water still covered great swathes of land on the plain below, sparkling in the newly risen sunshine that blanketed the world. Chaos's storm had taken its toll on the land.

"We need to keep moving. He'll be watching for us," Carling said as Galen joined her to look at the devastation.

"I hope no one suffered because of us," he said quietly as he took her into his arms.

"Not that I can sense. His focus was so engrossed on hurting me, he did not include others." She turned in his arms and put her own around his neck. "Did you sleep well?"

"I did. And you?" Galen asked.

"Almost too well." She smiled up at him.

"Your energy levels, have they recovered after your efforts yesterday?" The fleeting look of concern he had tried to hide did not escape her notice.

"They have, and I promise I will let you know if I am becoming depleted. We had best get moving."

"What about this place? Do we leave it, or can you do something with it?" Galen asked as he turned to look at the tent Red had supplied them.

"I can do something."

After packing away their things, Galen took their packs out of the tent while Carling put the fire out in the hearth. Stepping through the doorway, she waived a hand and the place they had made their own for the night crumbled away before his eyes, leaving nothing behind.

"You are very handy to have around, Carling," he told her with a wink.

"Don't get used to it. When we get back home, everything shall be done the way it is supposed to be. With hard work," Carling replied, trying hard not to let her own amusement show.

"But if you don't use your abilities, they will become unusable." Galen handed her the pack and she placed it on her back.

"No, they won't. I am a Sentinel, and our abilities do not leave us." She began to walk out of the forest, carefully picking her way through the debris from the storm.

"So, the new room, you could have built that yourself, out of thin air?" he asked catching up to her.

"Of course. But no one asked me. And anyway," Carling added mischievously, "I did most of the work felling and making the planks."

"But we did the building," Galen exclaimed, taking her hand.

"Again, no one asked me," she replied with a grin. "Shall we fly? It's a beautiful morning." Carling gave his hand a squeeze and without a word pushed off from the ground, taking to the air and heading south.

With the wind at their backs, it did not take the couple long to reach their next destination. Carling looked down on the town she had once called home and found it had changed a great deal in the few years she had been gone. The roads were straight as they had always been, but now they had spread further. The camp of the soldiers was now more permanent, with wooden and stone structures where once only tents had stood. The Romans were settling in for the long term.

Carling searched and found the people she was thinking of. Livia was now married and large with pregnancy. Benedictus had married one of their old friends and was finding that he was not as happy as he would have liked with her. The Governor she could not find, but she did find Serena, living with her daughter. Their lives had gone on as she hoped they would.

A column of soldiers was just leaving the newly formed gates and heading west. Carling pointed them out to Galen, and they followed for a way before leaving them far behind and heading to the mountainous lands that lay in that direction.

"The people here are not just Celts. I can sense an older—much older—tribe of people," Carling told him. "And they have kept their own gods still. We need to land. I need to talk to their gods."

"How about there, in that clearing?" Galen asked, pointing to a large green space in the dense wood.

"Looks good." Carling nodded, and the couple descended hand in hand until their feet disappeared into the long, dark-green grass.

"While you talk, I'll hunt. We need something for our meal tonight," he said unburdening himself of his pack. "But be wary, Carling."

"I will, happy hunting," she told him as he headed out.

Carling found the centre of the clearing and stood in it. She raised her arms out to her sides, palms towards the sky, and called out to the ancient gods of the lands she now found herself in. Slowly a woman appeared before her. She was bent and wrinkled, but Carling sensed this was a ruse.

"Who are you to call us forth?" the woman asked curiously. "You are not one of us."

"I am Carling, One True Child of the Sentinels of the North. I come from the sacred lands to seek your council and to give you warnings," Carling said, bowing her head to the woman.

"Warnings of what?"

"Chaos," Carling told her simply.

"To use his name, I feel you have steeled yourself with your charms of protection. You are the one to battle him, to defeat him." The woman nodded.

"Not defeat—imprison. There will be another who will defeat him," Carling told her.

"Long after we are forgotten, Child. What council does a Sentinel want with us?" she demanded softly.

"Chaos is sending his men into your lands. He means to overrun them and have domain over them."

"Our lands have already been overrun by the Celts. Where were the Sentinels then to help us?" the Goddess asked, taking a hobbling step closer to Carling.

"I do not know. The Celts were already in our lands when I was born," Carling replied, standing her ground.

"Your people still hold by the old ways and do not take on these new gods. Yet here they deliberately push us out and seek to destroy us, defiling our sacred spots with their ways," the woman spat with some venom.

"That does not sound like the Celts in the north. They wish to live side by side with The People, to learn and to assimilate into our families," Carling said worriedly.

"Not here. Their druids have been gaining in numbers for years, planting their sacred groves of oaks where they will. We would welcome these men of Chaos to rid our lands of them."

"The Romans are worse than the Celts. Go see for yourself what they have done already in the East. The land they take and destroy, the lives they waste without even a thought. These are not a kind and benevolent people. They celebrate and revel in the sight of blood and killing. Your people shall be put to the sword or worse." As Carling spoke, her skin glowed with the points of lights.

"Our people take to the mountains where the Celts refuse to go. We shall do the same with these Romans. We thank you for your warning, Sentinel. I shall pass them on to my brothers and sisters and we shall protect our own sacred lands. But I have a warning for you." She made another step closer to Carling. "He will not stop at our lands as he searches for you, Child. Be on your guard with your own children. He will use one of them against you."

The chill that went up Carling's spine made her shiver at the warning. "Thank you, wise one. I will heed your warning and keep my children close."

"They will come, Carling. Very soon." The old woman gave her a lopsided grin and then disappeared.

Carling stared at the spot where the old woman had been standing for a long time. Her words flitting through her head as she picked up the packs and moved closer to the trees. More concerned with the warning, Carling waved a hand and the red tent from their wedding night was now in place just under the trees. She started a fire with another wave and sat down on the ground in front of it while she waited for Galen to return. When he did, he was empty handed.

"It looks like it will be dried meat again," Galen said as he pulled at his pack to get at the food.

"Not necessary." Carling snapped her fingers this time, and a rabbit appeared above the fire, turning itself on a spit.

"Carling?" Galen queried quietly as he sat beside her.

"I talked to one of the gods. She took my warning and said they would protect their people, just as they had from the Celts. It appears as if the Celts that have invaded these lands are more war-like than those to the north. She also gave me a warning," Carling told him.

"What was it?"

"To watch our children. She said Chaos will use one to get to me."

"Then we will have to be very over-protective. Growing up in the valley protected you, and they will be too," Galen replied with some confidence.

"I will ask for the Ancestors to help to check the protection. It may have become ineffective over these last few years." Carling was still distracted by the news.

"There's no point worrying about it just now," he said gently and pulled her closer.

Carling woke with a start in the morning. The tent was gloomy as the sun had not made it into the clearing yet and was still hidden behind the trees that surrounded them. Carling lay on the bed with Galen snoring softly beside her. She waited and listened, holding her breath a moment to hear what had disturbed her. Again, another crack caught her attention and she sent out a thought, searching the trees, and found a man stalking their tent. In his hands he held a bow, and he was slowly creeping closer, trying to be quiet.

Carling sat up, and her movement brought Galen awake and alert, already half out of bed. She stopped him and placed a finger to her lips. With a thought, Carling froze the man in the trees and then went to race out of the tent.

"Carling, you may want to dress first." Galen laughed at her, eyeing her body appreciatively. "I mean, I don't mind, but you might get a bit embarrassed." He was reaching for his own leggings and pulling them on.

Pausing long enough to pull the tunic over her head, she left the tent and raced around to the trees, entering under the canopy.

Galen followed a bit slower. He found her walking around the man, peering at how he was dressed and what weapons he was carrying. "Are you going to unfreeze him so we can find out what he wants?" he asked, folding his arms across his bare chest.

"I think I will disarm him first." She began to pry the bow out of his hands and lifted the knife from his belt, passing them to Galen.

"You should step back before you let him go," he told her and moved backwards himself.

With a gesture, the man was moving again and jumped when he found them standing in front of him. His hand went for his knife and found it missing, then realised his bow was also gone and both were in Galen's hands. His stance was prepared for a fight, and he stepped back from the couple.

"We're not going to hurt you," Carling told him. The man started to talk excitedly, and Carling began to understand him and tried again in his language. "We are not going to hurt you."

"Who are you?" he demanded.

"We're friends you haven't met yet," Carling said gently.

The man looked her up and down, and Galen glanced at where he was staring. The tunic she wore barely covered her and he stepped in front of her. "Can you tell your mountain that I mean you no harm?" he asked.

"My husband is very protective," Carling said from around the broad back of Galen and then translated for her husband.

"You should go dress properly and then I wouldn't be," he said back to her with a laugh.

"Keep him here then. I'll be back." She raced away, pulled her leggings on, and ran back.

"You have pretty legs," the man said to her with a good-natured raise of his eyebrow. "It's a pity to cover them."

"You are not in a very good position to be passing me compliments. My husband doesn't like it. What is your name?" Carling asked him, now standing beside Galen.

"Bedwyr. And yours?"

"My husband is Galen, and I am Claire," she introduced them, deciding it was better to use the name she was once known by, rather than her own clarion call.

"Where are you from?" Bedwyr demanded.

"From the north. Why were you creeping up on our camp?" Carling asked him.

"I thought you were those men that have been crashing around—or the Celts."

"We are neither and will be out of your lands soon. We only came to get information on the Romans. The new men, not the Celts," Carling told him.

"Can I have my bow back?" he asked, eyeing up Galen.

"I don't think so, not just yet. Have there been a lot of Romans in this area?" Carling asked.

"They have been pouring in over the border of our lands for some time now. Why are you so interested in them?" Bedwyr asked her.

"Because they have threatened my family, and I don't like it when people threaten them. The Romans are only after one thing—domination."

"I didn't think it was for anything else. The way they attack the farmers, I have seen what they can do. They have not only threatened my family; they have killed them," he said with a mix of anger and sadness.

"I am sorry to hear that, Bedwyr. We plan to leave your lands today," Carling informed him.

"That is not what she said," Bedwyr told her.

"Who?"

"Blodeuwedd, the goddess. She came to me last night and told me to come this way to look out for strangers. I have to protect what is left of my family. She said you were different and gave her warnings. She also said that you would only speak the truth and to trust you," Bedwyr said with some suspicion.

"Your goddess never gave me her name. I gave her the same warnings I have given you."

"Her cryptic words to me explain how you managed to disarm me so easily. I am willing to accept that your name is Claire for the moment, for she told me something different."

"My secrets are not mine anymore, I see. I would appreciate if you did not use my other name. It could bring you more trouble than you were wanting," Carling advised him.

"I understand your warning. Now if I can have my bow and knife back, I can be on my way," Bedwyr said, holding out his hand.

"You may, and I wish to apologise for what I have to do now." She moved her hand and Bedwyr froze in place again. "Return his things to him, please, Galen." When Carling turned to him, he was looking curiously at her.

"What are you saying?" Galen asked her.

"Sorry, I thought I had switched back. He said he has already lost family to the Romans and that he was just trying to protect them. The goddess I talked to yesterday sent him." She took the bow and knife from Galen and returned them to Bedwyr.

"Are you going to let him go?" Galen asked.

"Of course I am. He poses no threat to us. But I won't until after we're gone. He doesn't need to know all that much," Carling told him as she headed back to the tent.

"I understood that when you used *Claire* again," he said, following along behind.

Carling packed up their gear, and they ate a hasty meal. After she had dismissed the tent and they had lifted off into the air, she released Bedwyr. The couple watched from on high as the man looked around him, confused and bewildered. They left him searching the woods as they flew towards the border.

From the air, they spotted dark, thick smoke billowing up ahead of them. It was caught up on the wind and spreading out. Circling around, they could see the damage wrought by the Romans as they passed through. Enclosures decimated, and bodies lay strewn on the ground beside the burning buildings. They landed and searched for survivors but found none. The bloodied and mutilated bodies of the children broke Carling's heart and fed the anger that was building inside as she checked each one.

Carefully, with Galen's help, they brought the dead bodies together and built a pyre for them, sending their souls to the care of their gods.

"Did you notice that there were no young women?" Carling said simply as they stood guard on the fire.

"I did." There was a fierceness to his tone that spoke of his own anger. "Another fact for which they will pay."

"Agreed," Carling said.

"With the ability to make time stop, like you did with Bedwyr, can you do that to the Romans? Can we kill them while they are in that state?" Galen asked darkly.

"It is an interesting idea, but it does not strike me as being a very fitting way for a warrior to behave. Taking a life while they cannot fight back," Carling explained.

"There is too much of the blood rage in you to see the simplicity of it, Carling. I warned you that it would take you over."

"Under the stopping of time, the Romans have no chance to defend themselves. I know we have free choice. I would like to think that they also have it," Carling argued.

"But he will not allow them. He will just keep sending them."

"I understand your frustration, and if I could, I would obliterate them all, but that would also mean killing people like Livia, who have gentle souls. There are innocents in amongst these Romans," Carling said softly.

"This is a waste." Galen gestured to the fire before them. "These people did nothing except live their lives in the path of the Romans. For what purpose did they die?"

"Now who has the blood rage?" Carling asked, gently taking his arm, and wrapping it around her. "The Romans will pay for what they do. Just as I will make him pay."

"There is one good thing. We don't have to track them. They leave a path wide enough to not miss. At least with the tribes, they tried to keep themselves concealed when they attacked."

"It is the arrogance that is passed to them from him. That sort of thing would not occur to him. I just hope none of these are family of Bedwyr," Carling said sadly.

They watched the pyre burn for a while longer and then left the enclosure. Carling looked back at what would have been an idyllic scene in the landscape and tried to imagine it full of the life it had only the day before. The young children playing, the older ones going about their chores. The adults talking and working, tending the fields and animals. Now the smoke that filled the air had no welcome of a friendly hearth—only loss and death. She wondered if they had welcomed the Romans, or if they had tried to defend their homes.

"There is nothing more we can do to help them. I wish to track down their killers and slaughter them," Galen said as he took her hand and turned her head to face him.

Carling nodded her agreement, and they rose into the air once more. They followed the Roman's tracks as they pushed further into the lands of these peaceful people and found them. They landed in a clearing away from where the soldiers had set up camp for the night, and Carling closed her eyes.

"There are twenty in this band. The captives are chained off to one side. They mean to camp here for the night only. The leader wants to reward the men before they go on, and it's not good news for the women," Carling whispered.

"Can you do something about that?" he asked eagerly.

"Wait here," she said and didn't wait for him to reply. Cloaking herself using the Hide ability, she crept through the underbrush carefully and stopped at the edge of where they were setting up for the night. Fires were being lit and pots put on to start cooking. As food was being distributed for the cooking pots, an image of a plant came to her and the properties that it held.

Carling searched for it, but she could find none around the area, so she produced it from a patch she knew grew in the valley. Tearing it in her hands, she walked into the camp still encased in the protective ability. Dropping pieces into each pot, she knew it was only a small thing she could do for now and looked at what else that could be done to help protect the women.

A high-pitched and terrified scream pierced the air, and Carling spun around to where it had come from. A young woman was being dragged forcefully by a man into a tent on the edge of the encampment, to the cheers of others nearby. Carling raced in behind them and waited until he had let the girl go, watching as she tried to crawl away from leering man. Remembering that the Romans were a superstitious lot and believed in ghosts, Carling used it to her advantage. She reached out a hidden hand and grabbed the Roman's shoulder, spinning him around to face her. His face was one of puzzlement and shock as he realised there was no one there.

"Leave the girl alone," Carling called out, stepping back out of his reach.

The man went white at the sound of the disembodied voice and tore out of the tent, tripping over his loosened belt that had fallen around his legs. The woman was huddled on the ground, her eyes wide with fright. Quickly Carling grabbed her arm and transported her to where Galen was standing. "Look after her," Carling instructed her husband hastily as she left them to return to the camp.

The sounds of the soldier explaining what had happened and the yells as they discovered the girl missing were great. They were peering around them, searching for signs of ghosts or anything supernatural while making signs to ward off any restless spirits. Carling couldn't help but enjoy their discomfort. She joined the closest fireside as the soldiers started to gather and talk about the goings-on.

"You will all die tomorrow," she whispered directly into the man's ear whom she had first scared and leapt back out of reach as he swung out with a large muscular arm, hoping to trap whatever it was that had talked to him. His eyes were wide with fright and his face drained of all colour while his fellow soldiers stared at him as if he was mad.

Carling went to the edge of the camp beside the women, and she picked out individual soldiers for the same treatment, only this time she used her mind. Planting the voice inside their minds to repeat the same warning every so often. Her victims kept looking around them, their faces terrified as they tried to work out where the voices were coming from.

"What in the Gods is happening here?" a loud voice called out as the Lieutenant came out of his tent to see what was going on.

"Ghosts, sir," the soldier nearest him said, staring around the camp in fright.

"That is rubbish. There are no ghosts here," he countered, and Carling saw the briefest flicker of panic cross through his eyes as he contemplated the thought. The message she sent to him was different to the others.

"Let the women go unharmed, or you will suffer a far worse fate in the morning."

"Who said that?" he demanded as he drew his sword and turned quickly, looking for the source of the voice.

"No one spoke, sir," the soldier said, stepping out of his reach.

"There was a voice," the Lieutenant said adamantly. "A woman."

"I've heard her," another spoke from one of the fires. "She said we will die tomorrow."

"One of the women are doing this," another yelled from further away, panic clear in his voice. "Kill them."

All heads turned to the women, who were huddled together. There were too many for her to transport all at once, and their chains tied them together. Her mind working overtime, Carling placed herself in front of them and gathered all the energy she could, calling out for help from the Ancestors.

Slowly she grew in size until she towered over the tallest of the men before her. Her skin began to glow with the golden lights, which were now racing under the surface. Quickly Carling released the invisibility and she stood before them, her face set and grim.

"You harm one hair on their heads, and you shall know my wrath!" her voice boomed out over the camp.

Weapons were quickly drawn, and one soldier foolishly raced towards her, his sword tightly clenched in his fingers, and a yell escaping his lungs. Carling called her own staff forward from the heavens and lashed out before he could get anywhere near her. A sickening crunch accompanied the blow to the head as she connected the end of the staff with his temple, and he went flying across the camp, landing heavily on the ground.

"Is there anyone else who wishes to confront me?" she snarled at them.

Two flanked her, hoping to attack at the same time. With lightning speed, she brought her staff down on the head of one, dropping him to his knees. Then she caught the other just under the chin, pushing his head back and felling him. She raised her staff again and stared at the men.

Again, she sent the call out for help to the ancestors, and she felt an answer.

"We are not warriors, we cannot fight," Orange's voice called out, reminding Carling of their restrictions.

"Help the women. That is all I ask. Get them to safety with Galen," she told him hastily.

Carling paced up and down in front of them and felt the energy working as they did as she asked. A cry of alarm went up from the soldiers as they witnessed the women disappear in front of their eyes.

"You are not one of our gods," the lieutenant said, trying to sound braver than he felt.

"No, I am not one of your false gods. I am retribution. I am revenge for the harm you have caused. I am your last battle. Your bodies will not be leaving these lands," Carling called out as she looked down on them. "I am the last thing you shall see. But not tonight. I bid you a comfortable night's sleep. We shall meet tomorrow, and you all will die."

Carling transported herself back to Galen and fell to her knees as she shrunk to her proper size.

Chapter Nineteen

"Can you see what they're doing?" Galen asked her quietly later that night from the side of their own fire. The women were huddled together, still frightened, but free.

"There is a lot of mess, The plant I put in their pots is working. Some are talking of running away tonight to escape tomorrow," she told him as she pushed a stick into the fire.

"We heard you from here," he said, grinning. "I couldn't understand what you said, but it sounded impressive, and I got the meaning."

"I don't want to face tomorrow," Carling told him quietly.

"If it helps these people, Carling, then we will keep to your word. They will die tomorrow."

"I frightened myself today. I killed those three men without even thinking about it. There was no hesitation," she said with a shake of her head.

"They were going to kill those women and do worse, just as they had killed their families. You were protecting them." He pulled her to him and held her. "They would have suffered under their hands if you had not done something. You protected them well, and they are safe now because of it."

Carling looked across at the women. Some were already asleep, but a few were staring at her. Her presence as their protector had frightened them as much as it had the Romans.

"I fear they don't trust me or look on me as a protector," she said in a low voice.

"They are frightened. What happened to their families is etched in their memories. Give them time and they will be telling stories of the woman who came to their rescue."

Still looking at the women, she brushed the mind of one of them and found the nightmare that played over and over in her memory. Carefully she pulled the memory from her and tucked it to the side, giving the woman the suggestion of sleep in its place. Carling moved from each mind, doing the same for those that were still awake. For those that already dreamed, she moved the horrors away for the night. The sleep she gave them was restful and restorative. They would still have to deal with what had happened to them, but tonight this was her gift to them.

"They will sleep now," Carling said wearily.

"And so should you." Galen pulled a blanket out of his bag and covered the pair of them. "Sleep, my love, and give yourself the gift of a good night's rest. You will need it for the morning."

They lay together in each other's arms, and as Galen felt her slip into sleep, he continued to stare into the flames. "Red, my Ancestor, give Carling dreams that are sweet. Let her rest for the night," he called out in his mind and felt the acknowledgement from his Ancestor.

Carling walked through the long grass beside the dancing brook and smiled. Home. It was always so calming and safe. She looked up and saw the little house in the distance, the smoke curling lazily from the hearth and her parents working outside. Her father was scraping hides and her mother grinding the grain. It was a perfectly idyllic scene; one she had witnessed many times in her life.

High up in the sky a large eagle flew over the valley in sweeping, lazy circles, calling out every now and then, flapping its wings only when it needed to keep up in the air. A bull stood in the meadow across the brook, and behind it on the hill, a ten-point stag stepped out from the wood and looked up and down the valley before heading back in amongst the trunks.

As Carling walked, across her path an adder slithered, the zig-zag pattern that ran the length of its body dark against the lighter shade. Shortly after it had disappeared, a large wolf came to her side and sniffed her hand. It raced away again, and Carling smiled as she watched it bound through the grass, playfully and happy.

A black boar with tusks that curled up from its mouth came out of the forest and trotted along the track to the house. Carling watched as it was welcomed warmly and lay down beside her Ma. From the path that led up to the stones, a bear shambled its way down the side of the hill, making its slow way towards her, and Carling went to meet it eagerly.

The fur was deep and course, and she clasped her arms around its neck, not fearing the large teeth or claws. It nudged her a little and then walked away, to go back up the side of the hill. Carling watched as it climbed and found a position to sit and look down on the valley.

The peace of her home was wonderful, and the sunshine was warm as Carling climbed the switchback trail leading up to the large rocks that pushed up out of the ground. The spring sparkled in the light from above, and the water tasted so sweet and pure as she drank before turning to the stones.

Carling had felt their pull from down in the valley. They stood as always, reaching up into the sky — seven great stones, one for each of the Sentinels. Pushing high and straight. Their surfaces rough and lichen covered. The energy thrummed and pleaded with her to touch them. She reached out and felt what was stored there.

It filled her up and eased her mind. She felt all the cares and worries flow from her body, the tensions that had built up from her recent task fell away, and she felt whole. Slowly Carling went from one to the other. She could sense their power, could sense all the gifts that they held of the knowledge of the universe imprinted on them from the Sentinels. She absorbed it all and nodded. It was all there, everything she needed to know and understood. Reaching the entrance to the stones, she stood in between the great pillars, a hand on each.

"Carling?" Galen called to her as he rounded the rocks.

She stood and watched him come towards her, his eyes the brightest blue, his smile as warm and caring as the sun. Carling took him in her arms and kissed him deeply and long. They lay where they stood, joining their spirits in the entrance to this, the most sacred of spots. It was beautiful and magical. Their bodies moved as one as they shared their love, and she cried out his name to the world and the universe beyond.

Smiling as she lay in his arms, she kissed him again. It was all so perfect and wonderful, and she didn't want to wake up. But soon Carling knew she should. Soon the world would rouse, and the new day would begin with the promise of battle. For now, she pushed it aside and just enjoyed herself with her husband.

Morning did eventually come, and Carling woke feeling at peace with the world. She moved and felt Galen's arm around her.

He pulled her closer and murmured in her ear. "Not yet. I have just had the most amazing dream." He kissed her neck and she sighed.

Carling stayed where she was, not wanting to move herself yet and smiled at the memory of her own dream as it came back to her. "So did I," she whispered back.

"It was almost as if you were with me," Galen said, his voice low and deep.

"I have a funny feeling I was. I think we were together somewhere, but it wasn't in our dreams. I don't know how to explain it," she replied.

"Then don't, but you can do that every night. I feel so calm and happy," he told her.

"That is the power of the stones."

"I asked Red last night to give you sweet dreams," Galen told her.

"Then I know we were there. In some other time, not our own. It felt different, but—"

"Stop analysing it and just enjoy the feeling my sweet, sweet love." He moaned, and she could feel him behind her.

"You forget we are not alone," Carling whispered and laughed when he groaned.

"Can't you keep them asleep, so we can…?" Galen's hand moved up her body.

"No, I can't." Carling pushed his hand back down. "They need to be away quickly this morning, back to their families—or whatever family is left. Could I ask you to escort them?"

"Don't ask me to leave your side, Carling. I will not do it." Galen leaned up on one elbow to look down on her.

"I won't then. But they need help. I can't just send them off without some protection."

"You can transport anyone, can't you? What about that man we met yesterday—Bedwyr?" Galen asked.

"I knew there was a reason I loved you." She reached up with her hand and pulled him down for a kiss.

Pulling away slightly, he whispered to her. "If we can't do the other, then we should stop doing this. Otherwise, you will make it very difficult for me to leave the blanket." He smirked at her.

"Then I had better get up and get moving, so as not to tempt you any further." Carling grinned back and slipped out from under him and into the cool mountain air of the morning.

Contacting Bedwyr was more difficult than she had suspected. After the fifth attempt, Carling gave up and called out to the goddess Blodeuwedd for her help, and the goddess arrived shortly after. The guise of an old woman was gone, and in her place was a strong young woman with a sword at her hip and long, flowing hair. She was beautiful, graceful, and stern looking.

"I would ask a favour of you, Blodeuwedd. From the Sentinels of the north, I ask your protection on these women as they make their way to find their families."

"You do not need to ask for that protection. I give it freely to our people. They will be looked after. You have our thanks for their release, and we wish you well for your battle today. We ask a favour of you, One True Child," Blodeuwedd said grimly.

"If I can grant it, I shall do so willingly. What is the favour you seek from me?" Carling asked.

"That we join you this day. That we be allowed to stand beside you as you fight for our lands. We do not want it to be known that we hid behind the sword and staff of the Sentinels while she fought our battles."

"We would be honoured to have you with us, to fight with us." Carling bowed to her.

"We shall join you on the battlefield. Take care, One True Child. Do not risk yourself unnecessarily in this fight. It could be harmful to more than just yourself," Blodeuwedd said cryptically and then vanished.

Carling rejoined Galen and shook off the comment. She turned to the women who were eating the meagre morning meal and sat with them. "I have assurances from Blodeuwedd, who told me you will be protected as you go home," she told them.

"We wish to thank you, Claire. Without your help we hate to think what may have happened," said the woman Carling had helped from the tent.

"I could not sit by and let it happen. No man has the right to do that. When you are finished, you should get going, and get as far away from here as possible. You will be helped."

"And what about you and Galen? You are not coming with us?" the woman asked.

"No, we have other business. I gave them a warning last night, and I mean to keep my promise," Carling told her and then stood. "I pass the blessings of our Ancestors to you and pray that you stay safe." She nodded to them and returned to Galen. The bags had both been repacked and he was waiting for her.

"Are you ready?" he asked.

"As much as I can be." She took her pack off him, and they headed towards the Roman camp.

Stopping just outside, Carling took the time to once more cloak herself before she headed closer to the camp. What she found were signs that Romans had broken camp and moved off in a hurry. As she headed back to Galen, she searched for them and found them further into the forest, moving away from them fast. She did a quick head count and found a few missing.

"We need to go above. I want to see what the terrain is like," Carling told him.

"Fighting in amongst the trees is harder than open ground," Galen replied with a nod.

"There are a few that have left the main group as well. I've found them trying to head back to the border."

"We will go back for those later." Galen took her hand. "Up we go."

Keeping to the tops of the trees, they flew fast to catch up with the fleeing Romans. Carling spotted the glimpse of red through the trees and pulled both up. They landed on a top branch and watched as they were trying to keep in formation. Their shields were up, and swords and spears were already out in anticipation of an attack. The horse the Lieutenant rode was stepping nervously as it picked up on the feelings of the men behind it.

From tree to tree they jumped, keeping up with the group below until they burst through the edge of the forest into a grassy valley. Carling looked at Galen and took a deep breath.

"You know what to do. You don't need me to tell you," Galen told her, then kissed her swiftly.

Carling jumped from the tree, her body propelled through the air and landed in front of the squadron of Romans. Galen landed shortly after, and they both shed their packs. Immediately the sword and staff burst into life in her hands, and she brought them up, ready to fight.

"Is this all you have to fight against us? One man and a girl?" the Lieutenant laughed, fighting for control of his horse.

"I can even the odds easily." Carling grew in size.

"And we are here to help our sister from the north," a voice said beside her.

Blodeuwedd, with sword in hand, was ready, and more men and women joined them. The sound of their swords being drawn hissed out into the world harshly.

"I think you will find us more than a match Roman," Carling called out.

The Lieutenant turned his horse and rode to the back of the troops and began to bark out orders for them to fall into formation. They moved with practiced ease into a wedge shape, their shields up protecting the mass, both from in front as well as above.

"Charge!" The cry came out from the rear, and the men began to move slowly at first, picking up speed as they headed towards the gathered group before them. Spears erupted from the openings, and they began to run fully.

Carling readied herself to meet them and was glad that she and Galen were not alone in this. With her staff, she swung out when the Romans came close enough, breaking the ends of the spears off, then bracing for the clash of the shields. With their battle cries now loud in her ears, she swung at the wall of shields, pushing the lead man off balance and into the fellow beside him. The opening was made.

Galen stepped into the break and brought his sword down, slashing through flesh and bone as he carved his way through the men. The sound of battle raged around her while she parried and stepped into the thrusts she made. Her speed made her weapons a blur as she took out two men at time. Not once did she worry about the gods who had come to her side or the fate of Galen as she pushed her way through the band of men. Her eyes focused on the lieutenant who was beginning to look fearful as his men were starting to drop one by one at an alarming rate.

Carling saw the moment he decided to flee, his eyes watching the decimation and the mutilations in front of him. He tugged on the reins of his horse, and it did not need much encouragement to take off at a run. Pushing off the ground, Carling chased him, her mind searching for that of the frightened animal and calming it.

The horse pulled up and stood still, no matter what the lieutenant did to get it to move again. Carling landed at his side and pulled him off the horse. He crashed at her feet with a clatter, the breath knocked out of him.

"When you have recovered you shall face me," Carling told him calmly. The gasping man tried to crawl away from her. "I don't think so." Grabbing him by the arm, she hauled him to his feet without any effort.

"Please...mercy," he cried out, stepping back from her.

"You did not give mercy to those people in the village—to the women and innocent children, to the men trying to protect their families. I saw what you and your men did, and I told you yesterday, I am retribution and revenge," Carling said darkly to him.

The sword she had been using winked away, leaving her only holding the staff. Carling lashed out with it while he was backing away from her. With a few quick flicks, she had him down on his knees, blood pouring from the broken skin where the staff had connected.

"I beg you, please. Spare my life," he called out again, desperately trying to loosen his sword with a shaking hand.

"Take a message to your so-called god. He shall not have these lands. He shall not have me." She struck out with a wide swinging blow that connected with the side of his head. The helmet he wore was no protection from the mighty staff she wielded as it caved in, breaking the bone underneath, and killing him instantly.

Carling stood over him for a moment, looking at the mess she had made and suddenly feeling very tired. The eyes that were pleading and fearful just moments before were now still and staring, the spark of life gone. Closing her own, she gathered herself together as a tear rolled down her cheek. Slowly she lifted off the ground and headed back to where the battle was now over.

Already the gods of the lands were clearing the mess, bodies stacked up and weapons put to one side. Blodeuwedd came to stand before her as she landed and leaned on her staff. "It has been an honour to fight at your side, One True Child." The goddess bent to one knee in front of Carling.

"Please do not do that. I am only a warrior for the Sentinels. I am not truly one of them yet. And we are not gods," she told the goddess.

"I do not show you fealty as a god, but in recognition for your skills. For your fight against those we should be banishing. I recognise the care you have for our people, and it humbles and shames me that we did not do something sooner," Blodeuwedd said with her head bowed.

"Please get up, Blodeuwedd. You are making me feel uncomfortable," Carling said, helping her rise to her feet. "Protect your people. Keep them safe. That is all that is needed."

"We shall. The other men who fled have already been taken care off. Bedwyr and his brothers were nearby and came upon them," Blodeuwedd said as they walked back to the group.

"That is good. If you don't mind, I would rather not stay for any celebrations. I would like to take my husband and deal with the killing in my own way."

"It is understandable. Take care, One True Child." The goddess embraced her quickly and returned to her brothers and sisters.

Once more, Galen had the packs in hand and was waiting for her. She smiled at him as she approached, and he reached out and pulled her in for a kiss.

"I need a bath," Carling said, then wrinkled her nose at him. "And so do you."

For the next few weeks, there were several more skirmishes of the same kind. Each time Carling and Galen stepped back more and more, letting the gods and goddesses take the lead. Bedwyr, with Blodeuwedd's help, was raising an army of his own, and an uneasy truce was built between the original tribes of the land and the Celts. United, they became a more organised and formidable force.

"It's time to come home, Carling. You have done all you can in those lands," the voice of Red called out to her in her dream. He appeared to her in his shape of a boar, the hair on his back bristly and course, the tusks white, curved, and sharp.

"I am tired Red, so very tired." Carling sat on the ground beside him. "But there are so many of them, and more keep coming. We have to stay to help with the fight."

"Those lands are in the hands of their gods. It is time you came home to prepare for your next great task," Red told her.

"And what task is that?" Carling asked.

"It shall be revealed to you when you arrive home. Your mothers and fathers miss you."

"And what of my aunts and uncles and my brothers?" She smiled at the animal.

"We all miss you, Carling. It is time. It is not your job to stop the Romans, Carling. It is your next life that shall do that. This life is still not over, and your tasks are still not finished."

"Why does everything have to be such a mystery," Carling whined. "Why can't you just tell me what it is I am supposed to do?"

"Because, our dearest one, where is the fun in that? Life is supposed to be a mystery, a journey of discovery and learning. You have on this journey learned and accepted your warrior side. Now is the time for a brand-new lesson, one I think you are well and truly ready for." Red instructed her.

"Why does it sound like you are laughing at me?"

"I would not laugh at you, my Niece," he told her, but there was a definite sound of mirth in his voice. "I am happy you come home to us. We shall expect you tomorrow."

"It will take us longer than a day to come home, Uncle," Carling said with a shake of her head.

"Not if you transport yourself. Once you have reported to Gart about what you have seen, then we shall expect you around midday."

"Is that an order, Red?" Carling asked him.

"It is not my place to order around the One True Child, not when she could send me off to the farthest reaches of the universe." The boar gave a series of snorts in place of a laugh.

"Could I?"

"Possibly. Get some rest, Carling. You are going to need it." He snorted again and disappeared.

Carling lay on the ground and looked up at the stars, a streak of light crossing over and leaving a golden trail behind it, followed by another. The noises of the camp around her were soft and slumbering as the men of Bedwyr's army slept around them.

It would be nice, Carling thought to herself, to sleep in one spot for more than one night. To return home to the valley and be at peace. Thoughts of Tarl'a and Mailcon came to her as did the vision of her brothers. It had been some time since she had thought of them, and now she searched out into the world for them.

Uven and Ru were in the middle of wedded bliss and fatherhood. Arilith, who had become one of the family so easily, was the same. They were settled and happy with their lives, living in the village around Gart's broch. Loc was a little harder to find. The change was so complete with him that she had to shift her thinking to find both him and Wolf. When she did, she was happy to see another litter of a pups around them and Loc a proud father. She smiled at the thought of how much he had changed.

Ma and Da were getting old, and she was alarmed to see how things were starting to become too much for them. The roof on the house needed repair badly, and Ma was finding it harder to climb the hill to the stones. It was time she and Galen went home, time to give their parents the help and care they needed.

"Red visited me," Galen said quietly.

Carling rolled over as Galen moved his arm to cover her, pulling her in close. "I'm pleased we are going home. He is right," she replied with a sigh. "It is time."

Chapter Twenty

Their first stop the next morning was one Carling was not looking forward to. The last time she had seen Gart she had just returned his injured son back home to him, healed but still weak from loss of blood. Now as they walked towards the stone fort and were greeted by people they had come to know well; she was feeling unsure of the welcome she would receive to her uncle's house.

"Carling, Galen," Elfin called out as he saw them approach. He ran to them and greeted them warmly. "Welcome back. How were your travels?"

"We'll discuss it inside if you don't mind, Elfin," Galen said with an arm around Carling.

"Cousin, I did not get a chance to thank you for saving me. Da told me what you did," Elfin said to Carling.

"Is Uncle Gart still upset with me?" she asked quietly.

"No, come see for yourself." He led the way into the large stone building and to the main hall of his father. Gart was sitting at a long table discussing a hunt they were planning. "Da, we have visitors."

Gart turned in his seat to see who had come to visit him and almost pushed the table over trying to get up. He had Carling in the largest of hugs before she could breathe, and she felt relief wash over her.

"I am so sorry that I spoke to you that way the last time we saw each other, Niece. It was so wrong of me. You saved Elfin, and I did nothing but yell at you," Gart apologised gruffly.

"It's all right, Uncle. You were in shock," she said, her voice almost lost in the embrace.

"You must be rewarded with lands to call your own. Name it, and it shall be yours," he told her, holding her now by the hands.

"Nothing, Uncle. I want for nothing. I'm just happy that Elfin came through it and is fine. What would I do with lands when I will be living in the most beautiful valley for the rest of my life?" she asked with a twinkle in her eye.

"Has something happened to Tarl'a?" he asked, concerned.

"No, just age. We have news for you," Carling said, becoming serious.

"The Romans?" Gart looked up at Galen.

"Yes." Galen nodded. "Can we talk in private?"

"We'll go to my chamber. Elfin, go fetch your cousins. They'll want to see these two before they go again," Gart called out to his son before leading the way further into the growing fort. The chamber had a large table covered in maps. "We've had reports of them just to the south. We found the group that you and Carling encountered just after you left us."

"There are more on the way, Uncle. The town of the Governor has grown very large, and there are more being brought over the sea every day. At the moment, they seem to be concentrating on the west. Here," Galen said, pointing where they had just come from. "The people there are organising themselves now, and I hope it is not too late for them."

"What about moving north? Are there any significant forces we need to be aware of?" Gart asked, his eyes shifting from where Galen was indicating to their own borders to the south.

"Not now, though we did go and try to see this morning. We saw a few of them, but they seem more concerned with making roads at this stage. It could be in preparation for later. You are going to need to be wary, Uncle," Galen told him.

"I remember the warning your mother gave me, Galen. And you, Carling; what do you see for our future?" Gart turned to Carling and found her dozing on a chair.

"It has been a very busy few moon cycles. I worry that it took more of a toll on her than she is willing to tell me," Galen said softly.

"She fought well?"

"Like no other warrior I have ever seen, Uncle," he said proudly, looking down on his wife and chuckling. "I am going to have to be careful if we ever get into a fight."

"Still no child," Gart stated. When he saw Galen's face, he added, "But she is still young yet. I am sure they will come soon."

"Perhaps once we are back home."

"No more adventures for you then, Galen?" Gart asked jovially, placing a hand on Galen's shoulder companionably.

"I will always be ready, Uncle. You just need to send word, and I will come running—if Carling will let me."

"I thank you for bringing this news. Our own with Foresight have given us the same warnings as your mother recently," Gart said, becoming serious once more.

"The Romans still have a few tribes to go through before they reach us. You may want to think about sending some of our people with the necessary abilities south to help our neighbours in delaying their arrival here."

"I think that is a good idea, my boy," Gart replied as the door opened.

Ru, Uven, and Arilith all walked through and greeted their brother. Galen crouched down in front of Carling and woke her gently. She blinked a minute before remembering where she was.

"I must be more tired than I thought," she said, stretching and standing.

"But still as beautiful as ever," Arilith said, the first to greet her.

"Don't let Ila hear you say that. She's already jealous enough," Uven said with a laugh.

"Is Ila jealous of me?" Carling asked him as she hugged Ru in turn.

"She doesn't like us discussing you," Ru told her.

"I have never given her any reason to be jealous," Carling said, a bit concerned. She had always thought she and Arilith's wife had gotten along.

"It is because this stupid idiot told her that you were his first love," Uven said, hugging her and picking her up at the same time.

"Put me down," Carling told him.

"Have you heard anything of Loc?" Ru asked her.

"Yes, I checked on them last night. He and Wolf have another wonderfully healthy and rambunctious litter of pups to contend with. And he could not be happier," she relayed brightly.

"That is good to hear. We worry about them. Before the change, I did offer to take both of them in and care for them," Ru told her.

"And I can imagine what our brother said to that." Carling laughed.

"How long are you here for? Are you back for good?" Uven asked them both.

"No, we are heading to the valley today. We have both been told it is time to go back," Galen told him, as he looked at Carling, happy that they would be going home.

"I visited Ma and Da two moons ago. They are both getting on but won't admit it," Ru said.

"We know," Galen replied.

"Do you want some company on the road. I could travel with you?" Ru asked.

"We have another way to travel. It doesn't take as much time as the road. Plus, won't Nila mind you leaving her with the children?" Carling asked.

"That's the reason he wants to get out. She is pregnant again." Arilith clapped him on the shoulder, laughing.

"How many is that now?" Galen asked with a chuckle.

"This will be number eleven," he said wearily. "But I love each and every one of them. Carling, is there any way you can help Nila stop getting pregnant? These two say that is beyond their knowledge."

"It is beyond mine also, Ru. You could just…you know…" Carling suggested with a hint of a smirk and raised eyebrow.

"But there is the problem. She is still the most beautiful woman in the world to me." He sighed.

Gart convinced Carling and Galen to stay for a meal before they left, and the brothers joined them. They spent a lovely couple of hours catching up on news and sharing their own from the south. Galen regaled them with stories of Carling in battle. When he looked over to her to confirm part of the story he was telling, he found her asleep again, her head down on her chest, hands clasped over her stomach.

"Time to get her home, Galen," Ru said from across the table.

"It is, but I don't want to wake her. She looks so peaceful."

"Call out to Red, then, or Violet—or any of the Ancestors. I am sure they will be happy to help," Ru said wisely.

"No need to call, Ru. We have been watching our daughter," Blue said, appearing in the centre of room.

"Welcome Ancestor," Gart greeted him.

"Gart, our blessings on your house. I would love nothing more than to stay and talk with you gentlemen, but we do need to get her home. She will rest and heal better in the confines of the valley," Blue told the gathered men.

"Heal?" Uven said, standing ready to go around the table and check on his sister.

"It is not an injury you can cure, Uven. It is a tiredness of her soul. The fighting she has done has affected her more than she realises, and the valley will help ease that," Blue informed them.

"I could go into her mind and help that way," Uven suggested.

"No. I know Red has been teaching you more on how to use your Mind Touch recently, but I would not go into my daughter's uninvited. You would not be prepared for how her mind works." Blue then turned to Galen, "Are you ready?"

"I am." Galen picked up their discarded packs and turned to his brothers. "Come visit us soon."

"We will, brother. Look after our sister, and give our greetings to Ma and Da," Ru told him, slapping him on the back as they hugged.

"Try and keep us away," Uven said.

"Keep well, Galen, and tell her to relax when she wakes," Arilith said as they clasped hands.

"I will have your chamber packed up and sent on to you," Gart told Galen.

"Thank you, Uncle, though I'm not sure there is much in there." He clasped his uncle's shoulder briefly before going to pick Carling up. Gently he lifted her into his arms, and she murmured a little at being disturbed. They each dropped a kiss on her head before Blue took Galen's shoulder and transported them to the valley.

No matter how many times in the last few weeks Carling had moved them about in the same manner, it still felt wrong to Galen. The sudden shift in position made him feel queasy, and it took a second to right himself again. He shifted Carling in his arms as Blue opened the door to the new room so he could place her inside.

"Not again! Are you ever going to bring her home conscious?" Tarl'a asked from the doorway.

"She is just sleeping, Tarl'a," Blue assured her. "Her mind and body are weary."

"If she would just stay in one place for longer than a few days, she would be fine," Tarl'a said as she fussed with the blankets, tucking her in as she had done as a child. She smoothed the blonde hair from Carling's face and kissed her forehead. When Tarl'a sat back, she had a small secretive smile on her face.

Blue, who was standing behind Galen, shook his head at her, so Tarl'a kept the insight to herself.

"Do you want something to eat, Son?" Tarl'a asked as she stood stiffly and greeted him.

"No Ma. We've just eaten with Uncle Gart and our brothers. The boys all send their best wishes."

"It is lovely to hear. Come, let her sleep, and tell us all about what you two have been up to," Tarl'a said, taking his arm and leading him out.

The seasons were turning, and the nights were getting cold. Galen banked up the fire in the hearth before he joined his wife under the blankets. Carling had slept on during the day and was still asleep. It worried him somewhat, but Blue had assured him that it was necessary for her to heal. He pulled her closer and kissed her cheek as he snuggled in with her.

"You're cold," she murmured sleepily.

"We're losing the summer," he whispered into her ear.

"I have been having the most amazing dreams."

"Do you want to talk about them?"

"I don't know how to describe what I saw. I know it was me, but it wasn't. I saw all my possible future selves," Carling told him.

"Are they as beautiful as you?" Galen asked her.

"We are all the same. We will not change."

"That will make it easier for me to find you." Galen smiled. "What did you see in these dreams?"

"Sorrow and loss, but love. So much love. Our lives are so intertwined with so many we know now. Uncle Gart I saw twice over, always my uncle. Ru and Uven and some we have not met yet. But always you are there."

"Of course. Did you think that I would let a little thing like dying keep us apart, my love?" He kissed her again.

"No, especially as Order bound us together with the lights from myself."

"Is that what the cord was made from?" Galen asked with a little wonder.

"A little was transferred to you that day," she told him with a nod.

"There is part of you in me?"

"Yes." Carling turned in his arms and lifted his hand from her. "See." She traced a finger over the skin in the back of his hand and a light sprung from it. "Mother told me the afternoon before our betrothal. It was necessary so that we can have children. I am only part human, after all. But even then, it does not seem to have worked."

"Give it time, Carling. As you say, you are part Sentinel. It may take longer for you to conceive." He took her hand and placed it on her belly. "One day it will swell with our child."

Carling felt her stomach and tried to imagine what the life that would grow there would feel like. Under her palm, she felt a tiny fluttering, like a butterfly caught in her hands. She pulled her hand away, thinking she was imagining it and then slowly placed it back. The same fluttering came back to her, and she searched for the tiny speck of life inside her. So small but growing strong, she found it, and she felt love for the child already.

"That one day may not be far away," she said with wonder, taking his hand and placing it on her stomach under her shirt. With her help, she let him feel the child that was growing inside her.

"So small," he said in awe, coming up on his elbow and looking down into her eyes. His own were large at the touch of the child. "I had begun to worry."

"I know you had. I was not fully asleep this morning when you talked to Uncle Gart."

"A child. Our child." He smiled and kissed her ardently.

"Our child." Carling laughed at his enthusiasm.

"When? How long?" Galen asked excitedly.

"I think at the end of spring."

Galen's hand was still on her stomach as he felt the small fluttering of the heartbeat. "A girl as beautiful as her mother, with blonde hair and soft blue eyes," he said, almost a whisper.

"Have you discovered Foresight?" Carling laughed up at her husband.

"I can't tell you how I know, I just know," he said, grinning.

Carling woke to the sound of male voices talking low outside, the companionable sound of two men working together. She rolled over and rested her hand on her stomach. Feeling the heartbeat that was there, she smiled to herself. It was an amazing feeling, the small child growing inside her. She rose and headed out the door of the new room to find Galen and Mailcon looking up at the roof of the house.

"It's all going to need to come off, Da, and be replaced completely before winter comes."

"With you here now, we'll get it done," Mailcon replied, crossing his arms over his chest.

"I could just fix it for you," Carling offered, slipping her arm around Galen's waist.

"No, thank you, Carling. I think we will do this the proper way," her father told her.

"Let's not be too hasty with her suggestion yet," Galen said slowly.

"No, Son. Good, honest, hard work never hurt anyone, and you'll appreciate it more. It was a lovely offer, Carling, but not this time, and not while this is still our home." He clapped his son on his shoulder then went to kiss his daughter. "The thatch won't cut itself. Tell your Ma that we will be back later."

"I will," Carling told him.

"I haven't told him yet," Galen whispered, having waited for his father to move away a little.

"Tell him while you work. Enjoy your time with him, Galen. And he is right about the roof. We will be here a long time." She smiled up at him.

"I will then." He leaned down to kiss her, then bent to pick up the scythe and reluctantly left her side to catch up to Mailcon.

Carling watched as he jogged and immediately began to talk with his father as they walked down the track towards the forest and the field beyond. Turning, she went to look for Tarl'a and found her coming out of the house with a bundle in her hands.

"Good morning, Ma," she greeted her.

"Good morning. How are you feeling, Carling?" Tarl'a asked and hugged her daughter.

"I'm fine. Feeling much more like myself than I did yesterday."

"Good. I don't want you doing much for the next couple of days until you have rested properly. Inside you will find some cakes I saved for you. Bring them out and sit with me while I work."

"Thank you, Ma." Carling ducked in and found the little berry and crushed grain cakes she loved so much and brought them out. They were still warm, and she savoured their taste, finally feeling like she was home.

Tarl'a was stitching a piece of fabric and Carling watched her work. Sewing was one thing that she always had trouble with, finding she didn't have the patience for the small stitches. Her Ma's fingers deftly pushed the bone needle through the fabric with speed and accuracy.

"What are you making?" Carling asked as she saw how small the piece was that she was working on.

"A gift," Tarl'a said with a smile at her daughter.

"It's awfully small. Is it for one of the boy's children? I know, it's for Ru's newest child. Nila is pregnant again," Carling exclaimed.

"Yes, I know. Galen told us last night while you slept. So many grandchildren I have. With Ru's now eleven and Uven's five. Also, Arilith and Ila's four that call me Granny. So many children." Tarl'a sighed happily down at her work.

"Loc and Wolf have had another litter also. I counted five when I looked in on them," Carling informed her before taking another bite of the cake.

"Another five," Tarl'a looked up at Carling and stilled her hands for a moment. "We are so blessed."

"Is there something wrong, Ma?" Carling asked.

"No, I'm just waiting," she said calmly, a smile tugging at the corners of her mouth.

"You know. You saw?" Carling asked.

"I did—yesterday when I tucked you in. Carling, I am so happy for you and Galen." She rose from her seat and came to her daughter. "A child to bless your union. I see three more. All healthy and hearty. Beautiful children."

"Thank you, Ma. Galen said that this one will be a girl. He says he isn't sure how he knows, just that it will be a girl and beautiful."

"I would have words with Order if I were you. That bond she used to tie you together may have passed a few new abilities to him," Tarl'a said, giving a knowing wink.

"I know. The words Order used in our betrothal were the key. That we would be equals. How can we be equals if he does not have the abilities that I have, or at least some?"

"He is to become a Sentinel?" Tarl'a asked curiously.

"No. But he will join them when he passes, just as you and Da will. Certain abilities have been passed to him, like Hiding, Foresight, Seek, and Stealth. Also Mind Touch, but he is unaware of them. I have not told him he has them, though he has been using them without knowing for some time now. Sometimes I suspect he does, that Red may have told him, but others I am sure he has no idea," Carling said, her thoughts tumbling from her.

"Maybe you should tell him. If he has them, then he needs to be trained," Tarl'a suggested.

"I didn't know how to. The fact that Order changed him without his knowledge, without telling him, may upset him."

"With the news that you are having his child, I don't think anything will upset him right now. I saw his smile this morning when he came to eat with us. It was all I could do to keep myself quiet. I have not told your Da yet, that was another difficult thing I had to do."

"Galen is going to tell him while they work."

"It is so good to have you both home. Your Da has been finding doing these jobs more and more difficult lately. He has put off fixing the roof all summer," Tarl'a said with a sigh.

"We are back for good, Ma. I am back to learn from the Guardian of the Stones."

"I could think of no one better to hand the title to than you, my daughter," Tarl'a said proudly, reaching up with her hand and cupping Carling's face. "I am so very pleased you have come back to us."

"So am I, Ma." Carling beamed.

"Once I am finished with this stitching, we'll go up to the stones and give your news to your mother and father. I think they will be wanting to take a bit more interest in this child. It was very hard for them after you were born, and they had to give you up."

"I understand it was." Carling placed a hand on her stomach and could not even begin to imagine how hard it must have been for them to do that.

"But they have made up for it since. Yellow visits quite often to bring me news of you. You frustrated her quite a bit while you in the south. And more recently with the troubles in the west. She was so worried you would be hurt." Tarl'a told her seriously as her needle flashed through her work.

"It has been a funny thing to go from one set of parents to two. Both of whom love me and worry equally."

"Now your wandering is over. We can rest a bit easier, Carling. And yes, your Da and I have worried as well. We worry about all our children and now our grandchildren."

"Have you seen this child's future, Ma?" Carling asked.

"You have the ability. You should use it."

"I have a fear. While we were in the west, a goddess of the people there gave me a warning. She said that he will use one of our children against me. I'm scared."

"Shall we go see now then, and rest your mind a bit?" Tarl'a said, standing and putting the sewing down. She reached for Carling's hand, and she took it, together starting up the hill.

The climb was a slow one as Tarl'a had to stop regularly to catch her breath. Carling was patient and waited for her Ma, but worried about the state of her health. Tarl'a caught one of her concerned gazes as they reached the top.

"I am fine. It is just the passage of time catching up with me. It happens to us all," Tarl'a told her.

"As long as that is all it is, Ma. If there was something wrong, you would tell me, wouldn't you?"

"Of course I would, my girl. Now come, let's see the future for your child."

Together they walked around the rocks and headed for the entrance. Before she entered Tarl'a touched the stones on either side.

Into the centre they both walked, and Carling joined her mother on the soft grass. Tarl'a closed her eyes and tilted her head back a little, accepting the touch of the sun's warm rays on her face. Carling watched as her mother's expression changed and shifted. She could see her eyes moving under the lids, rapidly following something until they fluttered open, and her focus trained itself onto Carling.

"I was confused for a little while. I thought I was seeing you as a child running through the meadows. She will be the image of her mother. Such a happy and gorgeous child, not as shy as you were though. Very outgoing and happy. But there is a darkness I sensed around her as she grows. It is something you will need to keep watch for, Carling. We should call the Ancestors and get them to reinforce the protections around the valley," Tarl'a told her.

"Thank you, Ma. Would you like me to call them?" Carling asked.

"I am not feeble yet. I can still perform my duties," Tarl'a said, but accepted Carling's hands to help her rise from the ground.

Carling stepped back to the edge of the circle and waited for her Ma to send out the call.

Her arms raised and her head thrown back, Tarl'a called out into the morning, "Ancestors, hear me. Come to us here at the sacred stones. Your council is wanted."

The words always puzzled Carling, especially now. They sounded so demanding but were always spoken so gently.

Slowly the Sentinels came in ones and twos, and finally Red arrived. Each entered the circle, and each stood before a stone. Carling felt she should join them, but instead hovered near Tarl'a, awkward and out of place. There was no stone for her to stand in front of.

"Our Guardian has called, and we have answered," Red intoned, and they stepped forward to greet Tarl'a and Carling.

"Ancestors, thank you for coming. We have a request, but the news must come from Carling first," Tarl'a said as she held Carling's hand.

Carling looked at Yellow and Blue and began to feel shy before speaking. She smiled at them and then took a breath. "I am pregnant," she told them quietly.

Yellow was the first to react and pulled her into an embrace, only releasing her to be enfolded by her father, Blue.

"This is joyous news," he said to her as he kissed her forehead. He released her to be congratulated by the others.

Last of all, Red kissed her cheek and held her close for a moment. "So, what is the request that you have to make?"

"I have seen a darkness around this child, and Carling has had a warning that Chaos will attempt to use one of her children against her. We hoped that you could reinforce the protections on this valley to keep the children safe," Tarl'a requested.

"Who gave you the warning, Carling?" Yellow asked.

"It was a goddess of the west tribes. Her name is Blodeuwedd."

"I'll go talk to this goddess. She may have another insight for us as to when," Violet said and left them immediately.

"We will, of course, look at the protections and build them up. But Carling, you could have easily done this. Why ask?" Green asked her.

"Because I wish you all to be involved. I wish all our children to know you. You will be part of their family, and we request your protection of them."

"That is something you did not need to request. It is already a given that they shall be protected. The line that you have started is important. Chaos will not be able to touch these children," Red vowed to her. He rose into the air and swept along the perimeter of the valley. Orange followed his brother on the other side.

"The girl will be born in the late spring. We must make sure everything is ready, Tarl'a," Yellow said taking her arm.

"I have already begun the sewing. I am sure that the cradle will keep Galen busy through the wintertime," Tarl'a told her, and Carling felt the companionship these two had come to feel over her.

Red and Orange returned, and their faces were puzzled.

"There is evidence of tampering with the protection. I found a small gap where this ridge dips down to the river. It is only the smallest of holes, and I have fixed it. I cannot tell how it even got there as there is no indication of who has done it," Red said.

"Could it be from when we first put it in place?" Indigo asked, coming forward and taking Orange by the hand.

"No. I looked as well, as soon as Red found it. There are definite marks of tampering," Orange told her.

"There have been no strangers here recently. Our visitors were light over the summer," Tarl'a told them.

"I suggest we all place our own down, you also, Carling. It cannot hurt to be prepared for anything," Blue said.

"We are in agreement, then?" Green asked around the gathered group.

"We still need to wait for Violet. She might have found something out," Yellow told him.

"She is on her way," Green told the group as he looked out over the valley.

Violet reappeared and reported what Blodeuwedd had said to her. "The prophecy, as they call it, was seen by her. All she can tell me is that he manages to connect with the child and to keep watch."

"It is not much to go on. Those gods can be vague. They do not practice their arts as we do," Red said quickly. "We must get this protection on the valley as soon as possible."

"We will, Red. Be patient, Brother," Orange told him.

"I will leave you to your work, Ancestors. This is something I cannot help with. Carling, do not overdo things. You are still recovering," said Tarl'a as she let Yellow's arm go.

"I promise, Ma. But a protection is something else, only part of the energy comes from within," Carling told her. "Do you need a hand to go down?"

"When I have trouble getting out of my bed in the morning is when you can aid me up and down this hill, young lady. I am not that old and infirm yet." Tarl'a smiled up at her daughter. "But thank you for caring." She kissed her cheek and left them in the circle.

"I worry about her sometimes. This coming winter will be hard on her, my daughter," Yellow said, coming to her side and watching as Tarl'a headed around the rocks.

"I will look after her, Mother. Now shall we get to work?" Carling asked the gathered group.

"Just a moment, Carling. You said that only part of the protection comes from within. Are you sure about that?" Red asked with an eyebrow raised.

"Yes, I am very sure, Uncle. The other parts come from the universe," she told him.

"What protection are you going to use? I only ask because the ones we have used in the past have come fully from ourselves." Red's curiosity was evident.

"It is the only one I know. It is to stop unfriendly eyes looking into the valley, by all means, either physically from the hill or on the mental plain. They will not be able to focus on one person. In fact, they will not see anyone in this valley. It will appear to be empty," Carling told him.

"This is a new one to us. I think it might be useful to you in your next lives if some of this information was to be recorded at some point," Red told her.

"It is a very interesting idea. We will have to talk more about it, but later. Now we have to set this protection up. If you would all please start, and I will lay mine down on top."

"Until later then, Niece. I am looking forward to many a long discussion about your abilities during the coming winter." Red winked at her and took to the air, heading out.

"Typical Red. He has been harping on about your abilities since you were born. But I agree, it may be a very wise decision." Blue kissed her forehead once more before taking off after his brother.

One by one they left to place their own special type of protection on the valley. In her mind, she could see each layer as it settled on the valley in a large dome of colours that dazzled her eyes. Finally, it was her turn, and she lifted lightly off the ground and held her hands out to her sides.

She called the protection down from the universe, and it answered her wishes, settling a final golden, glittering layer over the top of the Sentinels own. As she landed, they stood with her down inside the valley.

"The universe is alive?" Violet asked with a hushed voice.

"Yes, Sister, it is. You did not know this?" Carling asked, puzzled.

"No, we did not. How is it you know?" Blue asked her.

"The Universe gave birth to two beings. Chaos, who it found to be destructive, so it created Order, born from Chaos's mess. Order has been helped by the Universe to control and contain Chaos, and that is what her last task is. When I confine Chaos in the place that is being prepared, Order will be there to contain her brother. You cannot have one without the other."

"So, when the Ultimate One comes and destroys Chaos, Order will also pass?" Yellow asked.

"The Universe will be as it should have been from the beginning. Everything in equilibrium. There shall always be those that will have evil in their hearts, but also, they will be balanced by those with love. It is the plan of the universe to have more love in the world than there is hate. For those who are strong to be protectors rather than domineering and ruling. For love is stronger than hate." Carling took a deep breath and started to sag.

Blue and Red were at her side each holding an arm.

"I think that is enough, Carling. Time to get you back to Tarl'a," Blue said gently.

"I did not know I knew that," she said weakly.

Blue picked her up in his arms. "The universe knew what it was doing when it created you, Daughter. We were just the vessels to bring you life. Now your earthbound mother will have our hides if we don't get you back to her." He began the short walk to the house.

Chapter Twenty-One

The winter was a hard one, with snow that piled up around the house in deep drifts. Before the worst of the weather had drawn in, the little family group was visited by two very important visitors. Loc and Wolf came and were made welcome. Their pups had already left the den and the pair had journeyed to reconnect with their human family. Carling was very pleased to see them, and she took the opportunity of the long winter to help Galen learn the ability of Whispering. From that moment on, he spent a lot of time talking with Loc. He told her that it was the best gift she could have given him, apart from their coming child.

When the snows set in, it was day after day of whiteout conditions. It fell in great icy sheets and nearly covered the house completely. Every morning Galen would have to dig out around the large wood pile he and Mailcon had managed to set aside for the winter. Inside the house was warm and dry. The new roof was holding up and they had enough stores set aside to last, even with the two hungry wolves.

They all lived in the one room, the original part of the house. And to keep them from fractiousness, Carling told them stories of her time in the south. There were lots of tales of their childhood as well. It was a lovely time for Carling, and she was happy as her belly grew. She would hum away to herself as she sat, her eyes on the fire and her hands protectively on her stomach. Galen would watch her with the love he had bursting from his heart. She would turn her eyes to him and blush with how he looked at her.

Winter was not a good time for Tarl'a, as Yellow had warned Carling. She felt the cold more than she ever had, and her hands began to swell and were painful to move. Carling would sit and rub them for her, drawing out the pain without telling her she was doing it. The gnarled hands had trouble gripping the needle she loved to use, and soon she gave up sewing altogether. Under her tuition, Carling picked it up and became a competent seamstress. It was not the magnificent work her mother produced, but it would hold together and was useable. Carling also didn't want to disappoint her Ma, by telling her that she could have made the garment without the use of a needle.

It was not until well into spring that the snow began to melt and give way to the sun. The wind was still cool, and Carling was feeling very heavy and encumbered under her distended belly. She would sit with a blanket about her shoulders and watch as Loc and Wolf bounded among the emerging grass and snow drifts that still stubbornly held onto the ground. Another litter was on the way for the pair, and they were ecstatic at the thought. They would head out into the forest with Mailcon and Galen and disappear for the day searching for a den to have them in, declining Tarl'a and Mailcon's invitation to have them at the house.

Carling was very much looking forward to the time when she would have her own child. She was an active child that would kick and push on her stomach. Each morning she would sit and connect with the baby nestled under her heart, making sure that the little girl knew she was loved and cared for. She showed her images of the people who were waiting for her arrival. There was a flicker of consciousness within the child's mind, and she didn't push for it to come to life fully just yet.

This child would be like any other. There would be no extra abilities or anything else that would mark her out as being anything special. For that, Carling was grateful. She would have a normal life. She would grow and love and have children of her own without any dangers or extra responsibilities. But the dark cloud still hung over her.

It was as spring was turning to summer, and finally the last of the snow had melted from the valley and the hills that surrounded it, that the child decided it was time to meet the world properly. The first pains were just another annoyance for Carling, not realising that her daughter was in a hurry to be born. To ease them, Carling had gone for a walk through the meadow to the brook. She was following it in a slow waddle towards the river and where Mailcon and Galen were working. Being confined to the house was starting to really annoy her, but then she was at that stage of the pregnancy when everything was an irritation.

The sharp pain continued and was getting stronger, not less as she had hoped. As one large pain caused her fall to her knees and cry out, her waters broke. Looking around as the pain eased slightly, she saw she was quite a way from the house and nowhere near where her husband was.

"Mother, help me," she called out to Yellow and within moments she was there.

"It is all right, my daughter. I will get you back to the house and your Ma. It is only fitting she help you, she birthed you from my body." Taking her arm gently, Yellow transported them to the house and then helped her inside. "Tarl'a it is time."

"I didn't think this child was ever going to come. All right Carling, we shall get you comfortable and then have a look."

Tarl'a took over from there, ordering Yellow around to assist her. The women were soon joined by Violet and Indigo, who sat either side of Carling, holding onto her hands.

"I have sent Orange to fetch Galen," Indigo said quietly to her.

"We don't need him just yet, Indigo," Tarl'a said as she checked on the progress.

The door burst open, and Galen stood framed as he stared at the scene of Carling down by the fire, leaning back on her elbows, her legs bent and apart.

"Out!" Tarl'a yelled at him. "Stay out until you are needed."

"Better do as she says. This is women's business." Red was there with his hand on Galen's shoulder, pulling him out of the house and shutting the door.

The progression of the labour quickened after that, and Tarl'a was not happy. She was concerned that there might be damage done to Carling, but she did not voice her worries. She spoke to her daughter calmly so as not to frighten her and got her to listen. But the need to push was too great for Carling, and she obeyed her body rather than her mother.

It was only a matter of minutes before the baby was born, rubbed down with clean cloths and wrapped up, then placed on her stomach. Carling held her child for the first time, and the tiny bundle let out a great cry announcing her arrival. She did not notice what Tarl'a was doing as she looked into the face of her own daughter for the first time and caught the tiny hand that was waving around.

"You might as well let him in now," Tarl'a told them. Violet went to the door, and she didn't even have to say a word.

Galen was at her side in a few strides, kneeling with Carling and their daughter. He kissed his wife and then the tiny head of the baby. Mailcon entered next with Red, who had fetched him from where they were working. Red knelt on her other side and placed a gentle hand on the head of the child.

"Have you chosen a name for the little one?" Red asked softly.

"We have Ancestor," Galen said. "She is to be known as Claire."

"A very good choice," Red grinned. "I hereby claim you, Claire, as a child of my line. My blessings on you, daughter, and my protection for your whole life. May it be long and happy." He leaned down and kissed the baby's head, then kissed Carling on the cheek. "Well done, Carling. Congratulations. My love to you both and your daughter." He stood and made room for Mailcon to greet his granddaughter, to be followed by Yellow and Blue to give their blessings.

Soon the other Ancestors had all arrived and they came in turn to see the child and bless her. Just as Carling was about to hand the child to Galen to hold, a brilliant white light shone into the room and before her stood Order. The great Being raised a hand that swam with points of light. "The first of many children to bear the likeness of The One True Child. The line shall carry it down. With each generation only one shall come who resembles our most favoured child. Our blessings for her future, our love unlimited. Hail our One True Child, the mother of the line. Our daughter Carling and our son Galen, your lives have changed. Let your love flow for this child and the others to come," she bade them.

"Thank you, Order. We accept your blessings and your love," Galen said, standing to face her.

"Galen, you have been blessed with our most precious child. The other gifts we have given you now bloom and need to be used. We give you full use of those. You will need them to protect your family," Order said, stepping closer and placing her hand on his head.

Galen's eyes widened as the knowledge poured into his mind and settled in the correct places. Order removed her glittering hand and Galen fell to one knee. "Great Light, greatest of Beings, I promise I shall protect my family to the last drop of my blood, for now and evermore. Carling and our children are my greatest charge," he vowed solemnly.

"As it should be, Galen. Now rise our son, we do not need such fealty, only your love," Order said with a smile.

"You have that, Order."

"Good and done," Order said with a nod.

Out beyond the house somewhere, a bell peeled out in answer to the declaration. Carling remembered hearing it when she and Galen had made their vows to each other, and when Violet had changed Loc's lineage to Indigo. It puzzled her, and then the answer came, like it was whispered on the wind from the universe itself. It was the universe acknowledging the great vows and decisions that would change things. It was its way of agreeing to the vow.

"I leave you with the love of your family around you, Carling. Be at peace and enjoy being a mother. But also know the time for the great meeting is coming to hand. You must ready yourself and be prepared for when it happens," Order told her.

"I will Great Light," Carling said, holding her child close, fear creeping into the edges of her heart.

Order left them and soon the baby was taken from her arms, and everyone shooed from the room, so Tarl'a and Yellow could help Carling clean up and change. Very carefully they helped her sit comfortably and then they returned the baby to her to feed. As she looked at the tiny baby at her breast, she pushed the thoughts of Chaos from her mind.

The baby grew, and as the seasons changed, more of little Claire's personality came through. It soon became evident that Galen and Mailcon were her favourites. But there was also another that could make her laugh and giggle, and Carling often caught Red at the baby's bedside when she was supposed to sleep.

"Don't deny me my right to see her, Carling," Red said with a smile as he held the child's hand after she had told him off.

"I do not deny you, Red, only not when she is supposed to be asleep," Carling told him.

"I used to come and see you too when you were this size. You don't remember do you?"

Carling sat down beside the Sentinel and looked at him.

"You would have made a wonderful father, Red," she said to him gently.

"Thank you. I like to think I am a wonderful father to my line. This family is my work and my focus. Carling, you are just as much my daughter as Galen is my son. There has always been a special place for you in my heart, child. I watched over and protected you while you grew. I have watched you blossom into the most beautiful woman in the world and now…now you are a mother. I will watch over her, just as I did you. I will also watch out for you in your next life."

"I accept your protection over her and over myself." Carling picked up his hand and kissed his cheek. "Of all the Sentinels, Uncle, I feel the closest to you. We have always been able to talk, even if we do not agree on some things. I would not want to lose you from our lives."

"You will never lose me, Carling. We are tied in some unknown way. I do not mean in the way you and Galen are, but more like…"

"Like brother and sister?" she asked.

"Yes. Brother and sister is a good way to put it. I feel so protective of you—I have from the moment you were born," Red told her with a smile.

"Then stay with her, Brother. Watch over her as she sleeps and give her sweet dreams. But please get her to sleep." Carling smiled at him.

"I will, Sister." He grinned back.

Carling let his hand go and kissed her child. As she got to the door she turned and saw Red still holding Claire's hand and singing softly to her.

Between Tarl'a, Yellow, Violet, Indigo and Red, and Carling feeding Claire, Galen had to grab his chances to hold his daughter. Carling loved to see him talking and playing with Claire. He was so gentle with her and jealously guarded the time he spent with her.

With the summer came visitors of family and travellers seeking to see the sacred stones and speak to the Ancestors. The winter had slowed Tarl'a down a great deal, and the pains in her joints continued. Carling did as much as she could to relieve them for her. She assisted her mother with their trips up to the stones, and as the season went on, found she was taking the lead and letting her mother rest.

Late in the season, with Claire sitting on her knee, she looked up at Carling and said, "I think it is time for you to take over. Without your help every day, I cannot make it up there. I think one more trip is necessary to transfer Guardianship to you."

"Are you sure, Ma?" Carling asked, setting aside the sewing she was working on.

"I am. I can look after Claire while you go to the Stones. That is, if I can get Galen to let her go."

"He is her father, Ma. He loves her and she loves him. They have a bond, I have noticed. I can't get her to giggle the way he does." Carling smiled

"Fathers and daughters are like that. You were the same with your Da, and whenever Blue held you there was no one else in the room," Tarl'a told her.

"I thought they stayed away while I was small?"

"As you grew, they stepped back. I could not deny them the rights of parents. Claire is so like you as a baby." Tarl'a looked down at the bundle in her arms and smiled.

"Red told me he used to sit with me and play."

"He did. At first Mailcon did not understand why he was so fascinated by you, but I could see he loved you and would not hurt you. He used to wait until the boys would be out and playing before coming to sit with you. He became very good at babysitting."

"And as I got older?" Carling asked.

"He would watch from afar. He did not like having to pull back from being so close to you. That is why he was always there when you started to join me up at the stones. Are you worried about something with Red?" Tarl'a suddenly asked.

"No, I have talked to him about this. He is sitting with Claire as she sleeps. I feel better knowing that he protects her when Galen and I cannot."

"I can see it would be a comfort," Tarl'a said nodding, understanding Carling's fear of the dark shadow that hung over her daughter. She lifted Claire to her shoulder and patted her back. "We will go up tomorrow."

"If it is hard for you, I can fly you up."

"I think I would like to try that." She smiled at Carling.

Before they got the chance to go up the hill to the stones, more visitors arrived. Down the track, Uven and Ru came riding, and racing through the long grass came Loc and Wolf, followed by their puppies, all nearly fully grown.

"We were told to come home," Ru said, dismounting and hugging his mother. "Violet was most insistent that we make the journey."

"It is always good to see my boys," Tarl'a said, hugging Uven next.

Loc and Wolf were greeted just as warmly, while the pups stood back, unsure of the humans around them. Carling came out with Claire, and she soon lost the baby as Ru and Uven both insisted on a cuddle with their niece. While she was being taken care of, Carling greeted the wolves.

"Are you well, littermate?" Carling asked formally of her brother.

"We are littermate. We bring our pups to greet you. Indigo tells us the one is in this litter," he said proudly.

"I would be pleased to meet your offspring."

"They are not used to humans, pack-mate, and are a bit timid. If you would sit, they will come to you," Wolf said, nudging her hand.

Carling did as she was told and sat on the ground. With encouragement from their mother and father, the puppies slowly drew nearer to her. Soon she was surrounded by five happy wolf young as they licked and sniffed at her.

"You smell like Father," one said.

"You have a pup?" another asked.

"I do. Can I introduce her to you and your pups?" Carling asked Wolf.

"I would be honoured to meet your young pup," Wolf told her as she came to sit with Carling.

Carling turned to see Galen taking Claire from Uven and walking towards her. He knelt beside Wolf and held the baby in his arms.

"This is our pup, pack-mate," he said and allowed her to sniff the child.

Loc padded around and stood in front of his brother and niece. "She is beautiful, brother. Just like her mother." He then turned and made a noise to one of the pups.

Half the size of her parents and with a coat of silvery grey, a she-pup came running, and sat between them.

"Pup, this child's child will become important to your pup's pup."

The cub sniffed the baby and Claire reached out for the small wolf. Her hand connected with the head, and out in the distance a bell peeled.

"It is done," Carling said. "The connection is made and will be recognised in the future."

Galen reached out and gently extracted his daughter's hand from the pup's fur. He scratched the ears of the young wolf, and it gently bit his hand, then bounded off to play with its littermates.

"She is young yet, Brother," Loc told him with a suggestion of laughter.

"Carling, it is time. The Ancestors are waiting for us," Tarl'a called to her daughter.

"I'm coming, Ma," Carling replied as she stood.

"What's happening?" Galen asked, still on his knees.

"I am passing the Guardianship to Carling," Tarl'a told them simply. Mailcon was at her side and holding her hand.

"Are you sure, my love?" he asked her gently.

"I am, my love. I'm very sure. It is time to pass the torch onto Carling." She turned to her daughter. "I am ready, Carling."

They walked together to the base of the hill and the beginning of the trail. While the others all started up the track, Tarl'a and Carling waited at the bottom.

"Hold on, Ma, and don't look down," Carling told her as she put her arms around her mother. Lifting off gently they rose into the air, and she smiled at the sight of her mother with her eyes closed. "Ma, have a look."

Slowly Tarl'a's eyes opened, and she looked around. They were higher than the hill, and they could see far into the distance. Tarl'a gasped at the sight. She turned her head, trying to take it all in before they descended to the stones. "It is so beautiful," she said with awe.

"It is. I think the Sentinels kept the best lands for themselves. Our home is in the middle of all this wonder," Carling told her.

"Thank you, Carling. Thank you for showing me."

"You're welcome. Anytime you wish to come back up just let me know." Carling laughed a little.

"Once will be enough. The idea of all that space under me makes me nervous," Tarl'a admitted.

"The stones beckon us, Ma." Carling began to drop down slowly so her Ma could still see the magnificent sight until they reached the rocks. They stood there for a while as they waited for the others to join them. Loc came first, and he sat panting patiently waiting. The rest arrived together, as they went at the same pace as Mailcon.

Behind them the Sentinels came, all in a line, and followed the family into the circle. They placed themselves between the stones while Carling and Tarl'a stood facing each other in the centre. The family arranged themselves around the pair.

"Ancestors be my witness. I, Tarl'a, daughter of Red's line, Guardian of the Stones, do relinquish my role. Though the daughter that stands before me is not a direct descendant, she is of my family. The One True Child, Carling, daughter of Yellow and Blue, foster daughter to Tarl'a and Mailcon, wife of Galen, who is a son of Red's line, shall be my successor. Do you accept this woman as Guardian of the Stones?" Tarl'a asked formally.

"I, Red, speak for those that you call Ancestors. We, the Sentinels of Order, do accept Carling, The One True Child, to be your successor. Though she is not of my line, I have long watched over her—as have we all—and long have I loved her as if she were of my line. The children of Galen, my son, and Carling will be of my line and the line will continue and survive. Our blessings on you, Tarl'a. Long have you guarded our sacred stones. Our blessings on you, Mailcon, who have supported our daughter. May your life together be happy and full. Our love and our thanks we give you for your dedicated service. We have but one question to ask. Carling, One True Child, do you accept this role to commit your life to the guardianship of our most sacred of places?" Red asked her.

"I, Carling, daughter of Yellow and Blue, foster daughter of Tarl'a and Mailcon and One True Child, do accept the role of Guardian of the Stones. I promise to guide those seeking your wisdom and to tell only the truth to those seeking answers. I promise to dedicate my life to you, the Ancestors, the Sentinels of this land." Carling said, giving her vow very seriously.

"We accept your promises and do hereby name you Guardian of the Stones." Red stepped away from his place and came to stand beside them. "The transfer is complete. Daughter of my line, you have our thanks and blessings."

"Thank you, my Ancestor. It has been my honour," Tarl'a said to him.

Life settled down after the ceremony. The valley became quiet as the visitors left and the seasons turned once more. Carling and Galen both loved and adored their little girl, watching her grow every day. The routine they found to be easy and sweet, working with their parents and being a family. She did not miss the road or the excitement that had come with it. Home was the most important place to her, but she did worry about Galen.

Having been used to travelling where and when he wanted, she was not sure he was happy staying in one place. A fact that was confirmed for her when an urgent message came from Uven that Galen was needed by Gart. Carling did not argue, or even try to keep him at home. She saw he needed to go and be active once more in the politics of the land. So, she let him go.

For the whole of the winter, he was away from them. They could be together in other ways, but it was not the same. She soon stopped reaching out to him in their dreams and became sad and withdrawn. Not even Claire could comfort her. The little girl was nearly one and was fast developing for her age, pulling herself up on things and crawling. Red was a constant visitor at her side during these times she felt low, though she did not acknowledge him.

The Sentinel was becoming worried and called out to her family for help. He himself set out to find Galen, and what he saw, he did not like. Galen was drinking with a woman wrapped around him and laughing at something she had said.

"For a man who swore he loved his wife and child, you are looking like they don't even exist," Red said on the other side of the table from him.

"Ancestor, pull up a chair and have yourself a drink," Galen slurred loudly.

"I would rather not. Do you know what is happening with Carling right now?" he asked, leaning on the table.

"I check in. It seems to me she is not missing me much. She stopped our contact," he said, becoming sullen and pushing the woman away.

"Carling needs you. She is slipping away."

"What do you mean 'slipping away'? Is she ill?"

"In a way," Red told him. "She is finding it hard without you there. She does not talk or laugh. She does not play with Claire or even seem to notice the child is there. She is not eating either. It is like she has just stopped."

"She told me to go help our Uncle. Carling knew I would be gone all winter," Galen said belligerently.

"Yes, but she did not want to let you go. She saw the signs of your restlessness and knew she had to. Now I find you here with this woman?"

"Just a bit of fun, Ancestor."

"You do not deserve her, Galen. You find comfort in another's arms."

"Carling won't let me in. She has refused me time and time again. I got the message. She does not want me anymore," Galen said angrily. Slamming his cup down on the table, he stood to face his Ancestor. "So now maybe the way is clear for you to step in my place."

"What does that mean?"

"I have seen the way you look at my wife. The way you have always looked at her, Ancestor. You may have her fooled about only loving her as family, but you love and covet her. Now you are welcome to her," Galen yelled, his face going red with anger.

Red reached across the table and grasped Galen around the neck of his tunic. Within a flash, they had disappeared and reappeared in a large room. Galen recognised it from the descriptions Carling had given him. Red had brought him to their home.

The Sentinel pushed him away and he landed heavily on the polished floor, skidding a good way till his back hit the wall. Red was fuming and angry, going the same colour as his name. He paced back and forth in front of Galen, trying to get his anger under control.

"Tell me I am wrong, Ancestor," Galen said as he got to his feet, his fist balled together ready for a fight.

"You are wrong," Red rounded on him. "I love Carling, yes. She is my niece and sister Sentinel. I have protected and watched over her whole life, but I do not love her that way. I am destined to be alone of the Sentinels. Love in that way is denied to me. But I can love in other ways and do so with my whole heart. I adore Carling, just as I adore Claire. You are throwing away the love of your life. Why? Carling thinks you have forgotten them, that you do not wish to come back to them. I have been trying to get through to her for the past few weeks, but she ignores us all. She is slipping away in her mind, Galen, pulling back and feeling unloved. She will die without your love."

"A person cannot die if they do not feel loved," Galen scoffed.

"Carling can. You forget who she is, Son. You forget what is most important in her life—love. She may be the bravest and fiercest of warriors, she may have the most abilities the universe can bestow, but without the special love that you feed her, she is nothing. Her life and soul depend on feeling your love."

"She pushed me away!" Galen yelled at him.

"You should have hung on harder!" Red roared back. "You broke the connection Galen, not Carling. This is your wife right now." He waved a hand in front of Galen's face and showed him an image from their home.

Carling was lying on their bed, her eyes open and staring, but empty. Her hair, which usually was glossy and shiny, was lank and unkempt. Claire was in the crib he had crafted while they waited for her to arrive, screaming her head off. Tarl'a, moving stiffly in the cold came into the room and picked the child up to comfort her, wincing with the pains in her hands and legs.

"She is not even trying," Galen said, stricken, trying to step back from the image.

"I told you, she has given up." Red dismissed the image and walked away from him. "I had thought you stronger than this, Galen. I was so wrong. I thought you were the perfect match for her, am I wrong about that too?"

"I love her still. I thought she did not love me." Tears stood out in Galen's eyes and ran unchecked over his whiskered face.

"Where did this idea come from? How can you go from such certainty in your feelings for her to having doubts?"

"I don't know. The longer I was away, the more it crept up on me. I felt scared to go home, afraid that she would send me away."

Red stepped towards him quickly and placed a hand on his head. Closing his eyes, he ran through Galen's mind, and when Red released him, he stumbled to the nearest seat.

"It's him. Blue, I need you," Red called out to his brother. "Blue, I need you now."

"I am here, Brother. What is so urgent?" Blue asked, coming to stand near them.

"Take a look inside his mind. I think someone has been meddling," Red said, indicating Galen.

Blue looked at him and placed a hand against his temple. The search this time was gentler. When Blue pulled away, he nodded. "You are right. It is all wrong in there. This is why Carling is the way she is at the moment. How did you discover this?" Blue asked Red.

"By accident. I did mean to drag him back home, but it was the way he was talking. We may need to work together to get this sorted. I wish Order was still with us. The help of the Great Light would make it easier to remove."

"Remove what?" Galen demanded.

"The suggestion that Chaos has inserted in your mind, son of my brother. He has made you think that Carling does not love you anymore, which we all know is false. But to you right now, at this moment in time, it is an absolute truth. Because that is what he wants you to believe," Blue told him plainly.

"The sooner we have it out, the better," Red said.

"Yes, but not by you. You are too hasty and rough, Brother. We do not want to cause more damage. Green is our man. He can heal as I extract."

"You know more on this matter than I do. I will step back and let you both work. Green, your help is urgently requested." Red stepped back, and they waited for Green to appear.

"My brothers," he greeted them.

Blue hastily filled him in on what they needed to do, and they got down to work. Each placing a hand on Galen they accessed his mind, searching through every corner to find the location of the suggestion. It had been cleverly placed so that there were more than one anchoring points to it. With as much care as they could, they extracted the malicious suggestion, but it was still painful for Galen.

Soon it was finished, and Galen held his head in his hands. It felt lighter and brighter than it had in weeks. His mind immediately sought the connection the malicious suggestion had almost severed, and held it gently, feeding it with energy once more to strengthen it. He followed it back to Carling, a golden spark that was flickering at the end of the rope, and he gathered her up in his arms and held it close. The spark did not even move, did not recognise him. He pulled in his energy and forced it on her, pushing all he could into it. He found the love he thought he had lost for his wife and let it flow, surrounding and wrapping about the tiny glimmer of light.

A little at a time, the spark grew and became more aware. Again, he pulled his love around her tighter, letting it seep in bit by bit until she recognised him. The more he fed her, the more Carling grasped onto. The spark was now a single flame, desperately trying to grow and gain strength.

"My love," Galen whispered to her. "My love."

With a burst of blinding light, the small flame became an inferno of brilliant gold, flaring into both of their minds. She formed herself inside the light and rushed to his arms.

"Galen," Carling sobbed into his shoulder, her love pouring from her and healing them both.

"I am sorry, my love. I was foolish," he told her, stroking her hair, and kissing her.

"I thought I had lost you."

"Never again will I go from your side," he promised her.

"Come home, my love, come back to me. I miss you. I love you," she told him between kisses.

"I will come now, if Red isn't still too mad at me," he promised. "I will be there soon." With one final push of energy and love into her burning light, he left her side and felt the separation deeply. Opening his eyes, he looked at Red.

"I want to apologise for my words, Red. I did not truly mean them."

"I understand that my son. There is no need to apologise for something you had no control over. Are you ready to go home?" Red asked him.

"I am. I am grateful for your help, Ancestors," Galen said clasping their hands in turn. "Take me home, Red. Take me back to my Carling."

Another child arrived safely into the world of the valley nine months later. A beautiful girl with the promise of eyes that matched her father's and hair just as dark. When Claire was introduced to her little sister, she was immediately fascinated and held her tiny hand with her own. Brei would not settle unless Claire was with her, and Claire would become jealous when either of her parents would hold the baby.

Red was the only one she would go to without insisting Brei was with her. Their special bond was still there, and he became a visitor around the times that Carling and Galen needed him to look after the little girl. He taught her to sing, and her child-like voice became strong. He taught her games, and her little legs became sturdier.

Claire grew quickly. She was confident and determined. If she found something that she could not do, she would persist until she could. She was outgoing and laughed often, especially with Red, and often told her parents when visitors were coming down the track, then run out to greet them.

Chapter Twenty-Two

"Claire," Carling called from the doorway and looked out over the meadow. There was no sign of their eldest child anywhere, and she ducked back into the house. "Where does she get to?"

"I do not know. Have you tried asking her?" Galen asked, looking up from the bed he was mending.

Carling searched out over the meadows and hills and still could not find her. She began to worry that she may have tried to cross the ford and roam further out beyond their protected valley.

"I'm going to go look for her," she said, heading out the door, Galen followed her.

"You remember what you were doing at the age of six? You roamed this whole valley."

"I know I did, but I can't find her. She is nowhere in the valley," Carling said sending out another search. Beside her she felt Galen do the same.

"You go to the stones—she may be up there—and I'll head to the forest. Da, can you watch the other three?" Galen called back into the house.

"Leave them with me. They will be no trouble. Go find your wayward daughter. She gives you as much grief as ours did." The old man chuckled.

Sentinels

Mailcon was old and stooped now. Tarl'a had left them just after Brei was born. Carling had found her sitting out in her favourite spot, her face turned to the sun. On her face had been a small smile and Carling was grateful that she had gone peacefully. The passing of their Ma had hit them hard. She was always the guiding force, and it was only then that Carling felt the burden of the Guardian truly fall onto her shoulders.

The Ancestors promised that she was comfortable and happy and that she would once more roam the earth as one of their children. But which one had not been decided yet.

Now Mailcon hung on, always strong and healthy. It pained both Galen and Carling to see him starting to fade. But he made himself useful doing little jobs for them and looking after the children. He still had not lost his sense of humour and it was now twinkling in his eyes at the actions of his granddaughter.

Claire, at six, was busy all day. If she was not in the house helping her mother, she was with her father. If she could not be found with her parents or grandfather, then she was with Brei playing. But more recently she had taken to going off alone and that worried Carling. The warning from the goddess come back to her.

"Don't worry, she can't have got far," Galen said lifting off the ground and heading towards the valley entrance.

Carling herself headed towards the hill at the back of the house. Up she followed the brook that tumbled down the side from the spring, which Yellow had released at the beginning of time. She searched around the stones and out over the hills beyond. Landing on one hill she remembered a night so long ago now, when she was young and full of herself. The dents in the ground were still there, as were the burn marks from the blood that had escaped him. Sending out another search she still could not feel Claire anywhere.

"Red, Yellow, Blue, my family, I need you," Carling called as she reached the stones again.

"My daughter, what is the matter?" Yellow said coming to her side, alarmed at the worry on Carling's face.

"Claire is missing, Mother, we can't find her." Carling was starting to panic.

"I'll go look, she won't hide from me," Red said with a comforting smile and disappeared again.

"What if it's him, what if he has her?" Carling said her voice rising.

"Calm child. All will be fine," said Blue as he kissed her brow.

"I must go look." Carling headed out of the stones with her parents following. They spread out across the valley and were gratefully relieved when Red put out the call to them all.

"By the ford. I have found her," he said.

Carling materialised and found Red sitting beside Claire, who was looking worried.

"Where were you, Claire?" Carling chided as she picked her up and held her close. "You gave us all a fright. I couldn't find you."

"I was here, Ma. I was with a new friend," the little girl said, wrapping her arms around her mother's neck.

"A new friend." The news startled Carling and she followed Red's hand as he pointed the new friend out. In amongst the trees and scrubby bushes was a wolf, she appeared fully grown and had a silvery grey coat. Claire recognised her. Carling put the girl down as she acknowledged the wolf. "Welcome daughter of our litter-mate. Is all well with you?" she asked formally.

"All is well with me. I remember the smell of the young one. I have met her before," the wolf said, now coming out of the brushes.

"You have, Wolf. When you were just a pup, and she was just a baby. Do you bring news of our littermate and his mate?" Carling asked her.

"I do. My sire asked to bear the news to you that our mother has passed onto the ancient ones," the wolf said as she sat before Carling.

Carling turned to Galen who came to her side.

"Thank you for bringing us this news young one. Is our littermate near?" he asked, trying to stay formal.

"Our sire is near. The grief he feels for our mother is deep. Can I take you to him?" Wolf asked.

"We would be most grateful if you could, Wolf," Galen replied and followed the wolf into the forest.

"Ma. I was about to come find you when Uncle Red arrived, I promise." The little girl slipped her hand into her mother's.

"It is fine, Claire. But I was worried. I couldn't sense you in the valley." Carling knelt beside her girl.

"I was still in the valley, I promise. See, I am still dry." She showed her legs to Carling for confirmation.

"So I can see. It is something that I am going to have to look at, I think. You are too young for your abilities, so it can't be hide. What do you do out here on your own?" Claire asked.

"I make up stories and I wander the trees. They speak to me. They whisper their secrets," Claire told her excitedly.

"Secrets? They have been here a long time. What secrets do they tell?"

"There is one secret I like the most." Claire moved away from her mother and went further up the path to the clearing nearby. Carling and the others followed her and watched as she headed to a fallen and almost rotten log. From inside a hollow, she pulled out something and showed it to her mother.

Carling smiled at the memories that came flooding back. She took the old wooden sword from her daughter's hands and held it gently.

"They told me that you used it, that you came here to practice with Da. Is that true?" Claire asked.

"It is, Claire. A very long time ago now. It was before your Da and I...well before things were settled between us." Carling remembered the fight, remembered the words and fleeing from the stones. "This should go back to where it came from. It came from the trees and should rot down into the ground." Very carefully she placed it back into the hollow of the rotten log.

"They are grateful it has been returned, Ma," Claire told her. "They also say that Da is coming back. I like Wolf, she is lovely."

"Can you talk to Wolf as well as the trees?" Red asked her curiously.

"Yes, I understand Wolf. Can't you?" Claire asked him.

"I can hear them, yes, Claire, but you are young to be hearing them just yet. But then you always do like to hear stories." He grinned at her and held out his hand for her to take. "I'll take her back. You should wait for Galen," he told Carling.

"Thank you, Red. Mother, Father, will you stay with me for a moment?"

"Of course we will," Blue nodded.

When Carling was certain that Claire was far enough away she could not hear, she asked a question that bothered her. "My daughter—"

"Yes, she is young, Carling, but that sometimes happens with Whisperers. Remember Loc was the same," Yellow said with a comforting smile.

"But the trees?"

"She is sensitive. Sometimes Whisperers grow out of hearing the trees. Not many adults can still commune with them," Blue said, then added with a chuckle, "There is nothing to worry about, Carling. She is your daughter after all."

"I worry about her all the time. Every time I search for her future, I still see the darkness that surrounds her."

"As a mother, it is your right to worry. As The One True Child, it is your duty to protect her," Yellow said. "He would not dare attempt anything while you all still reside under the protection of the valley. You are safe."

"Carling," Galen called as he entered the clearing. She turned and found him with Loc in his arms. His muzzle was now grey, and he looked tired and thin. Galen put him down on the ground and knelt at his side. "Brother, our sister is here. She will help you," he said as he gently stroked the large head of the wolf.

"Loc, I feel your sadness. Your pain is not physical, and I cannot ease it, but you need to eat to survive."

"My sister, I cannot live while she is gone. She was my life and my soul. I feel empty without her," Loc said.

The young wolf came to her sire's side and lay down, resting her own head onto his flank and whined a little.

"Your daughter feels your sadness," Carling said.

"She is the only one of our cubs to have stayed with us. I brought her here to you, and your daughter. This is my last task. Claire and Wolf will be paired, thankfully not the same pairing as her mother and I," he whined weakly.

"We need to get him home to tend to him," Carling said.

"I'll carry him." Galen picked him back up into his strong arms.

They walked back to the house slowly and with some care so as not jostle the wolf too much. When they reached the door, Mailcon took one look at his son and burst into tears.

Galen took him inside and lay him by the hearth—the spot that he would claim when he and Wolf would come to visit.

Mailcon dropped to the ground beside him and ran a hand down his side. "He is so thin," he said, turning worried eyes to Carling.

"He is grieving, Da. Wolf has passed," she relayed the news gently with a tear in her own eye.

The young wolf stopped at the threshold of the house and continued to stare at the inside of the den of humans. Claire came to stand next to her, hardly a head above her own, and placed an arm around the she-wolf's neck.

"Will you try to eat something, brother, please," Galen pleaded with him.

"It would only prolong my life. I cannot live without my Wolf. I have brought my daughter to your den. I can now leave this world and join my love."

"What is he saying, Galen? What does my son tell you?" Mailcon asked desperately.

Galen looked up and shook his head at his father. Tears streamed down his face at the fate of his youngest brother. The gentlest of them all and the quietest.

"He does not want to live without Wolf, Da," Carling told him gently. "He wishes to die, so he refuses to eat."

"You cannot die before me, Son. It is not the way," Mailcon begged. "Indigo can help. Carling, please call her." He grasped her hand and held it tightly.

"I have already called for her, Mailcon," Blue said, standing behind him with a comforting hand on his shoulder. "She is on her way."

As the words left his mouth, Indigo appeared, and Carling moved so she could be nearer to Loc. Very carefully, she moved her hand from his head over his body, assessing his condition.

"I don't understand. Wolf and Loc were supposed to have so many more years ahead of them. We gave them this gift. How did Wolf die?" Indigo asked.

"You have not seen her spirit, Sister?" Yellow asked quickly.

"No, I have not accepted her into the spirit realm. Do you know where her body lies?" Indigo looked around them.

"No. We have only just found out. His pup may be able to tell you," Galen said, indicating the she-wolf sitting beside Claire.

"Hello, my young daughter. I am sorry for the loss of your mother. Did you understand what we were saying just now?" Indigo asked her.

"I did. My sire has taught me to understand the speech of humans. He says that I and this young one are to be paired," the wolf replied.

"Yes, that has been decided. Can you tell me where your mother lies?"

"I can show you. It is a long distance away. She died many days ago."

"If you could think of the place, I can then go to her."

"If it would help you, Great Mother." The wolf lay down and closed her eyes.

"Thank you, young one." Indigo stood and took Carling's hand. "Sister, I will need your help."

The world slid past them, and they came to the spot where Wolf's body was now decimated by scavengers. Her once glossy and dark coat was torn to shreds and blowing out into the world. The smell of the decomposing flesh assaulted their noses, and Carling placed a hand to her face to stave it off. Indigo knelt beside the body and waved a hand over the top of the corpse, and when she stood a tear tracked down her cheek.

"There was no reason for her death. I can find no injury," she said, still looking down at the pitiful mess in front of her.

"I will try to contact her spirit for you, Sister," Carling said, taking her hand.

"Thank you, Carling." Indigo wiped the tear from her eyes.

Letting go of Indigo's hand, Carling stood over the body and raised her hands over it. She closed her eyes and called out to Wolf, searching for the spirit which had not passed on yet. Finding the barrier between the worlds of the living and dead, she pushed on it, but it did not relent. Gathering herself, Carling tried again with a harder force of energy behind it. The barrier tore and shredded away, leaving a hole for her to reach through. Finally, she linked her mind to Indigo.

"Call for her, Sister," Carling instructed the Sentinel, the strain of keeping the tear open in her voice.

"Wolf," Indigo called. With the calling of the name, the Sentinel also sent an image of her. "Wolf, we call your spirit."

There was no answer from the other side, and Carling began to tremble at the effort. Indigo once more called and this time they had an answer.

"Ancient One, I hear you." The wolf stepped through the gap and Carling released the edges. As they merged, they left no mark of the tear that had just been there.

"Daughter, we will guide you shortly to your final resting place. But first, we must know what happened here," Indigo asked.

Wolf looked down sadly at what was once her body and then back up to Indigo. "We hunted, my mate and I, and we were successful. A rabbit each we had that night. I was sick from it. There was something wrong with the rabbit," Wolf told her.

Carling closed her eyes and used more of her precious stores of energy to look into the past. It was not much different to searching the future but trying to see what had happened in this spot many days ago took some effort. She saw the hunt and the takedown of the rabbit.

There seemed to be nothing wrong with the small animal; it ran with no impairment. Continuing to watch, there was no reason for the wolf to become sick. And then she saw.

Curled up together, asleep after the hunt and with full bellies, the pair of wolves did not see what came next. The landscape froze around her, and everything went deathly quiet. She recognised the signs of time being stopped, and she looked around, searching for the only other Being in the world who could possibly do such a thing. And he came.

Chaos strode through the forest where the wolves slept and gently touched the belly of Wolf. He stood and looked down at them with a satisfied smirk, then looked up, directly at her. "You see, Carling, I can use your tricks too. I know where you are, and I can get to your family anytime I like. Come to me and no more of them shall have to die. Except for this other, of course. I shall let you watch him die slowly." He grinned at her.

"I will never give myself to you. I have protected my family, and you shall not be able to get to them," she growled at him.

"You will not see me coming. You are still beautiful despite the brats you have pushed out. Come to me, Carling." He smiled and stepped towards her.

She felt the charm coming from him in giant waves with every step he made. Carling stood firm against him and smiled in return. "That will not work on me, Chaos. You forget who I am." With one last shot of her energy, she released the lights under her skin. They flared into life and were dazzling to the eye.

"I do not forget." He stepped back from the light, covering his eyes from their glare. "We can fix that."

"I don't want to. I am happy with who I am. This is not the time, and definitely not the place, for our meeting."

"You can glow and talk all you want. It will not make any difference. I will have you, and you will be bent to my will. And I will enjoy breaking you, your spirit, and your soul," he said darkly.

"Then I would not be me, Chaos. How can you say you want me, only to forcibly change me? It would do you no good and you would soon lose interest. That does not sound so good to me. If a man loves me, he would not want me to change, and the prospect of him losing affection does nothing to entice me." Carling cocked her head to one side, opened her eyes and changed her expression to one of innocence and disappointment.

"Do not play with me, Carling," he said, taking another step back from her.

"I don't seek to play with you. I just wish to understand your thinking. Or is your thinking just as confusing as your actions? I do not think much of your people. They create great works and buildings; they are resourceful and intelligent. Yet they are so destructive and blood thirsty. Was that your intention?"

"They shall overrun these lands. Those that you call sacred shall be defiled and obliterated, starting with the stones you hold so dear."

"More threats? I grow tired of this conversation. You only have one subject, and it now bores me. Maybe next time we meet we might have something else to talk about. It is something you should think about. I just have one more thing for you before I go," she told him and readied herself.

"What is that?" She enjoyed the hint of trepidation to his speech.

"Only this. This is the result of the love I feel from my family. I hope you enjoy it." She let the lights go from the restraint she had placed on them, and they exploded to their fullest for a brief second before she left. She heard his screams as the light burnt his eyes and his skin. His screams echoed down through the short space of time and were still ringing as she suppressed the lights once more and sucked in energy from the area around her.

"Sister, are you alright?" Indigo asked, helping her stand up right.

"I am, I just need a moment." She sucked in air into her lungs and leaned on Indigo until she felt she could stand on her own. "It was him. It was not the rabbit my dear, dear Wolf. He was the cause of your illness. He came in the dark and gave you the pain and the agony you suffered. He is also the reason your spirit did not find Indigo."

"I thank you, pack-mate, for your information. It does rest my mind to know that. I would ask one last favour from you," Wolf said slowly.

"You may ask, my pack-mate. It is the least I can do for you and for Loc."

"It is my mate that it concerns. I wish to see him one last time. Is it possible for you to take me to him?" Wolf asked.

"With Indigo's help we can take you. He is not in a good way himself. He pines for you and refuses to eat," Carling told her.

"Which is why I need to see him."

"Indigo, do you have the knowledge to do this? I find my energy is low, and I cannot gather it quickly enough."

"If you would give the knowledge to me, I can transport you both, my sister," Indigo said with some concern.

Carling placed a hand on her head and passed her the information. As Indigo inspected it, Carling walked away from the body of Wolf, finding that it was too upsetting for her to be near it.

"I am ready, Sister. Wolf, I need to have your permission to do this — to remove your spirit from the area of your body."

"You have my permission, Mother of Wolves," the Wolf said formally.

"Carling, your arm please. Lean on me for now, and I will get you home."

"Thank you," Carling said with a smile and accepted Indigo's help readily.

Leaning heavily on Indigo's arm, she felt the slip of the world around them moving to the valley, and she sat down outside, immediately feeling the onrush of energy the valley had. Carling took a deep breath and followed Indigo and Wolf into the room.

Carling noted that the young wolf had made it inside and was now lying down on the bed beside Claire and her sister and brothers. Mailcon and Galen were still seated beside Loc, their hands trying to give comfort to the emaciated wolf. Wolf stepped up to Loc and went to nudge him with her nose.

"My mate. Your time is not here. This is not the time for you to die."

Loc opened his eye and took in the spirit of Wolf and whined, "My love, I miss you. Why did you have to leave without me?"

"I was taken, I did not leave. I would never have left you, my mate." The spirit lay down beside Loc, her nose almost pressed up against his. "You cannot leave and follow me, my mate. You have a task to accomplish, and your littermate cannot do what must be done without your help. You must eat and get healthy—not just healthy but strong. Please promise me that you will do this, my mate."

"If this is what you wish, then I shall, though it gives me great pain not to join you," Loc whined.

"The pain will only be for a little while longer. We will be together again soon, and then we will never be apart. My time to go is now. Please, my love, get well."

Loc lifted his head from his paws as she called him her love. It is not the way of wolves to express such an emotion, though they felt it. "For you, my love, it shall be. I look forward to the day I can be with you once more. Farewell until then, my love."

"Farewell until then, my love," Wolf said, standing. She looked towards her daughter and the young wolf whined her own farewell to her mother.

"Wolf child, your time has come to pass over. We welcome you to our spirit world where your wisdom and knowledge will be appreciated," Indigo said. The wolf and Sentinel soon left, and a silence descended on the room.

From the bed the young wolf lifted her muzzle and howled out her grief of losing a mother who was close to her. Weakly, Loc did the same. Their howls cut through the dusk as the sun set and sent shivers up Carling's spine.

Loc kept his promise to Wolf, and with the care and attention of both Galen and Mailcon, they nursed him back to health. At first Galen cut his food into tiny pieces, grinding it to a paste to feed him until Loc began to complain about the mush. Each day saw the change in him as his coat began to shine once more. Claire and Brei would sit with him for long stretches of time, combing his fur, carefully getting the burs out.

Carling watched, amused as he would take himself outside when he began to get his strength back and roll in the long grass each morning. She followed him back inside to find the girls waiting with combs in hand ready to groom him once more.

Young Wolf, as she became known to the family, fit in well. She waited patiently for Claire to finish with her ministrations to her sire and then the pair would wander the valley playing together. Galen spoke often to Loc about their daughters and the bond that was forming already, although Carling knew it would all work out for the pair, she was happy Galen had found someone with firsthand knowledge of the Whisperer ability.

The seasons soon turned, and winter was upon them once more. The snow started to pile up and the wolves stayed with them during the cold months. The house was full of children and animals, and the noise would get to Mailcon. Every now and then, Carling would find him off by himself in the new room. Closing the door firmly between the two rooms, she would sit and talk gently with him while Galen dealt with the children.

They spoke of many things in those times—memories and hopes. And he would always take her hand while they discussed Tarl'a. Carling loved these moments and made sure that Galen had them too. Loc would sometimes join them, and Carling had an idea. "Galen, I need to leave for a little while. I'll be back later tonight," she said one night as they readied for bed.

"Where are you going?" he asked her.

"I need to talk to Order about something. It's important that I do it tonight."

"As long as you are back with me before morning, I will not stop you." He took her in his arms and kissed her.

"I'll be back as soon as I can." She kissed him back and disappeared from his arms, leaving him smiling and shaking his head.

Carling transported herself to the one place she knew she would find Order and was not disappointed. The lights under her skin were dimmer than they had been when she had last seen the Great Light. They moved slowly and sluggishly. She waited calmly and patiently to be noticed by Order as she finished what she was doing.

"Our child, we do not know why you come to seek our aid when you already know the answers you seek," Order said smiling as she turned towards Carling.

"Great Light, you are my oldest advisor. How can I not seek your advice? Especially when I have missed you so much." She walked towards the tall glowing Being and took the withering hands into her own. "Your time is short now; I can feel it. I wish to make use of you as much as I can—while I still can."

"Your company is always welcome, Child. The question of giving the ability to Mailcon is an easy one. You can bestow it easily, though I would ask Green first. That ability comes under his domain, and he may get a little upset if you were to just bestow it without his knowledge."

"See, you can still advise me. I will do as you suggest. How does your task go, Great One?"

"Slowly, but as you say, it is almost complete. See what I've done." Order gestured to the small room and the crystals that were placed around.

The room had changed much since the last time Carling had been there. There were more crystals jutting from the floor and some from the ceiling. Smaller shimmering sparkles could be seen embedded in the walls and floor, and she could imagine that with the sunlight streaming in, the display would be dazzling to the eye.

"The small crystals are your contribution, Carling. Some of them anyway. They are the shards of one of your tears you left behind. We have built on them and increased their clarity to become more effective."

"It is beautiful Order. I only wish it was not at the expense of you," she said sadly.

"I think there is a space over there in that corner that could do with a few more shards," Order said gently with a small smile.

"Are you making fun of me, Great Light?" Carling smiled back.

"That is what family is for, is it not, Carling? To jest and to tease. Love comes in many forms, our dear child." Order released her hand and made a rising gesture with her own. From the floor, a column of basalt rose up and stopped halfway to the ceiling. Placing a hand on the top, Order sent lights flickering down the rock, and they penetrated the surface. Slowly it changed from dark and black, to clear and bright. The transformation of the rock to crystal was a great expenditure of energy for Order, and she leaned against the column for a moment. Carling dashed to the side of the Great One and supported her thin frame, feeding her energy into it.

"That is enough, Carling." Gently Order pushed her away and stood on her own. "When you have confined Chaos here, the little crystal in your mind, which has been growing, needs to be placed here. The moment it touches this crystal shard I will finish my transformation and lock myself away in it."

"You mean to light this room for eternity?"

"Not for that long. Only until the Ultimate One can release me and destroy Chaos. Then I shall leave this world. You have seen we are tied, the Universe's children. One cannot survive without the other. That is why we were born to cancel each other out."

"Is there anything else I can do to help you, Great One?" Carling asked quietly.

"Yes, you can look after yourself and your family. I see that care and attention stretching down through the ages. That love that you all share will become necessary to your last life, Carling. She will need it as she faces her ultimate test."

"I'll make sure, then, that when I love, I love deeply and strongly for all my family and friends. Just as I have love for you, Order. You created me for a purpose, and I mean to see that purpose through, though I will miss you greatly."

"I will still be here, Child. I will know your love, even if you do not know me. It is time to leave now, Carling. I still have much to do to prepare for your last visit. Go with my blessings and my love on you always."

"My blessings I give to you, Order. May they strengthen you in your time of preparation and confinement."

With a touch on her head from Order's hand, Carling felt the world tilt and slide under her as she raced back home. She found herself in the house once more, the children huddled together with the young wolf, Loc laid out beside the blazing fire, Mailcon snoring from his bed, and Galen sitting up waiting for her.

"I thought you would be in bed," Carling said, coming to sit beside him and taking his arm, wrapping it around her.

"Did you get the answers you needed?" he asked her, gently kissing her head.

"I did. I also received an instruction for later. Galen, the questions I had were of a change for someone close to us."

"I figured as much. You wish to allow Da to understand Loc," he whispered in her ear.

"I do. I need to talk to Green and gain his permission first."

"Why not do it now? I am sure he would not mind."

"It is too deep into the night to call out to him. The morning will be soon enough." Carling yawned and lay her head on his shoulder.

"Before it gets any deeper, it is time for bed Wife," he said, smiling.

"It is, Husband. I will need your help to get Da up to the stones tomorrow."

"You will have it. Now to sleep."

Morning found them up early. The sun had not even risen from its winter slumber yet, and above them the lights in the sky glowed brightly, moving slowly across the stars. Mailcon had been woken with great difficulty from a deep sleep and was still grumbling as Galen picked him up and flew to the stones with Carling following.

There was no snow in the circle and the wind did not blow. The air felt warmer as they passed the entrance stones, and the grass smelled sweet after the powdery scent of snow. Mailcon shed the blankets that he had wrapped himself in as the warmth seeped into his bones, and he stood straighter and taller than he had in many turnings of the seasons.

"Uncle Green, we request your presence in the sacred circle of stones," Carling called out. She did not adopt the stance her mother had of head thrown back and arms outstretched. Having an intimate relationship with the Sentinels, she felt there was no need for such theatrics. When visitors arrived seeking the wisdom of the Ancestors, they sometimes found this lack of dramatics a little disappointing, and Carling became very good at picking which ones would expect such a display.

Green soon joined them in the circle and greeted them warmly. "I have come, Guardian. What is the wisdom you seek?" he said, grinning.

"Less formality would be nice, Uncle," she said, hugging him.

"So, my brothers and sisters all get to be called such, but I am still Uncle?" He raised an eyebrow at her.

"Brother, then. Though it does sound strange to me. I still think of you as a favoured Uncle."

"I will be called whatever you are most comfortable with, Niece," he grinned broadly at her. "How can I help you?"

"You have domain over a particular ability, and I wish your blessing to bestow this ability to Da."

"Which ability is it, Carling?" he asked, becoming serious.

"Whisperer." Carling looked to Mailcon, who stepped forward briskly.

"Is that why you have dragged me up here in the middle of winter?" Mailcon asked her, his eyes going wide.

"It is, Da, with the reasoning that you should be able to talk to your son, and he talk to you. I have seen you struggling whenever either

Galen or I translate for you. I thought that the times you take yourself off to the new room, you could speak to each other."

"It is one I am willing to bless with all my heart, Mailcon," Green told him placing a hand on his shoulder. "Carling."

Carling echoed Green's gesture and laid a hand on Mailcon's other shoulder as she drew in the energy from the stones. Slowly she opened up the part of Mailcon's mind that had been closed off, hiding the ability away from use. She brought it forward, and at the same time, imparted the knowledge of how to use it to him. When they had finished, he looked between the pair.

"I don't feel any different," he said, confused.

"We'll go down and see if it has worked, then, Da," Galen said, bringing the blankets to wrap around him to keep the cold out.

Green joined them on the journey back to the house and watched as Mailcon went to Loc's side. Gently touching the wolf, he tried out his first words.

"Good morning, my son. The day is beginning. Did you sleep well?" Mailcon withdrew his hand and waited.

Loc sat up and looked at his father, his head cocking to one side. "Good morning, my sire. I did sleep well. Too well by the looks of things. Changes have been made, changes that I welcome. It is good to finally be able to talk to you, Father." The wolf licked Mailcon's face, and he laughed, tears of joy spilling from his eyes.

Chapter Twenty-Three

Mailcon spent many a long day and sometimes into the night talking with Loc. They had so much to say to each other. Sometimes Young Wolf and Claire would join their conversations, which would illicit jealous stares and grumbles—usually from Brei, who felt left out.

It was at these times that Carling would make sure she spent time with her second child. The boys would follow their father to get wood and it would be just her and Brei. It became their custom, just as it was with Carling and Tarl'a, to go up to the stones each day.

The time spent up there did not necessarily include the Sentinels, but it was time where Carling could teach Brei the old stories. Making sure she understood who the players were in them. As she grew, Brei had questions about them. They were insightful and sometimes Carling could not answer them. Calling upon the Sentinels, they filled in the knowledge where she could not. It surprised her there was still some things she did not know.

"Growing and learning go hand in hand, Daughter," Yellow said to her on one of these particular days. "Even though your body has finished growing, your mind does not. It takes in new information every day and processes it. The Universe is wide and not one creature, including The One True Child, can know everything."

"Yellow, is Ma really your daughter?" Brei asked her.

"Yes, she is. I gave birth to her here in the circle with the aid of your Granny."

"So, if Ma is your daughter, doesn't that make you my Granny too?" Brei looked up curiously at the Sentinel.

"It does, Brei. And Blue would be your Grand Da." Yellow smiled at him as he held her hand.

"If you don't want to call us that, Brei, you don't have to," Blue told the girl.

"I think I would like to." Her beaming smile reflected the twinkling in her blue eyes. Carling believed it had to do more with her growing rivalry with Claire, than any sort of family connection, but she kept her opinions to herself.

As they had grown, Carling and Galen had found that Claire and Brei were becoming more and more competitive, not only for their attention and time, but with everything. Brei was jealous of Claire's ability to talk to animals, and Claire was jealous of the time Brei spent up at the circle with their Ma and the Sentinels. There were many arguments where Galen had to pull them apart before they did damage to each other.

Things came to a head when Brei's talent finally revealed itself. They always knew it would be Foresight, but the vision she had was not expected. Carling was grinding the grain late one afternoon when she heard raised voices from inside.

"Well at least I'm not the one to betray Ma!" Brei flung at her sister.

"I would never betray, Ma. What are you talking about, you toad?" Claire yelled back.

"I've seen it. You betray Ma to Chaos."

Carling walked into the house and shut the door behind her. This action immediately separated the two girls, and they turned to their mother.

"Claire, Brei, will you please sit down?" Carling asked calmly.

The girls sat on the bed side by side, and Carling had to hide a smile as she saw them hold hands. They may fight, but they were still close, and she was pleased to see it.

"This vision you saw, Brei—was it a dream, or did it come to you while you were awake?" she asked her youngest daughter calmly.

"It was this morning, Ma. It was after we had visited the stones. I stopped to pick some flowers."

"I remember," Carling said, nodding. "And how did the vision come to you?"

"I could see it in my mind. I could still see the house, but the vision was over the top."

"And what did you see, Brei. If you could give me as much detail as possible it would be helpful."

Brei moved a little uncomfortably on the bed, and she sneaked a peek at her sister, who still held her hand and was looking at her curiously.

"I saw a dark night. The sky was covered in dark storm clouds and a wind blew heavily. I saw Claire leave the house and head up the hill. There was a man waiting for her. I didn't like the feeling I got from him. He grabbed her and made her call out to you. He looked like he was going to hurt her. From the descriptions in your stories, I thought it might be Chaos."

"Thank you, Brei. That was most insightful. Can you go get your Da, please, and tell him to bring the boys home. I think they are fishing by the ford."

"Yes, Ma." Brei got up from the bed and started to head to the door.

"One more thing, Brei. Did you see when this would happen? Did you get a feeling of how may days?"

"Not really, but it felt soon."

Sentinels

"You can go now," Carling dismissed her. When the door shut, Carling turned back to Claire.

"Was it a true vision, Ma? Did Brei really see me do that?" There was fear in Claire's eyes.

Carling moved to the bed and sat beside her, putting an arm around her eldest child. "Before you were born, we received a warning that he would use one of our children to get to me. When we looked into your future after you arrived, both your Granny and I saw a darkness shadowing you."

"Ma, I don't want it to be me. I will never do that, I promise. I will stay inside. I won't go out," Claire told her mother desperately.

"You would go mad if you could not go outside. It is not in your nature to keep yourself couped up. You are thirteen summers. You are young, and the Sentinels and I have placed all the protections we could on the valley. It is why we have asked all of our children to never leave the valley, unless under the protection of us or the Sentinels. But in saying that, he is a tricky one and you are going to have to be on your guard. Make sure Wolf is with you wherever you go."

"I will, Ma. I promise." There was still fear in her eyes and Carling worried more.

"Can you find Gran Da and Uncle Loc for me. I think they went for a walk towards the brook."

"They did. They're looking for a fish that is very old."

"That fish died a long time ago. I think it is now his great, great, great grandchild that resides in that pool." Carling shook her head and smiled. "Did I ever tell you about the time I caught that old fish?"

"No, I haven't heard that story," Claire said brightly.

"Then I will tell it after our meal. Go fetch them. Tell them to leave the poor thing alone and come eat."

"Yes, Ma." Claire got up and ran, her golden hair catching the last rays of the sun as she opened the door, and she was out in a flash.

Carling and Galen sat outside with the fire late into the night. They had waited until after the rest of the family had gone to sleep before discussing the problem with Brei and Claire. They had been lucky with the girls that they had been able to start Claire's training with the help of Loc, and now that Brei had started her visions, Carling had decided that she would stay at home, and she would train her.

The problem of the vision was another issue they discussed. Carling relayed the vision to Galen, and he pondered it as he stared into the flames that were dying down.

"It will be soon then," he said finally.

"I believe so. I would like to get the children out of harm's way, but I am afraid to let them leave the protection of the valley." Carling lay her head her husband's shoulder.

"What about the home of the Ancestors? They would be well protected there. You could take them. I am sure Yellow and Blue would look after them."

"It is an idea—a very good one. I will ask them in the morning. But that still does not help with the problem of him coming. Brei was very sure of the vision. She saw Claire climbing the hill and calling out to me. I did ask if she could have been mistaken and, in the darkness, seen myself. But, she was sure. She said that our hair is slightly different."

"It is." Galen smiled. "Yours is like the golden sunrise and Claire's is more a honey colour."

"That is interesting. I wonder—"

"You can wonder all you like, Carling. It won't change the fact." Galen gave a chuckle. "But you are right, if she has seen Claire, then we need to get the children away soon."

Sentinels

They sat for a while in comfortable silence, listening to the crackle of the fire as it danced merrily with the sweet-smelling breeze. Above them the stars winked and sparkled against the black of the night. The moon was on the wane, a small sliver of silver, barely any light coming from the crescent.

"If he is coming soon, it will be on the darkest of nights, when there is no moon," Carling said softly as she looked at it. "He detests light."

"That will be in two days." Galen looked up at the sky and took her hand. "How is your sword arm? Do you need some training?"

"Those muscles have not left me. I know that you have been training the boys. They are young yet to start, aren't they?" she asked.

"I don't think so, and at the moment it is only play. How did you know?" he asked her.

"I keep my eye on everyone. Itis is already showing his Strength."

"He is—another of our children we can keep with us. And Gede. Have you seen what his ability will be?"

"I have, and his talent will take him far, like his Uncle Ru. It will be Tongues. I think also Itis will benefit from going out to train. I know you can train him, Galen, but you are sometimes a little hard on him."

"I am not hard on the boy," Galen protested.

"Galen, he is only ten summers. His Strength is only just coming in, and you have him working as if he were fully trained already. Elfin would take him in," she said gently.

"You may be right. But I will not stop training both to wield a sword and knife. You could also train them in the staff. I have never seen a person able to use one so effectively," he suggested.

"We will see. For now, I just want them safe."

In the morning, Carling sent Brei off with Galen and the boys while Claire took on her training from her Uncle Loc and Grandfather. She made the solitary walk up the hill with a worried heart and mind, and Yellow and Blue came quickly to her call.

"It must be important for you to come on your own, Daughter, and we have become used to visiting the house. What troubles you?" Blue asked her.

"I would like to take the children to our home on the island. Brei has seen him coming. I need to know they are safe and protected and ask that you take care of them for a few days."

"Of course we will. The children will be most welcome to our home. When will you bring them to us?" Yellow said, taking her hand.

"Tomorrow afternoon. We think he will come tomorrow night when there is no moonlight. In case he is around already, I don't want to alert him to the fact that the children will not be there. Brei has seen he uses Claire."

"You will call us to help you, Carling. You will not face him on your own I hope?" Yellow asked pointedly.

"I learned my lesson from the last battle we had. Of course I want you there. I will need your light to flare into the sky to weaken him."

"That is a relief. Bring them to us and they shall be protected, Daughter. It will be nice to spend time with them," Blue said, smiling.

"You spoil them already Father, and so do you, Mother."

"It is a pleasure, I believe, afforded to the grandparents of children. The parents are for discipline, but a grandparent's role is to give little pleasures." Blue grinned at her.

"Sometimes I do not know who is worse. You or my brother Red." Carling shook her head.

The next day there were no jobs or chores to do. The family spent the time they had together out in the meadows. They laughed and played and enjoyed themselves. They ate at midday out in the middle of the valley with the sun shining down on them, and the children lay back on the grass looking up and seeing shapes in the clouds.

"Who would like to visit the home of the Sentinels?" Carling asked as the afternoon was marching on.

"I would, Ma. I want to see where they taught you," Brei said first, closely followed by her brothers, Itis and Gede. Claire did not say anything.

"What about you, Claire? Don't you want to go?" Galen asked her.

"It would mean leaving Wolf, Da. I don't want to do that," Claire explained.

"It would only be for a little while. Your grandparents Yellow and Blue are looking forward to you coming," Carling told her.

"Will Uncle Red be there?" Claire asked.

"I think he will."

"If it is just for a little while, then yes I would like to go," Claire relented.

"Good, because you are all going this afternoon. I want you to run back to the house and tidy up your things, and then I will start transporting you," Carling told them. The children jumped to their feet and took off across the grass in excitement.

"Da, would you like to go as well?" Galen asked.

"No, I would not like to son. I know you mean well and wish that I am safe, but this is my home. I have lived here for a very long time. I will not leave it because there is a threat. Many times we have had threats come to the entrance of the valley, and each time I protected the place."

"If that is your wish, Da, then stay you shall. And you Loc?" he asked his brother.

"This is my final task, Brother, to help my sister. You will not be taking me anywhere, just as our father said. But I would be happier knowing Young Wolf will be safe. Could you also take her, litter-mate?"

"I will. She must be made safe," Carling said.

Back in the house the children were waiting for their mother, all lined up and neat. Brei stepped forward first. "Me first, Ma," she said, her face smiling brightly.

"Alright, you first. Take my hand." Brei ran to her mother and clasped her hand tightly. "Are you ready, Brei?"

"I am." She nodded eagerly.

Carling transported them quickly to the house of the Sentinels and held her steady as the girl righted herself.

"You will feel a little dizzy. It will pass."

"I'm fine, Ma." Gently Brei shook her mother off and looked about the massive room with her mouth slightly open.

"Welcome to our home, Brei," Red said as he got up from his seat and greeted them. "Carling, how are you, Sister?"

"I am well, Red."

"Blue told me that I should be here to greet our guests. Also, he has another message for you." He guided her away a little from Brei and whispered to her, "We will be ready. He has organised one of Lucan's granddaughters to mind the children when we come to help."

"Thank you, Red. I will be back shortly with the next."

"Do you want me to help?"

"No, I think it would be better if I escort them. Gede can be a little nervous."

"See you soon."

Carling transported herself back home and found the three waiting impatiently. Mailcon and Loc were inside and talking quietly with them, reminding them to behave.

"Gede, do you want to go next?" Carling asked.

"Yes, Ma," he said bravely and took her hand. At only eight, he reminded Carling of Loc, but had seen his future and found he would become more like Ru.

The transportation was easy, and when they arrived, he felt none of the dizziness his sister had. As soon as he saw Red, he was off and running into his uncle's arms to be lifted up high into the air.

"You are becoming very big, Gede. Soon I won't be able to lift you." He laughed with the boy.

Carling headed home once more and found that Claire and Itis had agreed he would be next. Boldly he held her hand and they left. At ten, Itis was beginning to become more responsible. It was a trait also of the Strength ability. She had seen it firsthand with Galen, and also Elfin.

When he met with Red, the boy held his hand out in greeting. "What, am I not good enough for a hug?" Red asked him seriously.

"Of course you are, Uncle," Itis said, grinning and hugged him hard to prove his strength.

"When will you children stop growing? I am starting to feel very old," he said as he crouched down and made a good imitation of Mailcon.

"Don't let Da see you doing that." Carling laughed with them.

When she arrived home to transport Claire, she found that there was someone missing. "Where is Da?" she asked Loc who was dozing by the fire.

"I think he went outside to talk to our brother," he said, lifting his head. He stood and left the house with her. Galen was stoking up the fire and looking out over the hills.

"It looks like the storm is coming in," he told them as they approached.

"Have you seen Da?" Carling asked. "He is not in the house."

"No, I haven't seen anyone since I came out." Galen sent out a search, and she could feel his worry. "He's by the brook." Without another word, he took off to the brook to find his father, Loc at his heels.

Carling turned back to Claire. "Go back into the house and stay with Wolf. Do not come out unless you hear us near. Do you understand, Claire?"

"I do, Ma. The storm is the same from Brei's vision, isn't it?" she asked quietly, looking at the big black clouds that were rolling in the sky. Flashes of lightening could already be seen within the storm.

"I don't know, Claire." Carling put her arms around her child. "Go inside. Stay there, and do not come out for any reason."

Claire left her, and Carling made sure the door was closed firmly before heading in the same direction her husband and brother had gone. She found them on the banks with the lifeless form of Mailcon lying between them. His body was soaked from the water and dark marks on his neck were clearly visible in the dimming light.

"He's dead. I don't understand. How did he make it out here passed me?" Galen asked her, a look of disbelief on his face.

"I don't know." Carling knelt at the head of Mailcon and smoothed the white hair from his face, tears dripping from her own. "Go in peace, Father of my heart. Ancestors here my plea. Guide the spirit of Mailcon into the arms of his beloved wife Tarl'a. Bring them together so they may be with each other for the rest of time or until they are reborn."

"We will look after him, Guardian," the voice of Violet came to her on the breeze, and she could feel the spirit lift from the lifeless body and leave.

"Farewell Father of my heart. Until we meet again," she said softly, bending over to kiss his forehead.

Both Galen and Loc said their goodbyes and then another call drifted on the gathering wind. A call that chilled Carling's heart and immediately stopped her tears.

"Ma, Ma, I need you! Help!"

It sounded so far away, and she knew it had been amplified so that she could hear it. Galen and Loc both heard it too, and their heads turned to the top of hill where the stones stood.

"Ma. Help me!" Claire called again.

Wolf came bounding up to her father. "I could not stop her. I could see her go, but I was powerless to move," she said desperately.

"It is alright, young one," Loc told her. "Carling, how do you wish us to proceed?"

"I am not sure what you are going to do, but I am getting my daughter back," she answered, gathering her energy to relocate herself to the top of the hill.

Galen took her arm. "Wait. You cannot go up there unprepared. I want Claire back as well, but he wants you to go up there hastily. He is depending on it," he told her firmly.

"Let go, Galen, or you will be coming with me."

"That is what I am going to do, Carling. But first I need my weapons," he told her.

"Fine!" Carling snapped her fingers, and at his feet his swords fell from out of nowhere. "Anything else?"

Galen stooped and put the belt on, cinching it up tightly, then took her hand again. "Now I'm ready." He gave her a smile she had not seen for some time. The last time was their final battle in the west.

"Hold tight," she told him, and they were on the hill inside the stones within a blink of an eye. "Wait," she said as he was about to head out.

Carling stood in the entrance and placed a hand on each stone. They vibrated with the force of the energy stored within, and she drew on it deeply. The amount she contained was overflowing and manifested itself into the lights that swirled and flickered under her skin. Brighter and brighter the golden points grew until Galen had trouble looking at them.

"Now we go get our daughter back," she said grimly. Her hands she pulled away from the sacred stones, and in their place came the golden sword and staff she had used so effectively in the past. A part of her, an extension of her arms and her strength.

They rounded the upthrust of rock and went to confront Chaos who held their daughter, a hand firmly grasping the upper arm of Claire.

"Ma, Da, I am so sorry. I heard you calling me, Ma, to go up to the stones." The girl sobbed.

"It's all right, Claire. It is not your fault," Carling said calmly, trying to give Claire a reassuring smile before turning glaring eyes to Chaos.

"You do make it difficult for me sometimes, Carling. But I am very enamoured with your daughter, an almost exact copy of her mother. So much younger and more pliable too." Chaos said, running a hand over Claire's hair.

"Let her go, Chaos. I am here to face you. You have gotten your wish at last," she told him.

"No, not yet I don't. It is only you, Carling, that I want." He pushed the girl away from him, and she stumbled and fell. Galen quickly rushed to her and pulled Claire to safety.

"Stay here," Carling heard him say and did not look to see where he had placed her.

"This is the moment, Chaos. Our time has come."

"The long-promised meeting of The One True Child and Chaos. Do you fear to face me alone?" he asked, looking now at Galen, and then past her husband, at the two newcomers to the hill, Loc and Wolf.

"I do not fear you. I do not fear being alone. I welcome my family. And I shall now welcome more." Holding out the sword and the staff to the sky, she called out into the increasing storm. "Mother, Father, Brothers, Sisters. I need your help. I request your presence to light up the sky as it has never been before. Come to me and give me your aid!" Her voice fell and the roar of the storm took over as the wind began to batter them in earnest. Lightening flashed around them, great bolts of electrical force scorching the ground where it hit.

"This is getting dangerous, Carling. Where are they?" Galen called to her over the noise of the wind, his body beginning to lean into it.

"Soon. They will be here," she told him confidently.

"Daughter, Sister, One True Child, we answer your call, and it shall be. Behold our light to aid you on your task. Our blessings on you, and may you be successful on this day," the voice of Blue called out to her.

Around them in a giant arc that spread from horizon to horizon, lights flared, each a colour of the rainbow. Slowly they started to arc up across the sky, leaving trails of bright sparkling light in every hue to meet in the middle. They stretched out to meet each other, and when they joined above, a great golden light shone down on the hill.

"We are now all here, Chaos. This light is mine and it shall be your downfall. We are stronger together than you are alone," Carling called out, her own lights brightening and her body increasing in size.

"I will have you as my prize, Carling, and those lights will be put out forever more. This land will live in darkness, and all shall be mine," Chaos roared at her, wincing in the strong light as he matched her size for size. In his own hands dark weapons emerged, shadowy things that looked evil.

"Spread out," she told them calmly.

Wolf, Loc, and Galen moved carefully around Chaos, keeping their eyes on him. Chaos surprised them by laughing at their hesitations.

"Your army is as ineffective as those in the west. At least those farmers had some idea as to how to fight. But I did enjoy crushing them under the heels of my army. And now they march to these lands," he taunted her.

"They shall not be here for long. And you will not be there to see it," she cried back.

Slowly Carling began to advance, finally tired of his words. Action was calling, and she felt the weight of the sword in her hand, eager to swing. Chaos came on, his dark weapon raised above his head. As they met, he brought it down with as much force as he could. Carling brought her golden one up and sparks flew from the edge. The sound as they hit was as loud as thunder—an ear-splitting noise. She brought her staff around and connected with his head.

Chaos pulled away and swung again. Bringing the staff up, Carling blocked it then swung around, slicing his shoulder. His dark blood oozed from the wound and dripped down his arm. Carling pulled back a moment and stepped to the side.

From the opposite side, Loc advanced and clamped his jaws on Chaos's left hamstring, biting deep into the flesh and shaking. Chaos cried out with the pain and slashed out at Loc. He let go and danced out of the way quickly, the blood burning the fur off his muzzle.

While Chaos was occupied with Loc, Galen advanced and slashed at his other leg. It was only a glancing blow, but it was enough for him to turn again. Galen ducked down as Chaos swung out wildly, limping from the damage Loc had inflicted.

"Stop now, Chaos. Stop and there will be no more pain," Carling called out.

"Pain is nothing to me," he cried back and healed the ragged gash in the back of his leg, leaving his other superficial wounds. Chaos leered at her. "I can heal myself as well."

"But the pain will keep coming. Can you replace your blood as fast?" she asked, stepping around him, circling while twirling her sword in her hand, loosening up her muscles and reawakening them.

"My blood is none of your concern. Send these lesser beings away, and just let it be us."

"But I do not choose to be alone. We will defeat you," she told him and leapt into the air, coming down fast.

Chaos brought up his sword and managed to get past the staff which she had moved to connect with it. The tip of his shadowy weapon grazed her arm. Carling ignored the slice as she pooled all her strength into the blow she brought down onto his shoulder. Her sword sliced through it, digging deep into bone and flesh. Her feet hit his stomach and pushed him away, pulling her weapon free from his body, and he went flying, landing heavily on the ground.

Before her eyes, he healed himself again. He got slowly to his feet once more and shifted his hold on the weapon in his hands. He did not see the young wolf advance closer to him, eyeing up his Achilles tendon.

"Stay back, Wolf. Go find Claire and protect her," Carling called out to her. "Go now."

The silvery wolf edged backwards and left the battle ground, and Carling lost sight of her behind the rocks. In her mind, she saw the reunion between her daughter and the wolf. What she did not see was Chaos advancing on her. Galen cried out a warning, and at the last moment she ducked to the left and rolled as she saw the darkness from the great cleaver-looking weapon reach out for her. The anger she now felt was directed towards herself for losing concentration on what was going on before her, but it was enough to spur her forward. As she gained her feet again, Carling lashed out with the staff and hit his ankles, sweeping Chaos onto his back.

Before he could get to his feet, Loc was there again to rake with his claws and bite down on an arm, giving Carling enough time to rise. Just as she got to her feet, she saw Loc go flying as Chaos shook him loose. The wolf landed heavily on his back and yelped out in pain. He got to his paws gingerly.

Turning back to Chaos, Carling brought her staff up and swung at the exposed head of the would-be god. The crunch of bones would have felled a lesser being, killing them outright, but Chaos staggered a little before shaking his head and coming upright. Galen rushed in while he was still dazed and cut deeper into the right leg of Chaos, slicing through tendons and blood vessels. The blood sprayed out and over Galen, burning his skin and making him cry out.

Chaos lost control of the leg and went down on one knee. Carling took advantage of his weakness and swung out, lashing at his sword arm. His hand began to spasm, and he dropped the weapon. When it hit the ground, it sizzled the grass underneath, and acrid black smoke rose from the ground.

Coming up from behind, Carling grew larger. With the increase in size, the lights flared from under her skin, making her look like she was on fire with flames of gold licking up her body. Wrapping her arms around Chaos before he could heal himself again, she transported him to the room prepared by Order.

In the split second of arrival, Carling called up the two pillars of crystal still hidden in the floor. They shot out of the ground, and she pushed a hand of Chaos into each one, trapping them with the light from her body. Sparking coils of golden rope—thick and strong—snaked along his arms and knotted themselves around the crystal. The light from the rope was added to that of the crystals embedded in the walls, brightening the room further.

Carling stepped back when she knew he was confined and breathed heavily at the energy she had used. Holding out her hand, she called forth the crystal of white and gold that had been forming in her mind. It appeared and sparkled in her hand like a giant jewel, perfectly formed and ready for use. She stepped to the platform Order had created from the basalt rock and placed the crystal in the centre.

"Chaos, this shall be your prison until the time of your death. You shall be confined here by your opposite, Order. Order, the time is now for your final act on this world. Your brother is here and cannot escape."

Order appeared, and the lights which were faded when she last saw the Being were now bright, and equal to her own.

"Our daughter, you have completed your task, and this shall be your final necessity. You are free now to live the rest of this life in peace. Go with our love and our blessings, our Child," Order said to her.

With a blinding flash, Order disappeared. The crystal on the column glowed brightly and sent its light out to catch hold from one pillar to another. Soon the light had spread to the darkest corner of the room, dispelling any space that may aid Chaos.

Chaos cried out to the universe for help. He screamed as the light blinded him and burned. The coils of golden rope tightened as he strained against his bonds, trying to find a way to flee away from the light.

"Why do you not kill me?" he called out in pain.

"I do not kill you, Chaos, because that is not my task. That is for another to do. I leave you now to your solitude and advise you to forget the world outside these walls."

"I will have my revenge, Carling. I will hunt you down and make you and your line pay. I will make you subject yourself to me. I will bend you to my will and break your spirit. Your mind, body, and soul will be mine to devour," Chaos cried out, straining against the restraints.

"You can try, Chaos. We will always be stronger." Carling left him then to his screams and returned to the hill.

Carling first went to Galen and ran her hand over his burns. They healed but left a ragged scar behind. He caught her up in his arms and kissed her deeply and long.

"Ma, Uncle Loc needs you," Claire called out from behind them.

The couple broke apart and turned to find their daughter kneeling beside the shallow breathing Loc. Fur had been burnt away from his face and head, and he was barely alive. Carling knelt at his side and tried to heal him. Nothing she did worked. There was nothing she could do, and she felt helpless.

"Indigo, we need you. Your son needs you," Carling called out in desperation.

The rainbow lights that had helped dispel the darkness now faded, and Indigo came to her side. She knelt and took Carling's hands in her own, stopping them from trying to heal Loc.

"He is dying," Carling cried.

"I know. It is his time, Sister. This was his final task, to help and defend you. He came to this hill knowing he would die tonight. He goes to see his love, and that is what he wants," Indigo told her carefully and calmly. "You need to let him go, Carling."

Galen sat at her other side and placed a large hand on the flank of his brother. "You fought well, Brother. Go with our love until we meet again." A tear slipped down his face, quickly followed by another.

"My love and gratitude go with you, Brother. My blessing on you and Wolf," Carling said gently, holding a large paw in her hands.

"It is time, Loc. Let go of the pain and find your Wolf. She waits for you to pass over. May you hunt together until your heart is content.

Wolf child, your time has come to pass over, we welcome you to our spirit world where your wisdom and knowledge will be appreciated," Indigo intoned the greeting.

With the end of her words, Loc took one final breath and let it out, his side going still. Young Wolf lifted her head and howled out into the night, quickly followed by Claire. Carling and Galen joined them in expressing their grief at the passing of their brother. Never more would they see him walking down the track, see him play with his pups. They felt the loss keenly and expressed it the way a wolf would.

Around them, the host of Ancestors gathered and kept their vigil until the family in their midst were finished with their outburst. Calmly and gently, they sent their love to them, enfolding them with their light.

Young Wolf nudged Claire and sought the comfort of her hand on her head. Claire, in turn, put her arms around the Wolf's neck. Galen pulled Carling in close and held her then helped her stand. It was then he saw her injury.

The blood flowed from the wound freely, drenching the sleeve of her shirt. The cut was ragged, black, and festering fast. Without a word, he split the fabric and looked closely at it. Galen picked her up and took her immediately to the stones. He pushed her arm against the largest of the stones and heard the sizzle as it burnt away the festering mess that was spreading. Carling screamed at the pain and gripped Galen tightly, trying to pull away from the scourging of the wound.

When he relented and she collapsed in his arms, he looked down at it. Blackness still affected the wound and her blood still flowed. Red placed a hand over the slice and concentrated all his energy into healing and purging the darkness that had been passed to her from Chaos's weapon. He was replaced by Orange, then Yellow, Green and Blue; finally Indigo and Violet. The wound stubbornly remained.

"The stone is the only way," Red said, still recovering from his attempt. "I am sorry, Carling. It is the only way."

"Draw up the energy from the centre of the earth, Daughter. Use it to heal yourself." Yellow was panting and shaking slightly from her effort.

Carling looked up, feeling the effects of the darkness as it penetrated further into her body. Sweat was beading from her brow, and dark circles marred her face under her eyes.

"Help me," she said quietly to Galen who gave her a short nod.

Picking her up once more, he brought her to the largest stone. Carling braced herself. "Don't let go," she pleaded with him.

"I won't," he promised.

Pushing her arm out, Carling leaned up against the stone once more. The stench from the burning was vile, and Galen kept hold of her. Inside her mind she reached out for the energy she needed to use, the pure energy that spun in the centre of the world. Drawing it up slowly, she fed it into the stone and the knowledge it contained did the rest. Burning the flesh and the infection away, she screamed once more until she passed out from it.

Galen held her up, cradling her as he determinedly kept her arm pressed against the stone. Red knelt beside him and placed a hand on her brow.

"A little longer," he said to his son.

"It will kill her," Galen pleaded.

"No, leaving it will kill her," Red argued. "Just a little more."

Galen gritted his teeth and obeyed his Ancestor, waiting for Red to tell him to pull her away. The flow of energy spilled over from the scourging of the wound and fed the lights under her skin. Glowing a deep gold they moved, flickering and pushing out towards the wound.

"A little more, Galen," Red said as he checked on Carling again, watching carefully the movement of the lights. "Now! Take her off now," he called, helping to move her.

Yellow was there, her hand going over the top of the wound and checking for the damage the slice of the dark sword had created. The swirling lights had quietened now that her body was not touching the stone but were still gathering around the fast-growing scar tissue. A black line stubbornly remained on her skin, an ugly reminder of the battle.

Carling opened her eyes and the first person she saw was Galen, who hugged her to him.

"Did it work?" she asked him.

"I think it did." He released his grip on her and looked up at Red.

"Yes, it has, Sister, though I suggest that you will not be swinging the staff or sword in that arm again. It may become weaker than the other," Red told her.

"I have no intention of swinging any weapon ever again. My task is done," she told them.

"Ma?" Claire came to her side and knelt on the grass beside her. "I am so sorry. I thought it was you. I heard you calling me, telling me to go to safety at the stones." There were tears in her eyes from watching her mother being healed.

"It is all right, Claire." Carling placed a hand on her daughter's face. "It was going to happen. We could not stop it no matter what we did."

"I want to get you home," Galen said, picking Carling up.

"I can walk," she protested.

"Not when we can fly," he told her and lifted them up into the air. "Red, see Claire and Wolf get home please," he called down to his Ancestor.

"It would be my privilege, my son," Red called back, standing between the girl and wolf.

"Where are we going?" Carling asked him, her arms around his neck.

"Somewhere we can be alone, just you and I," he said to her softly.

They flew through the air. The storm clouds now shredding on the remaining wind and the stars twinkling brightly in the moonless sky. Out into the valley he took her, close to the wood that protected the entrance. Glowing in the centre of the meadow stood the red tent. Lowering them down until his feet tickled the tops of the long grass, he finally landed at the entrance.

"What about Claire? We cannot leave her alone there. And Da—"

"The Ancestors will do their part. Everything can wait until morning. You need rest and my care and attention," he told her as he put her down on her feet. Opening the tent flap, he pushed her inside and made sure the doorway was closed behind them.

"I have to go fetch the children," she tried to protest.

"Again, your mother and father will be looking after them. Carling, stop thinking of everyone else, and for once think of yourself." He stepped up to her, his hands going to her face, and he kissed her gently.

"I am fine," she insisted, trying to move his arms away.

"No, you are not. You have just been through an almighty battle. You were wounded and were fading in front of my eyes. Now do as you are told," he said firmly.

"Galen, I just—"

"Not another word." Slowly he lifted her shirt up over her head and pulled her close. "Let me take care of you."

Chapter Twenty-Four

"Ma, are you awake?" Brei called out to her mother, who turned in her blankets and peered out of one eye. "Ma, it is not that cold this morning."

"You try telling my old bones that," Carling complained, pulling the blankets tighter around herself.

"How come Da can get up in the first rays of the sun, but you can't," Brei complained.

"How come you are so demanding and nagging this morning?" she sat up and pulled the blankets from her. The chill of the spring morning seeping into the warmth of her body as it slowly began to work for her.

"Grandmother and Grandfather are already here," Brei said testily. "And have you forgotten what today is?"

Carling stood and stretched, then went to her daughter and pulled her into a hug.

"How could I forget the most important day in your life, my daughter." She kissed her forehead and then moved away to a chest pushed up against the wall. Opening it carefully, she pulled out a cloth bundle and handed it to Brei.

"Your Granny made this for me for my betrothal to your Da. I wish I had the skills that she had so I could have made one for you, but I hope you will wear it." Carling handed it over to her.

Brie placed it down on the table and unfolded the cloth wrapping. Nestled inside was the soft fabric of the dress Tarl'a had embroidered. Picking it up, she held it out and stared at the fine line of the flowers worked in yellow and red. Time had not faded the beautiful and tiny stitching.

"It is beautiful, Ma. I would be honoured to wear it." Brei put the dress back down and ran to her mother's arms.

"You will need to wear a belt with it. Your best one would look well with it," Carling said.

"No, it won't." Galen came into the house, and in his hands a coil of soft leather hung. "This is for you, Brei. Like your Grand Da did, I made a new belt for you to wear." He handed the belt to his daughter and hugged her, dropping a kiss on her head.

Brei uncoiled it and looked closely at the fine work he had put into it. Etched on the smooth, flat surface were figures of animals—seven in all, one for each of the Sentinels.

"It is amazing Da. So beautiful." She immediately placed it around her waist to try, and it fitted perfectly.

"If you are going, Carling, then it should be soon. I have just seen the groom coming up the track," Galen said, kissing his wife on the cheek.

"He's early," Carling protested.

"I don't think he really cares." Galen grinned.

"Gather the dress and the belt together, Brei. It looks like we will be leaving earlier than I had thought. Will you tell Mother we have left, and let Father know that I will speak to him later?" she said, turning to her husband.

"Just go. I'll let them know." Galen kissed her again and then went out the door to head off the impatient groom.

"Ma, do I have to go to the island?" Brei asked as she tried to see out of the door before her father closed it.

Sentinels

"Yes. I had to, Claire had to, and now it is your turn." Carling took her hand and picked the dress and belt up with the other. "Here we go."

Carling transported Brei quickly to the home of the Sentinels and held onto her while she found her legs once more. She let her go and lay the dress over the back of the chair.

"Ma, Brei." A mass of blond hair waddled quickly over to them and into their arms.

"You are huge," Brei said to her sister.

"I am," Claire said with her hand rubbing her belly. "But I was not going to miss seeing my little sister getting betrothed."

"Not just getting betrothed, Claire. I am passing the Guardianship over today as well," Carling told them.

"Ma, I'm not ready. You still have so many years in you yet," Brei exclaimed in shock.

"That is lovely to hear, Brei, but it is what is happening. You were ready years ago, and your Da and I want to spend some time wandering again."

"But you made the vow to guard the stones. You can't just give it away," Claire said, looking between them. "Can you?"

"She can," Yellow said, coming up behind them. "Your mother's main task has been completed. She has raised you and trained you well, Brei. Also, there are other reasons, which you do not need to know about right now."

"Mother," Carling greeted Yellow.

"Daughter. It does not seem so long ago that it was your day."

"And I remember it seemed to take all day for you and Ma to decide what to do with my hair." Carling smiled at the memory.

"It was supposed to distract you." Yellow laughed.

"But it didn't. I still managed to sneak a peek at Galen."

"And also tried to go through me," Red said, coming to join them.

"What are you doing here, Brother? This is supposed to be for the ladies only. You are supposed to be putting fear into Brei's intended. I found out what you said to Galen," Carling said, her eyes narrowing.

"He was not supposed to say anything. And, Sister, I only came by to let you know that the rest of your family have arrived at the house. Now that my task is complete, dear ladies, I will leave you. Brei, you are looking beautiful already. Don't let them change you too much. And Claire," he said turned to his niece. "You look radiant."

"Thank you, Uncle," she said, accepting his hug.

"Have a lovely day." Red left them.

Violet and Indigo soon joined them, and they began to make a fuss over Brei. Claire went and sat down gingerly onto a chair. Carling came to check on her eldest daughter. It was the first time she had seen her since Claire had wed, and it was Carling's children that really had made her mind up to pass the Guardianship to Brei.

"You are not far away now, Claire. Was it really wise for you to come today?"

"I would not miss it, Ma. I just wished we lived closer to the valley, so that I could be closer to you, Da, and Brei."

"Do you not like living in Lucan's town. Are you not happy with Niall? Because when I check on you, you both seem very happy."

"Ma! You don't need to keep checking."

"I know, but I like to see how my children are doing. How are you keeping yourself?"

"I'm tired, feel heavy, and can't wait to have this baby."

"Do you want me to see how far away you are?" Carling smiled at her.

"No. So far we have rebuffed all attempts to see the future for both the pregnancy and the child. And today is Brei's day, our focus should be on her."

"But look. The Sentinels have her occupied," Carling said with a smile as she looked over at her daughter.

"What is really behind your retirement, Ma?" Claire asked her.

"I'm feeling a little stuck in the valley. All my early life I was not allowed to leave it. I love it. It is and will always be my home, but I want to go and travel. Both your Da and I have been getting a little restless of late," Carling replied.

"You always seem so content and happy."

"We have been very happy in the valley. But the time we went to the west was the best that we have had, and I want to do it again before we get too old."

"But from the stories you told us, it was bloody and hard for you."

"It was, but the time we spent together—just us—was wonderful. I want to travel our lands and visit the far-flung places that no one has seen before," Carling told her.

"Then you should do it. Just remember to come visit us on your travels."

"My girl, just try and keep us away." Carling took her hands in hers.

"Be happy, Mother." Claire stood awkwardly, kissed her mother, then waddled away to sit with her sister and give her own opinions.

Smiling to herself, Carling watched the group as they talked and argued good-naturedly. When she had discussed her idea with Galen, he had answered with such enthusiasm and eagerness that it surprised her. She had sometimes suspected her husband missed his wandering ways, but he had hidden his restlessness very well from her over the years. They had begun their planning then and there.

"I feel you near, Carling," a whisper in her mind breezed through. It was so quiet that she was not sure she actually heard it.

Shaking her head, Carling went back to her thoughts of looking forward to passing on her responsibilities. Brei was definitely ready at twenty summers. She was strong, and with her personal relationship with the Sentinels, it held her in good stead for guarding the stones.

"Carling. I can feel you near me," the voice called again, and this time she was certain it was not her imagination.

"Who are you?" she called out to the voice.

"You know who I am. I am still here where you put me."

Carling stood up quickly, withdrawing her thoughts from him and slamming up her defences. She moved herself to the hidden room and stood before him.

Still trapped in the giant crystals to each side, Chaos stood slumped. He seemed to be broken and tired. His body was wasted away and almost just bones. Carling almost fell for his charade, but there was one detail that was wrong. His eyes still burned with his anger.

"Please, Carling, free me," he begged, his tone as weak and broken as possible.

"How did you know I was near, Chaos?" she asked him, crossing her arms over her chest.

"Please help me," he continued with his farce.

"Chaos, I don't believe you," she told him simply, as if she were talking to one of her children.

Standing upright, his physique changed and became the muscular one she had known again. He flexed against his restraints and glared at her.

"How did you know?" Carling asked.

"When you trapped me here, you left some of yourself behind. Your blood from the wound I inflicted on you." He sneered at her.

Reflexively she clasped her arm and the scar that was hidden under her shirt. His eyes watched her closely.

"You could not burn it all away, could you? The darkness will remain with you until the day you die. What a waste it has been. You are looking old, Carling. Free me and I can make you look young again," he said cajolingly.

"You know I will not. There is nothing you can say to me that will make me want to free you. Enjoy your solitude." She made to leave, and his words stopped her.

"I will be able to find you no matter where you are in the world. Your gift of your blood will ensure that I can reach you, even into your next life. You made a large mistake there."

"And I will be able to deal with you each time you come for me," she told him vehemently. "You will never have me, Chaos. You can keep trying, but the Ultimate One will come. She will be born, and she will finally defeat you."

Chaos stared at her in astonishment at her statement, and Carling appeared delighted at his misunderstanding. "You didn't know. I find that amazing. With all your power, all your abilities, you could not see what your future holds. Were you so certain that you would prevail that you could not see that it is not my spirit that defeats you?" Carling began to laugh. "My job on this earth is as your jailer. It is my task to confine you and keep you here." Her lights flared under her skin, and their glow added to the light that already illuminated the room. "I go from this world as any mortal will. In my next lives I may not have the lights of the Sentinels in my veins. I may not even be as powerful as I am now. But there is one thing you can bet your life on: I will keep you here for as long as I possibly can until the Ultimate One comes to finally rid this world of your poison."

"I cannot die. I am immortal!" Chaos screamed at her.

"You are not immortal. The Universe is immortal, and you are but a piece of it, as is Order." Carling moved over to the plinth and the crystal orb that sat there. The light from within increased as she neared it. Her hand hovered over the top and sparks leapt to it as she fed some of her golden energy into it, boosting the intensity.

"Leave me then!" he roared at her as the brightness increased in the room. "But look for me, Carling. I will find you."

"I look forward to it, Chaos," she said with a smirk and left him.

Brei stood in the middle of the room with the women all standing around her passing their critical eye over how she looked. Her long dark hair had been brushed to gleaming and pulled back off her face. The dress fitted perfectly, and the belt set it off nicely. There was still something not quite right with it though, and Carling was loath to make any changes.

Stepping forward, she raised a hand and passed it over the red and yellow flowers at the collar and cuffs. As it moved, they changed colour. From the bright vibrant hues, they changed to an icy white, gleaming against the soft green fabric. Carling held her hand out and a small circlet of the same white roses appeared on it. Gently she placed it on her daughter's head and then stepped back.

"I'm sure Ma will forgive my changes and the way I went about them, but this is perfect." She nodded and they all agreed.

"Thank you, Ma," Brei said kissing her on the cheek.

"You are welcome. Now, shall we get you to your groom? I am sure that by now he would have been terrified enough by the men in our family." Carling took her daughter's hands in her own and transported them to the stones.

Claire arrived with Yellow and Violet, and Indigo appeared shortly after. The three Sentinel women moved to their places by the sacred stones and Carling and Claire left Brei in the centre.

The procession was led by Brei's suitor. Shae had come to them a few moons back in the middle of a terrible winter storm. He had said that he had been guided to their door by a voice that sounded like an angel.

And he had stayed. Shae was the son of Bevan, Faolan's son, and had told them he had heard stories of the stones from his father and grandfather.

Their love had started almost immediately after he arrived, still shivering beside the fire as Brei continued singing while she worked, filling the quiet of the house. His eyes never left her, and Galen became suddenly protective of his daughter. Carling had to pull him aside after a few days of the young man's presence, to remind him of how it had been for them, and he had promised to get to know the young man better.

Red, at first, was as on guard as Galen was, and did not like the fact the man was Celtic, rather than one of the People. He became a regular visitor to their hearth in the first few weeks, and Red found him to be worthy of Brei.

Brei, on her part noticed none of this, and as far as Carling could see, did not even notice Shae until one winter's day as she was making her way back to the house from visiting the stones. Shae had been outside helping Galen split logs for the fire and noticed Brei had stumbled in the deep snow.

Carling had to hold Galen back from going to his daughter's aid as she watched Shae help her up, and she saw the first signs from Brei that she had any interest in the young man.

"The universe has sent him my love," Carling had told her husband.

The procession Shae lead was a long one. Galen was at his side, still strong and healthy. It still surprised Carling that he could take her breath away with just one look, and he was looking at her now. His hair was only just touched with grey at the temples. His blue eyes still twinkled when they saw her, and Galen was still an ardent lover.

Behind Galen and Shae, came Carling and Galen's sons, Itis and Gede. Itis, the image of Galen as a young man, was now enlisted with his cousin Elfin's war band, which kept an eye on the border and the Romans that were fast approaching. Gede, with his blond hair and intensely bright blue eyes, had finished his training with Ru and was now a confident young man, working alongside his uncle.

Behind them came their uncles. Ru was finally starting to look his age. Always a good-looking man, his hair was now greying, and lines showed heavily around his eyes. He looked tired and sad, having just lost Nila in the last of the winter storms. Uven came next, as healthy as ever, with Cait on his arm. The pair never seemed to age, and Carling thought to have a word with him about it. Arilith and Ila came next. They both had become so much a part of the family that they were called Aunt and Uncle by the many children. Ila had finally gotten over her jealousy of Carling and had become a firm friend.

Bringing up the rear, lined up and smiling broadly, came the rest the Sentinels. With Red leading the way into the circle, they arranged themselves once more in between the stones.

Stepping forward, Carling left her husband's side to stand beside Brei and Shae. Reaching out she joined their hands together and lay one of her own on top and one beneath. "Brei, do you freely take this man, Shae, to be your betrothed?" Carling asked her.

"I do take him," she responded.

"Shae, do you freely take this woman, Brei, to be your betrothed?" Carling turned her gaze to him.

"I do take her." Shae's eyes were firmly on the face of his love as he answered quickly.

"These two come to the Sacred Stones to pledge themselves to each other." Slowly a cord of gold materialised and wrapped itself around their wrists. "Let this cord symbolise the love these two have. Let it never be sundered by anyone or anything. You are now tied to each other, heart and soul, mind, and body. The blessings of the Guardian of the Stones be on you. The blessings of The One True Child be on you. The love of your father and mother be on you both." Carling removed her hands and stepped back as Violet came to give her blessing, to be followed by each Sentinel.

Red was the last and he lay a hand on Brei's shoulder and one on Shae's. "Shae, you are not of The People, but a Celt. As we welcome you into our special family you will share our secrets, as will be the way of many a joining between our peoples. My blessings on both of you and my love for always. I shall guard your line and protect it to the very end." Red stepped back to his stone and resumed his place. As he did so, the cord around their arms seemed to melt into their skins, the feeling of the golden tie was still there and would remain so for the rest of their lives.

The hands of the Ancestors all raised, and the light brightened around them.

"Go now, and for all time live your lives together in love," they all intoned and then lowered their arms, waiting for Carling.

Carling stepped back to her daughter and took her hands, holding them gently. "Ancestors, be my witness. I, Carling, daughter of Yellow and Blue, the One True Child of The Sentinels, daughter of Tarl'a and Mailcon, Guardian of the Stones, do relinquish my role. I bring before you my successor, Brei, a direct descendant of Red, protector of the line, daughter of Galen and Carling, wife of Shae. Do you accept this woman as Guardian of the Stones?"

"I, Red, speak for those that you call Ancestors. We, the Sentinels of Order, do accept Brei, daughter of Carling, The One True Child and direct descendant Galen, to be your successor. Our blessings on you, Carling. Though you have not guarded our sacred stones long, you have served Order in other more significant ways. Our blessings on you, Galen, who have supported our sister, Carling. May the life you have together be happy and full. Our love and our thanks we give you for your dedicated service. Brei, do you accept this role to commit your life to the guardianship of our most sacred of places, and that of your line?"

"I, Brei, daughter of Carling and Galen, wife of Shae and direct descendant of Red, do accept the role of Guardian of the Stones. I promise to guide those seeking your wisdom and to tell only the truth to those seeking answers. I promise to dedicate my life to you, the Ancestors, the Sentinels of this land."

"We accept your promises, and do hereby name you, Brei, Guardian of the Stones." Red stepped away from his place and came to stand beside them once more. "The transfer is complete. Sister, you have our thanks and blessings."

"Thank you, my brother. It has been my honour," Carling said to him.

With all the ceremonies complete, they celebrated long into the night. Carling sat with Claire the whole night. There were moments during the day that had concerned her. With one particularly large wince, Carling placed a hand on her distended belly.

"I think it was time we got you home," Carling said quietly to her.

"I don't want to go just yet," Claire protested.

"I don't think your child will let you." Carling's eyes shined with amusement. "Brei, can you come here, please."

"What is it, Ma?" Brei asked as she walked to her mother.

"Out in the meadow, over the brook, is a red tent set up for you and Shae for the night." Carling stood and hugged her daughter tightly. "Say goodbye to your sister. I need to take her home before her—" She stopped herself before she gave the gender away. "Before her child is delivered here."

Brei left her mother's arms and went to her sister. "Claire. Do you want to know now, or shall I pass what I have seen on to you by Uncle Red later?" she asked her.

"Now. I want to hear it from you, Brei," Claire said, a hint of panic in her voice.

"A beautiful girl, so much like her mother, the sister I love. Hair as golden and eyes the same shade. She will grow, and you will be proud of her. Strong and capable, from her comes many more the same. She will not be The One True Child, but her many times great, granddaughter will be once more. Be happy and safe my sister."

"Thank you, Brei. I wish you all the happiness in your betrothal as I have in mine." They hugged and were forced apart when a contraction hit Claire and she doubled up in pain.

"It is time to go, Claire," Carling said calmly. "Galen, do you wish to come to?"

"If Red would take me—or Yellow or Blue. I don't think you could keep any of the Sentinels from this birth." He chuckled softly as he quickly kissed Brei's head. "We will be back soon. Has Ma told you about the tent?"

"Yes, Da, she has." Brei blushed in the firelight.

"Good," Galen replied.

Red came to his side while Yellow and Blue, followed by Green, Violet, Indigo, and Orange, all winked out from beside the fire.

Best wishes calls from her entire family came to Claire, and she welcomed them weakly, her hand clasped firmly around her stomach. Carling took her spare hand, and they moved quickly back to the little village by the sea. Lucan's Town, home of the guardians of the island.

When they arrived, Carling assisted her daughter to her bedchamber and sent off Niall with the men. His mother, Dealla, came bustling into the room and got a great surprise at the presence of the Sentinels. She was a no-nonsense type of woman and soon had them organised and out of her way, as she took over the birthing of the child.

The labour was not a long one, and as Carling had suspected, Claire had hidden most of it so she could be present for Brei's wedding. The birth was an easy one, and the baby was soon born, letting out a wail as she was rubbed down vigorously. On her tiny head, a small amount of blonde fuzz could be seen, and when she blinked for her first look at the world, she met two sets of eyes, exactly the same colour as her own would be.

"What have you decided to name her?" Yellow asked when she was finally allowed to see her great granddaughter.

"Not yet, Mother. We need Red here first." Carling told her as she gazed at the newborn.

"I suppose you are decent enough for the men to come in," declared Dealla as she tidied the mess away and hid it from male eyes.

The door opened swiftly, and Niall went straight to the bedside of Claire, gently picking up his daughter in his arms.

"She is so beautiful, just as you are," he said, bending and kissing his wife.

Carling looked up and caught her own husband's eyes, remembering him saying something very similar to her. His eyes crinkled at the corners as he recalled the same.

"Have you decided on a name?" Red asked the couple.

"We have, Uncle Red. We have decided on Breena," Claire told him.

Red placed a gentle hand on the baby's head. "We welcome you, Breena, into the world. I now claim you as one of my line, a direct descendant through your mother. I will protect and guard you until you leave this world. My blessings and my love for always," he told her then kissed her forehead.

"Thank you, Uncle," Niall said, looking up at the Sentinel.

"I will be checking up on her. My blessings on you both." Red stepped aside and let the others in to make their own. With a final farewell, they left the couple to get to know their child in peace.

"We will leave you also, Claire. But we will come visit often," Carling said as she passed the baby back into the arms of her mother.

"You look after them both, young man," Galen said as he shook Naill's hand and dragged him into a hug.

"I will, Galen. I so promised, and I will. The vow that my grandfather took still stands, Carling. It is still under our protection and will remain so," Niall said solemnly to her.

"Thank you, Niall. You and your family. Be safe and happy until we meet again," Carling said, taking her husband's arm.

Carling transported them out of the town, but not back to the house in the valley. Instead, she took him to the island. It was not the first time he had visited the place, but the last time he was not there long enough, or in any fit state to really take any notice of it.

"What are we doing here?" Galen asked her.

"I did not want to go back home just yet. I wanted a little time for just you and me," she said coyly, looking up at him.

"But we have guests. We cannot just ignore them. Especially with the Guardian being busy on her wedding night."

"Our children are all grown, Galen. When did that happen?"

"We were watching. Were you not paying attention?" He pulled her closer and held her tight.

"I was. It just seemed to go so fast." She lay her head against his chest, hearing his heart beating steadily.

"Now we are grandparents," he said with a little wonder in his voice.

"Yes, we are."

"And there is yet another little you in the world."

"She is not me. She will be her own person, just as her mother is. It is a cruel trick that they look like me," she said smiling.

"Not cruel. Beautiful." He tilted her head and kissed her tenderly.

Carling broke the kiss and took his hand. Slowly she led him off to her bedchamber and the privacy it would afford in case the Sentinels decided to come home.

Over the years, Carling and Galen travelled around the lands, finding hidden treasures and beautiful people and places. Their family grew and they were present for each birth. Claire had five children, with Breena the only golden-haired child in amongst the ginger heads. Brei closely following her sister with four, all boys, except for her youngest. A dark haired, very serious girl she had named Rowena.

Itis was only a few turnings of the seasons into his marriage, and his wife was expecting their second child. But their youngest son, Gede, was still not betrothed. He was a handsome man and was sought after by the ladies at Elfin's Broch. Ru had despaired to the couple on whether Gede would ever settle down, both knowing that he wouldn't. She had looked into their futures before they had left on their travels, and it had at first disturbed her that Gede wouldn't find a wife and find happiness that way, but he would still be happy.

Though they had received offers from all their children to live with them, Carling and Galen had decided that they would have their own little house. Deciding where to place it was another matter and they discussed it in detail. One spot that they both agreed was beautiful and peaceful was a loch valley. When they arrived on the banks of the loch, they found in the intervening decades, a little community had sprung up on the shores. Only a few family groups had made the one side of the valley home, but they were welcoming of the visitors.

A familiar feeling came to Carling as she looked out at the opposite shore across the dark waters. She had seen this place before and searched her memory for it. The hint of smoke in the air brought it back to her as she remembered seeing a house out on the water, which had been burnt. A shiver went up her spine.

Galen had decided where their little house should be set without even talking to Carling about it. At first, she wondered if he were going senile, until she saw the views from where he wanted to place it. It was on the hill opposite to the little settlement, a little way up from the shore. From there they could see up the valley both ways, as the loch bent slightly, it was perfect. The speed with which he and she built the house raised a few eyebrows from the community, especially considering how aged they both appeared, but there were some of The People in amongst these Celts already, and their abilities were accepted.

They had settled themselves in and became quite comfortable in their little house. They were protected from the weather and well provided by the arable land around them. Carling became known as a healer, and they would have visitors regularly at their door. Visitors often came to them from their family as well. One in particular was a regular and welcome guest, that of Claire's eldest, Breena.

It soon became apparent that the young woman had fallen in love with one of the young men from across the loch, as Galen had found them secluded away down by the banks. He had sent the young man packing, telling him that next time he saw him, the boy had better come seeking her hand. Two days later, the boy and his parents arrived at the little house doing just that.

With a granddaughter wed and expecting her first child, Carling was beginning to feel her age. Lying in bed one stormy night, she reflected over her life, and it amazed her the things she had done and accomplished. The people she had met along the way, their faces so clear in her mind. She sought them out to see how they fared and was saddened to see so many now left them. Ru had gone only a few seasons ago, still mourning the loss of his Nila. Uven was still with them, but Cait was not. Both Arilith and Ila had been lost at sea when the boat they were on was sunk by a storm as they travelled north. Their nieces and nephews were grown, with children and grandchildren of their own and spreading out over the lands. Carling sighed and rolled over.

The Sentinels came to mind. No matter where they had gone on their travels, they were there only a call away. She did not even need to call sometimes for them to come and visit. When she searched out for them, she felt a kernel of worry creep into her heart. Their force, which used to be so strong to her, was now beginning to dim.

This worry played on her mind for a few days until Galen stopped her one morning as she was going about her chores. "What is it Carling?" he asked, sitting her down on the bed.

"I'm having trouble feeling the Sentinels. Something does not feel right," she told him as he sat beside her.

"Then call them or find them. I am sure the Ancestors will be able to tell you what is going on, my love," he suggested tenderly.

"But that is it. I do not know if they will be able to answer me."

"Go to the stones. Enlist your daughter's help to contact them."

"Can you cope on your own for a day or two?" she asked him.

"Carling, I am not infirm yet. I will be fine. Go and get it sorted in your mind, because you are not here at the moment, and it is making me a little crazy having to fix things after you have messed them up," he chuckled.

"All right, then, I will go. Look after yourself." She kissed him and stood. "You, as always, give the best advice, my love."

"That is what I was created for. To be your support and your love. Give Brei a hug and kiss for me."

"I will." She kissed him once more before leaving him to an empty room and a sigh.

The stones had not changed one bit. They remained upright and in place, reaching for the sky. Made of the same dark rock as the island and embedded deep into the ground, seeking the energy force that lay at the centre of the world. Seven massive stones flat and carved by no man, set in a perfect circle. The largest was one of the entrance stones. Lichen was growing now on the rough surface of the rocks, not marring the aesthetics of them, but adding to the richness of their history.

Brei rounded the rocks and entered the stones, greeting her mother warmly. She was still a beautiful and hearty woman with many years ahead of her. "Ma, it is good to see you. How is Da?" she asked.

"The same as ever. Next time I promise I'll bring him. But this time I need your help."

"What is it you wish me to do?" Brei asked, her face turning to a frown.

"Can you call the Sentinels?" Carling asked.

"Of course. I don't understand. Why don't you?"

"Please, can you call them now? I just have this feeling that something is not right."

"Of course, Ma." Carling stepped out of her way as Brei stood in the centre. "Ancestors, hear me. I request your presence in the most sacred of places," she called out, her hands clasped together, and her head bowed.

The two women waited and waited for an answer. Brei was looking very uncertain and unsettled by the lack of response.

"Can you try with me, Ma?" she asked, holding out a hand for her mother to join her.

They clasped hands in the centre, and both called out the ritualistic request. Carling felt the message go out strongly and one or two answer it briefly. They stayed in the centre as slowly, one by one, the Sentinels arrived. Last of all Red.

"We have come as requested by the Guardian of the Stones and The One True Child. What is it you seek?" Blue called out to them.

"My mother, The One True Child, seeks your council, Ancestors," Brei said as she stepped away from her mother.

"My family, there is something happening to you all, and I do not understand what it is. I feel you pulling away from me and it saddens me a great deal." A tear formed in her eye, and she blinked it away.

"Our daughter," Yellow said as she came to embrace her. "Our love will be with you always."

"You are correct, Carling. Our time to depart for the shadows is upon us. Our lights dim and do not shine as bright as they once did. We have helped you as much as we can, and we must now depart to prepare for your next lives," Blue said, replacing Yellow.

"What are The People to do without you?" Carling asked, suddenly feeling very frightened at the prospect that her family would not be there.

"We will still respond to those who have a need and those that we need to help. There is much to be done and much to be planned. We will guard our lands as best as we can, but we need to be apart to do this," Violet said.

"Where will you go?"

"We go to stand guard and commune with each other. Will you accompany us to our resting places, Sister?" Indigo asked, taking her hand.

"It would be my honour," Carling told her.

The world shifted and they were in the lands of Violet to the east. The lands where Gart and now Elfin's broch was built by the sea. In a stand of forest was a clearing, a brook running through it, and Violet positioned herself in the very centre.

"We will be with you always, Carling," she said as Carling came to say goodbye.

"I will think of you always," Carling told her and stepped back.

As Violet disappeared, in her place a tree stood, already fully formed, and rooted well into the earth. The branches draped themselves down to the ground and trailed in the water as it flowed past gracefully, the bright green leaves reflected in the brook. Carling placed a hand on the trunk of the tree and felt the life force of Violet within the willow.

Indigo took her hand the world moved again. When it had settled, she walked with her sister to the centre of a meadow. There were no other trees around her.

"Won't you feel lonely here?" Carling asked her as she hugged her goodbye.

"No, Sister. My mind shall be linked with my brothers and sisters as we work together. I like the open space." She wore an expression of contentment. Carling let her go and stepped back to the others.

To mark her spot in her lands, a great ash sprang from the green grass at her feet. The branches spread wide and high into the sky. Once more, Carling felt her energy emanating from the great trunk.

Blue was next, and when it came time to say goodbye to her father, Carling had tears rolling down her lined and creased face. He had not changed in all the years she had known the Sentinels—none of them did—but she had aged. She held him close, lingering in his last embrace and kissed his cheek.

"I will miss you, Father," she told him quietly.

"And I shall miss you, Daughter." He kissed her forehead one last time and left her standing beside her mother. In his wake, he left a mighty pine tree that stretched high up into the sky. It was strongly anchored to the ground with roots that dug deep. She stopped and listened to the sound the wind made through the branches, tucking it away into her memory.

Green's lands were next, and the closest to the Romans. Carling did not feel comfortable being so near the border but pushed it down as she farewelled her brother. With his passing into the spirit realm, he left an elm tree, just as tall and strong as Blue's pine.

Yellow was next. Her lands lay just to the south of the valley. Carling held onto her, not wanting to let her go, her face awash with tears. "Mother." It was the only word Carling could get out before the rest were choked with sobs.

"I know my, Daughter. I love you too. If you ever need council, you know how to contact me or your father," she said gently. "Now I must go. This must be done before the night draws in."

Yellow opened her arms, and reluctantly Carling let her go. As she stepped back, she was supported by Red and Orange. Lifting her arms up into the air, Yellow faded out. In her place was a large Yew tree. It was bent and twisted, and already had some age to it, but solid and strong.

"Come, Carling," Orange said, placing an arm around her and gently taking her to his lands in the west.

"This is too hard," Carling said into his shoulder as she hugged him.

"But it is necessary, Sister," he told her.

Looking up at his brother, Orange passed her over into Red's care and strode away further along the banks of the stream they were standing on. The change was so smooth and subtle as he got further away from them. The tree sprung up clinging to the rocks that jutted from the ground. Bright orange berries bloomed from the branches, heralding him changing into a rowan tree.

"Show off," Red said, wiping a tear from his own eye. "I suppose it is my turn now, Carling."

Quickly, he shifted the world, and they now stood in the clearing by the ford at the entrance to the hidden valley. The valley of her home. She looked around and found that it had changed little since the last time she had been there.

"You are to be so close to the stones?" she asked him.

"It is my job to protect the line of the Guardians, so where else should I place myself. You left something here, Carling, a long time ago." Red went to a fallen log and reached into the hollow, pulling out the old wooden practice sword, then presented it to her, hilt first.

Carling took the sword and hefted in her hand, still strong enough to lift it up and feel the weight of it. She placed the point down onto the ground. "What do I want with a sword now? That part of my life is well and truly over, and it has been many years since I held a sword, or a staff for that matter," she told him.

"I have watched you grow, and you are still the most beautiful woman I have ever seen." He waved a hand in front of her, and for a few moments she was once again her younger self.

She looked at her hands, the skin now smooth and tight, the age spots faded. She lifted searching fingers to her face and felt the wrinkles fade away.

"So beautiful," Red said regretfully before changing her back.

Carling dropped the sword and placed her arms around his neck, pulling him close. Gently he kissed her, a sorrowful kiss of unrequited love, then pulled away. So briefly and softly their lips touched that there was no impropriety to it, a kiss between them that had meant more on one side than it had on the other. Red pulled her arms away from him and stooped to pick the sword back up.

"Pick me a spot, Carling. A nice spot near the track so I may see who comes and goes." He held the sword out to her again, and she took it back.

Carefully, she searched for the perfect place, looking up and down the track until she found a spot that pleased her. Off to one side of the pathway, set back a little, she placed the tip of the sword and looked up at Red.

"Here will be perfect," she said with a lump in her throat.

"You have chosen, well, I thank you. It is time for me to go. The sun is about to set," Red said. He moved to her side and took back the sword as she moved aside.

"I will miss you, Red. I will miss all of you."

"Admit it, I was your favourite." He grinned at her.

"Of course you were." Quickly she rushed forward and kissed his cheek one last time.

"Go with my blessings and my love," Red told her quietly. "I have loved you dearly, Carling." With his final words he plunged the tip of the sword deep into the ground. Great limbs of wood grew up from the old practice sword and tangled their way around him. They spread out in a wide circle, and it swallowed him up under the dark bark. Green oak leaves sprung from the branches, creating a thick canopy overhead.

"Go with my love also, Red," she said softly, her hand resting on the giant trunk.

Very slowly she started to walk up the track towards the house in the hidden valley, then stopped. It was not her home anymore, and she did not feel like being there, though she loved her daughter and her family. Carling pulled in the energy from the surrounding area, and for the last time, transported herself home to Galen.

She walked through the door and found him carving something small. Galen looked up from his work and put his knife and the wood down at his feet, standing to take her into his arms. Tears already coursing down his face.

"They have gone," she told him and burst into her own. He held her gently and took her to her seat by the fire, kneeling in front of her as he continued to hold and comfort her.

"You will see them again," he told her softly, wiping at her wet cheeks. As he did, streaks of lights flared as they had not done in years. "I did not think I would see you again," Galen admitted to her.

She lifted her hand to his face. "I would not leave you in that way. I could never leave you," she said, a fresh batch of tears falling.

"I thought Red would finally take you from me."

"I love him, but it is not the same love as I have for you. You are my heart and soul." She kissed him again and clung to him, saddened that he would think that.

"I have something that I made for you—well as a reminder anyway," he said, getting up from his knees with great difficulty. He bent down and picked up the piece he had been working on and handed it to her.

Carling held it gently in her fingers and stared at the amazing workmanship. The details were perfect, and it looked so real. A tiny miniature boar, complete with tusks and hair lay in her hands.

"It is beautiful," she said, marvelling at his work.

"Not as beautiful as you are, my love," Galen said, kneeling once more.

To be continued…

The One True Child saga continues…

The world falls into Chaos as the Romans lay siege across the lands, a young Carling finds herself alone, her family slaughtered, and trapped. Forced into slavery, her powers growing, can she escape and discover her destiny in…

DOMINATION

Book 2 of the One True Child Series

The thick and hazy mist swirled over the water and crept through the reeds at the side of the still loch as a ghostly white swan emerged from it, gliding silently as it looked for its morning meal. An eerie quiet had descended over the bank, punctuated occasionally by a crack of wood, and quickly followed by a splash, making the little girl hiding in the thick reeds jump at the noise. She shivered. Huddled amongst the reeds on the edge of the loch all night, she was cold, cramped, and tired. The noises that had frightened her during the long night were now gone, but she was still too scared to move. She hugged herself, trying to get warm, while her baby teeth chattered.

Her father had woken her and told her to hide. They had come again—the raiders who had burnt their home the last time—and so she ran. The light from the fire had brightened the dark night, and she sank down as low as she could to stay hidden with her hands over her ears as she watched the shadowy figures. But she could still hear the screams of her mother and the growl and shouts of her father as he tried to defend the family and their home. She also heard the men who attacked them. Their yells and cruel laughter as her baby brother had cried out with ear-piercing screams into the night.

Now it was quiet.

The grumbling of her stomach finally made her move and she stood up and stretched. Her clothing was wet and heavy, clinging to her legs. Walking along the shoreline, she made her way back carefully on quiet, bare feet as the mud sucked at them. The smell of damp ash filled her nostrils before she reached the wooden walkway to her home that sat out over the loch. She could not see it through the thick mist and started to make her way slowly over the little bridge, holding on tightly to the railing. The smell was getting stronger, along with another scent that stung her nose. Pieces of burnt and charred wood floated by her, bobbing on the small waves as she made her way closer.

The white mist parted before her with a burst of the early morning breeze, and the remains of their home lay in shattered and blackened pieces. Lazy coils of blue smoke lifted and shifted in the now moving air as the embers still determinedly consumed the wood. She stared at it. In the wreckage she could see her brother's small cot and beside it lay the charred remains of her mother, her arm resting protectively across the tiny bed. Of her father there was no sign.

A blue tattooed arm reached around her tiny waist and lifted her up, carrying her away from the dreadful sight. It stayed with her as she struggled and fought to be let go. With all her might she bit, and she scratched at that arm, trying to break free. But it held on tightly. She was put down, turned, and when she saw who her captor was, gave a great sob and clung to her uncle. She cried into his large shoulder as she finally realised her family was gone. He held her gently until her grandmother came to take his place. The old woman picked her up and carried the small child farther away from the shore.

"Breena and Carvorst need to be sent off properly. Talorgan, go fetch the druid," the gruff voice of her uncle told someone. "Get the child home, Ma. Bron is waiting for news."

The old woman carried the child for as long as she could beside the loch. The remains of the mist were still swirling and eddied around them, and the tears had long since dried. Her grandmother was telling her stories, trying to keep her calm and quiet. The girl loved the stories and remembered running to see her grandmother to hear them—and getting told off by her mother when she came back.

Grandmother put her down and stopped to rest. She stretched her back a bit and then held onto the child's tiny hand. They walked in silence along the little path, and whenever they heard a noise, she would stop and wait. Threading their way through a group of trees, they came to a clearing and a man stepped out in front of them.

He was tall and had a helmet on his head. A red cloak was gathered around him against the cold and damp, and his legs were bare except for the boots he wore, with their many laces. He held in one hand a spear and long shield in the other. With the surprise of seeing suddenly seeing them appear from the trees gone, he pointed the spear at the old woman and young child.

In a language she couldn't understand he called out. His voice was loud in the quiet of the morning and the mist that still clung to the shore, and it carried far. She heard other feet come running. The jangling of their armour rang out, announcing their whereabouts. Grandmother tried to get away, her fingers digging into the girl's arm as she began to drag the child along, but they were met by another man standing at their back. The shield was up, and the spearhead was pointed at the chest of the unarmed old woman.

Grandmother picked the little girl up and held her close. Turning all around, she looked for an escape, but there was none. They were surrounded and herded further up the track. The child clung to her grandmother's neck, her blue eyes open wide with fright at the sight of the men and their yelling. Tears spilled down her face, leaving clean marks on the sooty skin of her cheeks.

They were pushed into a clearing and found themselves hemmed in by a group of large men. Most laughed at the bedraggled pair as they moved through their ranks, while others were bored and looked away. Grandmother was led to stand in front of a young man with dark hair and hazel eyes, and she placed the girl onto her own feet but clung tightly to her small hand. The man looked down his large, hooked nose at the pair and spoke. Grandmother was forced to her knees and stripped. The man shook his head and a spear entered Grandmother's back, exiting through her chest as she screamed.

The child stood there in shock.

The blood splattered over her face, and she watched her grandmother topple to the ground when the spear was pulled from her body. She let out a scream of her own as the old woman let go of her hand and lay on the ground, gurgling dark blood in great clots from her mouth. The body was dragged away, leaving a trail of blood over the green grass and leaf litter. The child heard a splash as they threw her beloved grandmother into the loch…

Domination available April 2022
PREORDER NOW FROM ALL MAJOR BOOKSELLERS

Loraine Conn grew up on the outskirts of Upper Hutt, New Zealand. Her backyard encompassed the surrounding farmland, river, hills, and mountains which she wandered with her brothers and fed her imagination. After discovering a love for writing in English class at the age of eight, she continued to write in secret. It was not until much later in life that Loraine turned what she thought was a hobby, and something fun to do, into her first completed novel. Now married, Loraine moved from New Zealand to Perth, Western Australia in 2008, and became a stay-at-home mum. While caring for her family and after battling breast cancer, a series was born from a kernel of a dream. Loraine has now published the seven book fantasy series, The One True Child Series, and Realm of Dragons, Fight for the Crown. Both the series and book have been released with the American based indie publishing company Between the Lines Publishing, under their Liminal Books branch, using the pen name L.C. Conn. She continues her career with many more stories waiting in the wings to be released, and even more ideas to be written.

CONNECT WITH L.C. CONN

Email: raindropc1970@gmail.com

Facebook: http://www.facebook.com/LCConn

Twitter: https://twitter.com/ConnLoraine

Instagram: https//www.instagram.com/l.c.conn

Web Page: https//lcconnwriter.wordpress.com/